JUST AS SIN PRO
COMES WITH ITS OWN PUNISHMENT

A
FATE
SO
WICKED

K.E. AUSTIN

GILDED
INK
PRESS

A Fate so Wicked
First published by Gilded Ink Press 2024
Copyright © 2024 by K.E Austin
All rights reserved.

In loving memory of my mom.
May this story reach you in the stars.
12/30/59 - 2/3/21

ONE

The hushed whispers of urban legends circulated amongst the crowd as they pulled Lilian Quelling's pale, lifeless body out of the Dolorem River. With her sopping brown hair covering half of her bloodied face, she was nearly unrecognizable as they laid her onto the shore.

Trembling, I brought my hand to my mouth.

I couldn't move.

Couldn't speak.

Shock wrapped around my rigid spine, squeezing the air from my lungs as I watched the doctor's futile attempts to resuscitate her. It was too late.

Lilian was dead.

The hoard of onlookers grew larger by the second, shouldering past me to glimpse the fifth person who'd drowned this year.

"The fae are out of control!" a man shouted.

"When is this madness going to end?"

"Soon we won't be safe in our own homes!" someone else cried.

I tuned their conversations out. They didn't care that she

was someone's daughter. Someone's friend. No one knew her name—they only cared to satiate their morbid curiosity.

She happened to be the only person I'd trusted in Wendover. The one person who hadn't cared who my mother was.

My hand dropped at the realization she was none of those things anymore.

The crowd hovered over her body feigning their condolences in a covert attempt to gossip and spread fear. No one had seen a faerie in over five hundred years. The iron-laden river prevented them from crossing over. Yet, as I stood there, struggling to catch my breath and quell the tears from welling over, I couldn't help but notice the twisted panic that festered in my chest. What if they were right? What if the iron levels were failing?

"Elowyn discovered her wedged between the rocks about an hour ago," the watchman told the coroner. "It doesn't appear to be an accident. I suspect foul play."

Everyone fell silent as they spoke. Whispers of the fae evoked pursed lips and judgment.

They gaped at me openly: the illegitimate child of the disgraced lady-in-waiting, Deirdre Rosewood. *Lovely.* I didn't need to hear their thoughts to know they'd run with that bit of information—gossiping about my mother and me was the vultures' favorite form of entertainment. Nothing about our lives remained off-limits to them. Not even my mother's illness.

I squeezed through the sea of bodies, thumbing the ring around my index finger. Closer and closer to Lilian's mangled corpse. I hugged my arms across my middle to shield my skin from the crisp spring air and conceal the involuntary tremors that riddled me. My body didn't feel like my own as I approached, each step too heavy. Too fast. Like I was in a dream and my mind was asleep.

The coroner shifted on her feet as I neared, trying but failing to conceal the wince on her face. She cleared her throat before turning to the watchman. "Would you mind informing Mrs. Quelling we've located her daughter and to come to the morgue right away—"

Their conversation faded away.

My ring ceased all movement.

I stared at Lilian. Her once bright brown irises were now glazed over—wide with terror—as she stared off into some otherworldly place, her arms and legs bent in an unnatural position.

I pulled my gaze away from Lilian and looked at the coroner.

"It's almost nightfall, and we need to get her back before curfew." Concern pulled at the coroner's thick eyebrows, yet something stern under the surface of her disposition put me on edge.

There my friend lay, her young life abruptly ended, and all they cared about was how to dispose of her as quickly as possible.

I rested my hands on my knees to stop the world from spinning. This couldn't be happening. It'd almost be comical if it weren't so tragic.

Stars forbid anyone be out past dusk in fear of a faerie coming to snatch them away.

The curfew King Edgar had implemented ten years ago did little to prevent these drownings and disappearances. In fact, it prevented nothing. Every year, the Dolorem River claimed countless lives. Dozens of children and adults, even household pets and cattle, still vanished without a trace. It was hard not to wonder if the fae were truly to blame or if they were a convenient scapegoat to maintain order without an uprising.

"Are you okay?" The coroner's voice sounded far away as

she turned her attention to me, the ground swaying under my feet.

No, I should have checked on her sooner! I wanted to scream. She had come there to paint every Wednesday morning and every afternoon, and, like clockwork, I'd meet her to grab a bite to eat at the farmers market. The one day I slept in an extra hour. The one day I took the longer, scenic route.

A cold sweat licked my skin; the world spun out of control.

I darted over to the willow tree—everyone's attention on me as I spewed up the contents of my stomach on the yellow and white daffodils.

The coroner approached me like I was an untamed animal, holding her palms up by her chest.

No.

I shook my head, unwilling—unable—to listen to whatever tumbled off her lips. The murmur of the crowd rose an octave, and all I could hear were their condescending remarks. Their unnecessary opinions. The venom that hid behind charming tones.

With each step the doctor took toward me, the harder it became to breathe, and I retreated. Stumbling until my back was flush against another tree several feet away, my vision blurred with tears.

"I—I'm sorry. I must go..." I tripped over a root, barely regaining my balance before skirting around the trunk and taking off in the opposite direction.

Away from the river.

Away from the vultures.

Away from Lilian.

Lacking any real destination, I only knew that I needed to get as far away from there as possible.

So, I ran.

My legs burned, and I flew through the dense woods,

faltering as I dodged a low-hanging branch that missed my head by inches, only to careen into a thorny bush.

Blood trickled down my arm. Stains of scarlet mushroomed where droplets hit my white dress, but I pushed forward, continuing deeper into the forest. I needed to get away. My lungs threatened to catch fire the harder and faster I ran, but I pushed through it. Ignored it. Relished in the pain as my mind emptied, and I concentrated on the uneven ground in front of me. The only thing that existed was the next step, the next breath. All the pent-up frustration, anger, and sadness broke free with each stride. Running was meditative—my escape from everything. From everyone.

When I reached a clearing, I collapsed onto the grass—the exposed skin on my arms and legs itching from the coarse sod beneath me.

I didn't care.

My body buzzed with energy as I rolled onto my back, my pulse slowing while I caught my breath.

"Safe. I'm safe, just breathe," I whispered.

A soft breeze rustled the trees, cooling my flushed face as birds chirped and sang around me. I soaked it up—pretending for a minute that everything was normal.

That Lilian wasn't dead.

And my mother wasn't sick.

Wellington Castle's clock tower echoed in the distance, bringing with it memories of a carefree childhood, and I hummed along to the deep, brassy chimes. Here, I could be whoever I wanted to be. Get lost in nature and forget about all my responsibilities. I knew I needed to get home, face reality— be the dutiful daughter I was—and make sure my mother took her nightly medicine.

But I soaked up the sun a while longer, mesmerized by the snowy tips of the Wintercrest Highlands and how they glowed under the sun's rays. It didn't seem fair that such a beautiful landmark had to waste away in the abhorrent faerie realm east of the Dolorem River. It was hard to believe we once lived in harmony with the same vile creatures rumored to be hunting and killing our people.

I closed my eyes for a few more moments.

According to legend, five hundred years ago, King Broderick II persecuted all magical beings for a decade-long famine that had killed hundreds of our people. Believing magic was responsible for The Great Blight, neighbor turned on neighbor, and villagers began killing anyone suspected of wielding it.

After years of bloodshed, human and fae emissaries finally reached an agreement. The Iron Accords were formed, and fae were banished to Faerway.

To cross the river, under the Accords, meant death.

I struggled to find the sense in why the fae would violate the Accords or how, after a decade, there wasn't a single reputable sighting of those ethereal beings. Some argued it was because they used magic—*glamours*—to make themselves invisible. Others claimed it was due to mind control. I didn't know what to believe. I'd been more concerned about caring for my sick mother these past two years than worrying myself with baseless hearsay. However, after today—after seeing the fear frozen in Lilian's eyes—there was no denying something untoward was going on in Wendover.

It was just before dusk by the time I made it home. I'd succumbed to my exhaustion and drifted off to sleep, only to startle awake hours later, shaking and disheveled.

The smell of fresh cinnamon enveloped me as I pushed open the solid cherry wood door to our cottage, relishing the warmth of the crackling fireplace. I soaked it up and savored the comfort only home could provide.

Our tiny cottage was tucked away in the countryside, surrounded by rolling hills and vast farmland miles away from the city—where an exiled lady-in-waiting and her bastard daughter were fit to live. Filled to the brim with eccentric, mismatched furniture, and random knick-knacks, it wasn't much to look at, but it was the only home I'd ever known.

In fact, the threadbare textile rug in front of the robust fireplace covered the bloodstain on the hardwood from where my mother had given birth to me.

As I entered the foyer, I made sure to remove my mud-soaked shoes and set them aside. Then, I found the usual spot for my satchel and settled it on the wooden barrel, which was serving as an improvised table. The actions were familiar —comforting.

"Mother, I'm home!" I called.

A light shuffle sounded from the bedroom as she made her way into the hall, her sunken cheeks lifting into a forlorn grimace when she saw me. "Sweet child, come here. What'd you do to your arm?" She frowned.

I tried to keep it together. Tried to be strong so she wouldn't worry about me, but the second she held out her arms, I was no longer the brave woman I pretended to be but a scared little girl who needed her mother. My lip quivered as she scuffled over and wrapped me in her bony arms, her light floral perfume caressing my cheek.

She'd always been smaller than me—my height, she told me, came from my father—but the difference between us was becoming glaringly apparent as her illness consumed her. It pained me to see her wither away.

"She's dead." My words came out in choppy breaths as hot tears streamed down my cheeks.

"Who child? What happened?"

"Lilian ... she's—she's dead," I sobbed. "I found her in the river." My arms clung to her tighter. "Oh, my stars, seeing her like that—so stiff—I can't get it out of my head. It's all my fault, if only I'd gotten there sooner."

My mother had already sacrificed so much, and now she was putting her physical pain aside to comfort me. The knot in my stomach tightened. The grief and guilt collided in an internal war that would leave me as the only casualty.

When the royals discovered she was pregnant, the kingdom had thrown itself into madness with speculation. A lady-in-waiting was supposed to be pure. Meant to save themselves for someone in the royal court. When she had refused to disclose who my father was, they exiled her. Leaving her—us—to fend for ourselves. To this day, years after his death, she kept him a secret. Even from me. All for the sake of protecting his name. His leafy gold ring shimmered under the light, catching my eye.

I looked at it now. Over her shoulder. I wore on my index finger, set with small amethysts, the only clue I had as to who he was. A physical reminder of his absence, even in name.

She rubbed the back of my head, smoothing my hair as the tears dwindled away. "Don't blame yourself, Elowyn. You couldn't have done *anything* to prevent what happened."

"But what if I could? What if I was only a few minutes too late?"

"The what-ifs will drive you insane, child, believe me." She pushed a stray piece of hair from my face, her amber eyes searching mine. "You can't save everyone. This realm is a wicked place."

Swiping at my cheeks, I nodded, needing to talk about something else. "Have you eaten anything today?" I asked, in a poor attempt to change the conversation. She and I both knew her appetite was nonexistent these days, but I needed to busy my hands and distract myself from the turmoil of my mind.

"Of course I ate, child. And yes, before you ask, I already took my medicines, too." Her tone was soft, if not filled with a light scolding.

I huffed my disbelief as I padded over to the kitchen—maybe if she didn't always act like a child, I wouldn't have to treat her as such. Ignoring her lies, I fished around the icebox to see what I could make.

My hands jittered, but I clenched my fists in an attempt to ward them off. If I was going to make it through the rest of this horrible day—the next few weeks—I needed to stay busy.

So, if hyper focusing on caring for my mother brought me a semblance of sanity, then that's what I'd do. "I can heat some soup from yesterday?"

"No, I told you I was fine." She waved her hand as she shuffled to her bedroom, signaling the end of the discussion. "I'm going to lie back down. Quit worrying about me."

Gone was the once vibrant woman who danced and sang around the house. She'd been replaced with a hollow shell of her past self. Medicines provided temporary relief, but the doctors told us there was no cure. I held onto hope that things would turn around, but each new day looked bleaker than the last.

After placing a pot of leftover soup on the cast-iron stove and setting the flame, I left it to simmer while I washed up and prepared for bed.

Drops of blood stained the sink as I cleaned the cut on my arm. Images of Lilian flashed in my mind, and I steadied my erratic breathing, trying to shove them away. I knew there was nothing I could've done to prevent her death, but it didn't stop the sense of dread that settled on top of my chest, turning my skin to ice. I splashed my face with water and glanced in the mirror, noting the dark, tired circles. Being my mother's caretaker, the weight of today, all of it was carved into my features, slowly draining the life from me.

The soup had warmed by the time I finished changing. With each bowl that I poured for us, the kitchen became infused with the rich and delicious combination of garlic and onion, creating a savory blend that made my stomach growl.

My mother pretended to be asleep when I entered her room —an attempt to avoid dinner—and a usual occurrence that grated on my nerves.

"Not tonight, lady." Purposefully allowing them to clash together, I placed the bowls on her bedside table and shuffled through the clutter for the serving tray. The noise would wake the stubbornness from her. "You need as much energy as you can get, and the only way you're going to get that is if you eat." I grabbed her hand and helped her up despite her reluctance and placed the bowl on the tray in front of her.

"Since when did you become so bossy?"

"Since the day I learned how to talk, now get eating."

"Of course." She huffed a laugh before launching into a coughing fit, her face turning bright red as she struggled for air.

I combed through her dresser in search of the smelling salts, located them under a pile of papers, and then held one under her nose.

Within seconds, her shoulders relaxed, and she took a full breath.

"You need to quit moving these." I set them on her bedside table, next to the nightly medicine she *allegedly* took. "Why do you insist on letting yourself suffer for no reason?"

"Please. I wish someone would put an arrow through my—"

"Mother!"

"You're eighteen years old, Elowyn. You should be out enjoying your life, not sitting around here worrying about an old hag." She dipped the spoon into her bowl, only half filling it, and slurped it into her mouth. "See, I'm better already."

I grabbed my soup and sank onto the bed by her feet, warming my hands on the bowl. I hated how flippant she was, how she didn't care about her health—or how it affected me. What was I supposed to do without her? I'd never been alone. Who'd answer my endless questions and help me navigate this harsh realm? I wasn't ready to do that by myself.

Defeat weighed heavy on my chest. I wasn't ready to be alone.

"I'm only trying to help, Mother. Your quality of life would improve if you tried. You can't just roll over and die."

She shook her head. "Forever hopeful, just like your father. May the stars bless his soul."

What an impossibly stubborn woman.

I finished eating the rest of my soup in silence until my belly felt warm and full, then laid on my side, waiting for Mother to finish hers so I could clear the dishes.

Her knobby fingers shook from the weight of the spoon, sending liquid splattering out of the bowl. I didn't realize until then how much grayer her hair had become. There was still a slight auburn tint to it, but it was dull and coarse and nothing like the deep, rich color we once shared. I picked at the skin around my nails. It was hard watching her age—watching her illness eat her away. No one prepares you for that. She'd say it was inevitable and 'proof of a well-lived life,' but it was still gut-wrenching.

"Why don't you ever talk about him? My father?" I asked after a while. It was a conversation I broached lightly. And one I never seemed to get answers from. Still, curiosity always got the best of me.

She smiled absently, her spoon clinking against the glass. "It was years ago, child. He was the most charming, handsome man

I'd ever met." My mother slurped her soup with a brightness to her eyes now. The memories served as a distraction from the task she disdained. "But we had a secret love affair—and the stars weren't in our favor. It's been for your own good to know as little as possible."

Realization smacked me in the face, making my jaw go slack. "Mother, did you—you had an affair with a married man!?"

"What do you take me for?" She chuckled, placing her bowl on the nightstand. Her face glowed with sentiment as she shook her head. "A married man. No, your father and I were simply worlds apart. I knew it. He knew it. But I wouldn't change a minute for anything in the stars. I'd relive that sorrow a hundred times over if it meant I could see him again."

She curled into herself, draping a throw blanket around her shoulders to warm her thinned skin. My mother's longing expression wasn't one of sadness but of joy, and I couldn't help but relish her nostalgia. A past I wish she could share with me.

"That must've been some epic love."

My mother's eyes twinkled as she stroked my face. "An epic love I can only hope you experience one day."

I wrinkled my nose in response and collected our dishes. While it was something I longed for, after the day I had, love remained the furthest thing from my mind.

Two

The weeks following Lilian's death slipped away like sand through fingers. A hazy blur of discomfort and a realm lacking color.

I found solace in the early mornings, when the dew had yet to settle, and the house was still asleep. Taking a sip of coffee, I savored the bold, rich aroma and settled into the chair by the bay window, draping a blanket over my legs.

There was nothing I loved more than witnessing the sun and moon's forbidden kiss as he cast away her shadows and briefly warmed her heart. These moments were becoming fewer and farther in between, however, as Mother's health was deteriorating faster than usual lately. I didn't know what day of the week it was half the time, but I forced myself to get through the motions. *Keep moving.*

Thanking my lucky stars for Nurse Betrys, who came a few hours every day to relieve me of some of the stress. And with my mother's stubborn attitude, I didn't think I could manage it alone.

I enjoyed another hour of uninterrupted birdwatching before my mother's deep, rattling cough echoed throughout the house. Her fit started earlier than usual, I noted, setting my now empty coffee mug on the glass table before padding into her room.

"I told you to leave your smelling salts on your bedside table. Are they there?" I pulled her curtains open, let the sun in, and stretched, my joints popping awake. "Hold them up to your—"

My body froze mid-movement when I turned around.

Blood dripped from my mother's mouth. Deep crimson was splattered across her white comforter and thick droplets sprayed her upper body.

My breath caught as Lilian's mangled limbs slammed into my mind's eye. The haunting expression in her eyes. The terror that tore through me. I thought I'd moved past it—accepted it at least—but there was so much blood.

The experience was so vivid that it felt as if I'd been transported back in time to that very moment. Fear completely overtook me, rendering me unable to move.

My mother coughed again, breaking me from my trance, and I blinked away the images, remembering how to breathe again.

"Oh, my stars! What happened?" I jumped into action, yanking the blankets down to assess the situation, but my brain was a muddled mess. She'd never coughed up so much blood before.

Another lighter cough spilled from her lips, and more blood ran down her chin.

Wiping my shaky hands along my sleep shirt, I scanned the room with wild eyes, figuring out where to begin. "I-It's okay. Let's clean you up, get you to the infirmary. You're going to be fine." *Everything is going to be fine.* "I'll go—"

She clicked her tongue, swatting me away. "Don't be rash, my throat's dry from all the coughing. I'm fine." My mother settled into bed, perfectly content, and fluffed her pillows to her liking.

"Coughing fit my ass," I mumbled under my breath as I stalked over to her dresser, rummaging through her medicine basket for her figroot tonic. It was the only thing that made a difference in times like these. Bottle after bottle clinked together —there had to be over twenty different ones in that damn thing, and my trembling fingers couldn't hold on to a damn one. "You haven't been taking the medicines I leave out, have you?"

Silence.

I peered over my shoulder, and she averted her gaze, fiddling with the blanket as I pulled out an empty figroot bottle.

More. I should've done more. Berating myself for my lack of caution, I ran a hand along my face. I'd been so shaken up over Lilian's death, I must've forgotten to get some of her medicine refilled. How could I let this slip through the cracks? It was my responsibility to take care of her, and I'd failed.

I failed.

All because I was too absorbed in my misery to notice, and now my mother's health was in jeopardy.

I took a deep gulp, clenching the frigid, hollow glass bottle in my hand, the weight of guilt flooding my chest. "I didn't realize. There must be five different tonics in here that need refilling." It took me a moment to work up the courage to face her. "Why didn't you tell me? I would've gone back to Mari's."

"Because it's unnecessary, child. I'm fine."

I scoffed, my tone matching the frustration that scratched beneath the surface. "You keep saying that, but it's not. It's not fine. Look at your bed!" Pacing the room, I rubbed my temples to regain my composure. "I understand you don't want me to worry, and I appreciate it, but I already do. Stop fighting me every step of the way." *You're making it worse*, I wanted to say.

A silent beat passed before she nodded, resigning to my demands, and I loosened a breath. She'd always been stubborn. However, it'd only gotten worse when she became ill. I tried to empathize, but it didn't make it any less disheartening. Especially when my efforts had gone unappreciated. *Unwanted.* I was tired of pretending it didn't bother me that my mother didn't care about her fate. That she didn't care to fight. She was the only person I had left.

I needed her.

"Okay, then. Let's get this cleaned up, and I'll head into town to get it filled."

Leading her into the bathroom, I dampened a rag, wiping her neck and face clean of residual blood before bringing her a change of clothes. I wasn't prepared to face the loss of my mother, but with each passing day, the looming, oppressive cloud grew larger and more burdensome. Rationalizing it hadn't helped either. No amount of reason could make any of this better. The best, most logical thing to do would be to prepare for the inevitable.

But how? How could I compartmentalize a lifetime of memories and feelings to arrange for something so final?

I guided her back into the bedroom to fit the bed with new sheets and helped her into it, making sure she had everything she could possibly need at arm's length. It was unlikely she'd bother with any of it, even if she required it for comfort, but I wouldn't stop hoping she would.

I still wished she would fight ... for me.

"I'll be home in about two hours, okay? Maybe sooner," I said, setting a kiss on her forehead. "Don't go anywhere."

"Smartass. Please be careful." She squeezed her eyelids shut in pain as she laughed.

～

My horse, Sugarfoot, was in her favorite spot under the oak tree, grazing on the only remaining patch of shaded grass. She was a birthday present from a distant family friend. Gifted to me when I'd turned five years old, we'd been inseparable ever since. My companion was a righteous pain in the ass most days. However, she understood me better than most.

I fastened my cloak around my shoulders to protect my arms from the rising sun and rolled my eyes. She had an entire field to roam, yet opted for that one desolate section. Either she was incredibly lazy—or spoiled rotten.

Little did she know I hadn't come barring apple slices, so the joke was on her.

"Hey pretty girl," I cooed, stroking her brown and black, brindle fur.

She nudged me with her snout, demanding more. *Yeah, totally rotten.*

"We need to go into town to get Mother her medicine."

Sugarfoot shook her mane in protest. She hated when I interrupted her grazing. Not that she ever stopped—she was a damn glutton.

"I know, but her coughing fits have gotten worse, and I'm afraid if we don't..." I trailed off and cleared my throat. "We won't be long, I promise." With a kiss to her snout and a resigned grunt from Sugarfoot, I grabbed her saddle off the tree and strapped it to her back. Dodging her thrashing head, I fit her bridle next.

I wiped my brow and peered at her. "Seriously? We'll be back before you know it, you lard. Be good and I see a few apples in your future. Now quit it."

Sugarfoot nickered, but she let me finish, remaining calm as I pulled myself onto the saddle. I swore she understood what I was saying—even if she did the opposite half the time. Mother would say she'd learned it from me, as if the apple didn't fall far from the tree.

I tapped my heels into her sides once, twice, bringing her to an immediate canter before we leaped over the picket fence and landed on the cobblestone street on the other side.

Her hooves clopped against the pavement in a rhythmic pattern, sending birds scattering in the opposite direction. The crisp breeze kissed my face as I leaned forward, cueing her into a gallop. An untamed smile adorned my face as we raced down the road, my blood surging through my veins. I loved the rush of going fast. When it was me and Sugarfoot out in the open, we were invincible—the closest to flying I'd ever get. And despite her lazy demeanor, she loved it too and pushed herself as fast as possible. Acres of field to play and run, yet she saved her short bursts of energy for me.

An hour later, Wellington Palace loomed into view. Atop the hill, the colossal white granite castle cast a commanding presence over the city. Tall, angular towers reached into the sky like needles, while the expansive cathedral windows shimmered in the sunlight.

Ahead, the square bustled with activity as locals perused the outdoor marketplace, and sellers enthusiastically called out prices. The air was filled with vibrant chatter, the enticing aroma of street food, and the colorful array of goods on display, created a familiar blend of vitality. So different from the stillness of my life on the outskirts.

I pulled my hood over my face as we trotted through the center of it—an attempt to avoid unnecessary conversation. If there was one thing people in this town loved more than talking about someone, it was pretending like they didn't. It was exhausting trying to decipher who you could and couldn't trust, and with Lilian's recent passing, I didn't care to rehash it. I'd had my fair share of confrontation with the townsfolk over the years, and the last thing I wanted this morning was to deal with their fake condolences.

When we arrived at the apothecary fifteen minutes later, I tied Sugarfoot to an empty wooden post beside the other horses and gripped her by the bridle. "You better behave yourself this time," I warned, readjusting my satchel.

She stuck her nose in the air to avoid the glower I gave her.

"If I have to chase your ass down because you chewed through another pair of reins to go gallivanting throughout the city, I swear I'll turn you into a pair of leather boots."

Sugarfoot huffed, and I whispered one more threat before turning my back on her.

The bell above the door jingled as I entered the store. Jars of multiple sizes that each contained a unique mixture covered the shelves in product order, further organized by color and size. It was homely and welcoming—and the gas lanterns and candlelight provided a calming ambiance against the hunter green walls and dark wood.

Mari wandered out from behind the curtain as I browsed the center display tables, her face bright and tone joyous when she spotted me. "Elowyn, how are you, love?" She flicked her wispy blonde bangs out of her eyes as she strolled over to me, pulling me into a hug.

I set the crystal I'd been admiring back on the table when she released me and met her friendly gaze. "Honestly? I've been better."

If there was someone with whom I could share my feelings and who would truly grasp what I was going through, it was Mari. She'd become like an adoptive aunt over the years, and I felt safe confiding in her. Never once had she made me feel small or judged. Not to mention, she always went above and beyond for my mother. People like her were hard to come by in Wendover. When you found one, you held on to them firmly.

"I read about Lilian. How sad, she was so young. You two were close, no?"

I nodded, offering nothing more as she rested her forearms on the display table across from me.

"Hm. Such a shame," Mari continued, "and your mother? How's she faring? How are those smelling rocks I gave you to try?"

"They're amazing. She's able to take a full breath within seconds during one of her coughing fits."

"Oh, good!" Her hands clasped under her chin. "I'm thrilled to hear it. Those took weeks to perfect. How are they lasting? Do you need more?" Mari shuffled through her assortment of wicker baskets.

I shook my head, tracing a finger along the different canisters and bowls on top of the table. "No, they're holding up great. I'm actually here to pick up more of your figroot tonic. Mother started coughing up blood this morning, and with everything going on, I didn't realize she was out."

"Oh love, I'm so sorry." Mari flicked her gaze to her feet. The frown on her face tied my stomach into knots. "Mrs. Belmont came by yesterday and bought the last bottle. Her husband's fallen ill, you know. I should've known and set some aside. I just knew something like this would happen." She continued to mumble to herself as she paced the shelves, frantically looking for something, when she finally grabbed an unlabeled, deep blue jar. "This is a new pain elixir I've been working on if you'd like to try it? It's not quite as strong, but it should hold her over—keep her comfortable, anyway. Just until I get it back in stock? No coin necessary, it's on the house."

Mari handed me the elixir, and I weighed the bottle in my hand, defeated. "When will you get the figroot back in stock?"

She wrung her stained apron between her fingers. "Well, you see, that specific tonic uses the black seeds found in

Elkway." Her face grew pained, and she took a sharp breath, causing my stomach to drop. "Until Wendover can settle on new trade agreements with them, I'm afraid I won't be getting another shipment."

My hands rested on the table so I wouldn't tip over. I remembered reading about the negotiations in the paper weeks ago—and the hysteria from local business that followed. But I would've assumed they'd reached an agreement by now. How was my mother—our realm—expected to survive without Elkway's imports? They were our main supplier of medicine, grains, and lumber. Wendover wasn't impoverished by any means. We produced many luxury goods. However, none of that would matter if townsfolk started dying from the common cold.

"I'm sorry, love." Mari reached for my cheek. "You're the second person I've had to turn away today. If there was anything else I could do, I would. But I'm confident this pain elixir will help immensely," she reassured me.

I chewed my lip. My mother needed that medicine. There must be something else—some other way to get it. She didn't need to be sedated; she needed a solution. Any solution. I couldn't go back empty-handed.

The walls of the apothecary pressed in on all sides, creating a closeness that weighed heavily on my senses. Air felt dense, and an invisible force seemed to constrict around me, making every breath a laborious effort. The very atmosphere conspired to squeeze the breath from my lungs, my chest threatening to implode.

"Thanks," I mustered after a moment. "I'm sure she'll appreciate this." I dropped the jar into my satchel and headed toward the door, the wheels in my mind turning.

"Elowyn," she called out as my heel met the street. "I'll send word the minute I hear the shipment is on its way. If you need anything, my door is always open."

If she lived that long, I wanted to say. Instead, I muttered another 'thanks' and stepped out, taking a full breath of the damp mid-morning air. Without the tonic, I couldn't see her making it another six months.

Sugarfoot sensed my disappointment as I approached and nuzzled her snout against my cheek.

"I was too late." I ran my fingers through her mane, trying but failing not to feel sorry for myself—for my mother—for my neglect. Her death would be on my hands. My stomach revolted as last night's dinner made its way to the back of my throat. "What am I supposed to do now, girl?"

I ransacked my worthless brain, desperate to come up with another plan.

A young girl, no older than ten, walked out of the bookstore carrying multiple brown bags—her defeated mother followed closely behind. The amount of money my mother spent on books for me when I was about that girl's age was likely in the hundreds. If only I could go back to those carefree days.

Sugarfoot nudged me in the same direction, but I brushed her off, reminiscing about the stories of beautiful faraway lands inside those fairytales I read late at night. She'd forbade me from reading them at one point. Mother was afraid I'd become disillusioned with reality, so I'd sneak them into the bag when she wasn't looking and hide them under my mattress. I still had my favorite, albeit very worn, copy of *A Void so Dark*, about a faerie princess on the verge of death. Her dark magic had consumed her, but the sun restored her health using nightingale, a flower with magical healing properties.

Sugarfoot nudged me again, and I whipped around—a

threat hanging on my tongue—when an idea popped into my head.

It was outlandish. Improbable. Downright *delusional*. Yet that didn't stop the smile that curled up my lips. What if such a flower existed?

"Stars, you're a genius!" I rubbed the top of her head. "I'll be right back, girl!"

Not wasting another minute, I pushed aside all logic and took off toward the bookstore, skidding to a stop before the stained-glass doors. I inhaled the warm, earthy scent of used books and entered. There was nothing more peaceful than the inside of a bookstore, the thousands of pages begging to be read. Characters to fall in love with. New worlds to get lost in. If only there was enough time in this life to read them all.

Relying on my intuition, I hastened up the creaky wooden staircase, weaving through the labyrinth of shelves. I held onto the hope that, when the moment came, I would recognize what I sought amidst the array of items.

The store was usually barren for a Saturday, with maybe two or three other customers wandering about. The faint hum of the phonograph trickled throughout the space, playing a lovely, classical piece I'd never heard before.

Shelf after shelf.

Book after book.

My finger had been damn near rubbed raw from running it along the endless book spines. Doubt gnawed at my ribs—this was ridiculous. Pointless. Maybe Mother was onto something. Maybe those books had disillusioned me from facing the realities of the world.

My shoulders rounded. I should just accept it. Let my guilt swallow me alive. Go back home with my tail between my legs.

Then, I saw it.

The mythology section loomed ahead, dark and tucked into

the far back corner of the bookstore, away from prying eyes. The hairs on my neck stood up as a worn, leather-bound book, unlike the rest, caught my eye.

I pulled it off the shelf. Something ancient inside me knew this book didn't belong there—even holding it felt wrong. It was whimsical and alien and filled with odd symbols and incantations. A grimoire, I realized.

It called to me.

But what was it doing there?

When King Broderick II banished the fae across the Dolorem River, they'd taken all their magic left with them. And all magical instruments had been eradicated—burned. Questions buzzed around in my head as I flipped through the pages, passing different potions and concoctions. Until I spotted it.

> *Nightingale:*
> *A late-spring flowering perennial. Star-shaped petals.*
> *Deep red foliage with a black stem and angular leaves.*
> *Fully erect and fast growing. Blooms at night and withers the forthcoming morning.*
>
> *Location: Faerway*
> *Usages: To prevent and cure respiratory ailments and diseases.*
>
> *Instructions: Bring one cup of water to a boil. Add two crushed nightingale flowers (stem included). Add a pinch of dandelion. Add two dollops of honey and let the mixture brew until it reaches a deep violet hue and promptly remove from heat.*

That was it.

That's the same description of the flower in *A Void so Dark*. I shivered from the goosebumps that tickled my neck and flipped it over in my hands, examining the worn edges and sigils on the cover. Searching the book to see who it belonged to revealed it was nameless. No price tag either. It was as if the universe had placed it there specifically for me to find.

I didn't want to risk anyone else discovering it, and as much as I didn't want to do what I did next, time was of the essence, and I had little to spare.

Checking over my shoulder, I slipped the book into my satchel and hurried down the staircase, passing the clerk with a small wave before shouldering the door open. My heart lurched as my feet hit the street outside.

Sugarfoot snorted her disapproval—sensing my deception —as I raced along the flagstone to the only person who could give me answers. Confirmation.

Mari startled as I charged through her door next, fumbling with the jar in her hand. "Elowyn, love, are you okay?" she asked, her hazel eyes wide with concern.

I nodded and waved off her question. Then I breathlessly slapped the book onto the counter and pushed it toward her, opening to the dog-eared page. I pointed to the image of the nightingale. "Have you heard of this before?"

Her jaw slacked. "Where did you get this book?"

"Is it real?" I pressed.

She straightened her apron, her nose crinkling in disgust. "In stories from fae folklore, yes."

"So, is it true? Is there some way to get it?" My words were desperate, but I didn't care to shroud my tone in bravery now.

Mari closed the book and shoved it across the counter like it was infected. "Not any I'm willing to take. If it was real, and I'm not saying it is, I wouldn't touch that flower. That realm and river are cursed. Who knows what dark magic runs through it?"

I ground my molars together. The answer to my mother's problems was potentially right in front of my face, and she expected a few scary stories to deter me? If it were true, and the nightingale did exist, the harm of not trying heavily outweighed the risk of taking a chance. Living in a world without my mother was not one I wanted to suffer.

Dark magic be damned.

"Leave this be, Elowyn," Mari warned as if she could read my thoughts. "I know how hard it is to watch someone you love—"

"Die?"

She wrung her hands, a beat of silence passing between us before she spoke again. "The best thing you can do is spend as much time with her as you can. At least try it. The elixir I provided will alleviate any adverse symptoms. When the trade deal settles, you'll be the first person I notify."

Mari's words passed over me but didn't fully settle. I nodded, tucking the grimoire under my arm, noticing the way Mari's shoulders slumped in relief as it left her presence.

She added, "Please, promise me you won't get involved in fae matters. They're cunning creatures. And not to be trusted."

Although I nodded again in agreement, I was deep in fore-thought. My reassurance to her absentminded—at best.

Because I'd already made up my mind.

I was going to cross the Dolorem River, find the nightingale flower, and right my wrong. Even if it was the last thing I did.

THREE

"All we can do now is make her comfortable."

Rain drummed against the window, muffling the nurse's words. Not that I needed the natural dampener, the rumbling terror in my ears did that already.

She stood at the other end of the table with her wrists perched on the top rail of the chair, her black hair pulled into a neat bun. Betrys had been tending to my mother since I'd gotten back from the apothecary six hours ago, and the exhaustion that rolled off her was palatable. It only got worse when I broke the news about the figroot tonic.

Although she did her best to remain professional, I could tell Betrys was frazzled. More on edge. And I was there with her.

Dread clung to the air. The unspoken—ever-encroaching—reality had come sooner than I ever hoped.

Stars, Betrys had been part of our family for almost a year. I'm sure it pained her to speak those words as much as it did me to hear them. With an internal sigh, I stabbed the carrot on my plate, chewing as my mother's plate grew cold beside mine. It was a sight I'd grown familiar with, but soon there would only be absence.

"I'll start coming earlier in the mornings until she nears the end," Betrys continued. "If you need any help to make burial arrangements, I can bring some information tomorrow. We can look at it together."

My fork clinked against the plate, and I sat back to meet her soft gaze, my chest tightening. It wasn't that I didn't appreciate her offer—I did—I just hated how we were there because of my mistake. The main thing I was responsible for.

"Thanks, Betrys." I smiled. "I can take it from here. You should get home before this weather worsens."

She began gathering her things when Mother shuffled out of her room and shuffled towards the table. Betrys set her bag on the floor and tried to assist her, but my mother shook her off.

"Oh, no need to bother. I got it," Mother said as she pulled out the chair. "I may be dying, but I can still manage a few things."

I gave Betrys a knowing look, silently thanking her for her patience as she pulled her hood over her head and slipped out the front door.

"Mm. Doesn't this smell delicious?" Mother marveled, fanning the napkin onto her lap. "Lamb—my favorite. It's been a while since you've made this." She stirred the mashed potatoes, helping herself to a large spoonful. "What's the occasion? Don't tell me you dropped your father's ring down the sink again."

I chuckled. The fury that feeble woman emitted that day had shaken me to the core—there wasn't a doubt in my mind she'd have murdered me if we weren't able to retrieve it.

I wasn't ignorant. Cooking my mother's favorite meal tonight wouldn't ease the wrath. Not after I told her what I was planning. But I hoped it'd lessen the blow.

"Did you have any more episodes today?" I ripped into a

piece of lamb, working up the nerve to tell her what I'd planned this time.

She, like most in Wendover, was terrified of the fae. For a moment, I debated not telling her, but my conscience talked me out of it. If I didn't return...

"No, the pain elixir Mari gave you did wonders."

"Really?"

"Yeah." She nodded. "It knocked me out almost immediately. I guess she figures I can't be in pain if I'm asleep."

The clatter of silverware scraping against our plates filled the beat of silence that followed. My throat dried. I was more of an ask for forgiveness, not permission, type of person, and the inevitable argument looming ahead had me on pins and needles.

"I went to the bookstore today," I finally said, taking a sip of water.

"Is that so?" Mother poked at her carrots. "Don't you already have enough books?"

"You can never have enough books, Mother."

"Tell that to the five bookshelves bowing from the weight of all yours." She pointed her fork at me and shook her head. "Did anything catch your eye?"

I shoveled more lamb into my mouth to bid myself time, mulling over the best way to tell her. "Yeah, actually." The following words rushed out before I could retreat from them. "A grimoire. It was so strange too, like someone knew I needed it and put it there for me to find. It detailed how to brew an elixir using nightingale, a magical—"

"Enough." She slammed her hand on the table, startling me. "What did I tell you about reading those fairytales? Filling your head with *ridiculous* ideas."

My eyebrows pulled together. "It's at least worth trying!"

"This conversation is over." Her fork stabbed into the lamb.

"My life is not worth yours—put an end to whatever you're thinking."

Frustration itched to the surface as she continued eating, and my grip on the fork tightened. I wasn't afraid, hiding books under my mattress, anymore. I wouldn't allow her to be taken from me.

"So, I should sit back and do nothing? Why? Why can't you ever accept my help?"

"Because I've never asked for it!" Her eyes cut into mine—a look I hadn't seen since I was a child, and my chin quaked. "The fae are more cruel and evil than anyone can imagine. Do you know what they'd do to you over there, girl?" A flash of pain crossed her features. There was something she wasn't telling me —I could feel it in my bones.

"Have you—have you met one before?"

"I said this conversation was over, Elowyn." Her fork clanked against the plate as she set it aside, done talking and done with dinner. "Let it go. All of it," she demanded.

Maybe it was pure stupidity to push. Maybe it was months and weeks' worth of bottled-up fear and anger and grief. But this conversation was far from over.

"No"—I tossed my napkin down—"I've sat here day in and day out watching you wither away. Refusing my help either out of pride or guilt—or whatever stars-forsaken reason. But I'm done. I can't. Expecting me to sit back and do nothing when there could be a solution on the other side of the river is beyond selfish. It's idiotic!"

Mother pushed back her chair and weakly stood, looking down her nose at me. A vicious tone filled her words. "You're just like your father. Dead set on being a martyr, trying to get yourself killed. Now that's idiotic!" She turned her back to me, a coldness I'd never felt from her, and headed toward her room.

"Clean these dishes up and get to bed. You're clearly demented from a lack of sleep," she said over her shoulder.

A rumble of thunder followed in her wake.

I wanted to go after her—finish the conversation and get her to see my side—but it was pointless. She'd made up her mind, and I knew there would be no getting through to her.

So, I sat there quietly, listening to the rain dwindle to nothing as I bid my time, trying not to let her harsh words get under my skin. Being compared to a man I didn't know felt odd, but being a martyr when the alternative was loneliness felt right.

While I respected her concerns, I had my own that needed tending to. This was my mistake, and regardless of whether she wanted my help or not, I'd be damned if I didn't make it right. I was done feeling useless.

I'd prove to her and everyone else in this realm just how capable I was. That I wasn't a good-for-nothing bastard child. This needed to work. It had to. There was no other option.

～

Mother,

By the time you read this, I'll be halfway to the Dolorem River. I know you never ask for my help (or want it), but I can't live with myself if I don't try. You said yourself, the what-ifs will drive me mad, so I need to make this right. Hopefully, I'll be home before Betrys begins her shift. However, if I'm not, you'll find your morning medicines beside this letter. Take them.

You've always been there for me. Now it's my turn to be there for you.

Please forgive me.

Love, Elowyn

It was just before sunrise the next day when I set the letter on Mother's nightstand and tiptoed out of her room, grateful I'd be miles away by the time she read it. I didn't want to hear the string of curses she'd unleash when she noticed I was gone. Although she was sweet and docile most of the time, her anger was unmatched.

Pulling my cloak tighter around me, I felt the cool morning air against my cheeks, a stark contrast to the warmth I'd left behind in my bed.

The sun hung low in the sky as I stepped outside, bypassing Sugarfoot as I made for the barn. I scanned the building, sheathing a hunting knife at my hip while I stuffed a bundle of rope into my satchel. I grew up in the Elmhurst Woods bordering my home and spent countless summers outside, climbing trees, and hunting small animals for supper. While my mother never approved, it came as natural as breathing.

The hike through the forest to the Dolorem River would only take a couple of hours, a path I'd taken many times, yet as I left the barn, beads of sweat dripping down my back, I couldn't shake the feeling I was massively unprepared.

"Mother's going to be pissed when she finds out I left," I told Sugarfoot, scratching the bridge of her nose.

She shook her mane in agreement, and my chest tightened.

"I'll be quick." My words came out as if I were trying to convince myself, too. "If anything happens, keep an eye on her, okay?"

Sugarfoot's brown eyes gleamed with a hint of sadness, or maybe it was hope. I couldn't tell the difference.

Unshed tears forced pressure to build in my throat, and I debated forgoing the entire thing. Sure, Mother had Betrys to care for her in the event everything went south, and I knew I was completely justified in doing whatever it took to help her, but was it *right*? I huffed a breath; it wasn't the time to think about the moral consequences. Everything would be okay. I'll find the nightingale and get out of Faerway undetected. Everything would work out.

With a resolved nod, I kissed Sugarfoot once more and started toward the forest's edge. Further from home. From my mother and safety. Further from warmth and everything I knew.

"Cross the river, grab the flower, and come back home," I repeated over and over again.

My stomach fluttered with anticipation as Sugarfoot reared up on her hind legs—a final goodbye as I disappeared over the grassy hill.

Above, a flock of ravens cawed, and I startled, instinctively wrapping a hand around the hilt of my knife, readying for an attack. Every snapping twig, each rustling bush, sent my nerves into overdrive. Nothing dangerous lived in this forest, aside from the occasional wolf, but that wasn't what had me on edge.

Maybe it was guilt—or regret—but the deeper I trekked into the forest, the harder it became to ignore the impending sense of dread. I knew better than to let the impulse take control. Because when someone you care about needs you, there's no time to stop and think about the consequences.

Taking a right at the moss-covered boulder, I walked another fifty yards until I reached a narrow creek and followed the water downstream. The trickling of the brook eased the tension coiling around my shoulders. It let my mind wander.

Hopping from rock to rock to keep my boots from getting wet, I glided forward. Like running, being in nature was therapeutic.

My head buzzed as I inhaled the fresh pine air, becoming

one with the forest. Something about being out in the wilderness filled me with such wild energy. I wished I could bottle it and drink it on a gloomy day. So, I focused on that feeling, casting my worries into the wind and allowed my instincts to take over.

About an hour later, I reached the Dolorem River and plopped down on the rocky shore, the wide body of water glistening under the sun. Swimming the length of it seemed impossible. Daunting, even.

I poked my toes in, sighing in delight as I welcomed the refreshing, cold water on my sun-kissed skin. It wouldn't be any different from all the other lakes and rivers I swam in, right?

Standing, I fished the rope out of my satchel with a trembling hand. A quick trip into Faerway surely wouldn't raise any flags. I'd be in and out before anyone noticed. Hopefully, even before my mother noticed, then I could snatch the letter and pretend it never happened.

For all we knew, the fae could be long extinct. I'd believe anything if it gave me enough courage to cross. I repeated my mantra once, twice, honing into that tranquil feeling that filled me moments ago.

Shrugging the satchel off my shoulder, I pulled out the bundle of rope, tossed my bag aside, and tied one end of it around my waist and the other to a nearby tree.

It wasn't bravery that had my legs moving of their own accord to the water's edge—I was doing what I needed to do to help my mother. She'd do it for me. I knew she would, even if she'd deny it to prevent me from doing the same.

With one last glance across the river, I took in the barren trees that lined Faerway's shore and rolled my shoulders. Stepping into the murky water immediately made my heart race. Another few steps. My dress billowed around me.

I sunk down to my neck, wading through the water until the slippery bottom dropped away.

Using my hands as makeshift oars, I glided through the river, gently paddling my feet behind me, mindful not to disturb any fish in the still waters. All the horror stories seemed trivial as I floated and took my time to move through the river.

The water lapped against my body, cradling me in its weightless arms. I stared up at the pale blue sky, searching for images within the clouds.

Then, something slick brushed against my foot.

Fear pricked my skin, and I flipped over, noticing the way the air stilled and birds stopped chirping.

It's just my imagination running wild, I told myself. A subconscious survival tactic my mind designed to keep me alive.

But my heart wouldn't calm. And air whooshed from my lips in a panicked series of pants.

Something was off. I could sense it.

I warily picked up my pace, trying not to draw attention to myself, only to be yanked underwater.

The river swallowed my screams as I thrashed below the surface, attempting to shake my foot from whatever held me in place, but I was stuck.

My lungs cried for air. *Please.*

The muscles in my legs ached, and I pulled and pulled, tugging until I freed my leg. As soon as my head emerged from the water, sharp air filled my lungs from the inhale.

I propelled forward, pushing my body to move faster—quicker—when a spiny, gray fin breached the surface, swimming alongside me before dipping out of view.

My heart slammed against my rib cage as rough scales brushed against my arm. My foot. My thigh.

I tried to reach for the knife at my hip, but I wasn't quick enough. Sharp claws—teeth—dug into my calf, and I shrieked in agony as I was pulled back under the water.

"Come, darling, don't be scared. I only want to play," the creature sang.

I didn't stop to wonder how I could hear its voice underwater—or why it sounded human. Only raw, unadulterated adrenaline pumped through my veins as I ripped my leg away, repeatedly slamming my hands and feet into its armored flesh as hard as I could, until I escaped its grasp.

"What's wrong?" The creature flashed its needlepoint teeth as it caught up to me—wrapping long, spindly fingers around my wrist. Its sinister voice lit with malice as its grip tightened. "It'll be fun, I promise."

I sure as hell wasn't about to find out.

Holding my breath, I willed my arms to carry me through the water, leaving a trail of blood in my wake.

After jamming my uninjured foot into its gills, it retreated, buying me enough time to swim away. My gaze flickered between my escape and its shadowy form beneath me.

Vengeance curled up its mouth as it lunged, tearing its webbed claw through the air toward my back. My feet met the rocky bottom once more, and I ran up the bank.

Narrowly escaping its claws, I crawled up the beach.

Soulless, beady orbs locked onto mine as the creature lingered at the surface. Its dark, stringy hair splayed out in the water around it.

I collapsed onto my back and tried to find my breath. It snarled, snapping its teeth in warning before slipping beneath the murky water. I couldn't move—paralyzed from the pain in my calf. From fear. From whatever that thing was.

Then, I realized that it was all true. A wave of terror washed over me, turning my skin to ice. The rumors of the river losing iron. The rumors of the fae. They were all true.

What had I done? How was I going to get back?

I clutched a hand to my chest, unsure if I was going to pass out or vomit or both. My chest rose and fell with haphazard breaths. I needed to get out of there. *Fast.*

Bottling my panic, I tried to stand but stumbled forward, crying out in the pain from the three large puncture wounds marring my skin. I bit my lip to keep quiet while I tore off the hem of my dress and wrapped it around my calf. I'd seen illustrations of different types of fae before, but that thing? That thing belonged in the underworld.

With the gash beginning to clot over, I pushed myself up and limped over to the nearest tree, tethering the rope to its trunk. It was secure enough, I thought, testing its resistance, hoping it'd support my weight long enough to shimmy across.

My lip grew tender as I unsheathed my knife, limping deeper into Faerway's forest. Leaves and trees blurred together —what had I been thinking?

Blood rushed to my ears, and I swayed. I didn't know where to find the nightingale, let alone how long I'd last while wounded. Pain radiated up my leg again; slices of icy pain surged into my skull.

This couldn't be happening. Was that heinous water crea-ture responsible for Lilian's death? Stars only knew what else lurked inside the forest.

I staggered ahead, fumbling my way through the trees as I kept my attention on the ground, searching the forest floor for anything resembling the nightingale, but nothing came close. It was useless. A foolish mission. My mother was right. If I didn't get back soon, I'd come down with an infection, or worse, be killed by whatever else lurked in the foliage.

Stumbling, I stopped and slapped a hand over my mouth as my injured leg rubbed against a thorn bush—silencing a scream —when deep male voices sounded from my right.

I hobbled behind a tree to remain out of sight and inched my head around the trunk, holding back a yelp of fear when I saw them. All three men were tall and slim and appeared like any normal human, except their ears were sharp. Their faces more angular.

Fae.

Clad in leather armor that hugged their well-fitted uniforms, they each carried a sword at their back. Their lethal demeanor made me stifle my breathing. I didn't know if they were guards or common fae, however, there was no denying their otherworldly beauty.

My jaw slacked—transfixed by their swift, agile movements as they breezed through the dense evergreen forest.

The shorter of the three stopped a few feet away and sniffed the air. "Do you smell that?" He grabbed the hilt of his dagger and whipped around, tracking the scent.

"Human filth," one replied. "This way."

The trio altered their course, veering toward the same direction I'd just come, causing a surge of tension to grip my already aching muscles. The blood that tricked down my thigh now meant more than a potential infection. They could scent me.

How the hell was I supposed to get out of there with them wandering around? My mother's words echoed in my head: *"The fae are more cruel and cunning and evil than anyone can imagine. Do you know what they'd do to you over there, girl?"*

One thing was sure, I didn't want to find out.

So, I waited until they were out of sight before I crept around the tree, making careful to not step on any twigs. When I slammed face-first into a leather breastplate, my blood turned to ice.

I took in the large, polished boots twice the size of mine as I stumbled back a step. The three faerie men towered over me, hindering my escape. *Shit.* I swallowed hard, allowing my gaze to travel up the body attached to the breastplate I'd run into, stopping when I met a pair of emerald eyes glowering down at me with pure disgust.

My nails dug into my palms, and I matched his scowl with a heated look of my own. I knew the odds of leaving this forest alive were next to none, but I wouldn't go down without a fight.

And there was no way I'd cower to a faerie.

"Well, aren't you a little far from home?"

"Go to hell."

The faerie man chuckled—the deep, raspy sound matching his voice. "We're already there. Don't worry, this will only hurt a little."

I didn't have time to protest as an invisible cord wrapped around my body, preventing me from moving.

A smoldering surge of heat coiled around my limbs like an invisible serpent, its fiery tendrils licking at my senses. The warmth seemed to steal the very light from my vision, leaving nothing but a smoky haze in its wake. As the intensity increased, the world around me blurred, until, inevitably, I succumbed to the inky abyss of unconsciousness.

FOUR

Stomach acid bubbled up my throat, its acrid taste lingering, as I regained consciousness within the confines of an inky black dungeon.

Where am I? How long have I been here?

My pulse pounded in my ears, and I rolled over on the dirt-sodden floor, gagging on the old, rancid air, and stood up, crashing into the stone wall as my injured leg gave out from underneath me.

The pain. It was too much. I screamed, clenching my knee while images of the repulsive, reptilian creature flashed in my mind. As did the emerald-eyed faerie and his impenetrable glare.

Of all the illustrations I'd seen, nothing could have prepared me for the intensity that crackled in the air around him, the way it weakened my limbs. Or maybe it was the pounding headache chiseling away at my skull. My thoughts were lost in a labyrinth maze as I struggled to breathe.

Fear sunk its dark, unforgiving jaws into my bones, and a wave of hot terror ripped through my flesh. This couldn't be happening. How was I going to get out of here? I couldn't die. Not yet. And not like this.

But I couldn't move.

I tried pulling myself back up the wall, but my body wouldn't respond. Slamming my hands into the wall, I yelled in frustration until my lungs deflated. Until I had nothing left inside me. I was determined not to be consigned to an eternity of enslavement or compelled into a marriage with one of those repulsive and vile creatures—or any of the other punishments I'd read about.

My future wasn't meant to be this. I needed to save her.

I pushed the heel of my palms into my temples, desperate for the pain in my head to subside so I could think, but the all-consuming terror still paralyzed me.

What if I couldn't get back home?

My mother would die, and I wouldn't be there to say good-bye. She'd spend her last days wondering what happened to me, riddled with guilt.

The room pulsated as I found my strength and limped over to the iron bars, digging my nails into the metal while a searing hot pain radiated up my leg. Torches lined the stone walls on the other side of the door, emitting faint embers of light along the endless corridor. I coughed as the damp, putrid air choked the flames.

"Help!" my shrill voice rang through the narrow chamber—the sound foreign to my ears, "Please somebody help me!"

Over and over and over again, I begged someone to save me until tears stained my cheeks and my voice went hoarse. Over and over until I had no breath left to spare.

Only silence replied.

My arms went numb, and I dropped to the ground with a thud, gripping the dirt as I prayed someone would come to my rescue. Begged the stars to hear my prayers through choked, angry cries.

I couldn't live out the rest of my days in this dungeon—or enslaved to the faerie king.

Lilian had told me a story once about how he'd trap human souls inside a jar and keep them on his shelf as a collectible. In hindsight, it was a blessing Lilian had died, so she didn't have to endure this suffering.

I winced.

The horror stories were endless—all of which concluded indentured servitude or death. I needed to get out of there.

My entire body teetered on the brink of collapse, the sensation of my ribcage cracking accompanying each labored breath. All I wanted was my mother; to go back to last night and heed her advice. When the creature attacked, I should've swum back to Wendover's shore, not toward Faerway. It should've been the final warning.

Pulling my dress up, I examined my wound, hissing as the fabric lightly rubbed against it. I didn't know what infection looked like, but I was pretty sure wounds weren't supposed to ooze yellow pus.

I wiped at the lingering tears itching my cheeks, but it only created a trail of mud in its wake. Dirt clung to every inch of my body, every crevice. My white dress was painted black. I wanted to crawl out of my body—shed this skin like some reptile and slither between those bars. To go home. *Scream.* But my voice disappeared into the inky void I lay in.

A chill blanketed my body now that I'd stilled, so I hugged my arms around myself, desperate for warmth. It would've been easy to feel sorry for myself and blame the stars for this horrible twist of fate, but it was my fault. I knew the risks and did it, anyway. A suicide mission with willful ignorance.

A dry laugh stuck to my windpipe as I rocked back and forth, fighting to stay awake and find whatever semblance of strength remained when the heavy tread of boots against stone sounded from somewhere in the dungeon.

My neck snapped in its direction.

I attempted to scurry into the far corner of the cell to hide in the darkness, but my body turned to lead and refused to move. Instead, I lay there unmoving, holding my breath, the sound of my chattering teeth vibrating across my jaw.

The metal door opened with a whine, and the footfall grew louder, stopping inches away from my face. I wasn't sure if I was playing dead or if I was slipping into it, but when a guttural laugh sounded above, I knew for a fact my heart stopped.

I'd read enough stories about the fae to know they had keen vision and impeccable hearing, so I knew I wasn't fooling whoever entered my cell. Nevertheless, it didn't stop me from trying. Not that I needed to. My body was limp. Cold. My breaths came and went in shallow gasps. If this person wasn't there to kill me, whatever festered in my cut would.

The tip of a boot nudged me in the shoulder. Rough and uncaring. "She doesn't look good, man. The wraith's venom has probably spread to her bones. Are you sure this will work?"

"It has to."

The deep voices blurred together as unconsciousness pulled me into its grips. It sounded like there were two of them, maybe more. Their conversation blended with my own thoughts. Soon, I couldn't decipher whose was whose.

The floor tilted, and I held onto the ground—my eyelids fluttering open to see my mother at the far end of the cell. My fingertips itched to reach for her. Finding traction in the dirt, only for the river's tide washed her away. Crows cawed in the distance. Men laughed.

I shook my head, coming to—panic squeezing my chest. The way my imagination jumbled with reality, I couldn't guarantee anyone was there. But I couldn't take any chances. I couldn't go down yet.

"Please, no. No, no!" I flailed my limbs in every direction, fighting off invisible assailants, but I met nothing but air. My head weighed a hundred pounds, throbbing with each movement. I was desperate to escape. Reaching to the bottomless depths of my core, I searched for the strength to run, but only met emptiness.

A flash of golden light filled the room, scorching my skin like it did in the forest, licking my body like a blazing fire.

I screamed.

Cursed.

Begged for it to end—and my screams traveled to the edge of the world until there was nothing left.

Upon waking again, a heavy pang of disappointment squeezed my chest, its weight a palpable, leaden presence. I wished whoever came into my cell would've killed me. Spared me. Showed me mercy instead of keeping me locked away in a grimy dungeon while I awaited whatever punishment would come.

But there wasn't time to panic. I needed to keep as calm as possible and formulate an actual plan to get home without drawing suspicion. Over my dead body would I be married off to one of those demonic creatures.

Perching myself against the wall, I expected my body to scream in protest, but ... I was fine. Refreshed. Only the lingering fragments of a headache remained. I pulled my pant leg up and gasped. There was no gash. No yellow puss. Not even dried blood lingered in its place. It was as if the water creature—wraith—attack had never happened.

Like I imagined it.

Why would they heal me? Unless, of course, I imagined that too. Maybe I was going mad.

"Hello," a small voice squeaked.

I startled, scrambling into the far corner of the cell—as if the walls would suck me in.

There was a little giggle. "Oh, I won't hurt you, human." A fluffy tan and white animal, no larger than my palm, stared at me. Its big brown irises took up half its face.

My brows knitted together, and I pointed to my chest. "Are you ... did you ... just talk to me?"

Sure, I'd joke I could talk to Sugarfoot, but she never spoke any words. It was her mannerisms. A silly quirk, if you will. However, this creature, just like the one in the water, actually *talked*. I wasn't sure how such a thing was possible. And it made my skin crawl.

"I could ask you the same thing." Its bat ears twitched.

I rubbed my temples, and it grinned, clasping its paws together. It appeared to be a chipmunk or a mouse but with a long, curly tail. A woodland animal of sorts, but nothing I'd ever seen or talked to. It seemed harmless enough.

"I'm sorry. What are you?"

"A felk, obviously." It plopped down on its butt. "Do you have a name, human?"

I paused, wondering if I should respond. "Elowyn," I offered, submitting to the nagging voice inside my head telling me I could trust it.

"El-o-wyn," she—definitely a female—enunciated my name as if it were tasting it on its tongue. "I'm Pipion. But my friends call me Pip." Her pink nose flared. "You've been sleeping a long time. You smell funny."

I pulled the collar of my dress to my nose and inhaled, my face squinting from the stench. She wasn't wrong—I smelled awful. "How long have I been sleeping?"

"Three days."

"Three days!"

Pipion shushed me, waving her paws through the air. "Keep your voice low, they'll hear you."

I shook my head, still unable to grasp the fact I was talking to an animal. "Who's they?"

"King Harkin's guards. Some of them will do anything for that cruel man, you know"—she shuddered—"and with the trials starting, everyone's on edge."

I inched closer to keep my voice hushed, curiosity getting the best of me. "Trials? What do you mean?"

Pipion hopped onto my lap, ignoring my question, and my back went rigid. Her tiny paws tickled my leg as she climbed up my dress and placed her paws on my forehead.

I went to flick her off me, unsure what she was doing, when a quick flash of light flooded the room. Once it'd receded, I touched my face, making sure nothing was missing or disfigured. Unlike when the faerie man cast his magic, this was painless.

"What did you do?"

Pipion held up her paws. "You were dirty. I figured you wouldn't want to look like that in front of everyone. I can't fix the smell, though."

Everyone? I scanned the cell. "Are there other creatures in here that I can't see?"

"I've always wanted to talk to a human." She cocked her head. "But none of the other humans can hear me. I've tried countless times. Why can you?"

It was hard to be irritated with her elusiveness—not when her comment about the other humans had blood rushing to my ears. I could taste the small glimmer of hope hanging in the air.

"There are other humans here?" I kept my tone nonchalant and sat up straighter, not wanting to appear too eager.

"Yeah, they're all in cages like you."

"How long have they been here?" I asked. A pit formed in my stomach.

"A couple of weeks, at least. Some for longer. I'm not sure." Pipion's ears twitched, and she darted to the metal bars on all fours.

"Have any of them been able to leave?"

"I'm afraid not." Her bushy tail straightened. "He's coming, I must go. It was nice meeting you, Elowyn. Hopefully, we can talk soon." With that, Pipion snapped her paw and disappeared into the air, leaving me alone in the cell yet again.

I sank against the wall, confused.

I had to be going mad. There was no other explanation.

There was no time to find one either, as the faerie guard with the emerald eyes appeared at the door wearing the same uniform he had on the other day. My breath hitched—partly out of fear—but it was as if his presence sucked the air out of the cell. Dominance and power rolled off him, and I knew he could kill me in an instant if he wanted to.

"Get up." He leaned against the cell door and crossed his arms—his silky voice dipped in malice.

My gaze traveled along his broad chest to the dagger at his hip. Then I obeyed and sat up, my head lulling to the side as I glared at him. I had to stay alive, but I wouldn't submit to them fully.

He rested a palm on the dagger's embellished hilt and sucked his teeth. "I will not ask you again. King Harkin and Prince Bowen request your presence in the throne room. Either you get up or I'll drag you there myself."

I fidgeted under his intense gaze—and, clenching my jaw, I stood on quivering legs. He loomed over me, making my tall stature seem insignificant in comparison. But I wouldn't back down, not without a fight. So, with my shoulders squared, I refused.

"Is all this necessary?" I pointed to his sharp weapons attached to various parts of his body. "Surely you can't be afraid of a human."

"We can do this the easy way or the hard way. I'd prefer the latter, but it's up to you."

"You can't believe I'd go with you voluntarily, can you?"

He shrugged. "Suit yourself."

Before I could blink, the faerie guard was in my cell with his hand around my arm, a wicked gleam across his face.

I tried to weasel out of his grip, but his hold remained strong. "Let go of me!"

An irritated snarl rumbled deep in his chest as I hit and clawed at his chest. It didn't faze him. If anything, it fueled his frustration. "These idiotic and suicidal attempts at escaping would be funny if it weren't so irritating."

I spat at his feet. "You're one to talk for a lowly brute. I can see why humans think so little of you creatures."

His raven hair fell into his face as he grabbed both my wrists in one hand and pinned them behind my back. While my breathing grew ragged, his stilled.

"Does it feel good?" I thrashed with a grunt. "Overpowering someone half your size?"

He gripped my chin. "Keep testing me."

"Or what? You're going to kill me? Please, spare me the theatrics."

He clenched his jaw and shoved me forward, causing me to trip on my own feet, but he didn't care. The faerie man kept walking, kept forcing me further and further down the narrow corridor.

I peered inside each cell lining the way, trying to spot the other humans that Pipion mentioned, but I didn't see anyone.

Only rows and rows of empty cells inside a damp, cold dungeon that led nowhere.

We walked until my feet went numb before light appeared at the end of the hallway, blinding me. I half expected to enter a barbaric castle filled with tortured and crying souls, but the room before us left my jaw on the floor.

It was light and majestic—boundless and bewitching. Vines and flowers clung to the ceiling and wrapped around the columns. Large iridescent windows cast a spectrum of colors onto the marble floor, entrancing my mind, and for a split second, I'd forgotten I was in a realm crawling with foul creatures. Dancing light unfolded, and a shiver ran down my spine, a stark reminder that beauty coexisted with peril on this side of the river. Enchantment held hands with danger.

I saw them as we neared a set of double doors adorned with intricate carvings—the other humans. There were nine, each with a faerie guard at their side. I tried picking up my pace to reach them sooner, but the cruel guard held me back.

"You're not to speak to anyone until after you meet with the court. Do you understand?"

"Says who?"

"You sure are demanding for someone not in the position to make them." He huffed a laugh, keeping his attention ahead. "I don't care to listen to you drone on and on about trivial human nonsense."

I scoffed. "Trivial? I'd hardly call being held captive against our will trivial."

The guard jerked me to a stop out of earshot of the other humans. "Are you done?" His question sounded more like a demand.

"Not even close, you brute." I matched his scowl.

Loud, orchestral music played from behind the closed doors —the rich, graceful assortment of violins and flutes rang through the air, as did the murmurs of a sizable crowd. A symphony to accompany punishment. It was beautiful. Terrifying. Who knew what horrors awaited us in that room?

I shook my head. The fae were more deranged than I imagined.

"I hope you've gotten your snide comments out of your system," the faerie guard purred into my ear. The hair on the back of my neck stood at attention. "The king will not be as forgiving of your disrespectful remarks—so don't screw it up."

I ground my molars together. "Am I supposed to drop to my knees now or later?"

"When your insides are leaking onto the floor, don't say I didn't warn you."

With that, he seized my arm. A permanent bruise likely marred my skin, and he led me into the lion's den.

FIVE

The throne room was darker than the rest of the building, glaringly so, and it took a minute for my vision to adjust. Blue and green opulent light leaped along the cathedral ceiling and down the walls, while a golden throne sat high on a dais in the middle of the room. It was mesmerizing and intimidating all in the same breath, and blood drained from my face.

Days ago, my mother and I were eating dinner together, and now there I was: stripped of my dignity. A prisoner.

My life hung in the balance of this majestic room, leaving me powerless as they decided my fate. I twisted the ring around my finger, struggling to remain upright as my knees knocked together.

Cheers and hollers erupted as we entered, and one by one, we made our way to the dais. I loosened my shaky breath and forced my face into neutrality as I took in the rows and rows of fae bordering each side of the room, reaching to the very top of the vaulted ceiling. They were there to watch the punishment unfold.

My skin burned like molten lava under the warmth of the

candles adorning the metal chandeliers. Sweat beaded on my forehead, and I wiped it away, pretending there weren't hundreds of people watching me.

I hated crowds. Hated being the center of attention.

"Stop!" a blood-curdling shrill sounded to my right.

From the corner of my eye, a tall girl with honey blonde hair dropped to her knees. Tears streamed down her red, swollen face.

"Please, someone! Have mercy on my soul—"

Her abrupt silence had my head whipping in her direction. Her mouth was still moving, the veins in her neck straining, but nothing was coming out. It was as if someone had muted her.

"Apparently, she didn't get the memo," the faerie guard said, just above an audible whisper. "You're welcome."

I bit the inside of my cheek. Less than ten minutes around this prick and I wanted nothing more than to mute him and his condescending comments. I knew his type. The guards in Wendover held the same arrogance—like they were better than everyone because of the title they held. He was nothing but a power tripping, egotistical, arrogant, domineering asshole, who thought he could get away with murder because he had a pretty face. Well, I wouldn't put up with it.

The candles above dimmed, turning the throne room pitch black before a light shone on a bald courtier at the top of the dais. He gripped his jacket lapels. "Please rise for King Harkin Rathborne and the beloved Prince Bowen."

The fae court erupted into applause once more.

King Harkin made his entrance and settled into his plush throne. He was a healthy, wide-set man—and his blond hair glistened under the array of candlelight as he stared down his pointed nose with animalistic curiosity.

Prince Bowen followed closely after him, wearing similar royal blue robes and a jeweled crown like the king. Admittedly, he was handsome. A spitting image of his father—if he were thirty years younger and with a slimmer frame. Their beauty shouldn't have surprised me. They were all stunning.

Both men waved to their adoring court, soaking up every ounce of praise and admiration as if it energized them. It was disturbing. Borderline embarrassing, if I were being honest. King and Queen Wellington would never act like that. They were humble. The people's leaders. They cared about us and our realm.

This kingdom—whoever this king was—it was clear they held themselves in high regard.

I shuddered—unable to shake the suspicion that something wicked festered beneath the king's attentive façade.

The crowd went silent with the wave of the king's hand. "Sprites and pixies, faerie and nymphs, welcome to the tenth annual Seven Deadly Trials."

Another round of applause erupted before he silenced them once more, stopping and starting like a windblown flame.

My bones shivered. Trials? Pipion mentioned something about that, but what did it mean for us? A lump formed in my throat—that almost seemed worse than death.

A shapeless cloud appeared a few feet above the dais, shifting and expanding, waiting for the king to speak.

"Over five hundred years ago, the great blight almost decimated our world," he started.

Images formed in the cloud, providing a visual reenactment of events.

"We worked hand in hand with the humans for a hundred years, doing everything in our power to restore balance. Some of us went as far as depleting our own magic for the greater good of civilization." The cloud darkened and rumbled with thunder. "But none of it mattered. Humans turned on us—blamed us for the blight and labeled us as demons. Monsters to be hunted and slaughtered for false retribution.

"For another fifty years, humans persecuted our people, and we were on the brink of extinction until the establishment of the Iron Accords."

Images of a desolate Faerway flashed across the cloud's surface, showing the gradual transformation of their kingdom to the present day.

"They banished us west of the Dolorem River, to the wastelands of the world where they thought we'd fall over and die. But we thrived!"

Excitement and pride permeated the air. The fae chanted in a strange, unrecognizable language, while images on the cloud showcased the growth and fruition of their kingdom. I had to admit it was thriving without human intervention.

The king raised two fingers, and the room went silent again. "That same treaty established stipulations that would allow us to continue to live in peace. It implied each realm could execute any adversary found on their land in whatever manner they saw fit."

The candles encircling the throne room strobed as the orchestral music played in rapid succession, causing the crowd to go feral. A wicked gleam etched into their cruel faces. I fidgeted with my dress sleeves, ignoring the harsh cackles echoing throughout the room.

"However, because we are a kind, forgiving species," the king boomed, "we're gracious enough to give you humans a second chance. Show you the mercy that your kind didn't show us, give you an opportunity to go home."

My body went stiff as dread stabbed my gut.

He continued, "These ten individuals before us will go through seven trials, designed to put their virtues to the test and use their human nature against them." The king paused, flashing his sharp teeth. "The last one living may go home."

The last one living?

The hair on the back of my neck stood as I peeked at the other nine individuals, who were now my competition, their faces as grave as my own. This sadistic, cruel form of punishment was entertainment for them. I knew the fae were tricksters and loved wordplay, but this was something else. This was evil. Turning us against each other to fight for our freedoms, using our own motivations against us.

My jaw tightened, and I clenched my hands in front of me, containing my anger and trying so hard to push it down. My unease threatened to spill over. This wasn't how any of this was supposed to happen! My mother would die if I didn't get back home to her. I didn't have time to play an absurd faerie game.

Everyone's warnings came flooding in at once, churning my stomach. Flushing my skin.

The room was too small—too hot.

"Our competitors will receive upgraded accommodations as they take part in the trials, however, I may revoke or extend privileges depending on their performance. They'll also receive a faerie mentor to help them train and navigate these trials. After all, we want a good fight, don't we?"

The crowd responded in confirmation. They wanted a show. A bloodbath. They wanted revenge.

All the air evaporated from the room at once, choking me into submission.

The weight of the king's words was too heavy.

The flicker of the candles like needle pricks to my skin.

How am I going to get out of this alive?

The crowd cheered and whistled their agreement, and the king puffed his chest. This was barbaric. All because of what happened centuries ago? And he called their species kind and forgiving? I dug my nails into my palms.

More like vengeful and sadistic.

"Now let's meet our competitors. When you're presented, offer us your name."

A cold sweat coated my skin.

A tall, muscular guy who appeared around my age stepped forward. He looked like a carbon copy of all the Royal Guards in Wendover, with his dark brown hair shaved close to his scalp. A sentry ready for orders. He clenched his jaw as he stared at the king. "Kelvin Amhurst."

My eyes widened—his nasal tone was a striking difference from the king's deep, robust voice.

"Calandra Edgeworth," the slender girl beside him announced.

I turned to put a face to the meek voice, but she fell back into line as quickly as she came forward. I only caught a glimpse of a soiled leather shoe.

A shorter, stocky guy stepped up next. His tapered blond curls bounced with each step—his shoulder blades practically touching as he puffed out his chest. Pretension seeped off him, and I scrunched my nose. "Aeron Beckworth," he said with his chin held high.

My bones turned to water as the other competitors announced their names, anxiously awaiting my turn.

Jeston Willows, Irving Munoz, Martell Colt, and Sage Sulwyn, all of whom appeared to be in their late teens—Martell, possibly in his late twenties—and like everyone else, their clothes were dirty and tattered.

The guard nudged me forward, and my knees almost buckled from beneath me.

King Harkin glowered at the sight of me, and the room spun as I found my voice. "Elowyn Rosewood."

"Looks like you two are already off to a great start," the guard whispered as I wobbled back into line and bit my cheek.

I held back my thoughts on where he could shove his patronizing comments and could've sworn he chuckled.

The tall girl—the one muted from earlier—stepped forward, her face still swollen with tears. "Breana Flint." Her guard jerked her back into line, and she let out a voiceless yelp.

My heart twisted. I didn't know what everyone did to end up there, but I couldn't imagine a death sentence was warranted punishment.

A small boyish voice broke me from my thoughts. "Lewis Fields."

Lewis Fields?

I recognized his name.

Leaning back onto my heels, I glimpsed his towhead and remembered the story of the young boy who disappeared from Wendover earlier this year. The town's paper wrote about how his mother searched endlessly day and night for weeks. Months. Refusing to give up. They later admitted her into the asylum, going mad with grief. Had he been there the entire time?

Blood surged to my ears. I wanted nothing more than to run as far away from this place as possible. I didn't stand a chance—none of us did.

The fae talked amongst themselves once we had finished presenting ourselves, their pointed and judgmental leers scrutinizing our every move.

"You'll meet back here in one hour for your assessments." The king stood, and the court hushed at once. "These assessments will put your skills—or lack of—on display to gain the interest of a faerie mentor. They'll be your biggest hope of survival. Should you *not* win the attention of one? Well, you'll be disqualified," he announced. A cruel smile spread across his face, revealing his pointed teeth.

Disqualified. The world tumbled through my mind as I thumbed the ring around my finger—the stakes to save my mother just became impossibly high. I wasn't a killer. I couldn't remember to fill all my mother's medicines. How was I going to outsmart these nine other people, let alone the faerie king?

King Harkin squared his shoulders as the cheers dwindled, and he stood from the throne.

I shifted on my feet as our eyes met, sending a jolt of panic to my belly.

"See you shortly, competitors."

Despite the urgency that left no room for fear, my mind was a chaotic whirlwind, unable to untangle the jumbled thoughts bouncing around inside my skull. The stark realization struck me: I was compelled to take a life. *Oh, my stars*, I found myself grappling with the unsettling truth. One day soon, I'd have to end someone's existence. Take their life before they took mine.

You could cut the tension with a knife as we filed down the maids' corridor. I didn't know where they were taking us, only that the dampness in the air sliced me to the bone. None of us spoke as we walked in a single file along the stone path, each of our guards to our left as if we were the threat.

"Excuse me," a raspy voice uttered. "Where are we going?"

I peered at the front of the line to see who the question came from. It was the red-headed girl, Sage. Her frizzy braid flapped against her back as she struggled to keep up—the heavy chains likely weighing her down.

"To get fitted for your garments," her guard replied.

I noted how he wasn't as tall or muscular as the emerald-eyed faerie who'd captured me, but I knew better than to underestimate his abilities. He'd kill us in a second with no remorse.

Every one of these fae would, if given the chance, yet they deemed themselves merciful because they didn't.

It made me sick. Especially considering how many humans disappeared without a trace from Wendover every year—and how many more mangled bodies, like Lilian's, washed up on the Dolorem's shore. Given the barbaric nature of our punishment, the coincidence that the fae weren't responsible for the deaths and disappearances was too great to ignore.

Merciful my ass.

They herded us into a small room with floor-to-ceiling windows and walls of endless shelves filled with fabric of every color imaginable. An assortment of ornate rugs covered the stone floor and stained-glass lanterns hung from the ceiling. The colors made the space feel light but did nothing to improve my somber mood.

Plush furniture and a wood mantled fireplace sat at the north end of the room where the seamstresses stood, furnished with lavish candles and lush pillows. It was cozy. Warm.

A swell of homesickness formed in my belly. I hadn't felt warmth since leaving my bed all those days ago.

"Two lines of five each. Let's get a move on it," a random guard demanded, and everyone followed suit, breaking off into two rows.

Some of the other competitors were borderline malnourished, while others appeared as strong as the guards. I knew I fell somewhere in the middle, but it seemed to be such an unfair advantage. I couldn't kill them. I couldn't kill any of them.

It was unethical.

How could the faerie king put our virtues to the test when his own morals were corrupt? It was beyond hypocritical.

"It's almost unfair how easy this will be."

I folded into myself when I noticed Aeron's icy blue gaze inspecting me. He wasn't much older than me, I assumed, but the bags under his eyes made him appear years my senior. I couldn't help but wonder how long he'd been here. A silent beat passed as he continued to assess me, smacking his lips with distaste.

"With an ass like yours, it's a shame you don't stand a chance. Don't worry, I'll take it easy on you." He winked.

I knew he was trying to get under my skin, but I wouldn't play into it. I couldn't let myself get caught up in mind games and silly rivalries. Only one of us would leave here alive—I needed to concentrate on surviving with my soul intact.

The line inched forward, and my skin prickled with goosebumps.

Aeron continued to dissect me from his peripheral vision, harshly judging my every imperfection and calculating how he could use whatever flaws he searched for to his advantage. However, his leer wasn't the only one I sensed, and the gnawing suspicion heated my neck.

I turned to find the emerald-eyed faerie watching me. His face revealed nothing, and I wrung my hands—feeling like I was still on trial—before dropping them to my sides. Giving away my emotions so freely wasn't an option anymore.

The seamstresses gestured for us to step forward and then tapped our arms and legs open. As she touched me, I held my breath, her cold fingers shocking my skin.

Aeron snickered with Kelvin as she wrapped a cloth tape measure around his upper thigh, mumbling vulgarities, before he turned his attention back to the seamstress. "If you think I'm thick there. You should see my—"

I scoffed, disgusted. "There's no need to embarrass yourself. We can *all* see what you're working with."

His nostrils flared, a reply on his tongue when the raven-haired guard stepped between us. "Save it for the trials." He brushed Aeron to the side and addressed me. "Follow me to the dining hall."

I did what he asked, and hurried away from Aeron, whose murderous glare had me regretting my impulsive insult. I knew better and did it anyway—it's how I ended up in this mess.

"You'd do well to remember this is a game of life and death, sweetheart," Aeron called out after me, straightening his dirty, mustard-colored shirt. "I'd watch that pretty mouth of yours, too, if I were you."

Six

My eyes widened as I entered the dining hall.

Fae of various hues and species flitted around, ranging from diminutive ones no larger than my hand to others that stooped slightly to prevent their massive, iridescent wings from colliding with the candle chandeliers. It was an eccentric mix—overwhelmingly so—yet I found it oddly welcoming. I didn't get the same menacing feeling from them as I did from the ones in the throne room. These fae seemed friendly. Warm, like Pipion. And I questioned why they weren't in the main part of the castle with the rest.

Maybe they were prisoners like us?

The faerie guard left my side to join the rest of the patrol flanking the back wall, swords drawn and ready for violence. With a deep breath, I helped myself to the buffet—although I couldn't identify anything besides what was possibly chicken.

"They say if you eat anything in Faerway, you can never leave," a meek voice said from beside me. Her petite frame matched her tone, although her hazel eyes took up half her face. For the life of me, I couldn't remember her name. It taunted me —on the very tip of my tongue.

I huffed a laugh. "I take it you don't believe that?"

"Nah, I just don't care anymore. Being here for almost six weeks will do that to a girl." She adjusted the pile of brown hair on top of her head. "We haven't officially met. I'm Calandra," she introduced, extending her hand.

I placed my palm against hers. "Elowyn."

"When'd you get here? I haven't seen you around before."

"Three days ago, maybe? I'm not sure. I think they put me under some sort of sleeping spell."

"Well, welcome to purgatory." She spread her arms out in front of her. "Where the food sucks, the baths aren't guaranteed, and the guards are self-righteous dicks. I won't lie though —I'm looking forward to the upgraded sleeping arrangements, so I'm glad you showed up when you did. Those bedrolls are awful."

I arched my brow, loading a plate with a helping of sloppy brown mush. "Why would my arrival influence that?"

"The trials, girl. Keep up." Calandra scooped a helping of chicken onto her plate. "The king was waiting until we had a tenth human to begin, and voila!" She pointed her utensil at me and then to the tables behind her. "We'll be sitting back there. Come find us when you're done, okay?"

I remained where I stood, watching her weave through the dining hall—my eyebrows still knitted together. She was so friendly. I guess I'd assumed with a trial of life and death hanging over our heads, everyone would be cruel and standoff-ish. Human nature could be a fickle beast; the king was right about that. Still, it was a pleasant surprise, and I suppose it wouldn't hurt to form allies.

Especially when I already had an enemy.

I didn't know what I'd done to piss off Aeron. Maybe he was just that type. The *'I'm better than everyone because my biceps are huge'* type.

Dumping the last dollop of gelatin onto the rustic wooden tray, an unappetizing aroma wafted through the air, assaulting my senses. I hoped it tasted better than it smelled. Then, retrieving a utensil, I set out to locate Calandra and the rest.

The unpleasant scent lingered as I navigated my surroundings. There must've been a hundred tables trailing the length of the hall—each one packed with an assortment of fae. The room appeared to breathe with the pulse of each flame burning from the torches on the walls. A soft cadence of conversation enveloped the hall, muffling the sharp clinks and clatters of those who were enjoying their meal.

The atmosphere starkly contrasted with the grandeur of the main castle I'd stepped into earlier. It exuded a darker, grimmer tone, with a pervasive sense of filth hanging in the air. Even the occupants had a slight edge to them. It seemed tailor-made for the likes of us—repulsive prisoners.

"Honestly, I don't care if I die at this point," Calandra said between bites as I approached the table. "I'm just happy to be out of that stars-forsaken dungeon." She scooted over to make room for me.

"Same," the towheaded boy, Lewis, replied. His large gray eyes were dull and tone somber. "If my mother knew this was where I was, she'd wish me dead." He sighed, eyes appearing haunted. "I don't remember what flowers look like anymore."

His admission was like a knife to my chest. "Oh, they're beautiful," I chimed in and sat beside Calandra. "Colorful, vibrant petals in all different shapes and sizes. Some with long, vine-like stems, others short and stubby, with thick leaves. And their smell? Fresh, like a clear summer's night. However, some are pungent, like my late Aunt Violet's perfume." I scrunched my nose for emphasis, and he giggled.

"You look familiar," he said. "Did you use to sell jewelry at the outdoor market in Wellington?"

I nodded. "A long time ago for extra cash. My mother refused to buy me any more books until I read the ones I had. So, I beat her at her own game."

Calandra dropped her fork. "That's where I know you from! You're Deirdre's daughter?"

The downfall of being the infamous bastard daughter: most people recognized you. I couldn't place her, however. She must've been a few grades ahead of me in school.

Poking the food around my tray, I wondered if I should lie. Even the other side of the river was unsafe from scandal and rumor.

"My mother used to work in Wellington Castle as the prince's handmaiden," Calandra went on, "she told me—"

"That she got pregnant by some lowly servant and had to abdicate her title?"

Lewis's voice cracked. "Is—is it true?"

"Your guess is as good as mine." I slid the mush into my mouth. It tasted vaguely like mushrooms, but it wasn't horrible. Better than having to elaborate and explain myself. Something that proved worthless back home.

Aeron's laugh sounded before he appeared behind Lewis, carrying his tray in one hand. "So, you're the bastard child? I always wondered what you looked like." He leaned down, his hot breath stinging my ear, and I cringed. "I knew you were nothing special."

"Go back into the hole you crawled out of." Calandra threw the rest of her bread at him.

"Missed you too, babe." He laughed once more before taking his place at another table. A few of the other male competitors received him with boisterous laughter.

She flipped him the middle finger, turning her attention back to me. "Don't let him get to you. His bark is worse than his bite."

"How can you be so sure?" I asked.

"He's my ex-boyfriend. I dumped his ass right before we ended up here. Mister, *'I hate being told no,'* got mad and pushed me into the water. He jumped in when the tide swept me under. Next thing I know, we're both lying on the bank, surrounded by four fae guards."

"Are you serious? That's horrible."

She ripped into a piece of chicken. "I'll get my revenge during the trials. How'd you end up here?"

"My mother's sick, and I remembered the story of the nightingale, so I crossed the river to find it. I didn't make it far before the guards discovered me. That one, to be specific." I flicked my chin to where he stood on the back wall.

Calandra turned to look at the guard who hadn't stopped staring at me since I sat down. "Oh, Talon? He found us too."

"Same here." Lewis wiped his face. "He's the nicest of all the guards, though. He always gave me extra bread."

Under Talon's stare, my face warmed, and I glanced away. If he was the nicest that they had to offer, I didn't want to know who else lurked in the king's ranks. My chest tightened as I thought of my captor.

"How'd you end up here?" I asked Lewis, needing to divert my thoughts.

A frown replaced his bright features as he remembered the events.

Quickly, I reassured him, "It's okay if you don't want to talk about it."

"No." He shook his head. "No. It's fine." A moment passed before he finally started speaking. "I snuck out to skip rocks at the river while my babysitter was busy feeding the chickens. Everything was going fine. I got one to skip *eight* times when the tide rolled." Lewis frowned and seemed to fight for his next words. "But then I slipped on a slick patch of algae and fell in. I was almost out when some creature pulled me under."

I suppressed my horror but was unable to conceal the narrowing of my throat as I asked breathlessly, "Was it human-like?"

"Yeah! It had gills in its neck and these sharp fingers." He held out his hands. "I don't remember what happened after that, but here I am. My mother is probably so mad." His hand retreated to below the table.

The burden of his guilt pressed heavily upon me. I wiped my hands on the worn and tattered fabric of my dress as if trying to rid myself of the invisible residue left by his conscience.

This was cruel.

Lewis was so young—he had his entire life ahead of him.

How could my life be more important than his? How were any of our lives more important? To decide who was and wasn't worthy of life was for the stars and fate to decide—not measly humans. And certainly not the fae. Whatever happened, I'd make sure, somehow, someway, I'd get him back home.

I placed my hand on his. "Don't beat yourself up, okay? Your mother loves you, and I promise she's not mad."

Lewis wiped at his nose. "I know. It's just—"

"Fucked?" Breana said from beside Lewis. "If it makes you feel any better, my family and I were only a day away from making it into Elkway when our boat capsized, and I ended up in this stars-forsaken place. It's been ten months, and I still don't know what happened to them—my parents. Or if they're even alive."

My mouth gaped. "Did you get stuck in a storm?"

"Nope. No clouds or waves in sight. Something pushed our boat over."

"You don't think—" I began.

"That it was a fae?" Breana finished. "I put nothing past them. Why do you think I begged for death earlier?" She slurped brown mush that resembled pudding into her mouth and made a face. "Sorry about that by the way. I realize it was a smidge dramatic, but it was worth a shot."

While logically I knew I shouldn't, I couldn't help but like her. And Calandra. And Lewis. In different circumstances, I could see us being friends. It was a shame we were going to be forced to compete against one another in hypocritical morality trials.

"Five more minutes, competitors, let's hurry it up," a loud voice thundered throughout the hall. It came from none other than the emerald-eyed guard, his face as hard as stone.

"Say what you want about the fae." Calandra took a swig of her drink and set her cup down. "That man is fine."

I choked on my food, unable to control my surprise.

She smirked. "What? Like you guys weren't thinking it?"

My gaze trailed the room to meet his piercing stare once more. She was right. He could've been hand-carved from the stars themselves. Only celestial hands would be capable of sculpting such chiseled features.

But it meant nothing. Something told me he was as cruel, if not more vile, than the rest of them.

The corner of his lips twitched into a smile, and he winked.

Fucking *winked*.

I shifted in my seat, and a fluttering swarm of butterflies erupted in the pit of my stomach. Desperately, I busied myself in the contents of my tray, silently praying for the ground to open up and offer a merciful escape from his eyes—his mouth.

~

Candelabras lit the way as three fae guards steered us along a narrow corridor and into a secluded section of the castle, lined with wooden, embellished doors and oil paintings. The portrait's eyes followed us as we walked down the narrow hall, the same revolting look on their face as the rest of the fae court. Not even inanimate objects welcomed our presence in the castle.

The oldest of the three guards turned to us as we came to a stop at the end of the hall. "Your attire will arrive at your rooms shortly," he said, and although he appeared to be three times their senior, he was as fit and burly as the others. "Clean up, get dressed, and meet back in the throne room in training gear, ready for assessments."

Our doors unlocked on their own and pushed open with an invisible breeze, revealing identical, cozy bedchambers.

The guards left us to our own devices and made no effort to avoid shouldering past us as they disappeared around the corner.

I wanted nothing more than to curl up into a ball on top of the comforter and sleep for days. Escape this horrible nightmare; run away in my dreams.

But reality was never too far behind my dreams of escape.

An elbow to my mouth forced me back, and mass chaos ensued.

Everyone, all at once, began vying over the rooms, fighting each other to claim which one would be theirs. They'd been kept in cages for so long that it seemed it had almost turned them into the beasts the fae claimed they were.

My jaw fell open as Kelvin shoved Lewis and Martell—two of the smallest competitors—into the wall as he claimed the chamber furthest away. Aeron had someone in a headlock. Calandra had Jeston's arm twisted behind his back. Someone cried out in agony.

There was going to be a bloodbath before the trials had begun. Or maybe this was a trial in and of itself.

I tried to get out of everyone's way the best I could, but there wasn't anywhere to go. I was stuck in the thick of it, dogging hands and feet until the madness dwindled, and everyone claimed their rooms.

Sucking the blood from my teeth, I locked the final remaining door behind me—not trusting someone wouldn't change their mind—and rested my head against the wood. A four-post bed was the centerpiece of the room, underneath the same iridescent windows that encased the rest of the castle. I imagined how tranquil it must be to fall asleep under the kaleidoscope of lights, and my muscles ached, yearning for sleep. If only I had time. If only I hadn't got myself into this mess.

Seated on the bed, I drew my legs close to my chest as I sought comfort in the solitude. If choosing a room had been any indicator, the trials would indeed be messy.

In the blink of an eye, everything was irrevocably different.

I couldn't comprehend how one moment I was riding Sugarfoot without a care in the world, and the next, I was a prisoner in a deadly game of freedom. I was powerless. All I could do was watch as everything unfolded while straddling the dangerous line between life and death.

Could I take a life? I held my hands out in front of me, feeling detached from myself and my surroundings, as if I were an observer in my body. Stars, how badly I prayed this was a bad dream.

I pinched my forearm to no avail and let out an incredulous laugh. "Keep it together, Elowyn," I told myself. "Stay focused."

Running my hands down my face, I stood up and padded over to the bathroom. There was no need for a shower, I determined, not when we were going to be assessed—whatever that'd entailed. Instead, I ran the sink, cupped water in my hands, and splashed it onto my face repeatedly—until my nerves settled.

I drew in a sharp breath as I prepared to face myself in the mirror, anticipating the severity of my injury. My shoulders relaxed when I saw the cut and brought a finger up to touch it. It wasn't too bad, but it'd likely leave a small scar without sutures. It could've been worse, I thought.

Recalling the lacerations from the water attack, I rubbed the wound with water to clean it out. Without proper supplies, it wouldn't do much. But it did make me feel better—cleaner.

A knock sounded at the door as I was finishing up, and I hurried to answer it, finding the seamstress from earlier on the other side. "Elowyn Rosewood?"

"Yes?"

The seamstress nodded, scouring the three-tiered cart of various baskets beside her before checking the board in her hands. "In here, you'll find your training clothes." She dropped a small cloth bag into my arms. "Your trial attire is in this one. This bag consists of approved day clothes and these"—she dropped a fourth bag on top of the stack—"are your lounge clothes."

My arms strained from the weight, and I dropped them on the floor beside me.

"If you have any issues with anything, let me know," the seamstress finished and scurried off before I could thank her, already knocking on the door across the corridor.

I shut mine behind her and hunched over to pull the training leathers from the bag. Peeling the dirt-covered clothes from my body, I scrunched my nose at the smell that wafted from me and realized there was no way, with a good conscience, I could face anyone like that.

So, I hurried back into the bathroom to wipe myself down,

focusing most of my attention under my arms, until I no longer smelled like death. And river water.

I held the training leathers up to my body and shook my head—there was no way these were going to fit. She must've mixed up the bags.

Sucking in, I pulled them on, twisting and contorting my body to get them to fit, but the material clung to every movement. One wrong step and they'd rip to shreds.

Though, I must admit that they weren't half bad. The leather hugged me in all the right places, accentuated the little curves I had and smoothed out my waist. Some of the other humans had been there much longer than I had; their muscle tone had withered to almost nothing. Running a hand over the shape of my body, I forced myself to confront this advantage.

I tilted my head.

Loose, billowing clothing was my standard attire. Having my figure on full display made me uncomfortable. How could anyone see it as an advantage when some of the humans appeared half-starved in comparison?

Turning from side to side, from back to front, I checked every angle. I'd never been insecure about my body, but the longer I inspected myself, the harder it became not to feel self-conscious. After all, I was only human.

What a strange concept that was now—my mortality—and how truly human I was. Being around such beautiful, immortal beings was bound to do that. As was their flippant disregard for my life. It put things into a bleak perspective, that was for sure.

Three loud chimes rang throughout the castle, startling me, and I opened the door to peek into the hallway. Breana and Lewis's heads appeared as well—their faces as confused as mine as we waited for orders.

"Assessments are in ten minutes, competitors," the emerald-eyed faerie announced, his attention focused on me. "Get dressed. Be in the corridor in five minutes or forfeit the trials."

I fidgeted under his scrutiny, ducked back into my room, and pulled a ribbon from the bag before securing my hair out of my face.

With a shaky breath, I stilled my trembling hands before joining everyone in the hallway, keeping my gaze straight ahead to avoid the faerie guard.

Here goes nothing.

SEVEN

We filed into the throne room one by one, taking our spots against the back wall.

The entire fae court was still in attendance, jeering and taunting us as we entered. They were ruthless. Their shrills inhuman as they awaited their show.

There was no music this time, only the symphony of insults and derogatory comments. Nor was there opulent light dancing along the walls.

I drew in a sharp breath.

Taking in the scene, the padded mats sprawled across the floor seemed more like a choice of obligation than safety. Perhaps they simply didn't want dirty, human blood staining their floors. On each side of the room, two racks of weapons were filled with older equipment. My eyes flicked to the archery targets ahead, and I could no longer ignore the impending judgment, so I looked up.

Hemp ropes hung from the ceiling.

My mind wandered back to Breana's cries—would they step in if a human decided to misuse the equipment? Decided to find escape on their own terms?

I shifted my weight between my feet, hoping I didn't appear as nervous as I felt.

Sure, I might've spent most of my time outdoors growing up and was skilled on a horse, but none of that mattered in terms of physical combat.

I panned the line of competitors, gauging everyone's reactions—Aeron, to no surprise, was all too impatient to begin. He flashed his teeth in warning when he noticed me staring, and I averted my gaze, allowing it to travel down the line.

Kids. All of us. Forced to grow up or die. Some lives ending before they began.

Lewis peered at me through long lashes, a slight blush on his neck. Having my soul sucked out of me and placed on a shelf sounded much more pleasant than what the king expected of me.

King Harkin and Prince Bowen strolled into the throne room, waving to the wild and untamed crowd as they breezed up the steps of the dais. Their hand movements were lazy but practical.

The guards stood at the base of the steps with their arms behind their backs, faces like stone as they stared ahead. What good sheepdogs they were.

Despite my better judgment, my gaze kept drifting to Talon, the emerald-eyed faerie, whose sharp features and tall, lean frame stood out more than the rest. It was almost an unfair advantage; how elegant he was.

"Welcome back, competitors."

An icy chill ran up my spine.

I peeled my focus away from Talon and recollected my thoughts as the king settled into his plush throne. Prince Bowen followed, flirting with a beautiful pixie who appeared to be made of moss and oak.

"I hope you found your accommodations to your liking. As

I mentioned earlier, these assessments will put your skills on display for the entire court to see. Prove yourself worthy, and one of my guards here may volunteer to train you for the duration of the trials. To lead you to victory. However"—the king's round face glowed—"should you fail to attract the attention of one, you shall be escorted to your execution."

Execution? I bounced my foot; the room felt too small.

The other competitors gasped their surprise, whispering amongst themselves as they too processed the information. Past the barbaric trials, we offered no purpose to the fae. Watching us risk our lives was entertainment for them. Immortal beings, playing with disposable humans like we were nothing more than ants.

I wasn't sure if I was going to be sick or wanted to scream.

"The courtier will call you up in groups of two to perform a series of miniature tests. We'll judge you accordingly. The winner of each test will stay in until they're defeated." He pointed to the shapeless cloud floating high above the dais, displaying our names in alphabetical order. "My sentries will make their decisions at the end."

Vomit.

I definitely wanted to vomit.

The fae court's conversations ebbed to a faint whisper, and I watched as a select few made their way up and down the aisles with what appeared to be a cloth bag collecting coins.

My body went stiff, and I brought a hand up to cover my horror.

They were betting on us?

Just when I thought it couldn't get any worse.

I dug my nails into my palm. Did they think they could give us upgraded sleeping arrangements and we wouldn't question what sick angle they were playing? That we'd believe they were showing us mercy and be thankful? Maybe that'd work on people like Aeron, but I wouldn't sweep it under the rug and accept their so-called generosity as anything less than manipulation.

A hush fell over the crowd, a tangible silence settling like a heavy curtain that waited for the show to begin. The courtier moved purposefully to the edge of the dais. With a parchment scroll in hand, anticipation hung in the air, and all eyes focused on the impending revelation.

Calandra bumped me with her shoulder, her button nose wrinkling as she noticed my displeasure, and I shook my head, mouthing I'd fill her in later.

"The first test will be archery," the courtier announced. "Kelvin Amhurst and Aeron Beckworth, step forward, please."

The boys strolled to the center of the floor, bumping their knuckles together before they each grabbed a bow and readied themselves at the mark.

"On my cue," the courtier announced.

Kelvin and Aeron positioned their bows.

"Three. Two—"

A bell chimed indicating 'one,' and they let their arrows fly with a collective sigh.

Aeron's arrow barely landed on the edge of the board while Kelvin's hit a perfect bullseye. They bumped knuckles once more as Aeron made his walk of shame back into the line.

I contained my amusement—happy to see his ego fall a couple of notches.

"Martell Colt," the courtier announced next.

The bow was as large as he was, but his strength surprised me. His draw back was strong and steady.

"On my cue."

They unleashed their arrows at the bell, and Martell hit inside the inner circle with his, much better than Aeron's pathetic attempt. It was a strike to take pride in—at the very least—a notable accomplishment, if they were in any other setting.

However, that didn't matter, as, once again, Kelvin landed a perfect bullseye.

As he did again and again.

And again.

Beating out Calandra, Lewis, Breana, and Irving.

"Elowyn Rosewood," my name rang throughout the throne room, and I became lightheaded.

Approaching the mark, a tense silence suffocated my throat, and my breath hung in the air, caught between anticipation and trepidation. The fine hairs on my arms stood at attention, my skin prickling with the fear that coursed through me.

The bow was much heavier than I expected when I eventually picked it up—and the string damn near immovable. I let my breathing even out.

"On my cue."

Lifting the bow up, I drew the string back to my chin, my fingertips gripping it with a desperate intensity as if clinging to a lifeline. The subtle creak of the tensioned bowstring resonated in the air.

"Three."

My fingers slipped, and my arrow went flying, ricocheting off an invisible force and back toward me. I dodged out of the way.

The tip missed me by mere inches as it lodged into the ground next to my head.

I squeezed my eyelids shut, wanting nothing more than to melt into the ground below. But I refused to let them see me falter.

The fae court didn't hold back their laughter as I stood up and walked back to the line, my chin up and focused on the wall ahead, forcing tears to stay at bay.

Sage and Jeston's turn went by in a flash, neither of them losing control of their arrow, although neither one of them beat Kelvin, either. His name had a resounding nine tally marks beside it. Everyone else with nothing.

"Kelvin, you may approach the rope next."

I licked the cut on my lip, savoring the sting that accompanied it. A welcome distraction from my bruised ego when I caught Talon's glare. His eyes swept over me in a dismissive motion, as if the sight of me disgusted him, and I huffed a laugh —the feeling mutual.

Turning my attention back to the assessment, Kelvin and Aeron climbed the ropes, up and up, until they grabbed the flag. It was Aeron who had reigned supreme this round, and each round after that.

Until he went against Calandra.

He checked her up and down as she approached as if he was thinking, *'Give me someone challenging to go against.'*

So, challenge him, she did.

Calandra beat him out with five seconds to spare, wiggling her fingers to say goodbye as he stomped off the floor. I relished every second of his brooding.

A light snicker traveled around the audience when my name was called. Their jeers had become more and more distant, inconvenient, background noise.

I took a deep breath as I made my way over to the rope, touching knuckles with Calandra before we took our stance.

She was halfway up the rope seconds after the bell rang, but I wasn't far behind. Climbing trees and swinging on branches proved to come in handy in this test, but I didn't care if I won. Too focused on redeeming myself, I didn't notice I'd gotten ahead of Calandra, let alone grabbed the flag a second before she reached her hand up.

Although she bit back her disappointment, she still congratulated me.

I won the next round against Sage as well, but my streak ended with Jeston when my hand slipped, and I fell two feet before I could recover, giving him enough time to take the lead.

I felt gutted. Embarrassed. But I kept my chin held high despite the laughter from both my human peers and the fae court. No one would volunteer to mentor me at this rate. I'd need to step it up if I wanted them to take me seriously.

My hands fisted at my side as they trembled with nerves. Getting them under control was all I could think about, but nothing was working. I didn't perform well under pressure, let alone with an audience.

In frustration, I smacked the wall we all returned to after completing each assessment.

Breana gave me a weak smile, and I pressed the back of my head into the cool stone wall.

"Irving Munoz, to the sparring mat, please."

Wiping his brow, Irving picked up a wooden sword, weighing it in his grip as he took his place on the mat. He was nervous, scared, and I knew once Kelvin got a whiff, it was over. Little did any of us know, it was over long before we stepped foot in that room.

"The first match will be between Irving Munoz and Kelvin Amhurst," the courtier announced, "Each hit is one point. We shall declare the first player to reach five points the winner."

Kelvin wore a cocky grin as he swaggered to the center of the ring with shameless confidence—his masculine ego on display for everyone to see.

The bell sounded, and Kelvin wasted no time. He thrust his sword forward, missing Irving by a hair as he ducked for cover. Kelvin tried to come for his blindside, but Irving expected it and kicked his feet out from underneath him.

Kelvin jumped back up and swung, but Irving was faster and smacked the wooden sword into his side first.

"Point."

Kelvin rolled his shoulders, readying himself for the second match. Moments later, the bell sounded, and this time it was Irving who lurched forward, catching Kelvin off guard.

He stumbled back before he regained his footing and side-stepped Irving's attack. "That's all you got, pussy?"

Irving's lip curled up his teeth as he launched forward, faking him out before he spun around and connected his sword to Kelvin's thigh. "I'd be careful what you ask for, bud. You're zero for two." He wiped his brow.

Kelvin stepped to him, their noses touching before he shoved him. "Keep talking, and I'll have you eating your teeth."

Irving shoved him back, their faces growing feral, and the bell sounded once again. Kelvin didn't hold back this time. He swung and stabbed and sliced the air, strong-arming Irving into defense as he bulldozed forward, forcing him off the mat.

Kelvin didn't allow him time to reposition. As soon as Irving settled, he aimed at his head.

He blocked his attempt, but it left him wide open, and Kelvin used it to his advantage. With one swift kick to his gut, Irving hunched over, and Kelvin cracked the sword against his ankle.

Irving fell with a thud, letting out a cry as he clutched his ankle.

"Point."

The fae crowd went wild, demanding more—their insatiable hunger almost brought me to my knees.

"What's wrong, pussy? You can't get up?" Kelvin mocked, circling Irving like a vulture. "Not talking such a big game anymore, huh? Get up." He shoved the toe of his boot into his ribs.

Irving spat at him as he stood and limped into position, but the second the bell sounded, Kelvin kicked the inside of his knee, dropping Irving to the ground.

No sound escaped him this time as he fell, and the instant he hit the mat, Kelvin slammed his sword into his injured ankle once more—his swollen bone a nasty shade of crimson.

I silently begged him to get up, but each time he tried, his ankle would give out.

The bell sounded, and they declared Kelvin the winner as Irving scooped himself off the ground and crawled back to the line.

My stomach twisted into a hundred knots; my hands refused to remain still at my sides.

I prepared for my name to be called.

No one, not even Aeron, had beaten Kelvin. He was merciless. Brutal. And he'd do anything to win.

Breana nudged me with her elbow. "He favors his right side," she whispered, keeping her focus ahead, "try to stay as low as possible, too."

I nodded and took a deep breath.

"Elowyn Rosewood."

My gaze met the king's and then Talon's before locking onto Kelvin's black soulless stare.

His eyebrow—sliced open from his match with Martell—stained the tips of his blond hair red. The predatory snarl he offered to me—coated with the blood of a jab to the mouth—made me stiffen. As maimed as he appeared, like the fae above, he was ready to kill.

I picked up the wooden sword and got into the same position I'd seen everyone else take. I'd never sparred with anyone in my entire life, not officially, anyway. Or with wooden swords. In fact, I couldn't recall a single time I'd ever gotten into a fight—aside from punching Rhett Belmont in the nose in primary school for making fun of my large front teeth—but that didn't count. And it wouldn't be much use to me now.

I'd never gain the attention of a mentor at the rate I was going, especially when I had the least number of points. I'd be heading straight for the gallows if I couldn't last more than five minutes.

My grip on the sword tightened as the bell sounded.

Kelvin lunged at me, and I startled, almost tripping over my own feet. He laughed at my expense and turned his back to me, shaking his head in disbelief at the guards. I wasn't sure what his angle was—if he was taunting me or if he genuinely didn't believe I'd do anything—but I knew I needed to act while I had an advantage.

He didn't hear me sneak up on him or the sound of my sword as it flew through the air. It wasn't until I smacked him over the head with the dull edge that I earned his attention.

A light laughter passed through the room as he whipped his head around—blind rage written on his face.

"Point."

"You stupid bitch!" He seethed.

Sweat dripped down my back as he charged toward me, whipping his sword through the air. I lifted mine up to block it and struggled to keep him from overpowering me.

The wood creaked from the pressure.

My brow collected beads of perspiration.

He shoved me backward as he stepped away, swinging his sword at my knees.

I leaped to the side, remembering what Breana told me, and started for his right, but he twisted before I could make contact, and his sword connected with my ribs.

My knees buckled from the pain, and I screamed, curling my body into itself.

"Point."

"Not so tough when my back's not turned, are you, coward?"

I took a shallow breath. *Coward?*

I'd show him what a coward I was. Readying myself for the next round, I straightened and forced myself through the pain.

Kelvin spun and kicked out his leg, attempting to throw out my knee the same way he did Irving, but I leaped back, striking my sword on his ankle.

"Point."

A wink of satisfaction sparked inside my chest, and Kelvin yelled. It was a deranged sound, coated with mirth as he snapped his teeth. He enjoyed this. A predator in its natural habitat, enjoying every bit of the kill.

But the excitement clouded my judgment, and I became the prey. Too distracted to notice his advance.

He gripped me by the collar and threw me to the ground—the air fleeing from my lungs. Kelvin flung his sword, and I rolled to the side, barely missing his assault. I didn't breathe as he slammed it down again and again until he made contact—the wooden tip striking my back.

I screamed out in agony.

"Point."

He raised his sword again, but I staggered to my feet, pushing through the throbbing in my spine, and narrowly blocked his attack. The vein in my neck strained as I clung to the last bit of spite that remained, my arms bowing under the pressure. It couldn't let him win. No, not yet. We'd only just started, and I refused to go down that easily.

Kelvin's hair dripped with sweat as he fought to overpower me, his jaw clenched so tight he'd likely crack a molar.

I wanted to prove to the court, to the other competitors, that I was a worthy opponent. That I could hold my own. That, although I wasn't the strongest or most skilled, I still had plenty of fight in me. That they, too, would struggle to get rid of me.

Pure defiance pulsed through my bones, and I kneed him between the legs, putting every ounce of strength I had left in it.

He collapsed on top of me with a howl—our swords crashing onto the ground beside us—and he wrapped his bloodied fingers around my neck.

I gasped for air, digging my nails into his face, his shoulders, his wrists—anything I could get my hands on to get away. To *breathe*. His grip only tightened as he restrained me, pinning my legs to the ground with his own.

Veins surged beneath my skin, visibly bulging as a paleness crept over my face, drained of its usual color. A wave of light-headedness swept over me. Each pulse of my heartbeat became a discordant beat, an irregular and ever-slowing rhythm of defeat.

I didn't stand a chance like this. If only I could get up, I could take him on. *Fight*.

Panic tore through my flesh as the corners of my vision grew dark.

He was going to kill me. Forget about the trials, this was it—my fate was sealed. Only the sound of my choked breaths filled the deafening silence while the fae court sat at the edge of their seats. Just as my arms dropped to the ground and my body went limp, Kelvin released me, leaving me listless on the mat as he leaped for his sword.

I gasped for air and rolled onto my side, crawling to reach mine in a wretched attempt, but I was too slow.

Too weak.

"You didn't think you'd win that easily, did you?" Kelvin twirled the wooden sword between his fingers and reared back, connecting his foot to the side of my skull.

EIGHT

My eyelids fluttered open to find the king's courtier standing over me, his bald head gleaming under the candlelight. He nudged my shoulder. "Can you hear me?"

I groaned in response.

"How many fingers am I holding up?"

Several tiny, blurry fingers came into view, and I blinked. "Four," I guessed.

"Close enough."

He extended a hand to help me up, and my vision doubled. I rested my hands on my knees before I hobbled back to my spot on the wall with the other competitors.

"Are you sure you're okay?" Breana whispered, and I could hardly hear her over the high-pitched ringing in my ears. "Skulls aren't supposed to crack like that."

I rubbed the sore spot on my head and stretched my jaw—tact wasn't her strong suit. "Yeah, just peachy."

Of course, I wasn't good.

I was embarrassed.

Pissed.

But I couldn't let her know that. Even if we were allies, it was still everyone for themselves, and I couldn't let anyone see how badly Kelvin had gotten under my skin. Or the severity of my injuries. I rubbed the sore spot on my scalp and opened and closed my mouth to pop my jaw back into place. At least I'd held my own—longer than Irving or anyone else. At least I wasn't a coward.

Not that it mattered, as my name was still dead last, but I hoped it'd be enough. My belly cramped—it had to be enough.

The courtier jogged up to the top of the dais and held up a hand, waiting for the court to settle. "Thank you. Thank you. This concludes the assessments. Competitors, when your name is called, please step into the center of the room. Sentries, should you wish to mentor the named competitor, please step forward as well. Should there be multiple guards who volunteer, the named competitor may decide which one they'd like to pursue further training with. We'll begin with the highest ranking."

I anxiously fiddled with my ring, unable to keep still. The seconds ticked by with painful slowness. I wanted to get this over with—to know—to breathe. These last forty-eight hours of nerve-wracking torture had me wound up so tightly it threatened to split me in half.

"First up, is Kelvin Amhurst."

The fae court went wild as he swaggered to the center—no doubt the fan favorite—and bowed to the king. I kept my sneer to myself as four sentries stepped out of line, each as burly and muscular as Kelvin. To no one's surprise, he chose the largest of the guards and together stood side by side on the edge of the mat.

"Aeron Beckworth," the courtier announced next.

Five guardsmen stepped forward to claim him and, like Kelvin, to no surprise, picked the most intimidating one of the group. *Typical*. Meatheads always stuck together. I hoped their size wasn't a sign of skill or we were all screwed.

One by one, competitors' names were called, and they each selected their guard until it was only Lewis and me remaining. No one had yet to be turned down, and the selection of promising-looking sentries dwindled away.

I'd noticed, as the courtier had gone through the line of competitors, Talon hadn't stepped forward for anyone. He appeared bored, almost as if he had a hundred other things he'd rather be doing—how inconsiderate of us to waste his precious time. If only our miserable mortal lives weren't so pathetic.

"Lewis Fields."

Only one guard stepped forward for him. He was the smallest of the lot and didn't appear much older than Lewis, but he happily obliged, sprinting to meet his guard in the center of the ring.

A scant number of guards lingered, numbering less than a dozen, their presence a dwindling force. The chance of being picked stood on a knife's edge.

"Elowyn Rosewood."

The fae court inched forward in their seats as they awaited to see who would step forward, and I shifted on my feet.

The suspense in the air thickened.

"Does *anyone* here wish to train Elowyn Rosewood?"

Still, no one stood.

This couldn't be happening.

King Harkin gleamed with anticipation at the turn of events, enjoying every minute of my embarrassment. Calandra and Breana wore the same pitted expression, while Aeron and Kelvin beamed with delight.

No, no, no! I didn't get attacked by a wraith and almost died from infection for nothing. I prayed for the stars to take pity on me.

"This is the final request. Should no one step forward, Elowyn, you'll be eliminated."

Tick.

Tick.

Tick.

Dread wormed through my veins.

"I'll do it," a velvet voice drawled.

My entire body tensed as Talon strolled to the middle of the room with his hands in his pockets. Audible murmurs erupted, and the king raised a hand, silencing the bewildered court.

Against my accord, my legs carried me over to him—weak and trembling. Talon said nothing as we joined the other competitors on the side of the mat; the shit-eating gleam on his face told me everything I needed to know.

"Congratulations, competitors." King Harkin's thick brows knitted together as he eyed Talon. "You've all made it through the preliminary assessment. Trials will be held at the end of each week, beginning this full moon." He straightened his fur coat, lifting his cleft chin to survey his adoring court.

Their frenzied whispers were still in full swing.

Until the king's voice silenced them again. "Ten of you stand before us today, but only one will remain in the end. Freedom is a privilege for those who fight to keep it."

Walking alongside Talon on the way to the bedchambers, I couldn't help but sense the palpable tension emanating from him. Thick in the air. It wrapped around me like an unsettling shroud. It frightened me.

His stealthy demeanor unsettled me even more. He wasn't burly, like some of the other guards. No. He was angular. Sharp. A perfectly honed blade.

We stopped outside the embellished door, and he leaned against the frame. His intensity made me self-conscious. "If today was any sign of your skill level, I certainly have my work cut out for me. You're going to need all the help you can get."

"No one asked you to volunteer."

He folded his arms across his chest. "I was in a good mood."

"A good mood?" I scoffed.

Talon arched a brow as if it was absurd to believe he'd volunteer for any other reason. "Well, it wasn't for your athletic abilities."

I laughed—the sound raw to my own ears as I pushed my fingers into my temples. "Oh, how inconsiderate of me. Please lead me to the nearest mountain so I can scream your praises for the stars to hear!"

"I'm not sure you'd make it up that far."

His lips hinted at a smile while my glare promised murder. There was no way we'd survive training together these next couple of weeks. If I even made it through the first trial. This entire situation felt like a massive trap. I was damned if I did and would be killed if I didn't.

"Well, this has been fun. If you don't mind, I'm going to go into my room and get some rest."

With the twist of his hand, the door popped open, and he pushed off the frame. "Such a foul, foul mouth. Meet me in the weapons room in the morning. We'll begin our training at sunrise, firefly."

"At sunrise?"

Talon stretched his neck as he strolled down the corridor. His back to me as he spoke. "That's what I said. Be there ... or don't. Either way, I'll see you tomorrow."

I beat my fists into the back of my chamber door as it closed behind me and let out a frustrated grunt. The collision with the door only served to remind me of how sore my body felt.

Resting my forehead against the wood, I wished my mother were there.

I felt lost. Confused. I knew I needed to get it together—to be the strong pillar of hope and believe in myself the way she did, but this was bigger than me. And as much as I despised my circumstances, I knew I needed to pull it together, if not for myself then to prove everyone wrong, especially a particular dark-haired sadist with a god complex.

I couldn't see anything. At first, I thought I was back in the dungeon, but as my vision adjusted to my surroundings, I recognized I was in a small, confined cave.

"Elowyn, help me, please!" a woman shrieked.

I prayed I was hallucinating, but as I turned toward the sound, there my mother lay in her bed just past the boulders.

I raced toward her, only to be cut off by an avalanche of rocks blocking me in.

No!

The jagged walls came crumbling down, and I knew I needed to escape. I needed to get to her. I scoured the cave, but there was no exit. The air thinned with each breath I took.

Desperately, I pushed on the walls, searching for a weak spot. My palms scraped across the rock. My fingertips sliced into the rutting edges. Searching. For a trapdoor, a secret passage, anything to set me free. But I was stuck.

"Mother! Stay with me. I'm going to get to you, I promise!"

My knuckles turned blood red as I pounded on the walls, but it was pointless. There wasn't a way out. I was going to die and so was my mother.

There was nothing I could do.

A glowing figure appeared at my side. He was tall, with

sharp ears, and had a familiar essence. An essence I longed for my entire life. His honey eyes held decades of wisdom, and I knew I could trust him.

"Reach within, Elowyn."

"I don't know what that means!"

He placed a hand on my shoulder, calming me. "The quiet energy that simmers beneath the surface. Focus on it. Listen to it. You'll know what to do."

"How will I know?" I begged, but he faded away.

I yelled and awoke in my chambers, "Wait! Don't go!"

Sweat drenched the back of my nightgown as I sat up and pressed my palms into my forehead. The room was too small, too stuffy, and I needed air.

Hopping out of bed, I pulled back the silk curtains to find my haphazard reflection staring back at me and sighed. I hadn't had a nightmare since grade school—when Rhett and his cronies were bullying me. The stress of the trials and the mounting pressure to save my mother must've triggered them to come back with a vengeance.

I rested my cheek on the windowpane, my breath fogging the glass, in an attempt to cool myself.

Back then, my mother would make me a cup of tea and sit with me outside, making me count all the stars in the sky until I got sleepy. If the past had a history of repeating itself, I knew I wouldn't be going back to bed anytime soon. A luxury I couldn't afford with my first training session in a few hours.

Since tea wasn't possible, sneaking around the castle it was.

I wasn't sure if it went against any rules, but I needed all the help I could get. What were they going to do? Hold me captive?

Twisting my untamed curls into a low braid, I pulled the

door open and peeked my head out to make sure the coast was clear and slipped into the hallway.

Strings of illuminated light guided my way to the infinite glass doors in the foyer of the great room. I was half expecting to run into at least one person along the way, but the castle was as still as a statue—frozen in time. There were no guards at the doors, no locks or bars, nothing to stop me from leaving. I suppose there wasn't a point. *Where would I escape to?* I didn't know how far away I was from the Dolorem River or which direction to head. Not that I knew any of those details coming into Faerway, but I didn't want to navigate my way through nocturnal terrain.

I strolled through the gardens, taking my time, noting the lush shrubs and manicured lawn. There was nothing spectacular about any of it, nothing I hadn't seen before during a tour of Wellington Castle.

However, once I cleared the colossal-sized hedges and veered off the stone footpath, a deep neon blue waterfall came into view, emptying into a glowing lake. The plants and flowers and grass sparkled under the moonlight—appearing to dance in the cool breeze.

The nocturnal bugs emitted a gentle twinkle, casting a soft luminescence that played among the trees, causing them to gleam with an ethereal glow. A soft, refreshing scent of blooming geraniums drifted through the air. It was magical, and something in my soul vibrated to life, connecting me to the surrounding nature.

The gentle wind kissed my skin; a trail of goosebumps was left in its wake.

It was entrancing.

Like I was under a spell. I could've stayed out there forever, savoring the beauty.

"What are you doing out of your chambers?" a silky voice crooned from behind me.

I audibly sighed. "I'm sorry. Am I not allowed to enjoy the outdoors?"

Talon circled me with predatory ease, stopping to rest against the tree in front of me. "Despite your upgraded sleeping arrangements, you're still a prisoner."

"And prisoners get time outside." I folded my arms.

Talon licked his lip, studying me. His nearness was unnerving, as were his striking features. I didn't think it'd be possible for anything to overshadow the mesmerizing nature surrounding us. Yet there he stood, like he wholly and fully belonged there.

He was in his element under the inky darkness: it was a stealth soldier's perfect backdrop.

"Don't tell me a few harsh words have you running for the hills, firefly. I thought you were tougher than that."

"First of all, don't get used to calling me that. And second, you know nothing about me."

"Am I wrong though?" He tucked a hand into his pocket.

Not in the mood to deal with his *lovely* personality, I shouldered past him to stand by the blue lake behind the tree.

He followed me. His unbearable, looming presence like a nagging thorn in my side.

"I know you get off on torturing humans, but can you quit following me? There are acres of land to stand on. You don't need to be a foot away from me."

Talon took a singular step to the side, and I shook my head, unsurprised.

"I'm on patrol tonight. It's my responsibility to monitor you—at all times."

"Sounds more like a stalker, if you ask me," I mumbled under my breath.

He huffed a laugh. "Don't flatter yourself. That would imply I was, in some way, infatuated with you, but I can assure you that couldn't be further from the truth. I have a job to do, Elowyn. And I plan on seeing it through until you're released." He shrugged. "Or dead."

I fumed. All I wanted was space to breathe, but stars forbid I did that. I couldn't do something as simple as inhaling oxygen without someone sucking it up.

"It's not only my life at stake here, you know?" I faced him. "This isn't another day for me like it is for you. My mother and I don't get the luxury of living forever."

Talon clicked his tongue. "We don't live forever. I mean, granted, we're practically immortal. We age like gods—"

I scoffed. "Just when I thought you couldn't be any more of an ass," I said. "You've got to be the most arrogant, big-headed man I've ever encountered. Simply being around you makes me want to claw my skin off."

"Faerie," he corrected.

My eyebrows rose, not understanding.

"You said I was 'the most arrogant, big-headed *man*' you'd ever encountered. I'm a faerie."

An incredulous laugh escaped me as I hung my head. "Stars, you're insufferable."

Talon stalked toward me again, closing the gap he'd only just allowed. "Me? That's rich coming from you."

"What's that supposed to mean?"

It was his turn to laugh. "You've got to be the most hot-headed, mouthy human I'd ever encountered. I'm not your enemy, Elowyn. Drop the attitude."

"Rot in hell." Energy crackled between us as our gaze clashed.

Talon stood toe to toe with me, his hard body pressing into mine like an impenetrable wall. My arms brushed his chest as I folded them across my middle and pinched myself to calm my nerves. I didn't appreciate his condescending assumptions about me or his smug, self-righteous attitude. Like he somehow knew me. He was nothing more than a relentless thorn in my side, whose sharp jawline and hooded eyes just so happened to infuriate me.

"Don't think for one second that because I'm being tolerant, I'll keep putting up with this behavior," he snarled into my ear—a reminder of how quickly he could overpower me. "Now drop the attitude."

I couldn't help myself. The words spilled out. A final taunt. "Regretting your decision so soon?"

He licked his bottom lip, sizing me up.

I hated the way he studied me—even more the way my body crackled under his scrutiny as if it was going to combust into flames. My treacherous, untrustworthy body. I told myself it meant nothing, that anyone would have the same reaction to his nearness.

"Good luck finding someone else to train you, Elowyn." Talon stepped back and turned toward the castle, my skin growing cold from his absence.

I'd pushed too far. I always pushed too far. All reason flew out the window when I felt backed into a corner. It was how I'd ended up a prisoner in the first place.

Guilt rippled through me. Sure, I didn't like him, but without him, I couldn't compete in the trials. I might as well have kissed my only shot at saving my mother goodbye.

"Wait," I called out.

Talon paused but didn't turn around.

"Fine. I—I'll try to watch my mouth," I forced out. The words tasted acidic on my tongue. It was a loaded promise, one I wasn't sure I could keep, but if it kept me from the gallows, I'd make a solid effort. Regardless of how much it pained me to think about.

Talon turned his head to speak over his shoulder. "Get your rest, firefly. Training begins in less than three hours."

With that, he stalked off.

And I could finally take a full breath—however momentary it might've been. Something in his demeanor told me he wouldn't take it easy on me in the morning.

NINE

Wandering the castle in mindless circles, I got lost in the labyrinth of corridors and staircases while trying to locate the training room.

The disappointment that radiated off Talon when I arrived made me pause, and part of me knew it wasn't because I was late. He was no longer in his uniform and instead wore leathers like mine, putting his muscles on full display. His body —cruel and vicious and sculpted to kill—intimidated me.

His jaw fluttered, and I twisted the ring on my finger.

"We don't have much time until the next competitor arrives. Get stretching so we can jump into warmups." Talon turned his attention back to the well-honed sword he was sharpening, guaranteed to filet someone's skin open with one small nick.

I pulled my arm behind my head, stretching my triceps. "What exactly are we going to be doing?" I switched to my other arm.

"We're going to focus on building your stamina and working your core." Talon arched a brow. "You have quite a bit of work ahead of you if you plan on surviving the first round."

Sitting on the mat, I spread my legs open and reached my right hand to my left foot, my hamstrings crying from the strain. "Why do you care if I survive or not? What's in it for you? I mean, you've made it clear you're doing this out of sheer pity. Why bother?"

"You're here to train, Elowyn, not ask questions about things that don't concern you. We each have our parts to play—the less we deal with each other, and the less we know about one another, the better, right? Now keep stretching."

"Maybe I'll fail just to spite you."

He sheathed his swords and stalked toward me, crouching down in front of me. His hair tickled my cheek, and my breath caught as he commanded, "Get on your knees, and give me three sets of fifty push-ups."

A hundred and fifty? He was mad!

Talon stood and leaned against the mirror.

Stars, how I wanted to scratch that stupid, condescending grin off his face. Keeping my death glare on him, I lowered myself to the ground, wishing looks could kill. My arms burned after the second set, and I struggled to finish—pleading my elbows to keep extending. I didn't want to give him the satisfaction of not being able to complete a menial task, but it was exhausting, especially when it'd been days since I'd eaten anything of true substance. I dropped to the ground after the last one, my arms like jelly as I struggled for air. As a runner, my endurance was above average, but my strength was less than ideal. Especially when competing against some of those hulking machines.

He blinked, painfully unimpressed. "Pathetic—I've seen children do better than that," he spat. "Get up and meet me at the ropes."

Talon turned his back to me and strolled to the other side of the room as I continued to lie there, fighting the compulsion to throw the nearby weight at his head. I didn't know who this guy thought he was or where any of these fae got off on being cold and merciless, but it stoked something inside me.

King Harkin's sob speech about humans turning on the fae was outlandish—bullshit rhetoric spoon-fed to them over the years. It wouldn't surprise me if they'd created a blight just to watch humans starve for their own bizarre enjoyment.

Nevertheless, if I wanted to get out of there, I needed to play their games. And not only the ones the king was going to put us through.

With a resigned sigh, I got to my feet and followed behind him, internally cursing with each step. My vision followed the length of the rope to the ceiling, where it stopped. It was much longer than the one we'd climbed during assessments.

I gulped—falling from that height would break multiple bones.

"Any day now, human," Talon urged.

"Is that a joke?"

He picked at his short, jagged nails. "I don't joke, it's a waste of time. Just like what you're trying to do. Now get going."

I scoffed. I wouldn't be surprised if his motive for choosing me was to kill me before I could participate in the trials. An up close and personal piece of fae revenge.

My fists clenched at my side. So, either I died from training or died from the trials. Regardless, it'd be a miracle to come out of this alive, so screw it.

Play the game, I reminded myself. *Focus.*

I gripped the rope, the coarse texture scratching my palm, and pulled myself onto it. My feet locked around the bottom, helping to keep my weight distributed as I put one hand above the other.

Focused on my breathing, I kept my eyes locked onto my

hands. The risk of missing the rope and slipping like I had when racing against Jeston wasn't an option.

My arms were fatigued, exhaustion from the pushups setting in. I craned my head up to see how much further I had to go, only to find I hadn't gotten over ten feet off the ground.

Talon went back to sharpening his sword, not in any way interested in what he had me doing.

My arms ached as I continued upwards, and my palms became slick. Unable to get a firm hold, I slipped—my hands burning as I held on until my feet touched the ground.

"Again," Talon said without looking up at me.

My shoulders screamed at me to stop; I rolled them in circles, attempting to release some of the strain. "I don't think I can," I said, showing him my bright red palms.

He gave his sword a final polish before sheathing it. "I don't think I asked. I won't have you embarrass me in front of the entire court. We still have another forty-five minutes, so stop making excuses and go again."

"Does it make you feel good pushing around a girl half your size?" I huffed. "I don't see you doing this."

Talon flashed his sharp canines. "I was the youngest guard in Faerway in almost a century. These basic tasks hardly scratch the surface of what my training entailed. Take your self-right-eousness somewhere else and get back to work."

I bit my tongue until I tasted blood, remembering our conversation from last night—my stupid promise to be nicer. I'd hardly been making an effort, but it was better than actively trying to rile him up.

His smile grew wider as if he knew how difficult it was for me to keep my words to myself.

The youngest guard in Faerway history.

It'd be impressive if he didn't have magical fae abilities and wasn't a raging prick.

"Aye, Warwick," someone called out from the other side of the training room, interrupting our silent battle of wills. A golden-brown-skinned faerie stood at the entryway, his coarse hair in tight locks that reached his shoulders. He smiled widely in greeting.

"Try not to fall next time. It defeats the purpose of the exercise," Talon called over his shoulder as he jogged over to the faerie and pulled him into a one-armed hug.

I stood there awkwardly, deciding to appear busy with some stretches so I could eavesdrop on their conversation unnoticed.

"You joining us for drinks tonight or what? It's Roe's night to pay," the other faerie said.

"Yeah, where you guys going?"

"The White Oak. The woodland nymphs will be there, and I need you to wingman me—keep Roe from stealing every girl I try to take home."

Talon clicked his tongue, unsure.

"C'mon man, have you seen her? I can't compete with that. She does this shit on purpose."

Talon laughed—an unusual, melodic sound that didn't match his no-nonsense demeanor. He didn't seem like one to go out and have fun or have friends, to be honest. I wasn't sure what to make of him or why I found myself curious.

And I couldn't pull myself away, eating up every bit of their conversation to the point I forgot what I was supposed to be doing, enamored by his fluid, open mannerisms. That wasn't the same person training me. *Asshole.*

The faerie nudged Talon, flicking his chin in my direction.

"Why are you just standing there? I thought I told you to go again?" Talon demanded.

"Oh, I'm sorry. I thought you volunteered to train me, not bark out demands. I didn't realize I had to jump the second you told me to."

The hand he had rested on the hilt of his dagger tightened around it, and he sucked his teeth. "We're done here," he growled, dismissing me, "get back to your chambers."

"Make me." I jumped on the rope.

But I wasn't quick enough. Talon was on my tail in a flash; a lethal look played out on his sharp features that had me climbing as fast as I could.

"Get down here now." He tried grabbing my foot, but I was just out of reach.

I scurried up a little higher, clinging to the rope for dear life.

"You wanted me to climb this thing so bad, yeah? Well, you got what you demanded."

"And now you're trying my patience. Get *down*."

"I'll catch you later, Tal." His friend laughed. "Good luck with that one."

Talon ignored him and started after me. "Impossible, human. You have a death wish, don't you?"

My palms stung from the bristly rope, but I kept climbing, kept pushing, and hoping my hands wouldn't become slick again.

His fingers wrapped around my ankle—still raw from the metal cuffs—and I let out a yelp. The pain caused me to falter, and my other foot slipped, connecting with Talon's face.

A growl rumbled from his chest, and he charged after me with swift ease, slipping an arm around my waist and pulling me back.

We fell toward the ground, the distance twice as high as when I fell earlier. We tumbled and turned, and he pulled me to him, twisting before we hit the ground.

Cushioning my fall, his body lay under me until the air returned to my lungs. A beat too long to notice the golden flakes in his green eyes.

I shook the fog from my head.

His hand slid off my back, releasing me, and I jumped away. Being in such a precarious position, being so close to him—against his hard body—disgusted me.

Talon stood up, straightening his leather breastplate. "You immature, foolish human. I have half the nerve to lock you back up in the dungeons for that stunt. Showing off in front of the other guards." The veins in his neck bulged.

I clenched my fists. He had some nerve barking at me like I was scum. Treating me like swine. Screw him! I came here to help my mother—I wasn't some criminal.

Before I could counter, he added, "Why did I bother with you? I should've let you fall to the ground and break your bones. Go back to your chambers and remain there for the rest of the day. I'm sick of looking at you."

We silently battled it out before I turned on my heel, exiting the training room with a hundred different retorts on my tongue, but none of them came out. The only sign I felt anything at all was the sting of tears on my cheeks.

Talon Warwick—youngest guard in Faerway history—could go fuck himself.

～

I couldn't move my arms. Like at all. They burned with even the smallest of twitches, making it next to impossible to pull on my nightgown. Which, unlike my training leathers, was baggy—borderline frumpy.

My body strained as I lay on the bed, screaming in protest.

I tucked my knees into the shirt. It didn't take long before my eyelids grew heavy. It was everything I needed after training with that sadist of a fae. I couldn't remember the last decent night of sleep I'd gotten.

"They let you out of the dungeon, I see," a familiar voice squeaked.

I groaned, rolling onto my other side to see Pipion lying on my pillow. "Yeah, only to put me in another prison."

Her nose twitched. "At least you smell better."

"Thanks. I could finally take a bath and get the nasty river water off me. Although, I swear I still smell like sewage." Bringing a strand of hair to my nose, I took a sniff to double-check, but only the residual scent of soap and something earthy remained.

"I heard you almost didn't place at assessments yesterday. This surprises me."

"Why does that surprise you? Have you seen my ankles? They barely support me. Some of those other competitors look like they lift weights for fun. I got lucky. I don't know how I'll make it through the trials."

Saying it out loud made my insides crawl.

To think I'd believed getting across the river was going to be the most troublesome part about getting the nightingale. I hadn't had time to process everything that followed. Getting attacked, being imprisoned, talking animals, arrogant fae. Hadn't stopped to think about my mother or how she was doing. I'd become too focused on surviving. Too focused on my selfish mistakes.

Pipion scratched behind her ear. "I was told Sir Warwick volunteered to train you as well. Is this true?"

"Yeah, lucky me."

"Curious. Warwick has never taken part in these trials. Some say it's to spite the king." Her brown and white fluffy tail fanned the pillow, deep in thought. "This is very curious. The power. You'll be undefeated. Whatever the case, what's your plan?"

It was obvious from the second he had spotted me in the

forest he disliked me. There was no doubt it was mutual, either. So, it didn't make sense why he'd break his streak for me.

"I don't have one." I sighed. "To be honest, I don't think I'll survive the first trial."

"Its power is fatal if in the wrong hands and carries the weight of millions. Wield it correctly and expect him to listen, but abuse the privilege, and you'll forfeit the competition."

My eyebrows arched in confusion. "What's that supposed to mean?" Her words swirled in my head in a muddled frenzy as I tried to piece the riddle together.

"You'll understand soon, Elowyn."

"What does that mean?" I repeated. "How is that relevant to the trials?" A surge of annoyance washed over me. "What do you know, Pipion?"

She cocked her head, said, "Feel it, embrace it, but conceal it," and with a snap of her paw, disappeared as quickly as she arrived.

I sat there unmoving—positive I'd finally snapped. Letting out a frustrated groan, I grabbed the pillow above my head and pushed it into my face. No one in this realm was any type of help.

If I was going to survive, it was going to be out of sheer spite.

TEN

I'd been up since before dawn broke, pacing the length of my chamber floor as I awaited the summons to the first trial. This was it. Survival or execution.

My stomach cramped.

I was cold, yet hot and clammy all at the same time.

Fingering my ring, I tried to take deep, controlled breaths, but they were coming out fast and haphazard. I was panicking. I was terrified.

The beginning and possibly the end. It'd come so soon—a week had flown by, and I didn't feel prepared at all. All our training sessions went as well as the first. They started with basic warm-up exercises and ended with one of us saying something hateful and storming off. Other than being able to get through all three rounds of push-ups, I'd made zero progress. How did he think I stood a chance against some of the other competitors? Better yet, why did he bother to train me if he was going to set me up to fail?

I checked my outfit in the mirror for the fifteenth time, hoping distraction would find me. It was like the training leathers I wore, but heavier and more durable. The vest was stiff and buckled around my chest, stealing my breath away. The boots rose to almost my knees, and the black long-sleeved shirt and pants trapped my body heat.

Adjusting the gloves around my exposed fingertips, I pulled my hair into a braid and dropped the strand over my shoulder—the deep red tresses like stained blood against my outfit. How much bloodshed would I witness today?

The door squeaked open, revealing an overzealous Talon in the entryway. His good mood was unsettling—surely it wasn't because he was excited to watch me die. Maybe it was meant to provide some type of reassurance and give me a semblance of hope, but it didn't help. It only made me more concerned.

My knees almost buckled, struggling to keep me up.

Talon clasped his hands behind his back. "Trials will start soon. Are you ready?"

I tipped my head to the side. "Do I look ready?"

Three loud, ominous chimes sounded throughout the castle before Talon could respond. "I'm not familiar with human sayings, but you better hope so. Because that's our cue."

Letting out a breath, I fidgeted with the leather pants sticking to my skin. I wasn't ready. My lungs burned, straining for air. My chest ached.

One foot after the other, I approached the door as if my legs had a mind of their own, and I willed them to stop—retreat—but they wouldn't listen.

Talon rolled his neck, stepping in front of me. "I don't care how nervous you are or how intimidated you might be. I don't care about any self-deprecating thought you've had this morning or whatever nonsense kept you up all night." He slipped his hands into his pockets, and I wondered how he knew any of that. "You don't show any uncertainty, understood? You walk out of this room with your chin up, and it doesn't come down until the trial is over and you're back in here. Do you understand?"

I nodded.

"No. Say it. Tell me. Do you understand?"

"Yes," I whispered.

"Good." He sighed. "The other fae mentors will be watching. They'll notice any hint of weakness and will use it to their advantage. As will the other competitors. Don't give them any more reason to target you."

I nodded again and shook my arms to release pent-up tension. Maybe if I could fool everyone else into believing I was confident, I'd believe it as well. It was worth a shot—and the only semblance of a plan I had.

"Do you know what the king has planned?"

Talon shook his head. "I know as much as you do."

I wiped my palms on my vest. "Well, here goes nothing, I suppose."

He stepped aside, motioning for me to walk ahead of him.

The hall was empty when I stepped into it. My gulp audible in the piercing silence. "Where is everyone?" There were no maids or guards or echoes of whispers. Only the sound of Talons and my boots against the polished marble floor. The stillness threw me off guard further.

"They're at the arena waiting for you to arrive. The king loathes tardiness, so I'm making sure you get there with one minute to spare," Talon said and pulled his shoulders back, a phantom smile on his face, and my cheeks flushed. "You don't wait for anyone. Not for the king, not for the other competitors, and surely not for death."

He increased his stride, forcing me to keep up.

If that was supposed to make me feel better, it missed the

mark. I wanted to dart into a nearby closet and scream. Throw up. Cry. Anything but continue down this cold, empty hallway into the unknown, but that wasn't an option. I needed to keep going, keep moving. I couldn't let anyone—Talon included—see me falter. Despite the aching, gnawing terror that dissolved my bones and turned them to jelly, I lifted my quivering chin and put one foot in front of the other.

Our steps were in sync—calculated—when we entered the foyer, the grand staircase to our right. Dozens of fae filled the room. I recognized a few from the dining hall, the vibrant hue of their skin like a rainbow against the beige walls. The hum of wings purred in the background.

It was an opulent space. The dome-shaped skylight acting as a ceiling filled the space with golden light. Malevolence disguised as beauty. It made my skin crawl.

'Don't show any uncertainty.' Talon's voice replayed in my head, and I straightened, lifting my chin as we breezed through the crowd of servants and handmaidens—a few I, again, recognized from the dining hall. Prisoners, like me, paying their debt with indentured servitude.

I sauntered between them all until I made it outside—the bright sun blinding me instantly.

Gone were the neon and fluorescent colors. Golden, luminous accents that sparkled under the sun replaced them. From the cobblestone path and opulent bird baths to flower petals and the tips of trees, everything was gold-plated.

Nature in Faerway seemed to glow in the dark and glimmer during the day—as if it inherently enhanced the beauty of both the sun and the moon. However, while it was magnificent and breathtaking, it must've been magic reserved only for the castle grounds, as the land by the river didn't seem to hold the same ability.

"Stop admiring the flowers and keep focused," Talon demanded.

Whipping my head around, I turned to face him, only to be met with a knowing smirk. If only he knew that flowers were what'd lead me to his *pleasant* company in the first place. I shook my head in annoyance. "Bite me. It's the only enjoyable thing about this place. Need I remind you I could be dead in a few minutes?"

He huffed a sadistic laugh. "Enough with the melodramatics and turn around before you draw attention."

Biting the inside of my cheek to control my irritation, I focused my attention back in front of me—cursing him under my breath.

At the end of the cobblestone path, a pair of double doors appeared, distant but imposing, standing a hundred feet away. Squinting in an attempt to decipher the peculiar markings and symbols adorning the colossal granite slabs, I found myself unable to discern the meaning behind the intricate etchings. If I had to guess, it must've been the ancient language they'd chanted that day in the throne room.

The columns on each side of the door supported an invisible structure and wore opaque scales, complete with dragon statues at the base. My gaze wandered up to the golden crest floating above the doors—it was simple yet powerful, illustrating a lone image of a winged fae pulling a crossbow. Entwined around the base of the plaque and ascending its sides were two serpents, their forms coiled. Atop the plaque, a crown crafted from menacing daggers adorned the scene and added an ominous elegance.

There was no building attached to the doors—only a pocket between realms that opened on a breeze as we approached.

I faltered, unsure how something like it could exist. It wasn't natural. If magic could create a realm within a realm, there was no telling the extent it could go. How vast and powerful it was.

"Keep moving, firefly. People will start to wonder," Talon growled.

"I need a second to breathe, you damn busybody."

Sadistic fae.

Talking animals.

Life or death trials.

It was all too much—I didn't know how I could get through this—but there was no turning back now. I needed to focus on the reason I was there and fight like hell. My mother, the nightingale, saving her life, getting home.

I stepped through the doors and flexed my fingers. A cool breeze kissed my flushed cheeks.

Massive walls of mirrors lined the ground floor in a rotating maze as fae spectators filed into the coliseum. With a gulp, I descended the ivory stairs to where I spotted a few of the other competitors below. Kelvin and Aeron stood at attention as they awaited their orders. I took my time getting there, craning my neck up to take in the mirrors towering over us. It was dizzying. As were the rows and rows of fae that extended into the sky. I didn't like the vibes I was getting.

The pointed scowls.

The venomous cackles.

The exchange of gold coins and the tally marks next to our names—mine still at the bottom.

We were nothing more than cattle being herded to our slaughter.

Entertainment.

I lifted my chin higher, refusing to let them get under my skin. Refusing to offer them a performance.

Talon veered to the right and up the stairs to join the other guards on the viewing deck where they'd have a front-row view of the trial as I went to the left toward the other competitors.

"Don't choke," Talon mouthed as he took a seat, resting his elbows on the back of the seat.

I glared. He had such a way with words.

Ignoring him, I took my place next to Kelvin, below King Harkin and Prince Bowen's thrones. Neither he nor Aeron acknowledged me, thankfully. Stone cold, the two of them stared ahead.

I did my best not to fidget.

"Do you have any idea what we're doing?" a soft voice asked beside me.

I turned to my right to see Lewis—his pale blond hair disheveled.

"No clue. It's like some sort of circus."

"I hope not." Lewis shuddered. "I hate clowns. Elowyn, if King Broderick knew how cruel these creatures truly were..." He knew better than to continue his thought.

The coliseum fell silent as King Harkin and Prince Bowen made their presence, halting our conversation. It gave me an odd sense of comfort knowing we were all trapped together. I only wished we could all leave together. The thought that some of us might not be alive soon was paralyzing. How these might be some of my last moments.

King Harkin held up a hand and everyone, save for the competitors, took their place. "Good morning, sprites, and pixies, fae, and nymphs. Welcome to the first trial."

Just as they did days before, the crowd erupted into cheers and applause. They were eager thralls to their king's every word.

By instinct, I searched the crowd for the frustrating—but familiar—eyes of my mentor. Talon remained stoic, however, his gaze still locked on me.

I squirmed, shifting my weight from one foot to the other, and glanced at the king and Prince Bowen, trying to dismiss the way my skin burned from his gaze. He might've been sadistic, but he was beautiful—almost uncomfortable in a vicious kind of way.

The king held up his hand again, and the audience obeyed the prompt for silence. "This will be the first of seven trials designed to ensure there will only be one winner. There are no rules other than to complete the assignment of each trial. I have placed a veil around the audience, preventing them from using their magic to give aid or disrupt the trials."

"You will have one hour to exit the maze. There will be obstacles along the way designed to test your avidity. Incentives to appease your thirst. Those of whom that cannot escape won't be moving on to the next trial."

A deep rumble vibrated the ground beneath us, and we turned to find the walls of mirrors rotating in an irregular, haphazard pattern in the center of the arena.

How were we going to navigate an ever-changing maze in an hour? It was impossible. A recipe for failure.

Fear licked my spine, stealing the air from my lungs, and I turned around to find Prince Bowen smiling at us—his teeth sharp and bright in the dim light. The hair on the back of my neck stood. It was crude. Malicious. And something in his eyes —or lack thereof—unsettled me.

Evil.

Pure evil.

I thumbed the ring on my finger, willing myself to relax, but I couldn't shake the unease that gnawed at my insides.

The veil surrounding the audience shimmered to life, blocking them from view, and the arena darkened. The only source of light now came from the shrubs themselves, and I could've sworn twelve more sprouted from the ground.

"Keep in mind, humans, selfishness is insatiable and knows no end. May the one who desires freedom most, win."

With that, the king and the prince disappeared, leaving us to fend for ourselves.

ELEVEN

Everything happened in such a blur. I didn't have time to gather my bearings. My head pounded as I tried to think of a plan, ignoring the fear that stabbed me in the chest.

Aeron and Kelvin took off into the maze of mirrors first. I didn't see where Calandra went or Lewis or any of the others, and I was the only one remaining. A sitting duck in an inky void surrounded by stars only knew what.

Paralyzed.

Nauseated.

Time wouldn't wait for anyone, and the longer I stood here, the less of it I had. This wasn't the time to choke. I couldn't choke. Not now. Not with so much to lose. I wouldn't be a coward. I wouldn't give them the satisfaction.

My mother was counting on me to make it home with the nightingale. I couldn't fail her again.

Wiping the sweat off my brow, I sucked in a sharp breath.

The mirrors gleamed as they rotated, streams of light trickling out from between them. This was it.

I mustered up the same false bravado that got me across the

Dolorem River and forced my tense shoulders to relax. Using the darkness to my advantage, I kept to the shadows, moving along the back wall on high alert, before bolting toward the entrance—sliding into the maze as the mirrors closed behind me.

My reflection stared at me from every angle in an infinite string, mimicking my every movement. The dread on my face was undeniable—my skin sickly pale as I spun around, keeping my hands on the wooden thresholds as I searched for an open passage. My vision crossed from the optical illusion.

How the hell are we supposed to navigate this maze in an hour?

It was impossible.

I crashed face-first into a mirror as I rounded a corner, rubbing the sore spot on my forehead. Frustration itched to the surface, but I pushed forward, slamming into mirrors, time and time again.

A low, frustrated groan escaped me, a clear expression of my dissatisfaction with the lack of headway I'd made. And, on top of that, the fae above were likely cackling at our expense, enjoying our frenzied, pathetic efforts to escape. To them, we were nothing but lousy pests trapped in a death spiral.

A shadow flashed in my peripheral.

I turned, startling myself as I collided with my reflection. My hands fell abruptly to my knees, and my face blanched as adrenaline rocked through me.

Anxiety wrapped around my throat.

"Screw this!" I grumbled, smacking my hand into the glass. Every muscle in my body constricted—panic brewing beneath the surface as it disappeared between the panes.

I ripped it back and flipped it over, searching for any signs of injury, but found it unscathed. Relief mixed with uncertainty as I tried to make sense of how that was possible. If it was the mirage of mirrors playing with my mind or if I'd discovered some type of portal.

My head weighed heavily on my shoulders. Still, I extended a finger toward the glass, swallowing hard when it vanished once again.

Stumbling back, my back clashed with a wooden threshold, and I fell to the ground, scrambling to my feet.

No, that couldn't be right.

How could that be possible?

My pulse raced. I kept moving, glancing over my shoulder as the shadow crept out into view, following me. Hunting me. I veered left, right, making a mental note of each turn I made when the ground vibrated, knocking me off balance.

Trying to maintain my balance, I grabbed onto a wooden post while the mirrors moved and jumped into a clearing, but my bootlaces got tangled under the mirrors, causing me to trip and fall. Fear prickled my skin as the silhouette appeared to my right, approaching with animalistic prowess.

I yanked and pulled and cursed under my breath, but it wouldn't budge. My fingers trembled as it flanked me, surrounding me from every angle.

It was faceless. A murky silhouette that oozed malignant rage, watching me.

I tugged my foot once more, praying to make it out, when it dislodged, flinging me backward. A wave of relief flooded me as I made a run for it, not bothering to lace my boot.

Racing down the clearing, I struggled to breathe, choking on the fear that still had me in a stranglehold. I jumped at the slightest sound. Froze with each apparition—growing mad with paranoia. I didn't know how much time we had left, or how close I was to the exit, but I'd already spent too much time wandering through the maze.

I couldn't think straight. My reflection a ghostly reminder. I needed to get out of there before I lost it. Before my mind shattered.

Death called to me like an old friend. A promise of peace. A promise to take away all my suffering, the torture I'd experience for weeks to come at the whim of the fae king.

I made another right—skirting to a stop as Kelvin appeared at the end of the same hall, but I couldn't be sure that's where he was. My pulse rang in my ears as he copied me step by step, his brown eyes tracking me. I clenched my hands at my sides, desperate to get away from him.

"What's wrong, bastard? Don't tell me you're scared." His face pulled into a sneer. "You sure were brave during assessments. Where's that same energy?"

"Screw you."

Kelvin sucked his teeth. "I figured you'd say that. I enjoy games."

My chest tightened as he circled me, and I slipped into a cove, losing him for a split second before he reappeared behind me. I turned around—my back flush against the wooden post.

He continued, "You see, I'm making it out of here one way or another, so I'll give you two options." He paused. "One, you can run, or two, you can watch me kill him."

Kelvin jerked Lewis into view, his hand covering his mouth, and my pulse raced in my ears.

Lewis silently pleaded for my help. Eyes wild.

"Let him go." My voice shook as I spoke, and Kelvin's smile grew, enjoying the effect he had on me.

"Oof. Too bad that wasn't an option." He clicked his tongue. "I'll give you a few more seconds to decide before I make it for you."

"I didn't peg you as a coward. If you want to kill someone, kill me." I held my hands out in front of me, hoping to call his bluff. "Kill someone who'll put up a fight. Not a defenseless child."

Kelvin stepped forward. "Ah. But what would that prove, hm? I want everyone to know I'll stop at nothing and no one. That I'm not one to back down or fuck with."

Lewis thrashed, but Kelvin's grip on him tightened.

Horror surged through me as I raced to find where they were, to save Lewis, but all I met was my reflection at each turn. He needed to get back home to his mother—to live his life—he was just a kid.

My chest ached.

My nerves splintered in a million directions as I rushed through the maze.

Lewis shook his head, sniffling away his tears. "At what cost, Kelvin? Show some humanity."

I turned another corner and came face to face with them. Not their reflection. Not an apparition. *Them*. Lewis's chest rose and fell in haphazard intervals as I dashed toward him.

"That died a long time ago." A quiet, menacing tone coined around each word, but there was a hint of regret, too.

I was less than three feet away when Kelvin released him.

"Run! You can—"

Kelvin gripped Lewis's head and twisted.

The scream that escaped me muted the nauseating crack that followed, and I collapsed to my knees. I wanted to run to him. Hold him. Tell him everything was going to be okay. Tell him how much his mother loved him and never gave up hope.

I gagged as Kelvin released his lifeless body, tossed him aside like an unwanted toy, and stalked toward me. My fingers dug into the ground as if I'd float away. Tears streamed down my face.

My knees trembled, but I tried to stand.

All he'd wanted was a fair chance, and yet there he laid.

I tried to find my footing again. To scurry away from Kelvin as he inched closer. To finally run. "You're a monster!" I spat. "A waste of air. The moral equivalent of a disease-ridden swine. People like you never win!"

Kelvin closed in on me, his shrill laugh ringing off the mirrors, piercing my ears. "No, Elowyn. People like me *always* win. You want to know why?" He cracked his neck as my boots found traction. "Because we don't let trivial emotions override our logic. It's okay, I know you're scared. Go on, run. I'll give you a head start."

Sure, he might not let his feelings get the best of him, but if he made it out of there, he'd never be happy. He'd spend the rest of his disgraceful life depressed and alone.

Although I wasn't afraid of him, that was the dangerous thing about people like Kelvin—misery loves company. He had nothing to lose, and I wasn't about to be another casualty in his rampage. Nor was I that dimwitted to think I could take him on alone.

I turned my back to him and heeded his warning, weaving through the wall of mirrors, making significant ground when Aeron stepped in front of me, blocking my path—Kelvin right behind me.

They had me trapped, their reflections encasing me.

"Come out, come out wherever you are, Elowyn," Aeron's grating voice sang. "We just want to talk. You can't think you're going to make it out of here, can you? You don't stand a chance against us. Just like poor Lewis, isn't that right, Kelvin?"

"We'll stop at nothing to get what we want," Kelvin echoed.

I dipped into an open passageway. "Bite me."

Their reflections grew larger, and I squeezed my eyelids shut, scavenging my brain for a way out when I remembered the portal.

Kelvin and Aeron were nowhere to be found when I ripped my eyes open, and my limbs felt numb.

I didn't know where it'd take me, but I gambled anywhere was better than remaining a sitting duck as they stalked me from afar.

With a deep breath, I reached a hand toward the mirror, stifling my surprise as it disappeared behind the glass. I poked my foot through next, noting the cooler air when Aeron grabbed my arm.

"Where do you think you're going?"

I kicked him in between the legs. There was no time to debate. He let go, doubling over in pain, and I flung the rest of my body through the portal.

Everything around me exploded.

A kaleidoscope of colors twisting and expanding, as I folded like paper between pockets of air, spinning and tumbling, until I crashed into the ground.

I was still in the maze, that much I knew, but where?

I had no clue.

But I couldn't bring myself to care. I'd never experienced something so invigorating—so thrilling—in my entire life. Blood coursed through my veins like a raging current, forgetting the severity of the situation. Lewis's final screams.

I shook my head, remembering Lilian's body on the bank, and clutched my chest. Begging the visions to go away.

The mirror rippled behind me, a deep shout following from within—Aeron. Shoving the memories into the deepest parts of my mind, I leaped out of the way, taking off through another portal before he could catch up to me. One after another, I jumped through countless portals, getting steadier with each landing, before I stopped to catch my breath. Time was running out, and I had no idea how close—or far away—I was to the exit.

Lewis's death would be in vain. As would my mother's.

I twisted the ring on my finger, wondering how Calandra and Breana were fairing. If they'd made it out yet. If they were even alive.

Voices sounded from somewhere behind me, and I twisted around to find where it was coming from.

"Yes, sweet child, this way. That's it. Closer. Closer," a meek voice crooned.

I glimpsed the cherub-like faerie, a vynx, as legends called them, and glanced away. I wasn't familiar with most magical species outside of the fae—aside from the most dangerous, most documented ones. But there were hundreds of stories featuring these murderous shifters who disguised themselves as the thing you desired most.

Never aging, some referred to them as The Little Demons. Just one look—a passing glance—was all it took to lure you in for the kill.

"Oh, my goodness!" Sage, the frizzy redhead, appeared, cupping her face in astonishment. "Look at all those toys! I could swim in them! Stars, I've never seen so many!"

No, no, no. "Sage, it isn't real! The toys aren't real! It's a vynx!"

A blood-curdling scream sounded seconds later, and I cupped my face in my hands. I peered out of my peripheral, grimacing as the vynx dipped its chubby fingers into her intestines, its porcelain skin dyed red as it snacked on her insides.

Sage's head lulled to the side, and I recoiled, my gaze meeting the ground in front of me as I retched.

First Lewis, then Sage—humans and demons.

I didn't want to imagine what other horrid beings lurked between the mirrors. Six more of these trials lay ahead; I couldn't fathom what else they'd try to break us down. What other moral dilemmas we'd face or how much more I could handle. If I was strong enough.

Resilient. Sure, I learned how to carry the burden of my mother's illness on my shoulders, but this? This was something else entirely.

I forced my numb legs to move, running far away from the vynx. From Aeron. Before he came through the portal after me.

Mirror after mirror, my head spun from the endless apparitions, growing sick and tired of my reflection. Sick of the fixed landscape and the grim reality that stared back at me, unsure I liked what I saw. Who I was.

Was that the point of the trial? To face the mirrored versions of ourselves—the darker parts of our ego we keep hidden? My vision blurred. I wanted it to be over. I was going mad. Exhausted.

Stumbling through another portal, my head spun.

I collapsed onto the ground.

The incessant portaling was taking a toll on my body.

A mirror to my left rippled, and I spun around a corner, my foot slipping on a slick patch of marble, propelling me into another portal. My temple smashed into a wooden threshold, and I shook away the stars, glimpsing a set of oak doors attached to a copper archway between the flutter of my lashes.

That must be the exit—*it had to be.*

My shoulders slumped with relief as I got to my feet and made for the arch, running as fast as I could. A mixture of relief and uncertainty flooded me the closer I got. As grateful as I was for this trial to be over, I didn't want to imagine what else the king had planned. The training it'd entail. The cruel trainer himself.

But I knew I must face it—chin held high. For Lilian. My mother. *Myself.* Prove I wasn't the worthless bastard everyone thought me to be. Show them how capable I was, even if I had to fake it.

An object glimmered in my peripheral—a deep red shimmer that had me skidding to a stop and questioning if I was imagining things. A bundle of nightingale sprouted from the base of a mirror I'd just passed—blooming bright and full and owning the marble it sprouted from.

It called to me. Demanded my attention as I floated over to it on a light breeze, unable to stop if I wanted to.

Bells chimed in succession from somewhere above, the deep trill breaking my trance, and I stopped.

The countdown to the end.

The solution to every problem was right in front of me. If I could pocket it, take a bud or two, I could escape. Find a way around the water wraiths and get it to my mother. Save her. Put this torture behind me.

The bells continued, and a shudder ran through me as I took another step. All judgment leaped into a nearby portal. It was beautiful. I was so close.

Run!

An unusual voice shook me from my stupor, and I searched the arena, unable to locate where it'd come from.

Run! It demanded again.

The deep timbre came from within—an internal thought that didn't belong to me.

It would've been alarming if, when I peered back at the bundle of nightingale, it hadn't been replaced with the same grotesque creature who'd devoured Sage. Blood still smeared across its face.

Wind whooshed from my lungs as I bolted toward the exit. Sheer panic snaked around my chest, turning the corners of my vision black.

No, no, no. I ran as fast as my legs would carry me, begging, pleading, praying to make it out of there.

The vynx chased me—it's circular maw of fangs yearning for flesh. A hunter stalking its prey for the killing blow.

The bells chimed, and the vynx wrapped a hand around my leg, yanking me toward it. I flailed, digging my nails into the ground to keep from getting closer to its mouth—my heart rate spiraling into a dangerous rhythm as it pinned me to the ground. Its rows of teeth inching toward my face.

A final bell sounded, and the door to the exit closed, threatening to lock me inside.

No, I was too close.

Too much was at risk.

I thrashed under its hold once more before rolling over on top of it and kneeing it in the head.

It screeched in response, disarming it long enough to free my hands and wrap them around its head. I winced as I recalled Lewis's soulless body dropping to the ground and hesitated for a split second before I twisted—snapping its neck.

The vynx twitched.

I scrambled to my feet and darted toward the exit, the light on the other side shrinking with each step.

I was almost there; the fresh air on the other side brushed my face.

Time stood still as I took a sharp breath, dug my boots into the marble ... and leaped.

TWELVE

My eyes strained as I squeezed them shut—too afraid to find out if I'd failed or not.

There was no other option.

No backup plan.

I needed to be on the other side of that door.

Taking a deep breath, I peeled them open.

Instant relief washed over me. The arena had gone back to its original state. Gone was the moving maze and oak door, and in their place a well-lit coliseum and the thousands of fae observing above. The veil, too, had disappeared, and the sounds of the crowd overpowered my thoughts.

Letting out a sigh, I sat up and searched the crowd for Talon but didn't see him on the viewing deck. He wasn't anywhere.

I scanned the group of competitors next as I got to my feet, checking to see who was still with us.

One. Two...

There were only six that I could see, including myself.

Twirling around, I checked the board with our names and tally marks, and my body went cold.

~~Lewis~~

~~Sage~~

~~Martell~~

~~Jeston~~

Then, I spotted them.

Their bodies piled over in the arena's corner, waiting to be tossed out like trash. The visual of Lewis and Sage's deaths replayed in my head, and I cringed—wiping away the tears that rimmed my eyelids as I rushed over to them.

My body felt miles away.

I collapsed beside him, brushing Lewis's blond hair from his face, and choked back a sob.

Death had come too early. His pale blue lips. His still chest. He was a kid. Only a kid. They all were. Kids who wanted a chance to go home just like everyone else.

I kissed his forehead, my fingers trembling as I stroked Sage's porcelain face. I wanted to scream. Curse the king and escape this star-forsaken realm while I still could. Alive.

Disappointment panged my chest—if only the nightingale was real, I'd be halfway to the border by now.

"Well, well, well, wasn't that exciting!" King Harkin clicked his tongue, pleased with the chaos he'd created.

Prince Bowen's face was just as menacing. The crowd cheered, their shrieks piercing my ears. If this was what they did for fun, I didn't want to know what they were capable of when they were angry.

"Six out of ten survived the first trial," he continued. "And this was only the beginning! Who will come out the winner?" His lip curled with disgust before he returned his attention ahead. "Place your bets. The next trial is one week from today."

Everyone filed out of the coliseum, cackling to one another, and gossiping about who they thought would win.

"You hear them?" a slimy voice came from behind me. "They're betting on me to win." I peeked out of my peripheral to find Aeron lurking over my shoulder, his fingers laced behind his head. "You won't get so lucky next time. I'll make sure of it. Your luck will run dry, eventually."

I stood up, our noses at equal level as his coal-black eyes bore into mine. "Is that a threat?"

"And what if it is?" He took a step toward me.

"I'm not scared of you," I lied. "You're a disgusting maggot that kills innocent children."

"All the more reasons to watch your back if I were you. I will win this, and I couldn't care less who I hurt or must kill to do it." Aeron shouldered past me, not giving me a chance to reply.

I stood there motionless, mustering up everything inside me not to scream in frustration.

He had a point—the king said only one of us could make it out alive. They designed these trials to test our virtues. Not that I was perfect by any means, but I certainly didn't have it in me to kill my way to the top. If that was everyone else's plan, I was doomed. I could play defense for as long as possible, but eventually, I'd have to make a decision that'd haunt me forever.

My breaths became shaky as I held back tears. I couldn't do it. It'd been a week since I'd arrived, and my mother would only be getting sicker as the days passed. There was no guarantee of walking out of this place.

The stars above knew I stood a better chance against those water creatures than the monsters crawling inside this castle.

I'd gone back and forth on whether I should wait until nightfall to make my escape, but I figured the sooner I got out of this dreadful place, the better. Pulling my hair out of my face, I tied it with a ribbon and wondered how far I'd get before anyone noticed I was missing.

Hopefully far enough to buy me some time.

I poked my head out of the door to check the corridor and closed it behind me as I exited. All the servants and hand-maidens didn't seem to pay me any mind as I breezed through the hall, weaving around carts of food and cleaning supplies. Getting caught was the furthest thing from my mind as I pushed past the gothic doors at the end of the corridor, running alongside the golden shrubs and trees to remain hidden.

The foliage dwindled to nothing—exposing me before I could reach the forest ahead.

I paused to catch my bearings, checked over my shoulder to see if any of the groundskeepers were watching, and took off toward the wooded shelter. My legs carried me as fast as they'd allow, still exhausted from the trial hours ago, until I reached the sanctuary of canopy trees and vines that hid me from the castle view.

Slowing to a walk, I took notice of which side the moss grew and cleared a shrub of purple berries, using them to mark my location in the event I got lost. However, as long as the Wintercrest Highlands remained on my right, I should make it to the Dolorem River in no time.

The deeper I trekked into the forest, the darker it became, and soon, I could barely see my hand in front of my face. I wasn't sure how long I'd been walking and if it was the sun that had gone down or the thick covering of leaves above that caused my impaired sight, but I knew I needed to find the river before whatever lurked in the shadows killed me.

I trekked further into the dense woods. Déjà vu of my travels through the Elmhurst Woods played around me and how densely ignorant I'd been. Never could I have imagined I'd end up in this predicament—stuck in a deadly trial, fighting for my life.

Nor could I have dreamed up half the creatures I'd come across. While most seemed innocent and kind enough, others belonged in the deepest depths of the underworld.

I grimaced, the hairs on my arms at attention, as sticks and leaves crunched to my right. Every muscle tightened, on high alert, and I pushed forward.

Each snap.

Every rustle.

The faint clicks and buzzes above.

My body hummed in anticipation. It instinctively knew how to overcompensate for my lack of vision—tune in to the environment.

Another crunch sounded to my left.

And then behind me.

I straightened, readying my fist as I turned in a circle, keeping my breaths calm and quiet. Searching the forest.

A light growl licked the back of my neck, and I spun around, backing away before sprinting toward the nearest tree. It galloped behind me, hot breath dampening my skin.

In a sea full of evergreens, I couldn't find one suitable to climb, but picked up speed, sprinting faster until my foot caught on an exposed tree root, flinging me to the ground with a thud.

Panicking, I rolled onto my back, scurried away on my elbows, and ignored the burning sensation in my bleeding hands.

An enormous wolf prowled in front of me, its back lined with sharp spikes—its barbed tail splitting into two. It tilted its head at me as it stalked toward me, analyzing my every breath. Each blink. The pulsing vein in my neck.

I kept as still as possible, hoping, like a bear, it'd leave me alone when a frilled membrane fanned out from around its neck and it cackled, leaping on top of me.

Curling into a ball was the only way to avoid razor claws, and we rolled against the forest's rough terrain, writhing and squirming as I tried to get free.

There was no time to think—only act—as its fangs neared my neck, thick saliva dripping on my face while I kicked and kneed it in its thick coat.

A barbed tail whipped over its back, bludgeoning down like a hammer, and I jerked my head to the side, barely avoiding its attack.

I grabbed onto its sticky membrane and yanked, jumping to my feet, and it pulled back, hissing while it slashed a heavy paw at my legs.

The creature crouched, swiping its claws at the dirt as I caught my breath, keeping my hands clenched at my side while we stared off.

I wiped the saliva with my sleeve. "Come on, is that all you got?"

The wolf cackled and leaped forward again, its talons slicing through the air before it went limp and dropped on top of me —the weight of it cutting off my air supply.

I shoved my hands into its dense coat, trying to get it off me, but it wouldn't budge.

In fact, it wasn't moving at all, a vast difference from our frenzied struggle minutes earlier. I didn't know if it was dead or about to rip into my neck, so I shoved harder, the veins in my neck straining. Gasping for air.

The fanged creature suddenly lifted into the air.

I scurried backward on my hands as it floated above me, horror-stricken and out of breath, when it was violently tossed against a tree.

"Are you trying to get yourself killed, or are you just

stupid?" a deep, husky voice drawled.

My blood boiled. I didn't need to see who stood before me to know who spoke those eloquent words. Leave it to Talon to be a pillar of comfort.

I twisted around, my lip curling with disdain as he rested against a tree, cleaning his fingernails with a small knife.

"Have you been following me this entire time?"

He lifted a shoulder. "It would appear so, yes."

"And you didn't think to ... I don't know." I tapped my chin. "Help me?"

He pointed his knife at the creature wrapped around the tree. "I did. You're welcome."

I huffed, clenching my jaw.

"So, what's your plan, hm?" He flicked the knife into his sleeve. "Assuming the water wraiths don't kill you this time. You get across the river, then what?"

"I'd figure it out." My right knee twinged in pain as I stood, brushing my hands clean of soil as I met his pointed stare.

Talon tipped his chin in my direction. "You need help with that?"

I limped forward. "Nope. I'm all right. You can go back to doing whatever it is you do."

The beast twitched, and I froze, afraid any sudden movement would have it charging at me again, but Talon held out a hand, casting a golden light from his palm, and the beast whimpered. Its bones crunched before it stilled—forever.

My jaw dropped, and I whirled around to face him. "How did you do that?"

Talon clicked his tongue. "Simple magic. You've broken the Iron Accords by coming onto our lands, you know." He strolled over to me, my body turning to stone as he neared. "We'd be well within our rights to bring you back."

"Go to hell," I spat, remembering how to walk—my knee

aching in response.

He chuckled. The light, sultry sound coated with condescension. "You won't survive more than an hour after sunfall. Drop the ego and the act before you make this worse on yourself."

"I think I'll take my chances, thank you. Can you quit following me now?"

"So, that's it? You're going to give up? Go on a suicide mission? Throw in the towel? What about your mother?"

I turned on my heel, tilting my head back to meet his glare. "Don't you dare bring my mother into this!"

"That's who this is all about, isn't it? Why you came here in the first place, no? Your childish impulses are clouding your judgment. You need to get back to the castle—"

"You know nothing about me! Or my mother! Your king murdered four humans in front of hundreds of your kind for entertainment. Why would I stick around to be next?"

"Because you're a fighter. I thought you were better than that."

"Well." I let out an incredulous laugh that had an edge of insanity to it. "You thought wrong."

"Yeah? I know you're a stubborn pain in the ass. One that not only survived an attack from a five-hundred-year-old wraith but also didn't back down from a drowler, either. Now you're telling me you draw the line at a couple of lowly tyrants?"

"While this has been enlightening, I have a time-sensitive journey to make. It's been … it's been something. I won't forget about this soon enough. Thanks for everything." I only made it a couple of steps before an arm snaked around my waist, pinning me to a hard, taut body. "What are you doing? Let go of me!" I jerked in his grip, but I was no match for Talon's strength.

"You're delirious if you think I'm going to let you wander

off and die." His breath caressed the shell of my ear. "You're not the only one with something at stake here."

I thrashed, slipping out of his grip, and tried to make a run for it, but he caught me by the hem of my shirt.

In one fluid motion, he twisted me around and threw me over his shoulder.

I slammed my fists into his back until I bruised my wrists, howling my annoyance.

I was simply a means to an end to get whatever it was he wanted. Of course he'd try to keep me from leaving, but I'm sure he'd have no problem getting whatever that was without me. Another wraith attack was welcome if it meant getting as far away from this realm—and this insufferable guard—as possible.

In violation of the Iron Accords, my ass, they wouldn't waste resources for one measly human. Not during such an *important* trial.

I pounded on his back. "Let go of me, you barbaric son of a bitch!"

An invisible gag slapped over my mouth, preventing me from continuing, just like Breana in the throne room last week.

Talon stretched his neck as he carried me out of the forest like a sack of potatoes, and I seethed, muttering curse after curse at his back. I hated him—why did he have to volunteer to train me? I'd rather be in a ditch somewhere than over his damn shoulder. It was degrading. Mortifying.

I still had autonomy despite being a prisoner. I could understand if I did something deserving to be in this position—like kill a faerie. But all I was trying to do was help my mother. The *horror*.

"Not until you control yourself and stop acting like an infant."

I flipped him my finger as he continued through the forest,

keeping me perched over his shoulder until we reached the castle grounds. It couldn't be any later than high noon when we stepped into the clearing. The birds were back to singing their cheerful melody, and the land glimmered in gold. I hadn't realized how unnaturally dark it was in the forest until the sun blinded me. Or how cold I'd been until the sun bathed me again.

Talon flung me to my feet—the blood rushing back to my head—and I swayed.

"If I remove the gag, are you going to remain quiet, or are you going to make a scene and embarrass me?"

I pointed to my mouth, letting him know I couldn't answer, and he sighed.

"Thumb up for yes, thumb down for no," he finished.

We stared at each other, a silent challenge of wills as I contemplated if I should compromise. With much hesitation and defiance, I gave him a thumbs up, concluding if I was going to be forced to stay, I might as well keep what remaining pride I had left. Not that there was much.

He waved his hand, removing the gag with one dismissive motion, and I stretched my mouth, rubbing my cheeks, feeling like it was still in place.

"You could've asked me nicely, you know." I straightened my vest. "There was no need for the dramatics."

Talon's eyes narrowed. The skepticism pulling at his brows told me he knew I was full of it, and he sucked his teeth. "Next time, you can run all the way to the wards for all I care." He turned to leave, but I remained where I stood, confused by what he meant.

"Hey!" I followed him, my curiosity getting the best of me. "The wards? What wards?"

A bemused smile crinkled the corners of his eyes. "The ones the king put up to keep you from leaving."

Thirteen

Talon's unclothed back greeted me as I entered the room, his rippling muscles captivating my attention. The sun had begun its climb over the mountains, casting golden rays of light through the windows that encompassed him.

The sword in his hands gleamed as he swung and cut it through the air—his arm and back muscles tightening with each precise movement. Every motion appeared as controlled and steady as his last.

Something inside me stirred, and I bit my cheek to keep the inappropriate thoughts at bay. Men weren't built like that in Wendover. It was almost unfair how beautiful he was, and I hated myself for admiring him, yet I peeked again, unable to control myself.

"Twice now, you've managed to be late." Talon thrust the sword out in front of him. "It's impressive, honestly."

I opened my mouth, ready to defend myself, but his deadly dance held me captive.

His movements were unnaturally mesmerizing. He pulled back, spinning the blade around his body with a flick of the hilt, catching it in his opposite hand. "Please feel free to keep standing there and wasting my time," he went on. "I'd hate to inconvenience you."

I strolled toward him, careful to keep as much distance between me and that blazing piece of metal as possible. A glittering arsenal of weapons paneled the wall to my left, ranging from small daggers to long swords like the one Talon used.

He sheathed his sword at his hip as he approached, scooping his shirt off the ground, and pulled it over his head. I hated how effortlessly he walked—his stupid leisurely stroll—as if he wasn't capable of unspeakable crimes.

"Pick the one that calls to you."

Death didn't call to me, not like it did the fae. And now I was expected to connect to a weapon I'd potentially have to use to kill another?

I brushed a finger along the blades, pretending not to notice how his abs flexed and glistened with sweat. Or the way his nimble fingers ran through the damp hair that clung to his forehead. He was a flame-forged weapon. Who needed all these bayonets and knives when fae like Talon existed? Casting creatures like the drowler into trees with a flick of the wrist. Surely the swordplay was just for show—to mock humans.

I shook my head, refocusing my attention on the daggers in front of me. "How will I know which one calls to me?"

"Trust your instinct. It'll tell you."

"That's not exactly helpful."

Talon wiped his face with the hem of his shirt, and I looked away—too quick to be casual. "Pick the prettiest one, then."

I hummed my annoyance. Beautiful yet cruel. It made my blood itch. "How original. Need I remind you of the hundreds of sharp weapons at my disposal that I could use to kill you?" Waving a hand across the wall, I matched his haughty attitude.

"Don't get ahead of yourself, firefly. While your threats are well intended, they're futile. Do me a favor and pick a weapon so we can move this along."

My molars ground together, and I balled my hands into fists at my side. I knew it was reckless. I knew he could kill me with one swift flick of his wrist. But the rage he induced inside me surged to the surface, and before I could rationalize it, I grabbed the first hilt I saw and spun around, pressing the tip of the sword into his Adam's apple.

A drop of crimson blood dripped down his neck.

"Don't patronize me," I snapped.

"Interesting choice." Talon flashed his sharp canines before swiftly disarming me. His face inches from mine as he held the tip of the sword to my ribcage.

I sucked in a breath.

"Let's get one thing straight, hm?" A beat passed before Talon retreated with my weapon, wiping the blood from his neck with his thumb before licking the pad of it clean. "Blind rage can and will get you killed. Every single time. It's sloppy. Careless. Dueling is about technique, timing, and control. Normally, I'd have you focus on defense, but with your stature, I think homing in and improving your coordination would be more beneficial." Talon tossed my sword. "Catch."

I jumped to catch the flying piece of metal, but the hilt slipped out of my fingers—the blade clanking against the cement ground. "What in the hell is wrong with you?" Bending over, I picked it up. "You can't throw a sword at someone like that!"

"Apparently." He tsked. "Now it's scuffed. Try to catch it next time."

He was impossible—insinuating I was to blame. As if I was the one who had casually thrown a razor-sharp object at another person. As if that was normal. He made me want to scream. Or commit murder. Taking a deep, slow breath, I pocketed my newfound murderous tendencies and faced him.

"Wouldn't it be better to use props first?" I palmed the hilt, getting comfortable with its weight.

Talon arched a brow. "Why would we do that?"

"Oh, I don't know." I contorted my face with mock contemplation. "You could've hurt me?"

Something resembling amusement flashed across his face, and he gave me a half-shrug. If I didn't know any better, I would've bet that was his goal.

"Sword up." Talon's face twisted back into neutrality.

I leveraged the sword off the ground and rested it against my shoulder, the cold metal burning my skin through my top.

He shook his head, displeased. "Open your legs," Talon demanded. Sliding his hand between my knees, he pushed them apart and pulled my right leg forward toward him.

Heat flooded my body as I tried not to squirm.

"A good stance will give you leverage and better control." He stepped back and pulled his sword out. "When I go up, you go under. I'm going to switch it up randomly and increase my speed. Stay alert."

His blade flashed in front of me as I fidgeted with my grip.

I stepped back, but he matched my stride and took one of his own toward me, cutting his sword through the air again.

"Hold on," I urged. "I don't have a good grip."

"If you still think for one minute any of the other competitors will care when it's your life or theirs, you're poorly mistaken." He swung the blade at me again.

I lifted the sword out of pure frustration and met the motion of his attack, straining my arms to keep as steady as possible. Our swords clashed.

Talon nodded. "Perfect. Again."

Each swing became easier than the last, and the untamed

delight in his smile told me I was doing something right. My blood buzzed as he picked up speed, and I matched his pace. He stepped toward me, and I backed up before he could get close, learning to read his cues to expect his next move.

Over.

Under.

Under.

Over.

It was rhythmic. Calming—like I was observing myself from above. Talon's concentration never left my gaze, squinting with unrelenting focus. His attentive eyes would've been a distraction if I weren't so keenly aware that one wrong move would leave my blood at his feet.

Over.

Over.

My wrist was burning from the repetitive back-and-forth movements as we migrated throughout the room. Just when I thought I'd gotten the hang of it, Talon jabbed the tip of the sword toward my center.

I lurched back, ducking to avoid the strike as he aimed it above my head.

"What was that?" I demanded as we fell back into the basic swordplay I'd gotten used to.

"Don't let yourself get comfortable. Always be on the lookout for the unexpected."

My brows pulled together. I mimicked his movement, thrusting the sword toward his center and around his head. "Like that?" I asked.

Talon huffed a laugh and advanced toward me. "I have a hard time believing you've never used a sword before."

"Never said I didn't." I stepped toward him, and our swords clanked—the sound reverberating against the stone walls. I tried to hold my own against him, but I was no match.

Talon overpowered me, causing my sword to go flying from my hands.

I thought he'd stop—or allow me to pick it up before we resumed—but he only moved faster. I should've known better. Mercy was for the weak on this side of the river.

"Seriously? Let me at least grab—"

Talon's sword came flying toward my shins, and I stopped to jump, the blade nearly nicking my skin.

"Stop!" I exclaimed. "You almost cut me!" But it was pointless.

He was relentless.

I jumped.

Rolled.

Ducked.

I did everything I could do to avoid his blade and vigorous assault. My breaths came quickly, and my lungs burned. I was ready to surrender when my back slammed against the wall.

Then the tip of Talon's sword came to an abrupt stop at my throat.

He lifted my chin with the flat part of the blade and cocked his head. I tried slipping away from him, but he had me trapped between his arm and sword. My chest rose and fell erratically. Light notes of teakwood drifted off him, warming the air between us.

He used the blade to push a strand of hair from my face, his voice low and gruff as he spoke. "All it takes is one wrong move and your life is in someone else's hands, firefly."

I didn't dare breathe as he slid the cool metal down my cheek, my neck, remaining completely still until he sheathed it behind his back.

"Your corpse will be left to bleed out without a second thought."

I straightened the hem of my top, keeping my idle hands

busy while I tried my damnedest to ignore the way Talon's back muscles stretched his shirt thin. Or how the room grew to accommodate his presence as he strolled over to the weapons rack on a swift, windless current.

It proved to be in vain, however. His mere existence demanded attention—it made me sick.

"Please, I'm sure nothing would make you happier. What's in this for you, anyway? Why do any of you care if we win or lose?" I'd asked him the question before but never got a straight answer.

Talon grinned, using the towel on the wall to wipe the sweat off his face. "An abundance of wealth and eternal glory, obviously. Although even that's hardly enough to tolerate you," he mumbled that last part.

I clenched my fists and stalked over to him, my boots slapping against the stone. "Oh, aren't you hilarious? I didn't realize you doubled as a comedian. Here I thought you didn't joke around. What did you call it? A waste of time?" I snatched the towel beside his and blotted my face while we stared each other down with pointed hostility.

"You just can't help being a righteous pain in the ass, can you?"

"What can I say? It's a gift."

Talon pressed his lips into a hard line, tossing the rag onto his shoulder. "And what a pleasant one it is."

I sank deeper into the clawfoot tub, submerging everything—except my nose—underwater. It'd been almost a week since my failed escape, and I'd been nursing my internal wounds ever since. It would've been nice to know about the wards before I made an ass of myself. I'm sure King Harkin knew one of us would be desperate enough to escape; it made me wonder what I would've encountered should Talon not have stopped me.

A chill ran up my spine as I thought about it, kicking myself for falling right into the king's trap. As if having to show my face around the castle after that wasn't already punishment enough, Talon took our training up a notch.

My body throbbed, each muscle protesting in a discomfort akin to being engulfed in flames. Despite the solace sought in daily warm salt baths, the relief was only a momentary respite for my mind. Which, if I was being honest, merely slowed it down to a mile a minute instead of two.

I sucked in a breath and submerged the rest of my head underwater, savoring the deafening silence that encompassed me, focusing on the cacophonous rhythm of my heartbeat. Around me, my hair fanned out in the water like a crimson cloud.

My mother.

These trials.

Life.

Death.

Nothing mattered then. I was weightless—free. I was everything and nothing all at the same time. I could've stayed there forever if my lungs didn't cry out for air.

My pulse slowed, and my chest burned, and I wondered when my body would fight for survival. But it never happened.

Was I broken?

Or simply lost?

I sat up with a gasp and pushed my sodden hair out of my face, resting my head against the side of the tub. The water was getting cold—my fingers pruned—and I knew my bath was nearing its end. I sighed. Back to meandering around my chambers and being bored to death. Although I didn't like Talon or our training sessions, I enjoyed getting out of these stuffy four walls.

Wringing my hair over the tub, I stepped onto the slick marble floor, holding onto the nearby banister so I wouldn't slip. As elegant as the bathroom was, there wasn't a rug in sight. Or art on the wall. Or any knickknacks, for that matter. It lacked warmth and the smaller details that'd give it a welcoming feel. Only the bare necessities and nothing more. I was sure it was a purposeful reminder of our impermanence. In life, and in their castle.

I couldn't complain. At least I wasn't locked up in a dirt-covered dungeon. Only, being here made me miss home. Miss it in the most wistful, aching type of way. The soft crackle of the fireplace and the warm smell of cinnamon. Mother's soft humming. My wall of books.

A deep longing welled beneath my ribcage as tears leaked down my cheeks, and I muffled my cries into the towel. I'd been trying my best to keep my emotions buried, determined not to let them interfere with the trials and training, but something inside me opened the tap.

Silent tears welled up, and up and up, an unstoppable cascade streaming down my face, each droplet a wordless expression of the emotions that I couldn't share with anyone. Everything seemed to hit me like a loaded carriage. I worried about my mother and Sugarfoot and how they were doing—if they were giving Betrys a run for her money.

My throat constricted. Hundreds of thoughts and scenarios played in my head as I sobbed into the towel, praying to the stars I'd make it back to see them.

A soft whimper escaped by swollen lips.

This wasn't me. I didn't give up.

I couldn't.

So, I collected myself after a minute and finished drying off before heading back into the bedchamber to change. Gripping the brass knob, I pushed the door open, expecting to breeze through the doorway and to my wardrobe when I slammed into a tall, firm body.

My breath hitched as a pair of concerned emerald orbs analyzed me.

"What are you doing in here?" I demanded, clenching the towel tighter to my body. "Don't you knock?"

"I did. A few times, actually. I let myself in when you didn't answer." He cocked his head, his brows pulling together. "You've been crying?"

"No," I denied and squeezed past him—Talon's entire body filled the small space, making it difficult to maneuver around him.

"Then why are the whites of your eyes red?"

"Allergies." I wiped at my nose and pulled open the dresser drawer. "I'm not used to the pollen."

"Pollen?"

"Yep." I shifted my weight between my feet, feeling self-conscious under the weight of Talon's careful gaze. If he didn't believe me, he didn't let on. "What are you doing here, anyway?"

"Well, given your track record, I wanted to make sure you didn't try running off again."

"You're not going to let that go, are you?"

Talon raised a brow.

I huffed. "Yeah, thought so. Well, unfortunately for you, I don't plan on being a drowler snack, so..." I motioned to the door. This conversation was over.

"I see you're still pissy from our session earlier." He clicked his tongue. "What a shame. Guess I'll take this with me." He flashed a roll of parchment from behind his back, using the end of it to scratch his head.

My eyes widened, glimpsing the silver tin he held in his pocket.

Charcoal.

What I'd give to have something besides my own thoughts to keep me busy. A distraction. An emotional outlet.

Forcing my face into neutrality, I refused to give him the satisfaction of knowing my hands itched to grasp that coarse paper. To draw until my fingers went numb. I didn't even like drawing—that was Lilian's thing—I much preferred burying my nose in a book, but beggars couldn't be choosers.

Tightening my hold on the towel, I plucked out a sleep shirt and closed the drawer with a deliberate motion.

"Thanks, but I know better than to accept a gift from a faerie. It's never what it seems, and I already have too much to lose. Not to mention I have nothing to give you in return." I regretted the words the instant they rolled off my tongue, but I bit my cheek to stop myself from taking them back. "Do you mind?" I pointed to my towel.

Talon turned around, gripping the top of the bathroom door frame. The muscles in his back stretched against his shirt, pulling it taut.

I kept my voice steady as I continued, needing to fill the tense silence. "Humans aren't as ignorant as you think we are. We grew up learning your folklore."

Talon laughed, and not that unusual melodic sound he displayed that first day of training when talking to his friend, but a brutal, haughty timbre. Annoyed. "I have nothing to gain by tricking you."

I scoffed my disbelief, unwrapped the towel from my body, and laid it on the chair beside me. Talon kept his attention locked on the bathroom wall away from me as I pulled on my clothes—one slight movement and he'd see me naked. My pulse quickened, remembering the way he had looked at me before the trial. A gaze filled with something I couldn't put my finger on. The warm sensation that grew in my belly. The muscles in his forearm fluttered.

I absently licked my bottom lip.

"As flattered as I am, stop staring, Elowyn, and get dressed."

I coughed in surprise, brushing the wrinkles out of my sleep shirt. "What? I wasn't staring."

"You're practically burning holes into the back of my head."

I scoffed. "Believe it or not, Talon, just because you look the way you do doesn't mean every female is drooling over you."

His body shook as he laughed. "As underhanded as it was, I accept your compliment."

"That wasn't..." I sat down on the chair, running a hand down my face. "It doesn't matter. So, this *wouldn't* be a gift, then?" I pressed.

He turned around, twirling the roll of parchment between his fingers as he strolled toward the chamber door. "No, I said I had nothing to gain by tricking you. But if you insist, you can pay me back by winning the trials using whatever means necessary."

I put my hand on my hip. "Why? I already planned on doing that. It can't be that simple. What's the catch?"

Talon held out a hand, examining his fingernails. "Because despite your stubbornness, firefly, like I've told you before, I'm not your enemy. I want you to succeed. For both of our sake." He paused, slipping his hand into his pocket, and meeting my gaze. I held my breath as he added, "And maybe I was a little harsh today, so I thought maybe this would help encourage you or, at a minimum, put you in a better mood."

"Are you apologizing?" I bit my lip. I couldn't believe my ears—maybe swine could fly. Sure, he didn't come out and say the words, but it still counted. At least in my book.

Talon, however, didn't share my amusement. He tipped his

chin toward the table, and I followed his gaze, noticing the parchment splayed out with the tin of charcoal on top. How did he—

"Consider it an olive branch."

I whipped around to thank him, only to find the space empty, the door shutting behind him on a gentle breeze, leaving nothing but his fresh teakwood scent in his wake.

The parchment rustled from the wind, a small, simple gesture that meant more than I could put into words.

An olive branch. I could live with that.

FOURTEEN

A warm breeze kissed my face as Mother and I strolled along the footpath, tall pine trees on each side lining our way. It was nice to get out of the house and into nature. I couldn't remember the last time we'd done something like this or the last time she was so healthy, let alone had enough energy to go on a hike. It made my chest swell with happiness, seeing the sparkle return to her features and the pink blush back on her cheeks. It was like she was never sick.

After about a quarter of a mile, we came to a stop at a fork in the road, two signs directing the way.

Left: Lodge/Visitor Center

Right: Whisperwill Falls

I turned to her. "Do you want to head back or keep going?"

"You decide. I'm happy to do whatever you want."

"Well, I've heard the Whisperwill Falls are breathtaking, but the trail is a little more strenuous than this one, though. Would you be up for that?"

"If you think it's worth it, let's do it." She beamed. "Try to keep up slow poke."

My mother took the lead, walking at such a brisk pace I had

to jog to catch up. "Jeez, woman, what'd you eat for breakfast? You're running circles around me."

She laughed in reply, not breaking her stride until we reached the summit.

Propping my foot on a rock, I stretched my calf, baffled by how my mother didn't appear to have broken a sweat.

"Look." She nodded her chin to the horizon, and my mouth fell open at the sight before us.

A cascade of water surged down the side of the bluff, forming a waterfall that poured into a crystalline blue lake, its surface punctuated by jagged rocks. Branching off from the main waterfall, smaller ones wound around boulders, creating a sound that rumbled across the natural landscape and made my hand rest against my chest in awe.

"This is..." I savored the gentle mist on my flushed skin.

"Beautiful," my mother finished, and I nodded in agreement, unable to find more perfect words.

All I knew was that everything was as it should be.

And, for the first time in years, I believed all would be okay.

"Come on, let's go sit over there and eat these sandwiches. I'm starving." I placed my hand on her elbow.

I tried guiding her over to a flat rock away from the ledge.

Her foot slipped, and she lost her balance, tumbling to the ground. The satchel dropped from my shoulder as I tried reaching for her, but she slid too fast. Her legs went over the edge, and I leaped, catching her by the hand before she went over.

"Elowyn, help me, please! Help me!" she shrieked.

"Don't worry, I got you. Okay?" My feet shuffled behind me, trying to find a rock to cling onto to keep me from sliding off with her. "I won't let go. I got you."

A glowing figure appeared at my side—the one with the

familiar essence, but no identifiable features. "Reach within, Elowyn."

My feet dug into a rock, and I tugged, my hands growing slick with moisture.

"I don't know what that means!" I yelled, using every ounce of strength I had to pull her up the cliff. My arms were growing weak. I didn't know how much longer I could hold on.

My mother's color drained from her face. Her once glowing, vibrant hue turned ashen.

"This is all your fault. You killed me, Elowyn." Her eyes were sunken. "You left me to die."

My legs turned to liquid, and I slipped. "I'm sorry. I was trying to help. I'm sorry. I'm sorry. I'm sorry." Tears welled over as I clung to her for dear life, regaining my footing. "I'm trying!"

"Focus, Elowyn. Listen," the male voice spoke again.

I turned my head to see familiar honey eyes pleading with me, begging me to understand, but there wasn't time to figure it out.

My mother slipped from my grip, and I scrambled to recover, regaining my hold on her by the tips of my fingers.

"You ruin everything," she spat, "nothing but a disappointment."

I choked. "I know you don't mean that."

"Elowyn. Focus," the voice said again.

But it was too late.

My mother slipped from my grip and plummeted toward the rocks—a mocking smile planted on her face. As if she knew I would never save her. As if my failure was expected.

No!

Her face disappeared behind the misting spray of the waterfall...

~

"Mother!" I screamed, startling awake. Sweat dripped down my spine as I straightened, wiping the crusted drool from my cheek.

I took in the half-finished drawing in front of me.

The abrupt awakening left me disoriented, my head clouded, with the lingering echoes of the dream—the waterfall—still clinging to the edges of my consciousness.

"Oh shit!" I exclaimed, jumping out of the chair. "Shit! Shit! Shit!"

Racing to the wardrobe, I ransacked the drawers for my trial attire, turning my chambers into something resembling a pig pen. I couldn't believe I'd slept in.

Talon would be here any minute to escort me to the trials, and I wasn't remotely ready. If he were to find out I stayed up all night drawing, he might rethink letting me keep the parchment. There was also no telling the extent he'd punish me during training—a hundred and fifty push-ups would be child's play.

A knock on the door sounded, and I jumped.

"I'll be out in a second!" I yanked and stretched the fabric until I got it past my knees, squatting, and thrusting to get them to my thighs, but they wouldn't budge. Between the nightmare and the possibility of being late to the trial, the thin layer of sweat that coated my skin made putting on clothes impossible.

"Let's go, Elowyn, you're pushing the message we're trying to send." Talon's velvet timbre sounded from behind the mahogany doors, and I tripped, my arms straining to tighten the vest behind my back. "King Harkin will have your neck if you're not in this hallway in twenty seconds."

Tugging on my boot, I hopped to the door and opened it to reveal an annoyed Talon leaning against the frame. *Good.*

"Sorry about that. Girl stuff." I wiped the sweat off my flushed neck.

"Is that so?"

"Mhm."

He sucked his teeth. "I see. Do you mind?"

"Mind what?" I rested a forearm against the wall as I pulled on my other boot.

Talon outstretched his hand—his fingers grazing my temple, and I held my breath. "Your tardiness would have nothing to do with this, would it?" He held out a charcoaled smudged finger.

I laughed nervously, thinking of a reason that'd be on my face, however, the only thing that came out was a string of incoherent sentences. "Huh! Strange. Oh well. We need to get a move on it, right?"

Talon stepped in front of me, blocking my path, and I crashed into his firm body, engulfed by his warm scent and strong arms.

His hand met my waist, keeping a respectable distance between us. It did nothing to quell the way my skin burned under his touch. He drank me in, his gaze running down my body like a pair of gentle hands, and I shifted under the weight of his gaze, feeling meek and hyperaware of every inch of my body. There was never any doubt about how handsome he was. How strong. Lethal. Yet, those things never caused me to yield to him before. The golden flakes in his irises never caused me to falter in his presence. If anything, it irritated me.

But that look? That look was like drinking sunshine.

"Careless to stay up all night coloring, no?"

My body went rigid, but I kept his gaze, hyperaware his hand was still on my waist. "Don't know what you're talking about."

"No?" He poked his head into my chambers, clicking his

tongue when he saw the parchment and charcoal still splayed out on the table. "If you won't take this seriously, I suggest you speak up now."

I clenched my teeth but said nothing.

"I didn't think so. Are you ready?"

"Of course," I lied, "there's nothing else I'd rather do than chance death first thing in the morning." I pulled my arm away, and slipped past him, needing nothing more than to put as much distance between us and whatever that twinkle of longing was before it caught up to me.

The fae's ancient, primitive chanting spilled out of the marble doors and into the courtyard, drowning out my thoughts and birds chirping nearby. I thumbed my father's ring, hoping it'd bring me reassurance. Comfort.

Instead, every fiber of my being was on high alert. I couldn't fathom what the king had planned this time, or what risks lay mere feet away, but the chanting that pulsed louder with each beat of my heart was a nagging reminder I didn't have a choice.

"Try not to get yourself killed," Talon said as we stepped into the damp arena.

My vision adjusted to the darkness, and I huffed a laugh— the reminder wasn't necessary. I knew my mother was growing sicker by the day, and I needed to get home to her. There was too much to lose if I didn't. "Aw, you care about me. How sweet."

Talon stretched his neck. "No. I'm worried about my own standings. Winning aside, how you perform during these trials reflects on me. My ass and my reputation are on the line."

"Oh yeah, that's right. Gaining respect is much more important than my life. Silly me, how could I ever forget?"

I hated how deep he got under my skin and how easily he turned me into a murderous wretch. More so, the warmth he sparked inside me—a long-forgotten feeling I'd only experienced on a handful of occasions.

Stars, he was obnoxious.

Talon stopped walking and grabbed my elbow, keeping me from stomping away. "We may not get along or see eye to eye, but I'm not worried about you because I know you're going to come out of this alive." His grip on my arm was strong. Demanding. It was all I could focus on. "They might have skill and strength on you, but you have drive, and that alone is a force to be reckoned with. Put that stubbornness to work, Elowyn."

I gulped, nodding in agreement. Although I wasn't convinced he believed what he was saying, it calmed the butterflies that swarmed my stomach—proof an ounce of faith outweighed a hundred lies. I just hoped that'd translate in the trials.

His touch lingered for a beat longer than I expected, and my skin smoldered under it.

I needed to refocus.

I wanted him to let go, yet found it comforting all at the same time.

When he didn't, I distanced myself from him instead and descended the staircase at a deliberate pace, trying to push aside the conflicting feelings that lingered. His touch that lingered.

And I readied myself for whatever fate had in store for me.

A dense forest of evergreens filled the arena—so vast I couldn't see where it started or stopped. The fae audience sat in their usual seats high above, giving them a bird-eye view of the trials below.

It was dark.

Cold.

And storm clouds clung to the trees, blurring my vision.

I took a deep breath as I proceeded to the clearing in the center of the forest, the thick branches nicking my exposed skin with every step I took.

"Well, if it isn't the bastard child," a taunting voice came from behind me.

I didn't need to turn around to know it was Aeron. Refusing to fall into whatever web he was weaving, I kept moving.

"I'm surprised you showed your face."

"Why? Because you said a few threats? Unfortunately for you, I don't scare easily."

Lies.

Every word.

I trembled on the inside.

There wasn't any time to process the depths of my fear as I ducked and swerved around the sprawling trees. The overwhelming scent of pine gave me a headache.

"Don't eat your words too soon, sweetheart. Irony doesn't age well."

"Bite me Aeron, you're nothing but hot air." I stopped in my tracks and faced him, holding my arms out to my side. "Just kill me already. You talk this huge game, and try to intimidate everyone, but let's be honest, you're a coward. A coward who kills children to feel better about himself."

Aeron stepped toward me.

I flinched.

"Why so jumpy, sweetheart?" His menacing laugh snaked up my spine as he adjusted the collar of my vest.

I smacked his hand away, hating how my body had betrayed me and shown him the cracks in my mask.

"You know, I thought about letting you live until the final trial. It makes the most sense to guarantee myself the victory and all." He dropped his arm to his side. "However, I'm not sure how much more I can tolerate listening to your grating, holier-than-thou voice."

"Fuck off," I seethed as I proceeded to the clearing.

However, I didn't make it far when he gripped my braid and yanked me back.

I yelped in pain.

"You can't run from me this time, you worthless bastard," he promised.

I staggered back, frozen, and he marched ahead of me like the path was forged for his feet alone.

"Don't let him get inside your head," Breana said as she approached from behind, and I jumped. "I'm pretty sure I over-heard him crying for his daddy last night. His parents didn't hug him enough if you ask me." She pushed the tree branches aside, motioning me to go ahead of her while I rubbed the sore spot on my head.

For someone with such a small stature, she sure had a way of making you feel protected. She reminded me of Lilian in that sense—Stars rest her soul. I was doing this for her, too. Fighting for her justice. There wasn't a doubt in my mind one of these foul creatures was responsible for her death.

"I'd believe it." I waited for her to catch up. "The things people are capable of when they're desperate is terrifying." The thought made me cringe. How effortlessly any of us could adopt the same callous and apathetic demeanor as Aeron. It was a disconcerting realization, if I allowed myself to consider it. It wasn't only our mortality that hung over our heads, but our own morality would be tested, too.

Breana shrugged. "Let's stick close together, then. You watch my back. I'll watch yours."

"And what if we make it to the end?"

The possibility of lasting that long weighed heavy on my shoulders. If Talon thought I could walk out of there, maybe it was worth believing in myself. For Lilian. For my mother. Even Lewis and Sage.

"Then we draw sticks to find out who's getting out of this alive."

FIFTEEN

"Welcome competitors to the second trial," King Harkin boomed from his throne on the deck above.

Only six of us remained from the previous trials, and if that was any indication of how this one was going to go, I needed to heed Talon's advice and put my stubbornness to work. Regardless of how much it pained me to admit that.

'Worthless, bastard.'

Aeron's comment rang through my head, taunting me.

"As you can see, today's trial differs from the last," the king continued. "Today, you'll have four hours to tame a wild stag, using nothing but skill and, for a select few, weapons to help you advance. Those who don't make it back before those four hours are up will be eliminated."

Panic strummed my tightly wound muscles as I peeked at the board of names and saw mine third to last, behind Irving and Breana. An improvement from last week, but defeating, nonetheless. I knew it was based on our prior trial performance, but I couldn't help but feel like it reflected mine and Talon's training sessions. How was I going to make any progress when we couldn't stand each other?

I dropped my gaze to my hands when a dagger materialized on the ground before me. I paid little mind to who or what anyone else received, too occupied with picking it up and weighing the blade in my palms to get a good feel for it. It was light. Dull. It'd be useless taming a stag. It'd be useless taking down a rabbit in the Elmhurst Woods behind my home.

Pointing the blade down, I gripped the hilt, containing my disappointment.

"May you not let resentment get the best of you and lose sight of the goal. Let the trial begin." King Harkin snapped his fingers and disappeared with the rest of the fae court, just as they did before, a dark, ominous sky taking their place.

Calandra and I caught each other's attention before we disappeared in different directions and nodded a silent 'good luck.'

I ran deep into the forest, careful to remain vigilant of my surroundings and develop a plan. There was no way I could wrangle a stag alone. I'd need help. Team up with the others or trap it.

Savoring the wind on my skin, I ran, and my chest swelled. How I'd missed running. The freedom. The peace. The blocks in my mind crumbled with each step, and I took a deep, calming breath. I could use vines and branches to create a web of sorts, maybe leave a trail of berries to lure it to the trap and rope its legs together when it gets caught up in vines. It could work—dragging it back would be a different story—but I'd cross that bridge when I got there.

You're going to come out of this alive. Talon's voice played in my mind.

I'd figure it out.

The canopy of trees obscured my vision, making it hard to

see where I was going. It was like the woods I found myself in a week ago when I foolishly tried to escape. The same plaguing feeling that something was watching me clamped down around my neck, making it hard to concentrate.

It was too quiet. Tendrils of whispers hanging in the air, spewing degrading rhetoric.

"Worthless bastard!"

"You'll never be good enough."

"Your mother will die because of you!"

Skirting to a stop, I dropped the dagger and fell my knees, covering my ears to quiet the truth I desperately wanted to ignore. My throat strained from my screams when one, not belonging to me, rang in the distance.

The voices disappeared as quickly as they began, and I ran my hands down my sweat-covered face—scouring the forest to see where the scream came from—when I spotted Kelvin and Aeron watching me in my peripheral vision.

Fear prickled down my spine.

His words haunted my mind. *You can't run from me this time.*

Why were they set on tormenting me?

I needed to use the forest to my advantage and lose them before they got any closer. Remembering to grab my dagger, I took off in the opposite direction, running as fast as my legs would carry me.

But they closed in.

The pungent scent radiating off them singed my nostrils. I was vulnerable. Exposed. I hung a quick right into a shrub, sniffling a cry as the branches dug deep into my skin. One—or both —leaped in after me.

I pushed ahead, ripping the thorns from my path, and ignoring my blood-soaked sleeve as I exited. Swiftly, I veered to the left, slipping into the concealment of another shrub for cover. The foliage embraced me as I crouched, the dagger ready and clutched in my fist.

Their faces were flushed. Brows pinched tight. And they came into view, searching for me. Hunting me.

Time seemed to move at a snail's pace as I hid in the bush, holding my breath as they scoured the area.

Another shriek sounded in the distance, and like a wolf sensing blood, they took off toward their prey.

I waited. I didn't know how long I'd been hiding, but I couldn't stay there forever. Emerging from the shrub, I moved as quietly as possible, assessing my surroundings.

When I eventually stepped out, my body lurched and I fell face-first into a puddle of mud, causing the dagger to fly from my hand.

An impish giggle rustled the bushes beside me, and I wiped the sludge from my face, catching a tiny, bearded man with a round belly running away with my weapon.

A gnome.

"Are you kidding me?" I swatted at the puddle—splashing mud in my eye—and released a string of curses. Now I was wet and injured and without a weapon.

"Worthless bastard. You'll never be good enough," the wind whispered, igniting my insecurities.

I grit my teeth, mollifying my blood boiling. "Shut up! Fuck, shut up!"

Biting back the urge to cry as I stood, I knew I couldn't throw in the towel. There were too many people to prove wrong. Too much at stake.

My clothes sloshed as I walked, adding extra weight to each step. Through the thick mossy overgrowth, I trudged, collecting spindles of vines as I tried to find the best location to set up the trap.

The sun peeked through the awning, reminding me it was

mid-day, yet there were still no songbirds to be found. No woodland creatures. It was as if they, too, could sense the impending peril to come. The sooner I finished this trial, the less likely I was to be picked off by barbarians. Both human and magical.

I twisted the ring on my finger as I walked for what felt like an eternity.

The forest quietened.

There were no birds singing. No critters rustling in the bushes. Nothing but the sound of my own feet crunching leaves while I raided the forest ground, my shoulder weighing heavy with vine. The last thing I needed was another encounter with a drowler, especially when Talon wasn't there to save me. Fear tickled my skin, or maybe it was the dried blood that coated my arms. Regardless, I was a sitting duck out there in the open —exposed.

So, I picked up my pace.

The whispers in the wind were drowned out by the blood rushing in my ears, my entire body on pins and needles and numb from the insults. Thoughts of the last conversation I had with my mother were on a repetitive loop, a harrowing reminder of how it could be the last one we ever had. Her warnings had fallen on deaf, ignorant ears.

The 'what-ifs' were, in fact, eating me alive.

Soon, a small cave just large enough to stand up in came into view, and I ducked inside, tossing the vine to the ground. I slid down the back wall, keeping my sight locked on the opening, and curled into myself.

Water dripped from somewhere inside, as did the patter of small paws, and a calmness settled over me, even though I knew the seconds were ticking away. There couldn't have been more than two hours remaining, and I still hadn't come across a stag, let alone begun setting up a trap.

Anxiety sat on my chest, suffocating me as I emptied my boots and combed the deepest parts of my mind for a way through this.

"Elowyn?" Calandra's soft voice sounded before her head popped into view, glancing around the cave to see if I was the only one inside.

"Yeah, in here."

She let out a sigh of relief as she entered, taking a spot next to me on the wall, and brought her knees to her chest. She was dirty and flustered, and her blonde hair was tied in a frayed bun on the top of her head. A vast difference from the long, smooth strands she began with. "Kelvin and Aeron took off north." She caught her breath. "I barely made it up a tree in time to hide from them. They were circling you like vultures, so I screamed to distract them."

"They're going to kill everyone."

She bumped me with her shoulder. "And then they'll kill each other. So, they won't get out of this alive either. Their egos won't allow it."

I laughed. She had a point.

"Let's beat them at their own game, shall we?"

I couldn't give up until I'd depleted every ounce of energy I had left, regardless of how uncertain the future felt. Anything could happen. Though the future felt uncertain, and I couldn't imagine anything past this cave, I needed to win my freedom.

Calandra faced me. "What's with all the vines? Didn't you get any weapons?"

My shoulders slumped. "They're to set up a trap to catch a stag. I had a dagger, but a gnome ran off with it. What about you?"

She hummed her approval and pulled up her pant leg. "A couple of knives." She lifted her shirt to show me the ones she had hidden there.

I shook my head—she was armed to the teeth. Ten times more than I was. Bitterness itched toward the surface.

"I also got these," she continued, holding out her hand to show me a metal interlocking ring that covered her knuckles. "One punch wearing these would shatter someone's jaw. Here." Calandra slid them off and held them out for me to take. "You did better during the sparring assessment than I did. You should have them."

The weight of them surprised me as I slid them onto my fingers, flexing them as I got used to them. "Are you sure?" Guilt riddled me. She didn't need to help me, but for whatever reason, she was. It didn't go unappreciated.

"Yeah, you'd put these to better use, anyway. I'm more of a long-distance fighter." Calandra flicked her wrist, revealing another concealed knife she'd hidden under the cuff of her sleeve. Her words weren't misplaced. She'd nailed every target during the knife-throwing portion of the assessment—no one came close to her accuracy.

"Thanks." I pulled my now mud-free boots back on. "We should probably get going. Do you have any idea how much longer we have? I can't endure much more of the whispers." I stuffed the drenched wool socks into my back pocket as I stood and held out a hand to help Calandra up.

She placed a hand on her chest. "You heard them too? Oh, thank the stars, I thought I was going mad. I found if you hum, it'll tune it out." Heading toward the entrance of the cave, she fixed her bun. "You coming? I'm pretty sure I saw a stag just west of here from my vantage point in the tree. I can't tame the thing by myself." She flicked her chin toward the pile of vines.

I nodded, a mixture of relief and hesitancy stirring inside me as I lugged the spool onto my shoulder and followed her out of the cave. We couldn't get too comfortable relying on each other, I knew that. Not when only one of us could win.

However, her kindness was helping me get through this. If only I were as heartless as Aeron and Kelvin. This would be so much easier.

With Calandra's sense of direction, we navigated the landscape in no time. It was impressive how easily she guided us through thick, dense terrain. Not stopping or faltering once to recalculate where we were. *And I thought I had a good sense of direction.* We must've carved our way through a mile of tangled vines and climbed over fifty fallen trees, my forehead beading with sweat and my knee aching as we reached a small opening.

"Shh, get down," Calandra hushed as we kneeled behind the base of a willow tree. "Over there, look..."

I craned my head around the wide trunk—my eyebrows meeting my hairline at the sight of the stag in front of us. It was stunning. Breathtaking. Its white fur shone like the moon, illuminating the grass it stood on as its bone-white antlers stretched high into the air above. I counted nine points on each side and determined—based on its relation to the trees—it had to have been twice as tall as Sugarfoot.

It was a remarkable beast. Magical.

"Don't. Fucking. Move," a coarse voice rasped to my left.

I turned to find Irving standing behind Calandra with a sharpened stick to her neck and his other hand over her mouth as he tugged her back.

A yelp escaped me in surprise, wrapping my fingers around the metal rings. "Irving, think about what you're doing." I stepped toward him.

"If you even think about coming any closer, I'll stab her!"

I paused, holding up my hands. "Okay, I won't. I won't. Tell me what I need to do, so you'll let her go."

"I want her knives!" His eyes blazed with anger. "I won't let her go until she's dropped all of them!"

"Why do you need all her knives, Irving?"

"Because I have nothing! Don't you get it? I've seen how many knives she has. You can share, can't you, Calandra?"

Calandra bucked in his grip, tried to dislodge the knife from her sleeve, but he pushed the stick further into her neck, drawing blood.

"We can work together, okay? This isn't necessary. The king wants us to turn on each other—"

"I don't care!" he yelled. His face was pained, like he was trying to tune out his thoughts. *The wind.* "How am I supposed to get a stag to obey me if I have no way of getting it to submit? Why does she get to keep all the knives for herself, huh? What makes her better than us?"

"No one thinks she is better than anyone, Irving. I didn't get any weapons either," I lied, trying to talk him off the ledge. "I get it. But this isn't the way to go about it."

Irving seethed. "Spare me the bullshit. If you think for one second she's befriended you for any reason other than—"

Calandra pulled a knife out of her waistband, stabbed it into his hand, and forced him to release her.

"Screw you bitch!" he cried out as she jumped from his grip, kicking him hard between his legs. He dropped to the ground; a hand cupped his groin.

"Hurry! Go," she urged, and we raced into the clearing.

The wind ripped through my hair. My adrenaline pumping.

The stag whipped its head in our direction.

I skidded to a stop, putting an arm out in front of Calandra, motioning her to take my lead. "Shh." I held a finger to my lips. "Move as quietly as possible. One wrong move and it'll run."

She nodded and stepped back, letting me take the lead.

The stag bleated as I approached, and I dropped the vines to show it my hands. "It's okay, don't be afraid. We're not here to hurt you." I inched closer.

"What brings you here, then? Why all the vines?"

I blanched, twirling around to make sure Calandra was still standing in the same spot, her face unreadable. I sucked in a breath. Never would I get used to hearing an animal's voice inside my head, hearing its thoughts as if they were my own.

I looked back to the stag, speaking low so Calandra wouldn't hear. "The trials. King Harkin demanded we find and tame a wild stag and bring it back to the center of the forest or we'd be eliminated."

The stag huffed. "King Harkin is not an honest ruler."

"Yeah, I figured as much. But either we follow his orders, or he won't let us go home."

I took another step. And another. Until I was less than five feet away from the majestic creature. It towered over me—my neck craning as I took it all in—we'd need a ladder to climb onto its back.

"You're not supposed to be here," it said. "You're in grave danger. If King Harkin discovers the secrets you're keeping, he'll have you killed."

"What? I don't have any secrets." A million questions flooded my mind, like how I could talk to animals, for one. But I didn't let on, not wanting Calandra to see my distress. I stood straighter, wiping my palms on my pants.

"It's best we do not discuss this here, young one. You'll understand when you're ready. Until then, you must get to safety."

"Why does everyone insist on talking in circles around here?"

"The answers lie in between words. It's up to you to discover them. Come now, I'll bring you and your friend to the clearing. But you must promise me you'll get to safety and get away from this place as soon as possible. Far, far away."

"I promise." I was unsure what it was asking from me, but one thing was certain: if I were to win these trials and make it out to cure my mother, we would indeed move as far away as humanly possible.

The stag curled its front legs beneath its body, placing its belly on the floor as its hind legs followed, allowing us access to its back. I waved Calandra over as I mounted the back of the stag, getting a tight grip around its neck.

"Did you—were you talking to the stag?" she questioned as she positioned herself behind me. She curled an arm around my torso to keep herself balanced as it stood up.

"No," I lied. "Well, I mean, sort of. Animals react well to you talking to them. It helps them sense you're not a threat."

She said nothing in return. She didn't need to.

And maybe it was guilt, but I could've sworn I felt her questioning leer boring into my back. How could I explain it to her without sounding mad? I couldn't explain it to myself.

The stag took off at a brisk canter, silencing any further conversation—the trees and branches parting ways to make room for its vast antlers. We were untouchable from up there. Memories of Sugarfoot and me riding through fields together played in my mind and how I longed to do that again, but it wasn't time to reminisce.

We weren't to the clearing yet, and if I'd learned anything so far—it was to expect the unexpected.

The stag picked up its pace, leaping over small creeks and through pungent marshes, until King Harkin and the arena of faerie spectators came into view. A collective gasp sounded as we broke through the line of trees, and my face warmed.

Once again, I searched the crowd for Talon, finding him leaning back in his seat with his foot upon his knee. I didn't know if I wanted to smack him or match his smile. Such a know-it-all, pain in the ass.

We dismounted the stag as it came to a stop.

"Thank you," I whispered, not loud enough for any human ears.

My arm burned as we took our places next to Breana, Kelvin, and Aeron and waited for Irving to appear with forty-five minutes remaining.

I pressed my hand to my chest, relieved to find Breana alive and well, and couldn't wait to hear all about her experience at dinner that night. Curious if it was as eventful as mine and Calandra's.

King Harkin and Prince Bowen, however, appeared all but curious, annoyed rather, that we had the gall to stand before them. *Alive.* I wanted to flip them my finger in defiance but knew better than to test whatever lucky stars watched over me.

The timer ticked away, and less than ten minutes remained.

There was still no sign of Irving.

I shifted on my feet, unsure if I wanted him to show or not, wondering if that made me good or bad. I suppose it didn't matter at the end of the day. We were all going to do something —become someone—we didn't recognize, and we'd have to make peace with that, eventually.

A flicker of movement in the crowd caught my attention, and my gaze floated to Talon, who rose from his seat. Apparently, he'd seen all he needed to as he made his way out of the arena, a high-pitched scream followed by a familiar animalistic growl arising in his wake.

A drowler.

I looked to Breana and Calandra—our jaws slack with relief or fear—before everything went silent, and a line crossed out Irving's name.

King Harkin sneered, disdain coating every syllable as he spoke. "Congratulations, humans. You five live to see yet another day."

SIXTEEN

The front of my shirt was coated in a viscous layer of blood, staining the fabric with a dark hue as I hastened into my bedchamber. Clutching my arm tightly to my chest, the metallic scent hung in the air, an unsettling reminder of the injuries I'd acquired since journeying there.

I hadn't realized how deep the thorn bush had cut me. The adrenaline coursing through my veins must've masked the pain. I needed to clean it out and stop the bleeding, and it'd be fine. There was no need to worry. I'd dealt with much worse.

Peeling off my trial attire, I was in only my undergarments as I ran the bathroom sink water over the gash. Blood stained the porcelain bowl, and I muffled a cry, biting into the long-sleeved shirt to keep from making any noise. The last thing I needed was for the other competitors to hear I was hurting. Kelvin and Aeron would stop at nothing to play it to their advantage. Thank goodness for dark-colored clothes to disguise the wound—stars knew I was riddled with enough of them as it was.

My hand shook as I turned off the water and wrapped a towel around my arm, pulling it tight. The castle had to have an infirmary somewhere, but that'd be too risky. I'd need to wait until nightfall when everyone was asleep, so no one would spot me.

A sequence of loud bangs on my door had me jumping out of my skin, and I gripped the wall for support.

"Elowyn, you in here?" Talon's silky voice sounded on the other side of the wooden door, and I groaned my annoyance.

I looked at my bare body—my makeshift bandage—and back at the door. "Uh, I'll be right there!" I called out, searching my drawers for clothes to throw on.

Sure, there was a part of me that bubbled with excitement at the thought of his eyes caressing over me like they did earlier, but I knew that wasn't appropriate. I didn't know where these lustful feelings were coming from—or when they began—but I knew I needed to get a hold of them. Preferably in a vice grip and until I choked the life of them.

"If you don't open this door in two seconds, I'm coming in. I saw your arm."

My skin went cold at his words—he couldn't finish that sentence. Not in the hallway with prying ears. I ran a hand through my damp hair as I pulled on a pair of pants and grabbed a sleep shirt, but I couldn't get the sleeve over my tourniquet.

"One."

I tried again, stretching the sleeve as far as possible, but it was pointless. It wouldn't give.

"Two."

Without thinking, I dropped the shirt and raced toward the door, keeping my chest covered as I popped my head through the threshold.

I took in his hardened scowl. "Hey." My tone breathless and impatient.

Talon cocked a brow. "Hi?"

"How's it going?"

"Are you mad?" He tried peering into my room, but I stood on my tiptoes to obstruct his view. "Why are you acting strange?"

"I don't know what you're talking about. Just—uh, tired. My arm's fine. See? Everything's fine here. You can leave, now."

"You're a horrible liar, you know that? I'm not leaving until you show me your arm."

"How about you break me out of this hellhole first, then I show you?" I countered, placing a hand on my hip.

Talon sucked his teeth as he pushed past me and entered my room. "I'm not in the mood, Elowyn. Injuries aren't anything to play around with. Not here. Not under these circumstances." He scanned my room—his gaze landing on my trial leathers spewed on the ground and then on me.

Talon's gaze darkened as he took in my half-naked body, realization heating his neck.

The swell of my chest.

My bare stomach.

My body buzzed as I wrapped my uninjured arm around my middle, a poor attempt at concealing myself.

The air in the room grew tense.

We stared at each other, neither of us breathing. I waited for him to say something. Anything. Or look away. But he did neither.

Talon cleared his throat, focusing on the injured arm I held behind my back. He folded his across his chest—the veins in his arms bulging out of his olive skin. "Let me see your arm, Elowyn."

I shook my head. "No."

"I won't ask you again. Show me your arm."

There was no reason to hide it from him. I knew that. But I had it taken care of. I was going to find the infirmary tonight, and it'd be fine. There was no need to involve him—I could take care of myself. Just like I always had.

Talon raised his brows expectantly, and I extended my arm toward him. Maybe the sooner I went along with his commands, the sooner he'd leave me alone.

I bit my lip as he approached and took my hand in his, my stupid pulse pounding in my ears. He used his other hand to untie the towel, the brush of his knuckles tickling my skin.

I felt exposed as it dropped from my arm. It felt intimate somehow—as if he was undressing me. And the fear of showing weakness to such a commanding, lethal fae made me want to pull away.

"How were you planning to take care of this?" His voice was low and rough.

I steadied a breath. "I was going to sneak into the infirmary."

"Is that so? And do what exactly? Rummage the shelves until you stumbled across something you thought would help? This isn't Wendover, firefly. Pick the wrong salve and you'd have toes growing out of your arm."

I ripped my hand from his. "What am I supposed to do?"

His smirk turned into a full toothy grin, and I shifted on my feet, realizing I was still in my undergarments and hyperaware of every inch of my body. Every wrong sensation coursing through me.

"You could ask for my help."

Just when I thought he wasn't, Talon reminded me how insufferable he was.

"Yeah, and what's the catch? I think I'd rather take my chances growing toes."

"Honestly, Elowyn, when have I given you a reason not to trust me? Isn't it getting exhausting fighting me every step of the way?"

He had a point. I hated it when he had a point. And that deep, deep down, I think I did trust him.

Reluctantly. *Maybe not entirely.*

Perhaps it was the thick air clouding my judgment, but the fact was, something shifted between us. I couldn't quite put my finger on it, but it frightened me and intrigued me all at the same time. I knew I couldn't get caught up in it, though. These trials required my complete attention. Not to mention it was wrong. He was an arrogant, murderous, wicked, insufferable faerie.

However, there was nothing wrong with being friendly, right? It'd be to my advantage to stop fighting him, wouldn't it? I'd simply play nice for the advantage. No other reason.

Talon dropped his head, his onyx hair brushing his forehead. "I'm taking that as a yes." He flicked a small knife from his sleeve. It had unique markings whittled into the hilt, identical to the ones on the arena's entrance. "There's nothing wrong with asking for help every once in a while, you know," he continued.

My heart fluttered despite the fear that ran through me. How long had it been since I'd had someone to rely on, to lean on?

"In fact, it's a strength, not a weakness, to allow yourself to be vulnerable."

I took a step away from him. "What are you going to do with that?" I breathed, wrapping both arms around my middle.

Talon held his hand up at his chest, balancing the knife between his thumb and index finger. "I only need it to access my abilities. In order to heal you, it's blood for blood. I won't use it on you, I promise."

With a curt nod, I took a controlled breath, and he tipped his chin toward the chair. "Take a seat."

I did what he asked and sat on the velvet cushion, the soft

fabric caressing my back. Talon kept his gaze locked on mine—focused and sure—and I felt calm. Secure.

He kneeled between my legs, his elbow brushing my inner thigh as he reached for my hand. Was it on purpose?

My breath hitched at his touch, sending a shiver up my spine.

I watched his cheeks darken—as if he could sense the effect he had on me. And he guided my forearm on top of my knee.

Prick.

Talon placed his hand on mine, his palm up, and pushed the tip of the knife into his skin. He didn't so much as flinch as he dragged it across his hand, carefully ripping into flesh. But his chest rose and fell in steady breaths.

Blood pooled in his palm, and I couldn't take my attention off him. How effortlessly he could draw such a complex design. The way his veins bulged with each movement. And how his brows pulled together with such intense concentration, he didn't seem to notice his hair fall into his face.

I itched to reach out and push it back, but I didn't want to disrupt him. Didn't want to give in to the impulse. Instead, I only marveled at his hard work, trying to ignore the way his touch burned into my skin. Seared me with his fingerprints.

He removed the knife once the symbol was complete, and it glowed like the sun at high noon—harsh and with fiery promise. I felt the warmth and power that rolled off him as Talon closed his eyes, only reopening them once his blood and the carving had disappeared. His once emerald orbs blazed a deep gold color, and words became lost on my tongue. He was breathtaking. Ethereal.

My skin warmed in response to whatever this unfamiliar feeling was that coursed through me. I didn't want it to stop.

"This is going to sting a little," he warned, placing his palm on my wound. "Try to be as quiet as possible, okay?"

I could only nod as I took a deep breath, trying to ready myself, but he didn't give me any other warning.

Light emitted from his palm, and I stifled a cry. Without thinking, I gripped his shoulder for support. My head dropped, meeting his forehead as I bit back tears and reminded myself to keep quiet.

I felt his hand come up, his calloused palm gripping the nape of my neck to keep me still, and I melted into his touch.

"Breathe, it's okay. I'm almost done."

With a weak nod, I tried to do as he said, but I was restless, vague memories of those first few nights in that stars-awful dungeon floated into consciousness. I searched Talon's face—the bright, warm light. "It was you. You're the one who healed me, aren't you?"

Talon winked. "I couldn't let my champion suffer, could I?"

We shared a breath as the light faded, his hold on me never wavering long after the pain dissipated. My breaths remained heavy—for reasons unrelated to the magic—as Talon and I remained locked together.

He dragged his hand away from my arm and allowed his fingers to stroke my healed skin.

I quivered.

"You're good as new."

Good as new. I took his word for it, unable to pull my gaze away from his, transfixed as they reverted to their original color.

Talon flashed a sheepish grin. "This is usually the part where someone says thank you."

Huffing a laugh, my forehead rolling against his, embarrassed by my own thoughts. "I'm sorry," I breathed. "I'm so used to taking care of other people. I guess I forgot what it's like to be on the other side of that."

Talon's face was full of contemplation as he studied my features. I'd never wanted to know what someone was thinking so badly before in my entire life. "I should get back to my duties now." He pulled away from me at that, and my chest tightened.

Reality slammed into me. Our reality. Our differences. And I cringed. "Yeah, that's a good idea." What was I thinking? I couldn't believe I'd allow myself to be that unguarded. Especially with him. These twisted feelings were going to ruin everything. "So, um, when's the next training session?"

Talon flicked the knife back into his sleeve as he stood and straightened his shirt. His usual hard-set features back on his face, like nothing just transpired between us. I don't know why, but it made my stomach sink.

"Let's give it a day so you can recover. Meet me then in the training room at sunrise."

I nodded and turned for the door, exposed and self-conscious, as he strolled to the other side of the room. In an act of self-soothing, my arms folded across my middle.

"Have a good evening, Elowyn." His tone felt soft on my ears.

As soon as the door shut behind him, I yanked the sleep shirt over my head and stomped over to my bed, plopping down face-first, letting the comforter muffle my groan. I refused to give Talon any more thought or read into whatever that was. It was nothing—a guard helping his prisoner. I'd be better off not to read into it.

Yet, the way his touch lingered on my thigh begged to differ.

I flipped through our conversation in my head, processing every word, every touch, analyzing what it meant. If it meant anything. Wondering why his sultry voice stoked long-forgotten feelings inside me. How I wanted to punch him in the nose like I did Rhett Belmont, however, struggled to breathe when his gaze washed over me with subtle intensity.

It made no sense.

The longer I was in this star-forsaken realm, the less anything made sense.

I rolled over onto my back and stared at the mosaic painted on the ceiling, pushing my palms into my temples to soothe the developing headache. I didn't know if it was from the magic or my conflicted feelings about Talon. But I knew my brutish, handsome guard would be my downfall. That was, if the trials didn't take me out first.

At this point, I'd take whatever quelled these crippling thoughts.

SEVENTEEN

"Keep your arms up. Like this." Talon slid behind me and positioned my hands in front of my face. His smooth touch warmed my exposed skin, sending a wave of heat to my core.

I hated being close to him—how my body reacted to his nearness.

My skin tingled from his deft touch. It betrayed every logical fiber in my body, but I couldn't look away. Not from the beads of sweat that dripped down his tanned body, or the veins that pulsed in his neck. I imagined my tongue trailing up his salty skin—

The thought escaped me as quickly as it arrived when Talon materialized back in front of me, reminding me how much his fae agility annoyed me. It made training with him impossible. Infuriating, even. It was better that way. Disliking him. Entertaining these bizarre fantasies would be a recipe for disaster. An ending that would see me buried and him alive to tell the tale.

He got into a fighting stance, about to slip the boxing mitts back on, when he dropped his arms and sighed. "Stop dropping your elbows," he growled. "Getting hit in the ribs will suck, but it won't knock you out. You're leaving yourself wide open."

"What are you talking about?" I was confident they hadn't moved an inch. Then again, they might've sagged a bit while I was drinking him in. I shook my head, settling back into my stance. "This is where you put them."

Talon's hand latched around my neck and kicked my feet out from underneath me. I dropped to the ground—the wind knocking from my lungs—and he straddled my legs, pressing his dagger to my sternum.

His raven hair tickled my forehead. "Then tell me why it was so easy to overpower you? If I were Aeron or Kelvin, you'd be dead. That quick."

I sucked in a breath, squirming under his weight. Squirming because he could and did overpower me.

"Keep. Your. Elbows. Up."

My skin warmed. How could I focus when every touch, every glance, every fluid movement, had me questioning my sanity? The oddest part about it? I could've sworn his face softened as he searched mine.

I loosened a breath, regained control of my thoughts, and without wasting another second, slapped him in the face. Stunning him just enough that the dagger dropped from his grip.

Scurrying out from under him, I clambered to my feet.

Talon stood, his nostrils flaring as he sucked his teeth.

"That's it, firefly. Keep that aggression up." There was nothing friendly in his voice as he approached, and I folded under his intense scrutiny. "Get back into position."

I refrained from saying anything else that'd excite him more and did as he ordered. I'd never seen anyone's face light with such delight after being smacked in the face before—he was more deranged than I thought. However, the way my body tingled in response was even more concerning. Maybe I was just as deranged.

I threw my weight into the next punch, and then the next, releasing the fermenting anger, when Talon smacked me upside the head, startling me.

I paused, rubbing the sore spot. "What the fuck was that for?"

"You're not blocking."

Smack.

"Stop that!" I punched the mitt harder, pretending it was Talon's face.

A tense silence threatened to ignite the training room—only the sounds of my fists pounding leather filled the space.

Hit.

Hit.

Smack.

Hit.

Talon swung again, but this time I ducked, avoiding his attack, and popped up—kicking my heel into the mitt. He beamed. "Perfect. Again."

For someone stressing the importance of blocking, his right side was wide open.

I bit my lip. Oh, I'd do it again alright. Payback for his relentless assaults. I returned his smile before I spun around, kicking the top of my foot into his side, and sending him to the ground.

My chest puffed out, relishing in my victory, but it was short-lived.

Talon wrapped his long fingers around my ankle and pulled my leg out from underneath, the air whooshing from my lungs as I fell on my back. His movements were fast.

He grabbed my hands, attempting to pin them to the

ground, but I challenged him. His chest pressed into mine, his stomach.

My pulse quickened. I grunted and attempted to push against him.

Our legs tangled together as we scuffled on the ground, fighting, wrestling, each of us trying to get the upper hand.

Sweat slid down my neck; I tried to free myself, to calm whatever strange sensation filled my chest before it exploded.

But he dominated me. Again and again.

I kicked the inside of his knee as hard as I could, giving me enough time to regain my stance and stagger away from him.

He continued for me—his eyes ablaze. My breaths came more quickly, feeling the heat radiating off him. Off *me.* "That's more like it, firefly. Use your anger to your benefit, control it. Don't let it control you."

Reach within, Elowyn.

Talon slipped the mitts back on, signaling for me to get back into position.

I threw my fist into the thick leather, releasing all my frustrations, all my doubts into each punch—my breaths coming in sharp succession as I focused on each movement. My body hummed to life, singing to the sound of the deep beat.

Liberated and weightless, I ducked before he could smack me. Jumped before he could trip me. Struck before he pounced. Like running, it was meditative. Gone were my worries about the trials and surviving. I felt powerful, like I actually stood a chance.

"Good girl. Come on, give me four more. Put everything you have left in it."

His words fueled me, piercing the vast darkness that lived inside me and replacing it with warmth and light. I unleashed everything I had, biting back my delight as his grew wider, his sharp canines digging into his lower lip. Despite our many disagreements, he still rooted for me—took care of me. It was unfamiliar territory. This person—faerie—I'd been told to fear my entire life, despite my reluctance, was growing on me.

Kick.

Duck.

I threw one last punch and collapsed to the ground, the smile never leaving my face while my pulse returned to normal.

Stars, that felt good.

I felt good—and hopeful for the first time since I'd awoken in this vile realm.

The quiet solitude of the library was the perfect reprieve to escape my horrible reality. Just me and faraway lands that provided a temporary bandage to the harsh truth we were forced to face every day.

I propped my feet on the oak table, my nose buried between the pages of a leather-bound book, while Calandra and Breana discussed their latest training sessions.

Stacks of books climbed as high as the vaulted ceiling, and plush, velour seats wrapped around our bodies like silk. It didn't thwart the looming dread that clung to every inch of my body, or the haunting thoughts of my mortality, but it certainly helped. As twisted as it was, being in this library with Calandra and Breana provided a sense of normalcy. Balance. What better way to remain clearheaded and keep from going mad? Even if I had to pretend.

I flipped the page, deciding we needed to sneak out of our chambers in there more often. I'm sure we could spare thirty minutes after lunch most days.

"What about you, Elowyn?"

Peering up from my book, I settled on Breana and stretched the kink in my neck. "I'm sorry?"

"How's your training with Talon going?"

Calandra giggled. "Are his abs as delicious as I imagine? Ugh, what I'd give to take one of his *punishments*." She waggled her brows.

I bit my cheek, debating if I should tell her they were, in fact, extremely delicious, but kept that bit of information to myself. Admitting it out loud felt like a confession to something I'd been trying to pretend didn't exist. Feelings that shouldn't exist.

"Don't let his looks fool you. He's bossy and insufferable." I closed the book, placing it on the table. "And doesn't seem to grasp human limitations. We've struggled to..." I picked at the frayed book spine, pieces of it getting stuck under my nail. "Get along. But I think that's turning around. Thank the stars too, because we were two minutes away from murdering each other."

My cheeks warmed. I'd left out the part about Talon healing me and our non-intimate, yet awfully intimate, moment. We might be friends, but they didn't need to know about that. I couldn't chance them using it against me or for someone like Aeron or Kelvin, to overhear them talking about it. Not to mention the king.

It's not like it meant anything, anyway.

"I hear that," Breana said. "My guard smells like decade-old cheese that's been left out on a humid summer's night." She gagged for emphasis. "Every time he comes within a foot of me, I get lightheaded. To make matters worse, we train outside in the blistering heat, where he can ferment even more."

Mine and Calandra's faces puckered from the image.

"Mine makes me run laps until I throw up," Calandra said. "And then makes me drag these weights attached to my back."

The longer they went on about their situations, and all they had endured, the more and more trivial mine became. I shifted in my seat, trying to keep up with their conversation, but the guilt that riddled me made it hard to concentrate. Of all the stories I'd heard about the fae, maybe I internalized some bias against him?

No.

No, he *was* arrogant. He *was* a prick. Not to mention rude. And yet, despite all his negative traits, he was also oddly patient and kind. He'd taken care of me when I'd needed someone the most—twice—when he could've left me to rot. And after the way I'd been treating him, I wouldn't have blamed him.

My leg bounced under the table as I reminisced about how his magic filled me. His soft caress.

Calandra frowned. "You didn't hear, did you?"

I shook my head, offering her an apologetic smile.

"He went off on this rage-fueled tirade about how you cheated," she went on. "I heard he destroyed his entire bedchamber."

My head spun, trying to jump into a conversation that felt miles away, but I fell short. "I'm sorry. Who are you talking about?"

"Aeron, girl, keep up," Breana said, as if I hadn't zoned out for the last two minutes. "Talon restrained him before he got to your room, but it was scary."

"Let me get this straight. Aeron thinks I cheated and tried to attack me?"

They nodded, and I chewed my nails. Sure, I could talk to animals, but he didn't know that. Unless he saw me? Or he could do the same thing.

"How could I have cheated?" I asked.

"I guess because you rode out on a stag instead of dragging one in, bucking and bleating like we did. Stars forbid anyone shows up that piece of shit. Congrats, by the way, I meant to tell you," Breana said.

"I treated it the same way I would my horse back home." I bobbed my shoulder, hoping I appeared nonchalant and unsuspecting. "Sugarfoot was known to freak out from time to time. She's very touchy. So, I approached the situation like I would with her."

Calandra beamed and held out her fist. "And thank goodness for that. I don't care how you did it. I'm just glad we didn't end up like Irving."

"Thanks." I bumped my knuckles with hers and slumped back in my seat, astounded. If only I knew how dangerously close I was to being attacked. Killed. "Wait, you said Talon restrained him?"

"Yeah," Calandra spoke. "It was hot. He didn't need to put a hand on him, either."

Sounds of the drowler's bones crunching in the forest rang in my head—how effortlessly Talon had killed it still terrified me. Yet knowing he had come to my defense minutes before healing me made my insides warm.

"He didn't say any—"

"Why would he?" Calandra rested her forearms on the table. "It would've just caused additional stress. We debated telling you."

Breana nodded. "You had the right to know, though. Figured maybe you could use it as motivation."

"How? They're barbarians. He and Kelvin were seconds away from killing me during that trial. Going against them is next to impossible."

"Yeah, tell me about it. They ripped my sword away from me and were about to stab me with it when a stag wandered into view, and they raced after it. It was sheer luck I could wrangle one with some vine."

"Irving, too." Calandra added, "It was like he was possessed."

"Jealous." Their faces were expectant as they waited for me to elaborate. "Well, Irving was jealous that Calandra had weapons, and he didn't. If you didn't stab him, I don't think you'd be sitting here. The king himself said, 'May you not let resentment get the best of you and lose sight of the goal.' What if each trial is designed to bring out a different moral dilemma?"

Calandra straightened. "And use our human tendencies against us."

"In the first trial, the vynx were placed there to tempt us with the things we want most—to devour us if we went after it." I pulled my feet off the table and sat back in my chair, my head buzzing with theories. "Why?"

"It was all in the mirrors." Breana appeared deep in thought. "They showed us who we really are. The truth ... our greed."

"The seven deadly sins." Calandra cupped a hand over her mouth. "It makes the most sense—torturing us with our mortal shortcomings."

"And slowly pitting us against each other," I said.

Realization spread across our features as the weight of our epiphany settled deep into our bones. A silent omission that we could no longer trust one another.

The main door to the library popped open, and we twisted around, keeping our surprise hushed as a large silhouette appeared in the entryway.

They crept their head into the room, the sword on their back gleaming under the candelabra's light, and scanned the space.

A guard.

My back went rigid. We were never told we couldn't be in

here. A faerie implication, I'm sure, but I didn't want to find out what would happen if they found us out of our chambers.

He sniffed the air, and our eyes grew wide in silent agreement that we needed to get out of there as fast as possible before we—and our secret cove—were discovered.

We slipped out of our chairs and dropped to the ground, scurrying on our hands and knees to the side door, using the row of easels and drafting tables as cover.

Breana stifled a giggle. "We're so dead if we're caught."

"And it'd be no thanks to you"—Calandra shoved her arm —"get yourself together."

I tilted my head toward a nearby wall of books, motioning for them to follow, and one by one, we spilled into the small nook, collecting ourselves.

There was a five-foot opening between where we sat and the exit that'd leave us exposed, but I knew making a run for it would be risky. Especially when we no longer had our sight on the fae guard.

I poked my head around the stack to find him stalking in our direction, peering around every stack before he made a swift left.

It was now or never.

Urging them ahead, I felt the burn in my knees from the coarse rug beneath. I followed behind, a constant vigilance prompting me to glance over my shoulder every two seconds, ensuring I made for a watchful lookout.

Calandra chewed her lip as Breana reached for the brass knob and pulled the door open, motioning Calandra through first before she reached for me.

My torso was halfway through the threshold when I stopped, making one last sweep to ensure the coast was clear.

Breana unleashed a string of hushed curses, and I did as she demanded, slipping through the opening just as a black-toed boot stepped around the corner.

We took off down the hall, weaving through handmaidens and servants and their mile-high brows—not slowing until we reached our corridor.

Once we reached it, I slumped against a wall, out of breath, and paled, matching Calandra and Breana, who lay on the ground.

"That was so close!" Breana said.

Calandra laughed. "What do you think he would've done if he caught us?"

A beat passed before I spoke. "Probably make us fight to the death."

We looked at each other, and unable to control our laughter any longer, collapsed in a fit of giggles.

Eighteen

With a slow, controlled breath, I adjusted my grip on the knife and lifted my arm above my shoulder. Talon had left me to train alone. Apparently, he needed to 'handle something.'

While it was strange to train without him, I couldn't think of a better way to release all the pent-up frustration than throwing knives at an immovable target. However, I must admit, I strangely missed Talon's brooding, sarcastic commentary. And after my talk with the others in the library, I realized I didn't have it the worst.

Lowering my arm, I lined the knife up with the target—pulled back once more—and sent the knife flying. It twisted and spun straight toward the bullseye, rebounding off the wooden board and clanking on the ground below.

"Dammit!" I kicked the air.

I'd been at this for over half an hour and had yet to hit the target. I refused to leave the training room without landing at least one, determined to be productive. Winning on sheer luck once was pushing it. I knew I wouldn't get that lucky again.

Picking up another knife, I aimed, steadied my breath, and released—

Missed again.

Letting out a string of curses, I launched knife after knife at the board in a fit of anger, not caring if any of them hit, before dropping to the ground.

Panting, I held back tears, trying but failing to not feel sorry for myself. My hand slapped against the ground, and I took comfort in the sting.

I wanted to curse at the stars.

Scream at how unfair this was.

But it was pointless—no one could save me. I was the creator of the hell I was living in, and it was up to me to get out. If only I could be more cunning. Stronger. More resilient. Instead, time felt like it was running out.

With the third trial coming up in a couple of days, I could use all the help I could get. I'd taken the initiative and pushed myself—trained harder. Yet there I was, feeling more pathetic than I did before I'd started.

"I'd find your failure amusing if you weren't so delusional."

The hairs on my arms stood at the sound of Aeron's grating voice, wishing I hadn't thrown all my knives. It wasn't safe to be alone with him, especially not after what Calandra and Breana had told me. I estimated the distance between me and the closest knife. He was predictably unpredictable, and there was no telling what he'd do.

"I might be many things, but delusional isn't one of them. So, feel free to leave." I wiped my hands on my pants.

He didn't—Aeron kept walking toward me with a menacing glower on his face. The knife was less than a yard away. I could get to it before he did.

"What would be the fun of that? The training room is available to anyone. Plus, it appears you could use some help."

"I don't need any help from you."

Aeron stopped in his tracks and tipped his head back with laughter. It wasn't boyish and genuine like Talons, but dark and laced with venom. I used his hesitation to my advantage and hurried to my feet, scrambling across the floor to reach the knife.

Aeron stopped laughing when he noticed what I was trying to do and closed the distance between us in a flash, reaching for the knife before I did.

I scurried away from him, but I wasn't fast enough—he grabbed me by my collar and yanked me up to meet his scowl. Kicking him as hard as I could between his legs, Aeron dropped to his knees with a growl but kept the knife firmly in his hand.

"And here I thought we were becoming friends, Elowyn." He clenched his jaw and raised his head like a predator that'd been tempted. "Why'd you have to ruin it?" He stood up, focused on me as he pursued.

My legs slipped from underneath me as I hurried away from him, Aeron on my heels as I raced to where the knives lay near the target. Diving to the ground, I had one in reach when his body slammed into mine, knocking the wind out of me.

It felt like the training room walls were closing in.

I struggled to catch my breath, fighting and thrashing to get him off me. But it was pointless. My arm strained as I stretched it as far as it could go, desperate to reach a knife that lay feet away.

I was so close—if I could just touch one.

Aeron flipped me over, pinning me beneath his legs, and held the blade to my neck. "It's going to be so satisfying watching you bleed out. Seeing you take your last breath."

I kept reaching, refusing to give up. "Do it already," I snarled. "You want to so bad. Do it."

"And ruin the fun of making you anxiously bide your time

until I do?" He turned the blade onto its side and slid it across my neck.

I held my breath. Shivers wracked my skin as the cool weapon taunted me.

I heard the grin as he asked, "Where would my manners be?"

This couldn't be happening.

The tip of my index finger brushed the cool, slick edge of a blade, and I flicked it into my palm, getting a firm grip on the handle before launching it into his thigh. Aeron roared out in agony as he rolled onto his side, and I slipped away, readying my knife in my fist as I backed up.

He pulled the bloodied blade out of his thigh with a snarl and started toward me. "You stupid, worthless bastard. Have you not learned your lesson? Just when I thought you couldn't get any more ignorant."

My palm became slick with moisture, and I gulped. I knew better than to react before thinking—my stupid impulsivity was going to get me killed this time.

Aeron slashed his knife at me, and I ducked, remembering my lessons with Talon. He didn't think I'd fight back. He was too comfortable. Aeron thought he was in control of this situation.

And that was the same reason he wouldn't expect what I did next.

Coming back up, I threw my arm out as quickly as possible and punched him in the nose.

The snap that followed fueled me with pride.

He licked away the blood that dripped from his nostril and grabbed me. My back slammed into a hard wall; my breath caught—not from the impact, but from the long sword that appeared in my peripheral vision.

The tip of the sharpened blade dug into the crevice of

Aeron's Adam's apple, and his face paled. The familiar scent of teakwood enveloped me, and every nerve ending swelled with delight.

Talon.

"Put the knife down." His calm voice made my chest flutter.

I bit the inside of my cheek to keep from smiling, allowing myself to relax into Talon as he pulled me to his chest.

Aeron kept his snarl in place, refusing his orders.

"I will not repeat myself. Do as I've said, or you'll be disqualified from the trials. Or don't. There's nothing I'd enjoy more than tying a noose around your neck."

Aeron faltered.

I'd never seen him afraid, let alone anything resembling uncertainty. I imagined the lethal, pointed look Talon must be giving him to match his violent timbre. Likely the same one I'd seen a few times. How nice it felt not to be on the receiving end for a change.

Goosebumps erupted on my arms as his grip on my waist tightened. How was it that he made me feel safe? My guard, my captor.

Talon dug the tip of his blade further into his neck, cutting into his skin until Aeron dropped the knife.

He straightened his vest as he took a step back, the color returning to his face as his false confidence returned. "As if you fae deserve any respect."

Talon twisted his sword at his side and slammed the hilt of it into Aeron's head—knocking him out.

His body dropped to the floor with a thud.

"Disgusting waste of space," he mumbled and released his grip on me, wiping the residual blood on his sword across his pants.

I turned to face him—his expression cool and pleased.

"Thank you." I licked my dry lips, and his gaze flicked to my mouth before he sheathed his sword behind his back.

The air between us thickened as I read into his words, wondering if there was something deeper to them. Wondering if I dared to ask.

Talon's voice softened for only me to hear. "You need to stop letting him get to you."

"I swear it's a curse. I think my fight or flight is broken."

"That's why we train." He lifted my chin with a finger. There were no traces of malice remaining on his face, only gentle consideration. "And we'll keep training until you're the last one standing. We'll break whatever mental block is standing in your way, but in the meantime, don't let it break you. Yield to nothing and no one."

I nodded once, wishing I could live up not only to his expectations ... but to my own.

"Good." Talon dropped his hand. "Nice right hook, by the way, that's the girl I'm rooting for."

I allowed myself to smile, bashful and flattered, and my cheeks burned red. I wasn't sure how we got here, or if things would remain this way, but I could get used to it.

Somehow, through our training sessions and endless bickering, I found myself liking Talon. And that voice that shamed me for it—that warned me against it—was growing quieter. It was strange and made no sense, but no matter how hard I tried to fight it, something inside me refused to listen. He hadn't given me any reason not to trust him. He had defended me when I hadn't been deserving of it. Healed me when I lay dying. Protected me instinctively.

It was unfamiliar, yet a deeper part of me, the one I kept

silenced and locked away, yearned for that. Yearned to be cared for.

After years of being my mother's caretaker, I'd grown used to shouldering heavy burdens and taking care of myself. I didn't know how to process these strange, abhorrent feelings. There was no place for them. These trials demanded my attention—coiled around my neck, suffocating me with each passing day. However, it was getting harder and harder to resist the temptation that was Talon and not find solace in those rough hands.

Something clattered against the window, once, twice, breaking my train of thought.

I straightened in my chair. It was well past midnight—what could that be at this time of night? Surely it couldn't be an animal. Curiosity, not fear, had me setting the stick of charcoal down and craning my neck toward the window.

It almost sounded like pebbles.

Three repetitive taps followed, and I jumped to my feet, needing to satiate my interest.

I cupped my hands against the dark glass, my chest swirling with anticipation when I spotted Talon on the courtyard below holding a large brown bag in his hand. He flicked his chin up, using his index to motion for me to meet him outside.

My brows furrowed, wondering what he was doing out this late or why he wanted me to come outside. Training, perhaps? No, not at this hour. Not when there was a trial tomorrow. Surely, there had to be a good reason.

I hopped away from the window and changed into my training attire, tossing my sleep shirt on the bed. Using my hair as a curtain to conceal my face, I tiptoed down the corridor, shying away from the candelabra's light to avoid being seen. Not that anyone else was awake. Even the castle yawned, its foundation creaking and moaning like it was deep in slumber.

Guilt mixed with excitement as I took the maids' staircase to the grand room, slipping out the servant's door into the glowing courtyard.

My mother's life was in jeopardy. My life was in jeopardy, and I had the audacity to bubble with eagerness to see the same fae I wanted to strangle just days ago? Not only was it implausible, but the Iron Accords forbade it. Not that I wanted to *be* with him.

I did, however, want to run my hands through his hair to see if it was as soft as I remembered it on my cheek. And I did want to lean a little closer to scent him at an impossibly intimate proximity.

I groaned. This would be so much easier if Talon smelled like molded cheese. I envied Breana—maybe.

"Took you long enough." Talon extended the bag to me, teakwood and something I couldn't put my finger on rolled off him, blending into the balmy night air. "This was getting cold."

"What is it?" The inflection in my tone was hard to miss as I opened the paper bag and shuffled through the contents. "Oh, it smells amazing." There was a breaded chicken thigh, seasoned diced potatoes, and a slice of apple pie. My mouth watered, and I frowned, realizing how painfully starved I was for actual food.

Talon chuckled. It was an unusual sight, shy almost, and my skin burned from his gaze as he strolled backward toward the lake. "I was at The White Oak tonight having a few drinks when I got to thinking. That garbage the king feeds you isn't enough to sustain you. Not with the training I have you do. So..." He pointed to the bag.

'The White Oak. The woodland nymphs will be there.'

I didn't know why, but knowing Talon thought of me while surrounded by other beautiful, ethereal beings warmed my cheeks.

"Believe it or not, I'm not a completely barbaric son of a

bitch." He flopped onto the grass, resting his forearms on his knees, and I took the spot beside him.

Cloves!

That unfamiliar scent I couldn't put my finger on. It was cloves.

He'd been drinking. His face was flushed, his shoulders relaxed. I'd never seen him so casual.

"I've been around a while. My mother and sister would have my ass if they knew I wasn't being hospitable." He leaned back on his hands; the knotted muscles in his arms rippled under his uniform.

Talon's sudden transparency surprised me. I knew it was because of the ale, but if I were being honest, I enjoyed seeing this side of him. A regular person—fae—in his element, soaking up the moonlight. His sharp features cut through the shadows like a knife.

If I was being honest, I hadn't given his personal life much thought. It was hard to think anyone, myself included, had lives and interests that stretched beyond this castle. Beyond the trials. Being trapped here made it easy to be self-absorbed in my misery. But the consequences of thinking about them, those we left behind, became too much of a distraction to indulge in.

Talon didn't seem like the type to have a sister, though. The thought of them putting him in his place had me forcing back a smile as I took a bite out of the chicken thigh. "How long's a while?"

Talon pondered it, as if he was doing the math in his head. "Well, I'm twenty-three—"

I released a spat of air. "That's not a long time."

"Right, but a year for us is equivalent to five for you. I think that'd put me about a hundred and fifteen in human years?"

I humphed my surprise, imagining what he'd seen and experienced in that amount of time. "Oh damn, you're ancient then!"

He clicked his tongue and reached into my bag, popping a sliced potato into his mouth before I could stop him.

"Hey!" I laughed, waving a hand down my body. "Starved one here."

The bright smile that followed was contagious. I couldn't help but display one of my own, wondering when things between us started to feel light.

"No, we simply age slower. That hardly makes me ancient."

As much as I didn't want to admit it, I could never tire of looking at him. Even his eyes seemed to change shades of green, depending on his mood. It was fascinating, and I needed to change the subject.

"Do you get to see your mother and sister often?"

He sighed. "No, not exactly." Talon's tone was curt, hinting he didn't want to discuss the topic further, but curiosity had the best of me.

I finished with the chicken thigh and started on the potatoes before he could steal anymore. "Does being on the king's guard take up a lot of your time?"

"Your focus should be on the trials—it's best you don't worry yourself about it."

"Believe it or not," I said between bites, "just because I'm a human doesn't mean I have the mental capacity of a fish."

Talon pinched the bridge of his nose. "Can you drop it? It's just not something I wish to discuss with you."

I huffed a laugh. *Well, fuck you too*, I wanted to say. Instead, I poked around at the potatoes. "It all makes total sense now."

He was harder to read than the ancient language carved into the coliseum doors—his mood ever-changing like the tide. It was infuriating. I couldn't keep up. Hot one minute; cold the next.

Annoyance flared at Talon's nostrils. "And what's that exactly?"

"Why, you're such a prick. You keep everyone at arm's length, don't you?"

"I chose not to share my personal life with you—and I'm a prick? What makes you entitled to that information?"

I stood, snatching the bag in my fist, my appetite nonexistent and my patience worn thin. We couldn't go more than ten minutes without bickering. It was ignorant to believe we could get along. We were too different. Too explosive. "I don't feel entitled to anything, I just figured—"

"That I bring you food and suddenly we're friends? Need you forget this is a deadly competition?" Talon stood, towering over me, and I took a step back. His size—his demeanor—intimidating me. "I didn't volunteer to be your friend, Elowyn. It's best you don't lose sight of the goal by entertaining such outlandish fantasies."

"Fantasies?" I scoffed. "Wow. Could you be any more conceited? Excuse me for trying to get to know the guy I've been stuck training with for weeks. As if getting to know each other wouldn't work to our advantage. But you're right, how outlandish of me."

He stepped toward me, and I lifted my chin to keep his glare, hoping it wasn't trembling.

"You humans and your emotions," he snarled. "This isn't Wendover. You're in faerie territory—where such things will be used against you and cost you your life. So yes, it's foolish to allow yourself to be even more vulnerable than you already are."

Foolish to feel. How very faerie of him. How very *him* of him. I was done trying to make it work when he apparently cared so little. "Who are you trying to convince, me or you?"

The muscle in Talon's cheek fluttered, but he didn't reply.

"Yeah," I went on. "I'm sure keeping yourself closed off will work out great for you." I pushed the bag of food into his chest. A little harder than I should have. A little harder than I would've done a week ago. "Your mother would be proud."

With that, I turned on my heel.

But Talon grabbed my wrist, pulling me back toward him with such force the air whooshed from my lungs. He flashed his teeth in warning. "Don't you dare speak about my mother."

I ripped my arm from his grip and flashed him one of my own. "Careful, Talon, your vulnerability is showing."

NINETEEN

A pungent scent wafted out of the coliseum's marble doors and up my nose, burning my nostrils. There were no trees. No mazes made of mirrors.

Only five tables—each donned with three gold chalices—were arranged in the middle of the arena in a perfect circle. One for each of us.

A wall of potions and exotic plants flanked the side wall, wooden barrels with ancient lettering on the other.

Talon's arm brushed against my shoulder as we stepped inside and sent a wave of goosebumps down my skin. "You've been quiet," he stated. It was the first time he'd spoken since he arrived at my bedchamber this morning. After last night it seemed we were back to disliking each other and only speaking when it was convenient. Perfect. It wasn't like I needed the distraction. And that's all he was, a beautiful distraction. "What's going on inside that head of yours?"

I didn't know why he cared. It was clear my humanness was an annoyance for him. Letting out a breath, I let it go. Our argument, the tension, everything that hindered my ability to focus on the trial ahead. Everything that wasn't important.

"How I'm trying not to vomit." My nose scrunched from the harsh scent. I couldn't put my finger on it. It was harsh and synthetic. Unlike anything I'd ever smelled before.

It didn't appear like there would be any duels or knife fights, nor any physical combat—all my training so far had yet to prepare me for whatever this was.

I fidgeted on my feet, trying not to panic.

"It's a glamor to throw off your senses. My best guess? One or more of those chalices are mixed with poison," he said.

I squinted, straining to see the dark liquid inside each cup. Must be nice to have perfect fae vision.

"The king is a notorious alchemist. Some would argue he's the best in the realm. It wouldn't be the first time he's incorporated it into a trial."

I nodded my understanding, struggling not to show any fear. "How—how am I supposed to know which one is lethal?"

"You won't. You'll have to use your best judgment."

"So, I'm going to have to guess?"

His face was unreadable, however, his forehead creased.

"I'm going to have to guess," I repeated. "And pray for the best, aren't I?"

Talon nodded once. "Yes."

Awesome. I thumbed the ring on my finger, keeping my attention ahead. "Well, here goes nothing. May Lady Luck be on my side."

Talon squeezed my hand as I started down the stairs—his warm touch a welcome reprieve to my cold skin. I froze mid-step, but his hand was gone as quickly as I could blink. If it wasn't for the lingering heat that remained, I wouldn't have realized it happened at all.

"Your instincts will tell you what to do. Don't second guess yourself."

I clenched my hand into a fist by my side. I knew I was

testing my fate with each step I took, almost tripping when I peeked at the board of names.

I didn't know which was worse: another name crossed off the list or my name in bold at the top. One thing was sure, it did nothing to thwart the faerie court's sneers and scowls pointed my way as I claimed the last empty table. Their expectation for me to perform—to win—had bile crawling up my throat.

What if I disappointed them?

I brushed a finger along the side of each chalice once I reached them, ignoring Aeron's icy glare from across the circle.

But it was like the knife I lodged in his leg. Unmistakable.

"What'd you do to piss him off this time?" Breana chuckled.

"I may have stabbed him in the training room yesterday."

"You did what?" She didn't contain her amusement. "Spill. Right now. Who else knows?"

"Talon was there." I made sure no one else was listening and continued, "He hit him in the head and knocked his ass out."

She blinked her surprise before doubling over in laughter, and my gaze flicked to a bemused Talon on the deck above. The asshole was listening in.

I scratched my face with my middle finger, hoping he'd catch the hint.

"That's epic! What I would've done to see that. About time someone stood up to—"

The court erupted into cheers as King Harkin and Prince Bowen entered the coliseum, putting an end to our conversation.

"I expect you to finish telling me all the details when this is over." Breana turned her attention to the king. "Or I'll stab you in the leg." She winked.

I took a shaky breath, gripping the edge of the coarse table to still my hands. A million scenarios played in my head—most of which were about how I could get out of this alive. I didn't like my odds and how I was already gambling with my life. How many chances was Lady Luck willing to dish out?

King Harkin entered the arena, swathed in his rich silk robe and a jeweled crown on top of his head. The court fell silent; light giggles lingering in the air as Bowen winked and blew kisses to the nymphs in attendance.

I grimaced.

Sure, he was conventionally attractive with his wispy, blond hair and square jawline, but there was something beneath those brown eyes that was rotten. Wicked. Not to mention their blatant display of status made me sick.

"Welcome, fae, to the third trial." King Harkin puffed his chest out as he spoke. "Today we will test our human's judgment and put their attention to detail to the test. This is the most anticipated and *my* personal favorite trial thus far, as I contributed my alchemy expertise to ensure very interesting results."

He and Prince Bowen chuckled, although I wasn't sure what was funny, and I ran my hands down the side of my pants, drawing a sharp breath through my nose.

Why did Talon always have to be right?

"One of the three chalices before you are poisoned. Drink the correct one, and you may live. Drink the wrong one, and you must find the antidote before time runs out. Choose not to drink and seal the fate of another. Those of you who survive will be invited to dinner with the prince and me to celebrate your victories. Whoever discovers the antidote will be invited to attend our spring ball."

The court broke out in a whisper—visibly against the king's statement. But he waved off their remarks, his decision already made. "Altruism is a virtue most don't possess. It's a potentially lethal risk for those who might not be deserving of such sacrifice. May your ego not cloud your judgment. You have thirty minutes." With a snap of his fingers, he and the fae court disappeared, leaving us to fend for ourselves in the cold, bleak arena.

No one moved as the timer began ticking down, a menacing reminder that our lives hung in its balance.

Don't show any uncertainty.

I noted everyone's tells to distract myself. How Calandra coiled a strand of her brown hair around her finger. The way Breana's leg bounced underneath her. Kelvin's deep furrow between his brows, and the relentless glare Aeron kept on me—his head cocked as he assessed my every movement.

"How should we do this? Should we all drink at once? Take turns?" my voice echoed off the walls, and everyone turned to me at once. Just as the vultures had at the riverbank when Lilian was discovered. I regretted saying anything immediately.

"Why?" Aeron asked. "So you can pretend to drink and calculate your next move? Buy yourself extra time to plot the different ways you could stab someone in the back?"

"Get over yourself. Just because you're a scheming rat doesn't mean everyone else is, too."

Aeron snarled, preparing to respond when Kelvin spoke up first. "Why don't we go by age order? Youngest to oldest?"

Breana and I nodded in agreement. "Yeah, that works for me."

"Same here," Calandra agreed.

"You fools are actually going to drink whatever's in these cups?" Aeron gawked at us as if we were out of our minds as he circled his table, resting his hip against the edge. "Seems it's a better bet to chance someone dying. After all, it'll come down to only one of us in the end. Why delay the inevitable?"

"And who's to say we all won't die if we all don't drink?" Kelvin challenged. "The king didn't specify a death-to-drink ratio. For all we know, if we don't comply, we're dead. I don't know about you, but I haven't gotten this far only to die now."

Aeron shrugged. "That seems doubtful. Who would they have to parade around in these little trials of theirs if we all died? There wouldn't be any entertainment in that. My original comment stands."

"A coward's stance. We wouldn't expect anything less from you," I spat. "I, for one, don't want any blood on my hands."

He laughed. "You already do, sweetheart." Aeron blew me a kiss.

I recoiled, shifting my weight between my feet before reminding myself not to show the reluctance I felt. "Tell me, how's that leg feeling?" I asked.

Aeron lunged for me, but Kelvin interjected. "Enough! The timer is not going to wait for us to decide. If you don't want to take part, you're within your rights." Aeron sat on the table, and the chalices clinked together. "I'm twenty. Calandra, how old are you?"

"Seventeen."

Kelvin pointed to Breana next. "And you?"

"Twenty-one."

My shoulders dropped, relieved. "Eighteen."

Aeron chuckled, crossing his ankles. "Oh, this is going to be fun, please, ladies, first." He motioned a hand in Calandra's direction.

We slipped back into an uncomfortable silence as Calandra studied the chalices, picking the one on her far right. She mouthed a silent prayer, and without waiting another second, took a sip. I held my breath for what felt like an eternity, sweat licking my neck before she peeked them open and gave us a thumbs up.

My limbs went numb as everyone turned to me next.

I couldn't control my trembling fingers—or the way my head spun—as I reached for the center cup, gripping the table with my free hand to keep from falling over. There was no odor to the drink when I brought it to my nose, and I slammed it back down as if the metal burned my skin.

I picked up the other two chalices and smelled each of them, searching for something. A clue. *Anything* that'd hint at their toxicity, but they all smelled the same.

"Tick tock," Aeron chimed. "Any day now.

Chewing the inside of my cheek, I reached for the far-left chalice and brought it to my lips.

Stop!

Something inside me screamed not to drink it.

In a trivial attempt, I looked up in the direction Talon was sitting—not sure what I was hoping to find, as there was no one there.

Trust yourself, Elowyn.

Reach within.

I wished either of those statements made sense, but alas, it sounded like a bunch of hogwash. Grounding my molars together, I made a silent offering to Lady Luck.

And without wasting another beat, I grabbed the middle chalice and took a swig.

My lips burned.

A reaction wouldn't happen that fast, would it?

I hunched over and rested my head against the table, praying, begging, pleading that it was only my anxiety, and I was imagining the sensations. Seconds, minutes, an eternity seemed to pass before my ears stopped ringing, and my pulse returned to normal.

Finally, I stood, wiping my brow, and nodded.

Kelvin returned the nod, rubbed his hands together, picked up the middle chalice on his table, and took a large gulp. There was no second guessing. No hesitation. No signs of distress as he wiped his mouth with his sleeve, until he gripped his throat

—gasping, choking, and sputtering incoherent words—before he staggered backward and collapsed on the ground.

Aeron hopped off the table and rushed to his side.

Maybe it was regret or fear, but for a second, he looked like he was going to be sick. I'd relish in his misery if someone wasn't on the verge of death.

I glanced at the clock.

Twenty minutes and fifteen seconds.

It was Breana's turn. What if she also drank the wrong one? The deep wrinkles on her forehead told me she had the same fear. This was fucked. I bit the inside of my cheek until it bled as she reached for the left chalice and took a sip.

No one dared breathe.

The room stood on pins and needles as we waited for a reaction. The seconds ticked away, the timer running down with lightning speed when she held up her thumb.

Calandra and I released a collective sigh as the color returned to Breana's face, the invisible grip on my airway loosening.

Breana kneeled, holding her knees to her chest, and I rounded the table.

"No, no, get up." I linked my arm under hers, motioning Calandra over. "You can't give up yet. We still need to find the antidote."

"You must really want to go to that ball." Aeron laughed. "The trial's over. Give up the act."

"Are you serious? That's why you think I want to find the antidote?" I shook my head in disbelief. "It's not about the ball. It's about morals. Principal. Proving the king wrong. Kelvin's your friend! You should want to find it, too."

"That's the point of the trials, Elowyn! You can't be that dense. Only one of us can live, remember? Kelvin would make the same decision if he was in my position. You can be a martyr all you want, but unlike you, I'm getting out of here."

My blood boiled. "What makes you think you're any more deserving to be freed than the rest of us, huh? You act like you're so much better than everyone here. Prove it. Drink one of those chalices. Unless, of course, you're afraid you'll be wrong."

Aeron scoffed. "I don't owe you anything. Drinking a potentially lethal potion is moronic—"

"And yet," I interrupted, "three out of the five of us who drank are still standing. That appears like pretty good odds to me."

"You keep talking to me as if anything you say matters. If you're worried about saving him, get busy finding the antidote." Aeron waved his hand at me. Dismissed me.

I clenched my fists at my sides, containing the rage that radiated out of every pore in my body as he sat back on the table and stretched his neck. He made me sick. I'd never wished harm on anyone, but he could choke for all I cared, and I'd thank the stars for ridding the world of one less vermin.

Turning my attention back to Calandra and Breana, I rubbed my temples, attempting to collect myself. "Fae love wordplay, correct?"

Breana nodded and glanced around the arena before motioning a finger for us to get closer. Her voice shook as she spoke. "My grandma used to tell me the story about a fae king that was murdered."

"Murdered?" Calandra repeated.

"By his own brother." Breana grimaced. "It's said he used poison to do it. Tricked him into drinking it after losing at a round of cards. He played right into his brother's trickery, and it cost him his life."

The wheels turned in my head. "Wait, are you saying..."

She shook her head. Yes.

And my stomach dropped.

I knew King Harkin was evil, but to kill his own family because he was jealous? That was an entirely different level. Breana bit her lip as I came to the realization.

"Okay." I nodded. "But what does any of that have to do with wordplay?"

"Your guess is as good as mine."

"Tick tock, girls," Aeron chided. His feet swung back and forth on the table like a defiant child.

Kelvin twitched, foam forming at his mouth, and his body locked up. I wanted to punch Aeron in the nose again, but he wasn't worth my time. Not now, not when only fifteen minutes remained, and Kelvin was only getting worse.

I paced back and forth, mulling over the king's speech.

"*Altruism is a virtue most don't possess. It's a potentially lethal risk for those who might not be deserving of such sacrifice.*"

"Ugh, what does that mean!" I said aloud to no one, aware everyone was watching me with hawk-like intensity.

A lethal risk was a reference to the poison; I knew that much. But what—or rather, who wasn't deserving? I fiddled with the tail of my braid. If the king had killed his brother, he must've viewed him as some sort of competition. He probably thought he could do a better job. Felt he was superior, more deserving of the title than he was. His ego—his pride — got the best of him.

The competitors.

To find the antidote, we'd have to risk being poisoned to save the other competitors—who may or may not be worthy of saving. The antidote to pride was self-sacrifice!

I stopped walking.

Breana wrapped her arms around her middle. "What is it?"

"What if the antidote is in one of our chalices?" I asked, heading back to my table.

"Like at the bottom of the cup?"

"No, like the liquid itself." I traced the edge of the metal brim with my index finger and met her bewildered gaze. "Can you guys help me carry the rest of these over to him?" I gathered all three of my chalices into my arms and set them on the ground next to Kelvin. "One of these must be the antidote. It must be," I continued, grabbing the stem of the first chalice.

His breaths were coming in haphazard intervals as his lips turned an unnatural tint of blue.

"I'm going to need you to drink, okay?" I gripped his chin and pulled his jaw open, pouring a small amount of liquid into his mouth.

Kelvin's eyes rolled into the back of his head, and I reached for another cup.

And another.

And another.

Nothing was happening, though I wasn't sure what to be looking for either. My brows pulled together as I continued to the next cup. And the next.

"Nothing's happening, Elowyn," Calandra stated. "Maybe there's some—"

"No, this is going to work." I picked up a fifth chalice, repeating the process, knowing every second was valuable. Truth was, I didn't know if it was going to work. I could only pray I wasn't poisoning him more and more with each drop of liquid I forced him to take.

But the fae loved to play games. It'd only make sense that one thing that could save us would have the ability to kill us. I just hoped I wasn't making it worse.

"Five minutes left," Aeron's grating voice sang from the

other side of the arena. He leaned back on his hands, kicking his feet back and forth off the table.

"Screw you," I snarled.

"Looks like you'll have more blood on your hands after all. What a pity."

"Until you're man enough to drink one of these cups, nothing you say is relevant—"

Kelvin choked and twitched as a gurgle sounded deep inside his chest, and he went limp.

"No, no, no!" I panicked, reaching for the sixth chalice.

The seventh.

Eighth.

Ninth.

Two minutes and six cups remained. I was quickly losing hope.

Aeron chuckled from behind me. Breana chewed on her nails beside me. Everything was too much. The lights too bright, my clothes too tight. Panic festered under my skin as I poured more liquid into his mouth. Nothing.

I kneeled next to him, holding my head in my hands, and forced back tears. Not here. Not in front of the entire fae court.

Don't show any uncertainty. Keep your chin up.

We were at the minute mark, and the odds didn't appear to be on Kelvin's side. When, suddenly, he jolted upright, startling me as he gasped for air.

A cold wave of relief settled into my bones, and I sank into myself. "Drink all of it," I urged, handing him the last chalice I'd given him. "Just to be safe."

Kelvin chugged until there wasn't a drop left, and the color returned to his face.

I dropped my head back with a laugh, grateful my idea worked, and thanked every star in the sky—even Lady Luck herself.

When we finally rose to our feet, Breana tossed her arms around me and pulled me into a hug. "You're a flipping genius," she squealed. "I was worried for a minute there. Pretty sure I stopped breathing at one point."

"Yeah, you and me both." My gaze shifted between the timer and Aeron.

Ten.

Nine.

"When this is all over, I'm going to sneak into the kitchens and devour an entire chocolate cake." Breana chuckled under her breath.

The last thing I could think about was food, but I admired her for attempting to lighten the mood and holding onto the fleeting moment of hope that remained before fate came to collect one of us.

Five.

Four.

"Save me a slice?" I replied, keeping my voice steady.

Three.

Two.

My head spun as the timer hit one, and I silently prayed I'd live to see another day—but just when the world stilled, Breana threw her arms around my middle, and I stumbled.

I tried to catch my footing, to keep us from falling, but it was fruitless.

My legs were like gelatin; her body too heavy.

We slammed onto the marble floor, stealing the air from my lungs.

It went eerily quiet. The pulse in my ears tapering to almost nothing. Was I dead? I wondered how long it'd take for the nothingness to consume me. If it was going to be painful. Memories of my mother dancing in the kitchen played in my mind, her singing, running in the field with Sugarfoot, and flying down the cobblestone. The warmth of the sun on my skin.

I'd experience none of it ever again.

Or tell my mother I loved her one last time.

Guilt devoured me, but true darkness never came.

It took a second to register the pool of blood that outlined my body, forming small streams that traveled along the grout lines away from me. The metallic scent slammed into my nostrils, and I tried to push Breana off me, but she wouldn't budge.

"Breana, get up," I nudged her shoulder.

But she didn't move.

"Breana," I tried again.

And again.

"Elowyn." Calandra cupped a hand over her mouth as if she couldn't bring herself to say something.

It didn't make sense.

My body went stiff when I realized the blood wasn't mine, but Breana's.

I lifted my cheek off the sticky ground, stifling a gag. *No, no, no!* This couldn't be real. I clung to the balance between the past and present, wishing I could stay there forever. But I knew such a place didn't exist.

Slowly and deliberately, I lowered my gaze to the arrow that penetrated her skull. It was a perfect shot between her brows. My hands trembled as I pawed at her to push her off me and run away, but I couldn't. I was stuck. Covered in her blood. Drowning in the guilt.

She was dead.

Breana was dead!

TWENTY

I stood motionless before the floor-length mirror in the corner of my room. Dried blood covered my body—and smeared my leathers. My hair was a tattered mess on the top of my head.

Recalling Breana's lifeless body, I winced. Devastation weighed heavy on my chest, crushing my ribs.

Lilian's mangled corpse at the river.

The shrill of Lewis's scream.

I wanted to save everyone. Yet death surrounded me—there was no escaping it. Not in my dreams, not in the waking world. Not in this realm or any other.

My breaths came in deep heaves as the weight of Breana's body settled over me, cutting off my air supply. I clawed at my clothes as the surrounding walls closed in—everything was too much. Everything screamed to be acknowledged.

Too tight.

The silence too loud.

I dropped to my knees with a silent sob but was quickly brought back to my feet and met with a warm, firm grip.

Talon's warm scent enveloped me before his arms did, and I

melted into his touch. Secure and strong—everything I failed to be.

"It's going to be okay." His breath brushed my hair.

I nodded absently, unable to find words. Everything felt like a blur, like it wasn't real. I wanted to believe his words. Though how could I?

I wanted to cry out: *Stars help me!* But I didn't. I couldn't. My head rested against his firm chest, staring into the nothing-ness. "It was supposed to be me, wasn't it?"

Talon's silence was my confirmation. I'd heard the murmurs from the faerie court, noticed their sideways glances as I stumbled out of the arena. Breana wasn't supposed to be dead.

I was.

"You should get cleaned up, come on." He peeled the blood-coated strands of hair out of my face.

I barked a laugh, the sound foreign to my ears and dripping with sarcasm. He couldn't lie. For whatever reason, that made me laugh harder. Nothing about this situation was funny. Something inside me was fundamentally altered—either that or I'd finally reached the point of delirium.

Talon's voice dropped an octave as he stepped closer. "Elowyn, look at me." It was a gentle command. Soft and comforting.

But I refused it.

I could barely look at myself, let alone at him.

Talon exhaled and scooped me into his arms, carrying me into the bathroom, where he set me on the bench by the claw-foot tub.

My body was limp, and it took every ounce of energy not to tip over, wanting nothing more than to curl up into a ball in the corner of the room.

Talon left me and turned on the tub's faucet. Then tested the water with his palm, getting it to the perfect temperature before he took my face into his wet hands—those emerald gems fixed with concern. "You can't shut down on me now, firefly. Are you able to get in yourself?"

I shook my head.

"Okay."

I didn't dare breathe as he unbuckled my vest, pushing it over my shoulders and onto the ground.

His face remained neutral as he tossed it aside. "Lift your arms," he said, voice just above a whisper.

I complied.

Talon stood, gripped the hem of my shirt, and lifted it over my head—leaving me in just my brassiere—and my newly exposed skin pimpled from the cool air. Or from his deft touch as he grabbed my waist to help me stand.

"Here, hold on to me." He brought my hands to his shoulders, the vein in his neck pulsing hard.

His fingers worked the button on my pants, and he slipped the leather past my hips, lifting my legs out of each hole one foot at a time. My body felt far away—heavy—yet with every soft touch, every gentle caress, Talon unknowingly kept me tethered to reality. I knew it should've elicited a feral response, but nothing registered. My skin didn't smolder, my belly didn't flutter. I felt nothing. I was nothing.

The room seemed to grow brighter, and I squeezed my eyes shut. *Am I defective? Has my mind finally shattered? I should feel something. Anything.* I dug as deep as I could in search of an inkling of emotion but came up empty-handed.

Talon didn't try to remove my undergarments. Instead, he turned off the water and helped me into the tub, sitting at the edge.

I sank into it, savoring the warm caress as it kissed my body.

The water turned pink as the blood lifted from my skin while Talon gently scrubbed my arms and back with a rag. Time stilled, transporting me back to the Dolorem River, where Lilian's lifeless body had laid. To the mirror maze right after Kelvin snapped Lewis's neck and the cold touch of Sage's porcelain skin. Now Breana.

Talon might be able to wash away the proof, but what was the point if the memories remained?

"Tilt your head back." He lifted my chin to meet his demand, pouring water on my hair—the tub was now a deep shade of red. Even the droplets of water that rolled down my bare arms held the familiar crimson hue. Tears welled over.

This should be my blood.

"I know it doesn't seem like it right now, but it's going to be okay. Take this sadness, this anger, and pour it into the trials. Harness it." He sounded so strong. I wanted some of that strength. Yearned for it now more than ever.

Reach within, Elowyn.

I choked. "Yeah, that's easy for you to say."

Talon brought the rag up to my cheek—concern wrinkled his forehead. Stars knew I didn't deserve his kindness, and guilt tore at my chest.

"It won't be easy—it'll be one of the hardest things you'll ever have to do, but you must keep going. Don't let it all go in vain."

It already felt like it was. There was nothing but a bleak emptiness I wasn't sure would ever go away. Silence encompassed me as I sunk down to my ears. From the beginning, I'd known this day would come. One of us wouldn't walk out of a trial. But seeing the evidence swirling around my body and singeing the air with a metallic taste felt different from how I'd convinced myself it would be.

Talon brushed the wet hair away from my face, his sharp features softening, but he kept his thoughts to himself. I appreciated that about him, his ability to observe. To see me. That small, quiet part of me that yearned to be taken care of craved more.

More gentle caressing looks.

More unspoken understanding.

More.

He warmed something long forgotten. My hold on reality was slipping, yet something told me if I were to fall into the darkness, he'd be there to catch me. It was wrong. Selfish. How could I crave comfort—crave his touch—when Breana's family would never see her again? They'd never have closure, nevertheless comfort.

What kind of person did that make me?

Talon finished washing the rest of the blood off my body until my skin was raw and helped me out of the tub. "Are you able to get dressed?"

I nodded, hugging the towel he wrapped around my body close to my chest.

"Good. You should get some rest. I'll come check on you later, okay?"

I wished that it wasn't so hard to express my feelings. To tell him how much his kindness meant to me, but there I stood, tongue-tied. Wanting yet failing, per usual. "Thanks," was all I could muster just before he paused, turning around to face me, "for helping me," I fumbled. "You didn't have to do any of this, but I, uh, it means a lot. So, thank you."

He dipped his head, onyx strands brushing the tip of his nose. "Someone has to make sure you don't destroy the entire realm." Talon winked. "Get your rest now, firefly."

∼

It had been twenty-four hours, sixteen minutes, and five seconds since Breana was murdered. Not that I was keeping track. No, I was desperately trying to forget. Forget about the trial—and my existence. This corrupt faerie realm. And its handsome guards. How each day that passed, my mother was only getting more and more sick.

Turning onto my side, I pushed the pillow into my face, blocking out the harsh afternoon sun that assaulted my window. I'd slept practically every minute since Talon helped bathe me. Though I never bothered to change.

Even now, I hated I was awake. However, hunger gnawed at my stomach, making it impossible to get comfortable.

Throwing the pillow across the room, I reluctantly sat up. A shimmering note on my bedside table caught my attention.

Hope you got enough rest.
Meet me at the northern edge of the forest at dusk.
- T.W.

I bit my lip, setting the note back onto the mahogany table. It was wrong how my body hummed at the thought of seeing him again. How I longed to be near him. My friend had just been killed, and I had the audacity to have these lustful thoughts? I tried to convince myself it meant nothing, that it was simply a byproduct of loneliness and raw need, but a nagging, persistent voice told me it might be something more.

"You're alive." Pipion's small voice caught me off guard.

I startled, turning to find her sitting at the foot of my bed.

"Sorry for showing up unexpectedly. I needed to see for myself that it was true."

I almost brought up her unexpected appearance, but I reconsidered. Instead, I hugged my knees to my chest, thankful for the company. "What do you mean?"

"There were rumors the king was going to kill you. But you escaped. How?"

My limbs went cold. "I'm sorry?" *A plot to kill me?*

"How'd you escape?"

"I—I don't know. By accident. Stupid luck if you could call it that." My insides turned. I'd begged for luck! Begged Lady Luck to get me out alive, and she'd listened. Taking Breana's life in return. My bones turned to liquid as the realization of what I'd done settled over me again like a thick cloud of rain. "Wait. Who told you the king was going to kill me?"

"You don't know yet, do you?"

"Know about what?" I tucked a strand of hair behind my ear.

Pipion scratched behind her ear with her hind leg. "If I were you, I'd thank your lucky stars. Twice. Someone up there is watching over you."

"Pipion, what don't I know? Why was the king going to kill me?"

"You'll know soon enough. I must get back before they realize I'm gone. I only needed to make sure you were okay."

"Who are they? Pipion, please—"

"Stay alive, Elowyn. No matter the cost, stay alive."

She disappeared into thin air.

My shoulders fell, guilt and confusion plaguing me. I shouldn't be alive. I should be dead, decaying deep within a forest. And it wasn't a secret that was where I should've ended up. Apparently, it was the talk of Faerway. The king had planned for me to die—wanted me to die—and decided before the trial had even begun. It was getting harder and harder to hold out hope. For my mother. The cure.

I should've been happy to simply escape with my life. Relieved, even. Yet, there I sat. Perplexed and disappointed.

∽

The birds nesting in the canopy above chirped wildly, almost as if they were warning us of impending danger, but I didn't care. I couldn't care. Not when I was trying to catch my breath. My head fell back against the tree with a painful thud, and my chest cramped from dehydration.

I felt Talon's presence before I heard him, the energy that rolled off him choking what little oxygen remained.

"Why are you stopping?" he asked.

"I'm tired." I groaned. "We've been walking for miles. My legs have had enough."

He shook his head, annoyed with my theatrics. "We're almost there, firefly. Just a little further."

"You've been saying that for the past thirty minutes and yet..." I took a deep breath. "A little further never comes along." Dropping my hands to my knees, I let my head fall between my arms.

"The reward will be worth the pain, I promise. Keep moving. Come on." He offered his arm, raising his brows expectantly. "I know you can do it."

I looked at it—like it would bite—unsure if I should take it or smack it away. It meant nothing, I told myself. He was simply taking pity on me, and I'd be stupid not to use his help. Not if he insisted that I finish the hike. I knew him well enough to know I'd get nowhere fighting with him. It was a simple, humane gesture. That was all.

Still, when I placed my hand on his forearm, energy coursed down to my core.

"I won't think twice about kicking you in the balls if you're lying to me."

Talon laughed. It wasn't his usual dark, condescending laugh, but boyish and authentic. It made my chest warm. "Violence looks good on you, firefly. If you took half the anger you showed me and directed it at Aeron, you'd be untouchable."

My head spun from his intoxicating scent as we strolled the narrow dirt path, his muscled arm like steel. I felt safe—like I instinctively knew he wouldn't let anything happen to me. I bit the inside of my cheek. "And here I thought the fae couldn't lie."

"Oh, we lie all the time. We can't tell direct lies."

I blinked at him. "That makes no sense."

"Sure it does. A lie is saying something you know to be false. However, some fae, the malevolent type, can be extremely deceptive. They'll play on your words, find loopholes, and mislead you, but they'll never directly lie to you."

"That's not reassuring." I shook my head. "How is anyone able to determine what's true and what's not?"

"Ah, that's the point. We're not all like that though, most of us have good intentions. Still, your human fears of us aren't unwarranted."

"You mean to tell me capturing humans and making them fight to the death doesn't scream welcoming?"

Talon laughed again.

I continued, "How do I know you haven't lied to me?"

Only the crunch of twigs beneath our boots responded, and my hand grew clammy around his arm. I didn't know what I wanted to hear, or why it mattered. Half of me hoped he had. Maybe then it'd shake whatever those festering sensations were that fluttered in my belly every time I was near him.

"A long time ago, firefly, I made a promise to a very powerful faerie to do everything in my ability to protect Faerway."

My neck twisted up at him, surprised. Talon kept his focus ahead, but I swore his lip twitched with amusement. I rolled my eyes and waited for him to speak again.

"It may not seem like it currently, but I've made good on that promise thus far, and I don't plan on screwing it up by sabotaging myself now. So, like I said before, I have nothing to gain by tricking you."

We shared a look, one with no malice or suspicion—just pure sincerity—and I loosened a breath. I didn't know why, but I wholeheartedly believed him. Trusted him. He hadn't given me any reason not to; he'd only proved time and time again that I could. A blush crept up my cheeks as we fell into a peaceful silence, my hold on his arm never wavering until we reached a small glade.

The golden forest gleamed in the sunlight, specks of light escaping in between the leaves. It was a vast difference from the Cursed Forest that I'd found myself in the other day. This was serene. Peaceful.

I let go of Talon's arm and sat on the moss-covered floor, the fuzzy plant providing the perfect cushion. I soaked it all in. A light wind brushed my hair, and I swore a tendril of faint giggles chimed in the distance.

"Oh, my. This is breathtaking. What is this place?"

Talon took a seat next to me, his leg brushing mine, and I tensed. "Once a month at dusk, all the adolescent sprites gather here to get their wings and take their first flight. We call it 'The Flight of Lumen.'"

The moss cradled me as I lay back, taking in the large ray of light coming in through the center of the glade and savoring the cool air on my flushed cheeks.

Magic showered over us kindling my soul. I inhaled the soft pine. Home. It was the closest I'd felt to it since crossing the Dolorem River, maybe more than I'd ever experienced, if I were to be honest.

The moss bed dipped to my right, and I lolled my head to the side to watch as Talon lay down. He tucked his hands leisurely behind his head.

"Why did you bring me here?"

He licked his bottom lip, thinking. "It wasn't always like this, you know—Faerway. It was once a harmonious realm where you didn't have to fight for your freedom. Feel trapped." His jaw muscle feathered, and he turned to me.

I itched to touch him, feel his soft skin under the pads of my fingers, and finally give in to the temptation that lurked beneath the surface, but I kept my arms firmly across my middle.

He sighed and looked away. "I understand what you're going through more than you realize, firefly. I've lost people important to me as well. This is where I come to escape and clear my head. Thought it might do you some good, too."

My gaze drifted along his sculpted jawline and straight nose to his hooded eyes, trying to find the slightest hint of deception, but I came up empty. "How can you possibly understand what I'm going through?"

Talon's lip twitched into a frown.

I couldn't help but wonder what haunted those emerald gems, but it disappeared as swiftly as the wind, replacing it with a tight grin.

"That's a conversation for another time. Look"—he nudged his chin toward the center of the glade—"it's starting."

I wanted to ask him what he meant, but I didn't want to upset him like that night in the courtyard. So, instead, I reluctantly followed his line of sight, not seeing what he did. "Where?"

He placed a gentle finger on my chin, his touch burning into my flesh, and moved my head toward the ray of light. "Right there." His voice was a gruff whisper, and I pinched my arm, punishing my treacherous body's reaction.

With a sharp breath, I observed the light, but only dust particles trickled through the stream.

I searched and searched, yet I didn't see anything. So, I stood, my bones whining. "I'm going to get a better look."

Talon nodded and remained where he was as I wandered into the center of the glade. The faint tendrils of giggles grew louder the closer I got, as did the rapid sound of wings buzzing. I glanced back at Talon, and he smiled—the warm one that made my chest swell—as he encouraged me to keep going.

I bit my cheek and turned back around, my brows arching to my hairline as they came into view.

There were hundreds of them. Sprites of all varieties flew and danced in between the warm rays of light like a harp, their wings beating as fast as a hummingbird. They laughed and sang as they glided through the air, flipping and twisting with unadulterated happiness.

"Come here and see this!" I yelled.

I marveled at how some appeared sharp and angular, while others were softer and cherub-like. There were sprites that resembled leaves and twigs, and others shaped like insects and birds. All of them, however, were no bigger than the size of my thumbs, their wings ranging in all shapes and sizes.

Talon appeared on the other side of the stream and dipped his hand into the light. The sprites giggled and danced around his nimble fingers, and I stepped closer, following his lead. The sudden warmth traveled up my arm, down my spine, filling every empty nook and cranny of my being.

The flutter of their wings tickled the tips of my fingers, and I laughed, unable to contain it. I'd never seen or experienced something as mesmerizing or delightful in my entire life. Their blithe spirit unfolded like a flower, and joy glowed inside me.

My fingers accidentally brushed against Talon's knuckles, and I pulled away, meeting his gaze under heavy lashes.

He kept his hand up, reading my reaction—waiting. Curious.

I bit my lip, slowly holding my palm to his until our skin nearly touched. The energy that crackled between us was almost as intoxicating as the warmth of the light. It forced me to draw a shaky breath, letting my fingers caress the tips of his. Over his calluses. Our gazes never leaving each other.

Though his face was unreadable, he didn't move, didn't retreat, allowing me access to touch. *Feel.*

The forest vanished.

The Flight of Lumen faded into nothing.

The only thing that existed was me and Talon as I laced our fingers together. A sense of calmness washed over me, forgetting about every challenge and trial that lay ahead when Talon closed his hand around mine and squeezed.

His features softened, like he too had finally taken a full breath and, one step later, the distance between us closed. Our chests pressed together with each rogue breath, and I reached up, gliding my fingers down his jaw.

Talon leaned into my touch, pulling me closer until we shared a breath. My grip on his tightened, and I stood on my tiptoes, ready to give in to impulse, when the stream disappeared behind a cloud, leaving us in the dark. In the cold.

Reality slammed into me, the icy splash of air waking me from a stupor as if I'd been drunk off the light.

"Oh, my stars!" I jerked away from his embrace, slamming my hands into his chest, embarrassed. "What was that?"

Talon took a step back, his head cocked as he observed me, confused. Or was he also embarrassed?

My fingers traced my mouth, mortified we'd almost kissed, and I paced the forest floor—imagining if his lips were as soft as I dreamed about. *No, no, no.* I couldn't think right. Crossing my arms across my chest, I ground my molars together to keep from shivering, missing the warmth of the light. Of Talon.

This wasn't good.

He pushed a hand through his hair and let it linger at the nape of his neck. His thoughts and gaze were somewhere else entirely, and I craved to know what distracted him. Was he thinking about—

No! I turned around, shaking my head. Shaking sense into my thick skull.

"Elowyn," Talon tried, my name like molasses on his tongue, sending a pulse to my core.

I waved my hand. "Don't."

Whatever that was, whatever this was, it needed to end. *Now.* It was reckless. Irrational. Stupid. And I'd almost lost control.

I whirled around and stormed in his direction, angry. At Talon—at myself—I didn't know which, finding it increasingly more difficult to concentrate the closer I got to him. Why couldn't the castle be in the other direction?

Talon touched my arm as I brushed past him, and I froze, his touch melting me in place. "Where are you going?" he asked.

"Back to the castle." I yanked my arm away and continued ahead. There was no way I could face him right now, not when my heart was in my throat. "Where else would I be going?"

He walked along beside me with his hands in his pockets, keeping his distance. "I see. So, I take it we're not going to address what just happened?"

I tripped on my feet. "What?" There wasn't a shot in hell I was going to address anything, but the way his eyes burned into the side of my head, I knew he wasn't going to let me avoid it. "Oh, sorry. Yeah, it was beautiful. I've never seen anything like that before. So stunning. Thanks, uh, thanks for bringing me here. That was nice of you."

Talon huffed a laugh. "You know that's not what I'm talking about."

"What are you talking about, then?"

He stopped walking, and I followed his cue. "I see. That's the game we're going to play, then?"

I wiped my palms on my pants.

It was a silent battle of wills, as neither of us dared to look away first, but I told myself it was for the best. Nothing good would come from these feelings—only pain and disappointment—and I wasn't in the market to lose more than I already had. My focus was on the trials. To save my mother and get home. This growing desire be damned.

"I don't know what you're talking about." I pinched my brows together for emphasis.

He sucked his teeth, huffing his disbelief, but said nothing more as he continued forward.

The trek back to the castle was painfully tense and awkward. Though I had no right, I wished I knew what was going through his mind again—and desired it more than I wished to evaporate into thin air.

TWENTY-ONE

The blue river water glistened under the sun's rays as I stood at the edge of the bank. It was hotter than usual for this time of year—my skin blistered with heat as sweat dripped down my back. I needed to cool off before I made the trek home. A quick dip to revitalize myself sounded perfect. But I wasn't ignorant of the stories about how dangerous and unpredictable the river was. Or of the evil fae that lived on the other side.

Sugarfoot neighed from behind me as if she'd read my mind.

"Please, no one's seen a faerie in over five hundred years."

She snorted in response.

"For all we know, they no longer exist. Besides, I'll be quick." I pulled my dress off over my head. "I promise."

She kicked at the ground as I poked my toes in first, adjusting to the temperature before I walked in. With a delighted sigh, I rolled onto my back and let the gentle waves cradle my body, savoring the river's cool and gentle caress. My eyes were closed for all of two minutes when my foot brushed against a rock, startling me out of my trance.

I tried to swim to the shore, but I was stuck.

Something had caught around my ankle and was keeping me trapped in place.

Trying not to panic, I reached down to free myself when I caught a pair of unblinking eyes staring back at me.

I screamed—the sound dampened by water—as I attempted to thrash my foot out of its grasp.

But it was unmoving. Like a metal statue that had rusted over.

"How could you do this to me, Elowyn?" Their voice was familiar.

The sun above disappeared behind a cloud, making it hard to see.

"Elowyn, help me. Please, how could you do this?"

My chest ached as I ran out of air, straining to see through the murky water, when I noticed her.

My mother.

She was pale and lifeless, and her skin had pulled away from her bones.

I couldn't control my gasp, inhaling a mouthful of water. Choking and coughing, I reached for her bony fingers, my vision growing darker with each passing second. I wouldn't make it. The pressure building in my lungs was too much. They burned. Wrung themselves empty for the last bit of air that remained.

My mother's eyes were hauntingly alert as she watched my body go limp, unable to fight any longer. If I didn't breathe soon, I'd join her.

"This is all your fault," she said through a lipless mouth, and I took my final inhale, succumbing to my fate.

A glowing light appeared beside me.

A star coming to collect my soul—but it reached inside me, filling me with life until warmth returned to my body.

"Don't give up, Elowyn." A deep voice boomed inside my head, *"Don't give up!"*

~

I jolted awake—wheezing—and shook the nonexistent water from my ears. It took me a second to remember where I was.

The gold floral wallpaper. The four-post bed. The rich mahogany furniture, and the musty stench of old air.

I groaned. Still trapped like a criminal.

Peeling my sleep shirt away from my neck, I flung the blankets off my legs and padded into the bathroom. I was about to splash cold water on my face when I stopped myself. The clawing feeling of drowning still clung to me. These dreams were getting stranger and stranger—if only I understood what they were trying to tell me.

Reach within.

They were more vague than the bullshit fae rhetoric everyone gave me. I didn't need the constant reminder my mother's life was in my fingers, balancing on splintered wood. Simply being there was the reminder. One wrong decision would cost her everything. I knew that. It was impossible to forget. And as selfish as it was, I wish I could. I wished for one minute I didn't have the nagging reminder looming over my head, threatening to eat me from the inside out.

Maybe that was the reason I entertained the stupid fantasies about Talon. Not because I was painfully alone but to forget.

I slammed the water off without touching it and padded over to the window seat, resting my shoulder against the glass pane. Stars sprinkled the inky night sky, fighting with the moon to illuminate the world below. I basked in the soft light that cascaded through the window, wondering what my mother was doing. If she too was looking out her bedroom window at this very moment and thinking of me. If she hoped that I'd find my way back home or if she'd resigned herself to the fact that I was possibly dead.

If she was even alive.

I shoved those thoughts as far away as possible. I couldn't think about that. I refused. Denying the existence of those thoughts was the only thing that kept me from slipping off the edge. It was the small voice at the back of my head that kept me sane. If she was already gone, there would be no point in even continuing.

Keep fighting.

Three loud knocks rapped at my door, interrupting me from my morbid thoughts, and I stilled. The last person to show up at my bedchamber at this hour was Talon, but I'd be willing to bet I was the last person he wanted to see. Not after this afternoon. Not after I'd almost kissed him and pretended like nothing happened.

Curiosity, or rather undiluted hope, had me hopping off the window seat, my ankles cracking as I hurried to the door.

No, maybe it was Calandra needing someone to talk to. Not that she ever needed to before. Two more loud knocks echoed throughout my room, but I pulled it open before they could finish the third.

"What is wrong with you?" I whisper-yelled to a disheveled Talon on the other side of the door. "Are you trying to wake everyone up?"

Talon said nothing. Instead, he held out an intricate blue and gold envelope and shoved past me into my room, lacing his hands on top of his head. A whiff of smoke and cloves trailed in behind him, just as it did the night he'd brought me food.

My belly swelled—he'd been at The White Oak.

"Sure, come on in, I guess," I said, flipping the envelope between my fingers and shutting the door behind him. "Why couldn't this have waited until tomorrow?" It was a genuine question, however, as soon as I spoke the words, I realized it came out with more of a bite than I'd intended.

"You're impossible." Talon turned around.

I inhaled sharply. His eyes glowed a lime green—from the ale, I assumed—and were accentuated by the flush on his cheeks. It was entrancing. Radiant in the sun, an inky shadow in the dark, and vibrant when intoxicated. I hadn't before realized the depth and range of his beauty.

"And stubborn, you know that? Not to mention downright infuriating at times." He ran a hand through his hair, clenching his fist at his side. "Stars, half the time you open your mouth, I want to strangle you."

And he had the charm to match—lucky me.

I leaned against the bedpost and ripped open the letter. I didn't know what his angle was or what he was getting at, but I didn't care to find out. To think I'd almost felt bad for what happened earlier. Thank the stars we hadn't kissed.

"Wow Talon, you sure know how to make a girl feel special—"

"That. Right there, that's exactly the type of shit I'm talking about. I'm tired of your immature, futile human games. We nearly kissed, and you're acting like a damn child!"

"Me?" My skin blazed as I closed the distance between us, slamming a finger into his hard chest, and he swayed. "You're the one who just stormed in here with a bone to pick, all because I changed my mind. Now that's childish!"

"Do you hear yourself? I don't give a shit that you changed your mind!" He stepped toward me, our chests inches apart, and I retreated, but he kept advancing—one step for every word he spoke until I was flush against the wall, trapped. "I have a problem with the fact that you're too self-consumed with your own bullshit, you can't pull your head out of your ass far enough to woman up and own the things you do."

"I'm too consumed with my own bullshit?" I scoffed and met his fixed glare. "Enlighten me, Talon. Because if I remember correctly, the only reason I'm in this predicament in the first place was because I was trying to help my mother. Who are you to judge me anyway, huh? You're the one with impossibly high walls that refuse to let anyone in. Seems like you're the one who needs to pull their head out of their ass."

He huffed a laugh and leaned down, his lips brushing my ear and sending defiant goosebumps down my arms. "Tell me, firefly. Are you deflecting because I'm right or because you're too cowardly to face the truth?"

Anger thrummed through my veins—that was it—I'd heard enough.

I wasn't a coward!

He could be an ass all he wanted, but I'd be damned if I stood there and took it. I already had too much on my plate. I didn't need to deal with this too. Screw it. Screw the trials. *And screw him!*

Without waiting another second, I craned my arm back and let it fly, hoping to blemish his flawless skin when Talon caught my wrist.

The muscle in his cheek tensed as I fought against his tight grip and struggled to get free, but he pinned it against the wall, foiling my attempt. I sucked in a breath as his body pressed into mine, painfully aware of every single place we connected.

A subtle fervor weighed thickly on Talon's lashes. "I've trained you better than that. I'm almost insulted."

I bit my cheek and swung my other hand. It was inches closer to meeting his cheekbone this time, but he grabbed it just before it could make contact and held it to the wall beside the other. I bucked from his touch. From the heat radiating off his body—from mine. My breath quickened, our chests rising and falling together.

His features softened. Yet anger danced with desire as his thumb idly caressed the throbbing vein in my wrist. Gentle. How could two vastly different emotions feel almost identical?

He dropped my hands, leaving his on the wall like a cage around my body, but I didn't try to fly away from his confines. The longer those emerald eyes bore into mine, the less I wanted to run, but rather melt into his touch. Maybe it was the last two days' worth of emotional turmoil. Or maybe it was a severe lack of judgment.

Whatever the reason, I lifted onto the tips of my toes and kissed him. Hard and deliberate, needing to release this annoying pent-up frustration.

Stars. His lips were like pure silk, and my head buzzed.

As his arms fell to his sides, he pulled me towards him, securing his rough hands around my waist to ensure that I wouldn't float away. He held my head to his, his fingers entwined in the hair at the back of my neck, and I willingly surrendered, welcoming his tongue greedily as they collided in a nimble rhythm.

We pawed at each other. Touching, feeling, clawing at whatever we could get our hand on like two scavenged animals.

Needing more. I moaned, arching into him. More. Like he was sunshine, and I was the darkest, coldest night in winter.

His hands found their way to the hem of my shirt, his calloused fingers grazing my stomach. The underside of my breast.

I sighed and allowed him access to my neck.

Talon's tongue lapped and sucked and stroked. His hair tickled my jaw, and my eyes rolled back into their sockets. I held his head to me as he gripped the back of my thigh and wrapped my leg around his waist, pressing his hips into mine until I was flush against the wall.

Selfish. Needy. Yet it wasn't enough.

My leg tightened around him, eliciting a guttural moan from Talon that made my insides throb, and I bit his earlobe to keep quiet. Then I reached down, slipping my fingers past his waistband, and grazed the trail of hair below his navel.

But then he was gone.

Off me in a flash and across the room like I was infected. Like my ice had started to smother his flames.

I tugged my shirt back into place, my stomach in a hundred knots and face flushed while we stared at each other.

His pupils were wide with disgust? Confusion?

Shit, I couldn't tell. I couldn't focus. I thumbed the ring on my finger as if it would magically help me figure it out. I should've been glad he'd pulled away, yet as I stood there, awkwardly, I couldn't help but feel rejected. What did I expect? It was absurd. Thoughtless. It meant nothing. My eyes flicked to his swollen red lips while my lungs learned how to breathe again, and my legs learned how to hold me up on their own.

What was wrong with me?

Talon cleared his throat, the subtle sound like a train horn in the tense silence, jarring me. "I, uh, I should probably go—"

"Yeah." I nodded. "Yeah. That's probably a good idea." I wanted to tell him to stay. To kiss him again to make sure I wasn't dreaming, but I couldn't bring myself to say it. I didn't want to risk looking even more like an idiot. The quicker we could forget about this encounter, the better off we'd be.

Talon nodded too, a reassurance for himself it seemed, but said nothing else as he strolled out of my bedchamber.

His absence left me ten times more confused than when he initially showed up.

I gathered my breath, shook the tightness from my limbs, and picked up the envelope that had fallen to the ground.

Flipping the envelope over in my fingers, I plopped onto my bed. The king spared no expense on his stationary, I noted, admiring the golden paper and the detailed insignia stamped in wax. Anything to distract me from Talon's moan echoing inside my skull.

I refocused, pulling out the handwritten note:

> *Ms. Elowyn Rosewood,*
> *It would be at the pleasure of the crown if you would join me and Prince Bowen in the grand hall tomorrow at dusk. A celebratory feast awaits you to celebrate your and the other competitor's success in making it this far. I anticipate your company.*
> *Sincerely,*
> *King Harkin*

What exactly did he want to celebrate? Us murdering each other? What a sick, deranged man.

I slapped the letter back onto the table, raking a hand through my hair, mortified and repulsed. The last thing I wanted to do was break bread with that sociopath. Yet as I laid back down and buried myself under the blankets, something told me it'd be a certain someone's rough, greedy touch I'd have to worry about most.

TWENTY-TWO

The doors to King Harkin's personal dining hall opened on an invisible breeze that carried a savory aroma. Inside, a long, ornate table dominated the center of the room, and food covered every inch of it. Ham and turkey. Bread and butter. Potatoes. Vegetables. Bowls of fruit. Cheese platters. Cakes. Pies. Endless bottles of wine. There was enough of it to feed a small village—it must've taken all day to cook everything. Or a snap of a finger.

Calandra appeared at my side, her stomach grumbling to announce her presence, and hazel gaze locked on the massive spread before us. "Is all this for us?"

I shrugged. "Maybe our guards will be joining later?"

A hearty marble fireplace took up half the back wall, over-shadowing the fifteen-person mahogany table in the center. From the vaulted ceiling hung an opulent gold chandelier, its flickering candles creating an enchanting golden ambiance that bathed the maroon walls. The elegance this room held was unlike anything else in the castle—unlike anything in Wellington Castle at that.

We wandered about the space, marveling at the portraits of

previous kings that hung in thick gold frames against the lush crimson walls.

I trailed a finger along the chair rail, stopping before a painting of an ash-blond king in royal blue robes and a bejeweled crown identical to the one King Harkin donned. The gold plaque under the bronze frame gleamed under the candlelight.

King Gareth Rathborne.

A chill ran down my spine. The slain king—the brother betrayed. They shared the same hair color and jawline, however, that's where the similarities ended. King Gareth's demeanor was warm. Trustworthy. He carried himself like a true dignitary. A leader. Nothing in his appearance hinted at the vile and carnivorous nature King Harkin and the prince oozed.

His eyes were honey-coated and wise. There was something familiar about them I couldn't put my finger on.

Speaking of the repulsive *majesty* himself, the king's voice crooned from the far side of the room. "Well, hello, humans."

I straightened.

He looked like an ant compared to the giant fireplace, his and the prince's gaudy floor-length cloaks trailing a foot behind them. "So nice of you to join us. Please, take a seat."

With a quick flick of his hand, the fire roared awake, and the smell of smoked cedar mixed with the food.

Aeron shouldered past me, sitting on the king's left, across the table from the prince. Our plates and silverware magically appeared in front of us, and our wine glasses filled on their own as I took my place—albeit reluctantly—next to Aeron. I slid my chair over an inch to avoid our shoulders rubbing together and shot Calandra a dirty look, who chuckled at my expense. As if this was ideal for any of us.

Flapping the linen napkin open, I laid it across my lap, brushing out the wrinkles while we looked at one another expectantly. Nervous.

Kelvin, of course, was the first to dig in, helping himself to a large scoop of beans and then a thick slab of steak. It wasn't long before everyone had their plates full, stacked high with various dishes and glasses half empty. Except mine. My porcelain plate remained unsullied.

Prince Bowen's mouth twitched, his brown eyes latching onto mine. "Don't be modest, Elowyn. You all have earned this. Please, try the wine, it's delicious." He motioned a finger at my glass.

The stars above knew how hungry I was, and I didn't want to be rude, yet I found myself hesitant to accept their generosity. Would the consequences of rejecting their kindness be worse?

I thumbed the ring on my finger and grabbed the stem, held the rim to my nose, and sniffed. *Here goes nothing,* I thought. With a silent prayer, I tipped the glass, letting the contents dribble between my lips and suppressing a moan, savoring its rich, dense flavor.

My chest warmed, and I sunk into my seat, taking another sip.

And another.

And another until it was gone. I craved more—as if I hadn't known how thirsty I was until I'd tasted the wine.

"Tell us, humans," Prince Bowen began, lacing his fingers behind his head. "How does it feel to eat like the filth you favor?"

King Harkin choked on his wine. "Now, Bowen, don't spoil their treat just yet." He dabbed the napkin against his mouth. "What I think he meant to ask is if you are enjoying yourselves?"

Aeron shook with laughter. "If this is how filth eats, then I'm an uncultured swine."

The king and prince smiled widely, pleased with his reply, and puffed out their chests.

Unable to ignore the gnawing hunger clawing at my stomach, I stabbed a fork into the fatty part of the ham and carved off a thick piece. Along with some turkey and peas and bread, and anything else I could get my hands on. I loaded my plate until the white porcelain was no longer visible, and when there was no more room, I piled food on top of what I already had. Kindness wasn't something they showed often, so I might as well enjoy myself while it was being offered, right?

Every manner my mother had taught me flew out the window as I stabbed my fork into the salad—the tangy vinegar dressing made my taste buds scream in delight—and I funneled as much as I could into my mouth. A little bit of meat. Some veggies. A slice of chocolate cake. There was no rhyme or reason to what I ate, only that I couldn't get enough.

Kelvin looked as mad as I felt with gravy-stained lips and sauce-coated fingers. The raging fire had sweat dripping from his brow, and greasy fingers smeared debris across his forehead as he wiped at it.

Placing my fork on top of my now empty plate, I discreetly burped into the napkin, releasing the pressure in my stomach. My wine glass refilled on its own as if it knew I needed to clean my palate before diving in for seconds, and I gulped it down as quickly as I did the first time.

My stomach screamed for more.

More.

More.

King Harkin drummed his fingers on the table, filling the silence between the clatter of the silverware. "It's truly remarkable, isn't it?" he said to Prince Bowen. "Humans are fascinatingly indulgent creatures. They never fail to meet my expectations of them."

"And they think we're the superfluous ones."

I shook my head, dismissing their passive-aggressive

remarks, and reached over the table to grab another spoonful of veggies when Aeron snatched the spoon from my grip.

My jaw opened on a hinge, and I turned to face him. "What the fuck? You just ripped that from my hand!"

"Oh, quit your bitching. There're a hundred other things to pick from." He shrugged, splattering the veggies onto this plate. "Just get something else."

"*You* get something else." I reached over the table and snatched the veggies off his plate with my hand and shoved them into my mouth. No utensil—licking my fingers clean.

He snarled as he snatched the bread off my plate and took a bite.

"What's your problem?" I demanded.

"You're my problem!" Crumbs sputtered from his mouth as he talked, landing on my cheek.

I leaned back and wiped my face.

"You think you're better than everyone else because you've won a few trials. Get over yourself. I think sharing your food is the least you can do."

"Stars, could you be any more ignorant? Shame I don't care what you think." I ripped the bread from his hand just as he went to take another bite and tossed it into my mouth, chewing dramatically.

He clutched the edge of the table, his face as red as the king's cloak.

"What are you trying to prove, Aeron?" Calandra asked. "If it's that you're a complete ass, you're doing a great job." She took a gulp of wine. "The king invited us to this feast, and you're acting like an animal. It's embarrassing."

The king's smile grew wider as we bickered, and the prince leaned over the table expectantly. It wasn't until that moment that I realized their plates were empty—no crumbs or residual food marred the spotless porcelain. I didn't know what the fae customs were, but back in Wendover, the king and queen were usually the first to eat.

My stomach hollowed—should we have waited for them to make their plate?

"It's fine, Calandra. He can have it." I gave him a sarcastic smile before repositioning myself in the suede chair. My fingers brushed through the ends of my hair. "He'll get what's coming to him."

Aeron helped himself to more turkey. "Yeah, says the bitch who's screwing her guard. Be honest, that's the only reason you've made it this far, isn't it?"

I gripped the napkin in my lap, my fingernails digging into my palm as I willed my anger back into its reservoir. I felt everyone's eyes on me, and my neck burned. Who did he think he was making such wild accusations? In front of the king, nonetheless. "Believe it or not, Aeron, but women don't need to sleep with anyone to be successful."

"Yeah, no. I'm aware. I was talking about you specifically." He pointed his knife at me. "What were you moaning about the other night? These walls are thin, sweetheart." He winked at me and tore into a turkey leg.

I grabbed my fork—tine side down—and went to stab it into the top of his hand when an invisible force wrapped around my wrist, preventing it from making impact. I bucked in response.

"Now that is enough," King Harkin bellowed. He fingered the air and released my arm. But pins and needles lingered where the magic had held it in place. "I can assure you, Aeron, our realm strictly prohibits relations between fae and humans. Not to mention my guards are the most loyal, rule-abiding in the realm. I have heard enough quarreling. Today is about celebrating your victories. So, please." He waved a hand at the feast before us.

I poked at the food on my plate, afraid if I looked up, everyone would read the guilt on my face. The king couldn't find out what had happened between me and Talon. It was a lapse in judgment.

Meaningless.

And it would never happen again.

Regardless of how the taste of his lips made my toes curl.

Shaking my head, I took a sip of wine, puckering at the harsh tang that filled my mouth. Gone was the rich, bold flavor, replaced with a bitter taste, and I forced the liquid down with a gag.

Kelvin arched a brow, but I forced my face into neutrality and finished loading my plate again, not wanting to draw any more attention to myself. It didn't make sense how I wasn't bursting from my clothes; I'd never eaten this much in my entire life. I knew if I kept going, I would become sick, yet my body acted of its own accord—my logic blurred—and I took another helping of casserole despite it.

I chewed and chewed, my jaw clicking as I struggled to eat the rubbery texture. Like the wine, it was no longer moist and palatable, but sour and stale. Glancing around the table, everyone still joyously stuffed their faces—a far cry from the disgust brewing inside me.

The more I chewed the dryer my mouth became, and I discreetly spit it into the napkin and set it down, wishing I had water to rinse off my tongue.

Prince Bowen and the king shared a look and leaned back in their chairs, eyeing me with careful assessment.

My throat itched, sweat clung to the back of my neck as the large fireplace continued to burn, and I took a sip of the wine, hoping to wash it down, but the metallic taste made the contents in my stomach slosh. In hopes of easing my discomfort, I rubbed my tongue along the roof of my mouth, piecing together the flavor—notes of iron and salt.

It almost tasted like blood. *It tasted like blood.*

I flung a hand over my mouth to contain my cough—gag— once. Twice. Trying to clear my throat and rid my palate of the wretched taste, but relief never came.

Calandra, Kelvin, and Aeron were too busy stuffing their faces they didn't seem to notice, or care, that I was choking. After nearly popping a vein in my forehead, I finally cleared the lump in my throat and spit the slimy ball into my napkin.

I froze.

The hollow sensation in my stomach spread to every limb when I saw what it was.

I whipped my head over to the king, who shook with laughter while the prince wore his signature vile smile.

A maggot.

A fucking maggot!

The room spun as an acidic, putrid stench strangled the air and burned my nostrils. I saw it then: the table, once covered with fresh, delicious dishes, was replaced with week-old left-overs, covered in mold, and crawling with bugs.

Like the filth we favored.

I dug my nails into my thighs, my eyes watering. I tried but failed to control the vomit that inched up my throat, spewing everything I'd eaten onto the ground next to me.

My body violently rejected everything I'd consumed.

The cackle of the king's laugh raddled around inside my skull as I wiped my mouth. I didn't know if I was going to throw up again or pass out as I sat up, my head throbbing with each movement. No one else seemed to notice—they were too absorbed, still stuffing their faces.

If they could only see what they were truly eating.

He had tricked us. Lured us here under false pretenses, only for it to be another trial. My limbs went numb as the realization slammed into me like a bag of bricks.

Gluttony: the fourth deadly sin.

"It's a trick," I croaked—my voice hoarse from vomiting. "A trick. It's a trick. Look." I cringed as I pointed to the cobbler Kelvin was eating, averting my eyes as tiny roaches crawled between the crust.

His brow furrowed as he inspected the spoon and shrugged, dumping it into his mouth. I gagged, pleading for him to stop, but he wouldn't. He was consumed with hunger.

As if possessed, my hand reached for the fork, gripping the cold metal between my fingers, and stabbed a piece of molded turkey. I looked to the king, who drooled with anticipation as my hand inched toward my mouth.

I refused to open. Refused to willingly eat any more of the spoiled food.

But it didn't matter. The fork pushed against my lower lip, but try as I might, I couldn't turn my head. The magic working against me was too strong.

"In many cultures, Elowyn, it's a sign of disrespect to refuse the food that's been prepared for you," the king said as the prince turned red from silent laughter. "I insist you keep eating until everyone is finished."

Tears stung my eyes as I challenged him, but my lips parted for the rotten meat despite it, unable to refuse the magic any longer.

I gagged as I chewed—the thick slime coated my mouth.

What was the point of this? To make us sick?

Bile mixed with the rotten meat, and tears rolled down my cheeks. There was no way I could keep eating until everyone was finished.

Forcing my hand back to the table, I dug my nails into the

wood. The king's magic wrapped around my arms like vines. Or puppet strings.

Calandra went to reach for her wine, but I kicked her under the table, and she startled.

"It's not wine!" I pleaded.

She pulled her arm away and rolled her eyes, taking a sip regardless.

I clenched my jaw. "Please, just taste it!"

She swished it around in her mouth as my hand reached for the browned salad, terror licking the back of my neck.

"Stars, truly taste it!" I yelled again.

She grimaced in response, but I could tell she was trying.

"Yes. Yes! That salty flavor? That metallic tang?" I pushed, watching her expression, "Blood. It's blood, Calandra, and this food's spoiled! Come on, snap out of it. *Please.*"

The wine glass dropped from her hand when it clicked, and she slapped it over her mouth. I couldn't provide any more comfort though as one by one my fingers wrapped around the stainless-steel spoon, and involuntarily scooped up another helping of salad. Dead flies were mixed in like grapes, and my throat tightened. I couldn't eat anymore. *I couldn't.*

A sharp pain clawed inside my stomach as if it was trying to escape.

"Don't you see this is an illusion?" I screamed across the table to Kelvin, who deliriously kept eating. "I know you guys are animals, but honestly, when have you ever been this hungry?"

Prince Bowen bit his lip, a vile eagerness stretched across his features as I chewed the salad. He and the king beamed with delight, and it made me simmer with rage. How King Harkin sat on that throne and said they were a kind and forgiving species with a straight face was beyond me. This was nefarious.

"Please stop eating." Calandra sobbed in between bites of raw chicken. "I beg of you."

I gagged. "Wake up!"

Aeron placed his fork down and arched a brow—sharing a look with Kelvin, who tore into a piece of raw steak.

"It's a glamor. All of it!" I cried.

"Elowyn," King Harkin drawled, crossing his legs. Stars, how badly I wanted to smack that smug expression off his face. "Did you forget our conversation already? It's disrespect—"

"Focus on the smell." I cut him a sideways glare. "And the texture. It's spoiled, Kelvin. Focus. This is a trick."

He examined the piece of steak on his fork, twirling it around to see every angle before putting it into his mouth, squinting as he chewed.

I held my breath, the putrid smell becoming harder to stomach by the second.

It took less than two rotations of his jaw before Kelvin spit it out—his face turning green as he took in the horror surrounding him. Vomit tumbled from his mouth and onto his lap. He tried to flee but was stuck in place, the king's magic forcing him to remain at the table, too.

"What did you do to us!" he demanded and thrashed against the invisible cords.

Prince Bowen let out a squawk of delight, tipping his head back with laughter before abruptly turning serious. Wielding his emotions like a weapon. "Why, we're giving our guests the feast they deserve." He deadpanned. His sudden change in demeanor was alarming, as was the way his eyes danced between us with wild intensity.

Aeron remained oblivious as he licked his mold-covered fingers clean. Bugs raced up his forearms that'd fled the item he'd just consumed.

"Come on man, wake up," Kelvin pleaded. His nails sunk

into the blackened turkey crawling with ants. "Your plate is swarming with maggots, man. Don't do it!"

"Please," Calandra cried.

Kelvin thrashed against the magic that held him—us—in place and begged him to listen.

King Harkin and Prince Bowen practically fell out of their chairs as they watched Aeron set the turkey down and close his eyes, searching the deepest parts of his mind for a semblance of self-control.

The incantation that bound us to the table—the same one making us move against our will—snapped when Aeron opened his eyes and released us from its claws.

Kelvin and Calandra ran from the table without a second's hesitation, their chairs crashing to the ground in their frenzied escape.

The room crackled along with the fireplace as Aeron's grip on his knife tightened, his face pained as he looked up at the king.

He launched out of his seat toward them, spilling dishes as he leaped onto the table.

My heart slammed in my chest.

"Ah, ah, ah." The king held up a hand. Aeron froze midair. "After the hospitality we showed you, that wouldn't be very smart, now, would it?"

Aeron's forehead wrinkled in pain as, one by one, his fingers were plucked off the knife until it fell from his grip.

"There you go, much better," the king continued, nodding to the prince, and they stood to leave. "Now get back to your chamber before I decide to make an example of your disrespect. And you." He looked at me, and my bladder threatened to empty. "Get yourself cleaned up. The ball begins in a few hours. It'd be a shame if you were late."

TWENTY-THREE

I kept my hand planted over my mouth as I sprinted down the corridor, trying not to vomit all over the polished marble floor. It felt like I had maggots crawling up my throat—cockroaches swimming around in my belly. I couldn't take a breath. Too afraid that the putrid smell of the decayed ham had permanently singed my nostrils.

I paused, catching myself on the ivory wall as my stomach violently churned. Their laughter and mocking, smug satisfaction haunted my mind.

Aeron hurried past me, his shirt soiled, and it took every ounce of self-preservation to push myself off that wall and keep walking. Keep moving. I'd be damned if the king or any of the fae court saw me in such a state—

"Chin up." Talon looped his arm around my waist and helped me off the wall. I staggered into him, holding onto him for dear life—my anchor. "Focus on your breathing. We're almost to your chamber."

I did what he said, stopping and restarting multiple times as I became too engrossed by his touch. We never should've kissed. Training with him was already next to impossible—as was pretending I didn't feel any sort of attraction toward him. How was I going to face him every day now? My insides knotted, and I forced my vomit back down.

"Only a couple more steps," he urged, pushing open my chamber door.

I raced to the bathroom and emptied the contents of my stomach into the toilet—my back straining from the force as if my body tried to purge whatever magical incantation festered inside. I felt heavy and weak. Clammy and dizzy. Resting my head against the seat, I wiped my bottom lip and noticed how the room seemed to pulsate in my vision.

I savored the moment of calm that passed over me, bracing myself on the rim as my mouth watered and bile splashed into the water.

My body fell limp. There was nothing left—yet the sensation lingered and threatened to wrap its claws around me and squeeze until only a hollow corpse remained. If this was what death felt like, I silently begged her to find mercy and put me out of this star's awful misery.

"Do you need any help in there?" Talon asked from outside the washroom.

I could tell by his clipped tone that my nausea was contagious and had found its way to him. A strong, powerful fae, uncomfortable with a little vomit? Priceless. I smiled. Against every miserable instinct, I smiled.

"No." I flushed the toilet. "I think I'm good now."

I caught his chiseled profile resting against the door frame as I padded over to the sink to rinse my mouth. He flexed his jaw. Those jaded eyes lost in a memory. Stars, he was beautiful. The veins in his forearms bulged as he adjusted his stance, and my chest swelled, recalling his firm grip on my hips. How truly commanding and dominating he was.

My arm brushed his as I walked to my bed, toward a large

decorative box that sat on top of the comforter. A shiver shot up my spine. I tried to ignore the effect Talon had on me, but my body forced me to acknowledge it—a memory now imprinted inside me. I half hoped he'd reach for me, pull me toward him like he did last night, and warm my balmy skin.

But his touch never came.

Disappointment ate away at me, and I knew I couldn't let it show. So, swallowing my pride, I brushed a hand over the gold box, admiring the silk red bow.

"Did you bring me this?" I twisted the bow around my index finger.

Talon appeared at my side and shook his head. "No, it was here when we arrived. There's a note." He reached for the small tag at the base of the bow and read the message aloud for me, *"Looking forward to your presence tonight at the spring ball, can't wait to see you fill it out. Until we meet at the Grand Hall at dusk. Yours, Prince Bowen."*

"The prince?" A sense of dread washed over me.

I pulled the periwinkle tulle dress from the box. Layers and layers of fabric billowed free, weighing heavy in my arms. The puffy satin sleeves were as thick as clouds, the corset embroidered with iridescent sequins. It glowed under the candlelight above, reflecting harsh and blinding hues.

Talon pursed his lips, trying but failing to conceal his amusement.

"Why would he send me a gift?" I added, "I can't accept this."

He shrugged, slipping his hands into his pockets. "Then don't go."

"And let the king know he won? No way."

He shook his head, letting out a breathy laugh. "So risk being indebted to the prince. I'm sure that'll work out well for you," he chided and strolled toward the door, indifference rippling off his words.

Irritation bubbled up inside me—how could he stroll into my room last night, kiss me stupid, and then act like it never happened? Like it was nothing—like I was nothing.

"You just don't want me to go," I said to his back, placing my hands on my hips in defiance.

Talon flashed me a wolfish smile as he turned around, approaching me with ghostly calmness. "No." He stopped an inch short of me. His warm, woodsy scent was a remedy for my queasiness. "I just think you're being foolish."

I scoffed. "Foolish? How am I being foolish?" My eyebrows pinched together with anger.

"You're smart, firefly." Talon licked his lips, his eyes darting to my mouth. "I'm sure you can put the pieces together."

"Stop calling me that."

He brushed his fingers along my jaw, and my lips parted for him. "Why don't you get some rest? I'll tell the king you're sick and can't attend tonight."

I huffed a laugh. "Oh, I get it. You're back to being a condescending prick, noted." I flashed him a fake smile. "I'm more than capable of making my own decisions, thank you. Please, do me the favor and see yourself out."

Talon flexed his jaw, his body turning to stone as he stared at me, but I held his gaze. "My pleasure," he said.

If he wanted to act like nothing happened, that was fine by me. Pushing my feelings aside came second nature—I'd done it my entire life. From school kids teasing me to my mother's sickness, to this damn trial. I had it perfected.

Whatever asinine feelings I had toward him wouldn't be any exception.

Yet, it didn't stop the deep, sinking ache from forming

inside my chest as he walked away. His silent dismissal told me everything I needed to know.

The door shut behind him, and I collapsed onto the bed, willing my nerves to settle and my heart to calm. As much as I hated to admit it, Talon had a point. I couldn't wear that dress unless I wanted to be indebted to the prince, but I'd be damned if I didn't go to the ball either.

Rubbing a hand along the back of my neck, I rolled onto my stomach. There had to be something else—another way. I surveyed the room, ransacking my brain for any ideas, when my eyes landed on the mulberry wine-colored curtains.

The perfect solution slammed into me like a stampede of horses: I'd make my own.

I sat up on my knees—the only thing I needed was a pair of scissors and some thread. Surely, I could whip something up that didn't require those things, but I had a point to prove. A statement to make. This couldn't be half-assed.

Jumping out of the bed, I slipped out of my chambers, keeping to the shadows along the wall.

I breezed down each hallway.

Whispers came from ahead, and I ducked into a nearby enclave, keeping as still and quiet as a mouse as two fae guards passed. I couldn't understand what they were saying, their voices low and muffled, but I relaxed into the wall when they didn't spot me.

Once they rounded a nearby corner, I continued and eventually slipped inside the textile room to my right. The room was empty. No fae seamstresses in sight as I shuffled through the drawers and cabinets. I thought about the consequences—the moral dilemma—if any, should someone learn anything went missing. It wasn't lost on me how easily they could link it back to me after I appeared in a one-of-a-kind dress and my curtains were missing chunks of fabric, but I didn't have time to dwell on it.

What was the worst they could do to me that hadn't already been done? I'd return the items before anyone noticed, I told myself, and pocketed a pair of scissors and a plum-colored spool into my vest, making sure the coast was clear before I wandered back out of the hallway.

Now returned to the safety of my chambers, I locked the door behind me and removed my curtains from the rod to splay them flat on the floor. I might not have had my mother's treadle sewing machine to help me get this done in a timely fashion, but I had a couple hours to spare, and it wasn't like I hadn't been in this predicament before. Mother's machine was constantly malfunctioning, so I'd learned how to sew by hand in a pinch.

Folding the fabric in half, I cut it into two pieces and laid the panels one on top of the other. I cut out a pattern I knew from heart, starting from the base and up the sides, working my way to the neckline. It was a basic dress template I'd used before, but instead of the short sleeves I'd typically cut, I went with a more whimsical bell-shaped sleeve that'd flow with every movement.

I sewed the panels together next, pulling and tugging at the thread to get it to bunch for the most flattering drape on my body. I did the same with the skirt, my fingers growing sore as I left enough fabric to trail along the floor and used a spare piece of fabric to tie the two sections together and cinch my waistline.

Wiping sweat from my neck, I picked the gown off the floor and laid it on the bed while I undressed. Sewing it took much longer than I'd expected, and I needed to hurry if I planned to be on time.

Slipping the delicate fabric over my head, I twirled in front of the floor-length mirror, admiring my work. The smooth, soft fabric was classy yet shapely. A vast difference from the dress the prince wanted me to wear. The color brought out the red strands in my hair, and for a moment, I felt normal. As if I wasn't stuck inside a prison disguised as a beautiful, enchanting castle.

Heading into the washroom, I released my hair from the bun on top of my head and allowed my tresses to flow freely over my shoulders. Coating my strands with water, I curled my hair around my fingers, twisting and turning in different directions to accentuate my curls.

I wished I had some blush for my cheeks to make me look more alive after the ordeal of earlier. To conceal the perpetual exhaustion that hung below my eyes. But, like everything else, I needed to make the best of what I had.

With a quick pinch to my cheeks, it was the best I'd be able to do. I was ready to go. A ping of melancholy jabbed me in the ribs as my reflection stared back at me one last time—I always tried to avoid it. The vacant and detached eyes that stared back were a harrowing reminder of how much I'd already lost. How much King Harkin had stolen from me.

Not tonight, I told myself. Tonight, I'd show the king how he'd never smother my fire.

TWENTY-FOUR

Loud orchestral music played from behind the closed doors of the Grand Hall. The rich, graceful melody of violins and flutes rang through the air, as did the murmurs of a sizable crowd.

The symphony of our death.

The hairs on the back of my neck stood as the haunting memory of being herded into the throne room to learn of our fate replayed in my head before all hope vanished. Wiping my hands down the silk dress, I lifted my chin and pulled the ornate door open.

Large candle chandeliers hung from the trusses—the ceiling, enchanted with thousands of night stars. Unlike I'd seen it before, an entire twinkling cosmos lined the upper rafters of the room.

My breath hitched.

Tea light candles wrapped around columns that resembled tree trunks. An assortment of wildflowers and moss covered the walls, and vines hung along the banisters. The polished floor glittered under the lights. It was magical. Like a miniature forest inside the castle.

Coming to a stop at the edge of the rustic staircase, the music receded, and the fae court below halted their conversations and paused their dancing to look up at me.

My chest heaved from the sudden attention, but I steadied my chin. I wanted to bolt—regretting my decision to come.

Then I saw him.

Time slowed as Talon and I locked eyes, my pulse returning to normal.

I took one step after the other, the wood cold under my bare feet. Closer and closer to him. His formal uniform hugged his body in all the perfect places, accentuating his large arms and built frame. His hair was haphazardly slicked back, and I mused about how those strands felt in between my fingers.

I didn't pay any mind to the cruel smirks and amused expressions from the rest of the court. None of it mattered while his eyes caressed my body. Mischievous thoughts ran across his features, but when I blinked, they were gone.

As if I'd imagined it.

When I looked again, Talon was in deep conversation with a forest nymph at his side, her fingers lightly stroking his forearm. And he laughed, that boyish smile of his on full display.

My hands tightened, and I stumbled, my foot slipping from underneath me, when a hand snaked up my back, catching me before I tumbled down the stairs.

"Careful, Elowyn," a familiar slimy voice croaked from beside me.

My skin rippled with unease at Prince Bowen's hand on my hip, and I forced back a grimace.

"You look breathtaking," he continued, shamelessly eyeing my cleavage. "Although, I am disappointed I don't get to see you in my dress. However, this one"—he ran a hand down the sleeve—"I must know who designed it and give them my full appreciation."

I gulped, my eyes darting over to Talon, who was now whispering into the nymph's ear. She giggled and my stomach sank. "I—uh, I did." I shook off his touch. Outing myself be damned; at this point, I'd welcome the punishment.

Prince Bowen moaned, looking me up and down once more. "Are you thirsty? Would you like me to get you something to drink?"

"No. No, that's okay. I'm okay. Thank you."

"Please," he insisted, "it would be my pleasure. It's quite delicious, too, if I say so myself. Wait here, I'll be right back." He disappeared into the sea of fae before I had a chance to politely decline again, although something told me he wouldn't have taken no for an answer, anyway.

"Don't drink anything he gives you," Talon's voice said from behind me.

I felt his presence like a vice grip around my chest, pulling me toward him with dominating force. But I kept my eyes straight ahead. "I'm sorry, are you talking to me?"

"There's no need to be immature, Elowyn. I'm only trying to look out for you."

"Oh, that's rich." I scoffed, daring a glance at him. "I'll take that into consideration. You should get back to your forest nymph now. You wouldn't want to keep her waiting, would you?"

Talon circled me. "I didn't realize you were the jealous type."

"Jealous?" I seethed. "More like disgusted."

"Don't let your emotions override your logic, firefly. Heed my advice. Or don't. But don't come crying to me when your plan goes up in smoke."

"Screw you," I said through a wide smile as Prince Bowen made his way back over to me. Thankful to be relieved from Talon's company.

He huffed an annoyed laugh and slipped past me, bowing to the prince as he headed back to the center of the ballroom. Talon didn't waste any time pulling the nymph in for a dance, holding her close to him. They swayed to the music.

I couldn't care less what he did—or *who* he did, for that matter. It was none of my business. He thought I was jealous! *Ha!* Of course, his ego would make him believe he was a gift to this world. Ultimately, though, he was like every other male that walked this planet. Disappointing and selfish.

"For you." The prince extended one of the glasses he held to me.

I took it from him, smelling the contents inside. It was a tart and sour mixture that made my cheeks tingle, and I scrunched my nose, making no effort to take a sip. "Thanks."

"It's safe," he urged. "I promise. Look." He grabbed the glass from my hand and took a large gulp, keeping his eyes on me the entire time. Stars, I hated the way he looked at me. It was wrong. Unnatural. "See, no glamours this time. Now, I insist," he went on, his tone dripping with honey. "Drink. Lest you want to offend me."

With a resigned sigh, I looked to Talon, his focus on me with hawklike intensity. I was damned if I did and damned if I didn't. It's not like he could save me or cared enough to try. That nymph had him captivated.

Before I could talk myself out of it, I sipped the contents of the glass in its entirety, thumbing away the residual juice from my mouth when I was done.

"Well," the prince marveled, "this will be an interesting night. Come now, let's dance, shall we?" He hooked his arm around mine and led me to the dance floor, not giving me an opportunity to protest.

Not that I would. I was feeling instantly lighter.

Willing.

Eager.

When King Harkin's large frame stepped in front of us, blocking our path, it put a damper on my mood, and I pouted.

"Ms. Rosewood." He extended his hand.

His casual tone made me giggle—it was so off-putting. So, disarming. And yet, I placed my hand in his, smitten, as he kissed the top of my knuckles, his amber eyes lingering a second too long on my ring.

"I'm happy you could make it."

I tugged my hand from his. "Okay," I said and wiped off his touch on my dress. Both the prince and the king were extremely vile and yet I couldn't help the blush that spread up my neck.

"May you have a wonderful evening." King Harkin shared a look with the prince before strolling off, allowing Prince Bowen the opportunity to lead me.

I noticed Talon gave me a disapproving scowl as we breezed onto the waxed floor, and I bit back my amusement—flipping him my middle finger before resting my arms over the prince's shoulders. As my hands settled onto the smooth material of his suit, the drink settled into my bones.

We danced and swayed as one—the room blurring together in a kaleidoscope of colors. The music, a serene melody. My skin warmed further, my cheeks and chest flushed, and my thoughts felt far away.

I laughed, unadulterated, and felt as free as a bird.

The prince twirled me around the floor, also seeming to enjoy each passing moment.

Gone were my fears about surviving the trial and saving my mother.

My conflict about Talon, forgotten.

Breana's death, a mere distant memory.

Twirling and spinning until I tripped and crashed onto the floor.

A loud cackle escaped my lips, surprising me, and I laughed even harder, enjoying the fact I didn't have a care in the world. Sprawled on the cool floor in a fit of hysterics and unable to get up, I lay there staring up at the chandeliers, unable to differentiate them from the star-filled sky. I didn't want to get up; I could've laid there forever.

"My, my, aren't we enjoying ourselves?" The prince extended his hand, his face wild with amusement, and I hiccuped.

"Sorry." I giggled, covering my mouth.

"Oh, don't be silly. You've nothing to apologize for. Here." He lifted me into his arms.

I felt like a wet noodle as he held me, my head too heavy for my shoulders. My feet slipped out from underneath me again, and I clung to him to stabilize myself.

Prince Bowen flashed me a curious smile. "This is my favorite symphony." He continued, "Dance. Dance, Elowyn. Entertain us. Entertain *me*."

Letting go of his jacket lapels, I giggled into my hands and stumbled back, crashing into another hard body. My eyes crossed as I tried to look at him, blinking them into focus. His features were sharp—cruel—as an inhumane smile spread across his dry, cracked lips.

"Hello," I drawled, wiggling my fingers dramatically in his face before fluttering off in the opposite direction.

I spun and spun like a table totem, ricocheting off fae like a blind moth to a flame—laughing and howling and embracing anyone I could get my hands on.

Their cruel faces were lit with merriment as they passed me around like a rag doll. Stray hands. Grips that were somewhat too tight, but it didn't seem to bother me. Soon, the nausea from earlier bubbled back to the surface.

Another spin. And another, until my eyes lost focus, and all sense of direction went with it. I stumbled, falling to my knees, and my skin cried out. My stomach twisted.

I doubled over in a fit of laughter, tears forming in the corner of my eyes. I'd drawn the attention of the crowd of fae that now surrounded me—their bony fingers pointing in my direction as they loomed over me.

Gawking.

Laughing.

Talon appeared at the front of the crowd, his hands in his pant pockets, and his lips pulled into a taut line.

Disappointed. *Figured*.

I rolled my eyes. "Ugh," I groaned, splaying my legs out in front of me, and pouted. Dirt stained the hem of my dress. "Why do you have to be such a fun sucker? You always fun the suck." Another hiccup escaped me, and I slapped a hand over my mouth, giggling into my palm.

At least his face had become my center of focus, my vision no longer spinning out.

Talon nodded to someone behind me as he swaggered forward, gripping me underneath my armpits—yanking me to my feet. My head lolled to the side as he carried me, keeping his arms fully extended out in front of him like I was infected and contagious.

It was degrading.

As if I was an infant.

I laughed, kicking my feet in the air.

He carried me like a sack of rotten potatoes until we reached an empty hall and, without warning, dropped me to my feet.

I collapsed onto the floor with a hard *thump*.

He pinched the bridge of his nose, attempting to contain himself before he jerked me up, pinning my body against the wall. "Why do you insist on being so stars damned pig-headed?"

"Pig-headed?" I dropped my head back against the stone wall as I convulsed with giggles when he forced a soft and peppery tart into my mouth. "What the f—" I attempted to spit it out, but Talon beat me to it.

He held a hand to my jaw, forcing my mouth to close. "Swallow it," he demanded.

His eyes dared me to defy him, but I knew better. That look was a threat. A promise of atonement. I wanted to push him—see exactly what he was capable of—but instead, I chewed, keeping my eyes locked on his out of spite.

I swallowed the dry lump of taffy, repressing a gag, and, as if on cue, a cloud lifted from my thoughts, and my head was clear. My vision refocused completely. The lights were no longer blinding. Nor did I feel like an outsider in my body.

A hot, searing wave of emotion flooded me, and I cringed as blacked-out memories forced themselves to be remembered. How I'd behaved. Embarrassment and shame coursed through my veins, turning them to ice, and tears welled in the corner of my eyes.

Talon held me against the wall, keeping me from running off. "I told you not to drink that juice," he growled, his lips grazing my ear.

I bared my teeth. "Don't you dare patronize me."

"How'd that turn out, hm?" He continued, "Besides making a complete ass of yourself knowing full well you have a target on your back."

I tried to shake him off me, but his grip on my waist only tightened. "Screw you," I spat, shoving my hands into his chest, but he didn't budge. "You have some nerve lecturing me when you were looking super cozy with your forest nymph while it was all unfolding."

"That's what this is about, isn't it?" A knowing grin pulled at his lips. "The nymph."

"Stars, you're so arrogant. Let go of me!" Heat crawled up my neck. It wasn't about her. It was him. Talon and his stupid hooded eyes. His stupid smile. The way he made my heart hiccup. Made my nerves ignite. I hated him. Hated that I liked him.

I tried wriggling free once more, but his right hand came up, his fingers grazing my neck before he cupped my face. I wanted to be mad, but I felt myself melting despite it.

"That forest nymph is only a friend, Elowyn." He ran his knuckles along my jaw, stopping above my collarbone.

My breath hitched—his touch like a branding iron on my skin.

"Don't you dare believe for one second I've been able to stop thinking about those soft fucking lips on mine, over and over and over again." His grip on my waist tightened, and I arched into him. His nose brushed mine as he kissed the corner of my mouth. "Your sweet taste is still on my tongue, firefly. If you only knew how badly I wish to do it again."

Talon's confession took me by surprise, and I stilled, my lips parting.

I felt weightless—wanting. Knowing I wasn't suffering alone with the same hungry thoughts had me soaring from the flesh and bones that chained me to the ground. The show he put on with the nymph was impressive. Convincing, even. Yet with every laugh and touch, he had been thinking about me.

The air in the hall thinned, and my chest rose and fell haphazardly. "What's stopping you now?"

Talon rested his forehead against mine and smiled, our lips lightly brushing. "You have no fucking idea what you do to me."

I held onto him tighter, and he nuzzled into my neck. A wave of goosebumps exploded over my body as his lips met my skin.

"If anyone were to find out." He sunk his teeth into my neck, and I moaned, my fingers pulling his hair.

"Show me." It almost sounded like I was begging.

I breathlessly waited for his next move as he kissed the now sensitive spot, filling my core with need before he gripped my chin. Every nerve ending launched into overdrive.

He leaned in—so close I could almost taste the cloves on his tongue—when his eye darted to the dark end of the hallway, and he released me. "Someone's coming."

My body went cold from his lack of touch like a flower starved for light when he interlocked his fingers with mine.

"We need to go." Without warning, he pulled me along with him and took off down the corridor.

My legs strained to keep up as he made sharp, unexpected turns, ducking into nearby enclaves and secret passageways, all the while keeping me anchored to his side. I'd have tried to memorize the routes for a later advantage, but my mind was clouded with his closeness.

My heart thumped wildly in my chest in fear of getting caught, yet it was exhilarating in the same breath.

Talon was right.

Maybe I did have a penchant for trouble.

TWENTY-FIVE

Talon placed a hand over my mouth, silencing me as he shut the door behind us. A wicked gleam lit his eyes. The heavy thud of boots passed by a few seconds later, disappearing down the corridor, and we erupted into laughter.

"Holy shit, that was close." Talon chuckled breathlessly. He dropped his head back against the wall, his Adam's apple bobbing as he swallowed hard.

My body hummed along to the alluring melody. I was so engrossed I didn't notice we were still in each other's arms until he looked down and his hair tickled my forehead. I should've left well enough alone and stepped back from his embrace—put an end to these feelings once and for all. Forget about what happened in my bedchambers and the hallway. But I couldn't resist the allure of the flame.

I reached up and pushed it out of his face.

The tips of my fingers caressed his jawline, sending a blazing warmth straight to my core, our chests rising and falling together as one. Stars, his skin was so soft, I couldn't stop touching him. Exploring him.

Neither of us dared blink as I let my fingers drift to his cheek, to his lips. His collarbone.

There was no logical reason for it. No explanation or warning. I don't even think there was a word to describe it, but something intrinsically shifted inside me. As if he awakened a part of my soul that'd never rest again. It was a dangerous line to walk, and one I shouldn't cross.

Talon rested his free hand on the center of my chest. "Your heart is racing." His lips were inches away. Oh, how simple it would be to close the distance and damn it all.

But impulsivity had landed me in this mess in the first place. I knew it wouldn't be my way out. I told myself it was for the best as I slipped from his arms. I told myself there was no other choice as my body protested every movement.

"Come on." Talon kissed the side of my head, leading me into the massive kitchen.

My eyes widened at the size of cast-iron stoves and wood-burning ovens. It was the last thing I'd noticed, too consumed with Talon to give a damn. There were hundreds of copper skillets and saucepans hanging from the walls and a barrage of storage closets and chillers. It was magnificent. The amount of cooking I could get done—

I frowned. My thoughts wandered to my mother alone in our small cottage. If she was eating. How she was fairing. There were only three more trials left before I could go home, and yet it felt more unattainable than it did a month ago. I couldn't believe so much time had passed, and it was even harder to remember life outside of the castle walls.

Talon lifted me by the waist and spun me around, planting me firmly on top of the wooden cooking station. "I should warn you, I'm pretty good in the kitchen."

I arched a brow. "Is that so?"

"Mhm. I make a mean sandwich." He winked, shrugging

off his suit jacket and tossing it onto the counter beside me. His dress shirt underneath pulled taut against his chest as his long, slender fingers unbuttoned his cufflinks—pushing his sleeves up his tanned forearms, one by one.

Just as he did last night, Talon looked so normal. In his element, even. There was no mistaking what a powerhouse he was. No, his tall, lean frame was impossible to ignore. Those hands—his arms—etched to perfection with years of training behind them.

I cleared my throat, averting my eyes to anything that wasn't a six-foot-something fae guard that dominated my thoughts, and fidgeted with my bell sleeve. "Do you think anyone will come in here?"

"It's not likely." Talon rinsed his hands. "Fae balls, parties, any gatherings that include faerie juice and music, are guaranteed to last well into the early morning hours. No one's going to be leaving anytime soon." He turned off the water, dried his hands, and faced me. "You would've danced until you died if I hadn't hauled you away."

I huffed a laugh. "Of course. Why would the king do anything that wouldn't benefit him?"

Talon strolled over to the crisper, grabbing a couple pounds of packaged chicken and salami. "I had half the nerve to let it happen, since your stubborn ass has to do everything the hard way."

He placed the meats onto the table beside me, heading back to the crisper to dig out a wooden box of assorted fruit and cheese next.

I grabbed the round of uncured ham, juggling it in my hands. "Isn't anyone going to notice you're gone?"

Talon shrugged, walking back over with the wooden crate tucked under one arm and a loaf of bread in the other. "It was an oddity I even showed up in the first place."

"You don't normally go?"

"I don't usually have a human girl to babysit." He winked again, snatching the ham from the air before I could catch it.

I flipped him my middle finger. "You know what I mean."

Talon pushed his hair out of his eyes as he reached for a chef's knife, keeping quiet as he chipped away at the link of salami. He was deep in thought, seeming to contemplate whether he should let me in. If I was trustworthy of such information. I couldn't help but imagine what he'd experienced in his lifetime. Everyone he'd encountered. Surely, he must have his reasons for separating himself from the fae court, yet why did he remain part of it?

I rubbed my palms against my thighs, nervous about opening up, but if it'd help him do the same, it was worth a shot. A truth for a truth.

"Back home, I was the infamous bastard child of Deirdre Rosewood. The disgraced lady-in-waiting who couldn't keep her legs closed." My mouth went dry. "I was teased relentlessly growing up. Mostly in primary school, but that sort of thing sticks with you, you know? My mother moved us out to the countryside to distance ourselves from most of it. From all the gossip and whatnot, but she never let on that any of it bothered her. She never let it dull her light. How anyone could remain optimistic despite all that slander." I shook my head, disgusted with the memory of how they treated us.

Talon eyed me from his peripheral vision as he sliced a block of cheese, waiting for me to continue.

"I always blamed myself. For being born, for her getting sick. All of it. As stupid as it is, I thought ... I don't know. I guess I thought that if I could find her the cure, people wouldn't think I was useless."

Talon set the knife on the counter and picked up a slice of bread, topping it with chicken and cheese, tomato, lettuce, salami, and a smear of dressing. He stood in front of me, my legs straddling his frame as he cupped my chin.

"You have nothing to prove to anyone, Elowyn. You're not useless. Far from it, now open," he ordered, placing the sandwich at the edge of my lips.

I did what he asked, and he slipped it into my mouth. The bold flavors erased all memories of that horrible feast.

Talon was right. I hadn't realized how badly I needed to eat. I took the rest of the sandwich from his hands, and he hopped up on the counter next to me, picking up one of his own.

"I grew up in Rahway." His eyes were fixed on his lap where he held his sandwich. "It's about a day's journey north of here. It was a close-knit town, safe. But then one day, faerie poachers showed up and slaughtered half the people. Including my parents."

Oh stars. My stomach sank. "Faerie poachers?" I yearned to reach out and touch him. Somehow show my support, but I kept my hands in my lap.

He lifted his shoulder, taking a bite of his sandwich. "That's what they told us. It's why I joined the guard. I thought maybe if I could find who did it and deliver justice for my family, then everything would be right again."

Talon's comment about how he understood what I was going through became all too clear. I hated we had that in common.

"Was it?"

"I don't know." He looked sad, mustering an indifferent smile when he noticed me watching. "In my twenty years in the guard, I've never come across a poacher. Not once." Talon tore off a piece of his sandwich and tossed it into his mouth. "Then King Gareth died, and King Harkin rose to power, and everything went downhill."

He picked at his sandwich for a moment before finishing it,

his eyes haunted by distant memories. Not in the same way my mother's eyes were when she talked about my father—with nostalgia and fondness. No. The look in Talon's eyes was painful. Heartbreaking, even.

I placed my hand on his knee, and he topped it with his, interlocking our fingers.

A silent understanding.

"Breana told me a story before she died about the fae king who was murdered by his brother. Was that true?"

Talon inched back, sitting cross-legged on the table, and motioned for me to do the same. "It depends on who you ask— the court is largely divided. King Gareth was my mentor. When I heard the rumors, I couldn't think straight." He pulled my legs onto his lap, and I leaned back on my hands. "He took me under his wing when I needed it the most. So, I confronted the newly appointed king in front of the entire court."

"I threatened to leave," Talon continued, mindlessly running his fingertips along my knees and thighs. "He didn't appreciate that. As you can imagine. The king stripped me of my title. Demoted me. And in my position, that's worse than death. Yet even though I ridiculed him in front of his newly inherited court, King Harkin wasn't about to lose his strongest guard. Not completely."

Talon's fingers inched past my knees, caressing the outermost parts of my thighs. Simple. Easy. I couldn't remember the last time I felt that way with a male. With anyone.

"What'd he do?" By the way his jaw set, I knew it was a difficult topic. I reached out, lightly grazing my nails along his forearms, needing to touch him—comfort him.

"He knew my little sister meant the most to me. I'd do anything for her. So, he imprisoned her for my mistake."

My back went rigid, my hand dropping from his arm. "Are you serious?"

The hard-set expression on his forehead told me everything I didn't want to know. Every time I thought King Harkin couldn't get any more repulsive—

How could his court tolerate such a corrupt ruler?

"He began the trials shortly after and came to me with a proposition. If my human won, not only would he rank me back to my former position, but he'd release my sister as well."

My eyebrows furrowed. "But you've never participated?"

"My sister made me vow I wouldn't. Told me I'd be selling my soul if I did, fully convinced the fabled princess would soon return to take back the throne."

I arched a brow. "The fabled princess? Wait, but wouldn't that mean—"

"That King Gareth had a secret child?" Talon shrugged. "It was a risk I was willing to take."

I let out a breath and sagged further back on my hands, my head dizzy with the new information. Was he ever allowed to visit his sister? How many other people did the king imprison—threaten—to keep Faerway in order?

He plucked a grape from the stem and popped it into my mouth, letting his thumb finger linger on my bottom lip. "I see those wheels turning, firefly. Don't worry yourself about any of this. This is my fight."

That was easy for him to say. "But what if I don't win?"

"What if you do?"

I shrugged. It felt more like a pipe dream than reality, if I were being honest. After hearing that, was I to truly believe the king would let anyone walk out of here?

"Look at me." Talon lifted my chin to meet his gaze. "Don't do that. Don't run away in those mad thoughts of yours, you're only going to get lost. You're more than capable. And brave. And strong. And insufferable. And stubborn." He cupped my face, threading a strand of hair behind my ear before he kissed the tip of my nose. "I should probably get you back to your chambers before we get into any more trouble." He released a breathy laugh.

I kissed the other side of his smile. "It seems I have a proclivity for it."

Talon nodded, giving my thigh one more squeeze before he hopped off the table, helping me down after him. The edge of his thumbs came dangerously close to the underside of my breasts as his hands slid up my sides.

But his touch never came.

I wondered if it ever would. If either of us dared cross the line more than we already had, we'd risk losing something more than our lives.

He grabbed my hand, pulled me into his chest, and kissed the crown of my head. "You're going to drive me mad, firefly. What am I possibly going to do with you?"

There were a few things I could think of.

TWENTY-SIX

There'd only been one time in my entire life that I'd ever truly been scared. When my mother first got sick, it felt like my entire world came crashing down. Like everything around me sped up, and all I could do was watch as it all passed me by. I was only a child. A child that suddenly had an enormous weight to carry all by herself. The pressure to remain strong. Although I knew most of it was self-imposed, the baggage was agonizing to carry.

Yet, as I stood at the top of the landing that led into the arena, looking out across the mountainous terrain, to the tall, narrow plateau in the center—my heart lodged in my throat—I knew in my bones that this was a close second.

Much to my relief, Talon had already disappeared to his place at the observation deck, far, far away from me. If I caught one more whiff of his inebriating musk, I was going to shove him into the bottomless ravine. I needed to focus, not drool over his lingering touch on my thigh from the other night. To say our walk to the arena had been tense would be an understatement. Just like our training session had been yesterday.

I was convinced the entire kingdom could hear the deafening silence between us. Our energies biting and snapping at each other like two starved wolves. Pretending there was no chemistry between us—pretending nothing forbidden happened behind closed doors—was getting harder and harder to do.

My stomach twisted into a million knots as I held onto the splintered railing, my hands trembling and slicked with moisture as I tried not to look down. It wasn't that I simply feared heights—they petrified me.

One foot after the other, I told myself, taking long, deep breaths. Everyone's eyes lingered on me as I made my way to the plateau, Aeron and Calandra in my sights.

"Can you walk any slower, Rosewood? I'd like to get this over with," Kelvin sneered from behind me. He quickened his pace, causing the bridge to sway, and I clutched the railing with both hands, my torso hanging over the edge as he shouldered past me. "What's wrong, fae fucker? Having second thoughts?" He walked backward and mocked me. "I can give you a quick push. Ya know, spare you the embarrassment, give you an honorable death."

My knuckles turned white as he imitated moaning sounds, deliberately swaying the bridge back and forth at my expense until he hopped onto the plateau.

I shut my eyes, willing my nausea to settle. It continued to swing underneath me, creaking with each movement.

The moment my feet touched solid land, I collapsed to my knees and kissed the lime green grass in gratitude. If making it across that bridge was any testament to how the trial was going to go, I was going to need to step up my game. My training sessions had improved, and I was feeling more confident than ever defending myself—a perk of repressed sexual desires. Although, I'd think Talon would disagree, having threatened me on more than one occasion to keep my attitude in check.

I needed to hone that. If I could, I'd be okay.

"Welcome back, humans. You all are looking more nourished since the last time we saw each other." King Harkin cackled, provoking the bloodthirsty fae court that howled their amusement, and I fought the urge to roll my eyes. "Settle down, settle down," he went on, sitting back in his throne. "We have an interesting trial ahead of us today. One with much higher stakes than the ones before. Today, competitors, your patience will be challenged. Your morality threatened. Four of you stand before us, but only three may leave."

I turned around to find the dilapidated bridge gone, surrounded only by clouds and the faerie court above.

Calandra gave me a somber smile as she tipped her pointed chin to the board—her name in dead last.

I sucked in a breath, hoping it wasn't a premonition to come, before sending her a reassuring but subtle shake of my head.

It had been a week since the potion trial. A week since Breana walked into this very arena never to come back out. Somehow it felt like it was merely hours ago. In other ways, it felt like years. Yet there we were again, destined to relive the same ending. Our lives once again, dangling in the king's hands.

I swallowed—not daring to wish for anything this time.

"Four competitors. Two swords. The bridge to the exit will reappear when one of you has died. Good luck."

My eyes darted to Talon as the veil shimmered to life, my heart pounding against my rib cage. "Whatever means necessary," he mouthed before the bright blue sky enveloped him and the rest of the court.

A second passed, and no one moved, the swords in the center of the plateau glistening under the sunlight, taunting us.

Aeron and I watched each other, gauging each other's next move when he broke from his spot, running full speed toward the swords. I didn't waste any time as I took off after him, refusing to be a sitting duck—not when we were this close to the end. If he could, I knew he would take both weapons and anoint himself the bringer of our deaths.

Kelvin trailed close behind me, attempting to outrun Calandra, who was on his heels. It was a recipe for a dog pile—a game of chicken to see who'd skid to a stop first.

Aeron and I reached the swords first, each of us grabbing one at the same time, narrowly avoiding each other as we halted to a stop. I extended my sword out in front of me—readying for his attack—and its weight strained my arm as I backed up to where Calandra stood.

Whatever means necessary.

I held my ground, Aeron closing the distance between us with stealth-like ease.

"You don't think you stand a chance, do you?" He thrust his sword toward my stomach.

I leaped back, and he laughed, turning his attention to Kelvin, who flanked his side.

"Look at her, man. I almost feel bad about how easy this will be." He swung his sword at my legs, and I tried to block, but I wasn't quick enough. The tip nicked my pants, drawing blood, and I stumbled back, catching my balance before I fell onto my back.

I spat at his feet. "Go to hell."

"Aw, we're only playing." Kelvin smirked, his brown eyes almost black.

Aeron clicked his teeth. "You like to play games, don't you, sweetheart?" He jabbed his sword at me again, but this time I blocked it, the sound of metal on metal piercing the air. Aeron gave me a sleazy smile before adding, "It'll be fun. We'll take it easy on you, I promise."

"And when you're done bleeding out, we'll move on to

you, princess"—Kelvin pointed to Calandra, who stood behind me—"I wonder how far that fall is? A five hundred feet?"

"I'd guess a thousand," Aeron answered. "Your mangled body will look like a drop of blood from up here." He used the tip of the sword to scratch his scalp.

I launched toward him while his guard was down, my blade catching his thigh before he could position his sword to block, ripping into his flesh.

"You fucking bitch!" He seethed, swinging his sword through the air.

I rotated out of the way before it could make contact, wielding my blade out in front of me, readying to block.

His counterattack never came.

Instead, he laughed, resting his blade behind his neck as he strolled toward me. "You've got nerve, I'll admit. But you're only making this harder on yourself, sweetheart. Keep pissing me off."

Kelvin and Aeron split up, attempting to cattle us to the edge of the plateau, but I dug my feet into the ground, keeping a hawk-like focus on Aeron as he circled in front of me. "Keep your back to mine, Calandra." I faced off with him—my pulse pounding in my ears as Kelvin disappeared from my peripheral vision.

"How adorable," Aeron mocked, his expression bordering on feral.

This was a game to them. One death would give them the win. Two would mean an advantage in the next trial. A sick, deranged game they'd stop at nothing to win.

"You think you're going to save her? I hate to break it to you, but both your bodies will be at the bottom of the ravine when we're finished here. Sorry, you won't be able to save your mommy."

I bared my teeth at him. "Keep underestimating me, Aeron."

"Did you hear that, Kelvin?" He yelled behind me, "She thinks we're underestimating her."

Kelvin howled in amusement. "You were right, Aeron, she is delusional."

A faint buzzing sound hummed in the distance, growing closer and louder with each passing second until a large black cloud came into view. My eyes strained to see what it was—stretching and yawning as it moved closer.

The sound oddly familiar.

I peered over Aeron's shoulder. "What is that?"

He rolled his eyes. "Honestly, sweetheart? You're going to need to be a little more creative than that. That's the oldest—"

"No, I'm serious." My eyes grew wide.

Wings.

Hundreds and thousands of sprites barreled toward us, their razor-sharp teeth jutting out of their mouths, itching for a taste of flesh.

"Duck!" I yelled as I dropped to the ground, dodging the fleet of sprites as they swarmed above, blocking out the sun.

Calandra fell to the ground with me, attempting to cover her head and neck as they nipped at the skin on her hands.

I crawled over to her, batting away the sprites that flew overhead, and somehow my hands escaped injury. I'd lost sight of Aeron and Kelvin, although their deep screams exploded from somewhere behind me.

"Hail King Gareth," one chanted as it buzzed past my ear.

I curled into a ball, stopping short of making it to Calandra, who cried in agony. One after another, the sprites flew over my head, evading me, chirping words of encouragement, and whistling their praises.

My brows knitted together so tightly that my forehead

ached. I didn't know why they spoke to me, let alone what any of it meant. Why weren't they attacking me? Was this part of the trial? Retaliation toward King Harkin? Surely, he'd put a stop to it if it were—

Before I could analyze it any further, the arena went silent, and the sun returned overhead, warming my back.

The sprites were gone as quickly as they had arrived, the only proof of their appearance being the tiny chunks of skin missing from the other competitor's limbs.

I shuffled to my feet with my sword in tow.

Aeron's back was to me as he examined his injuries—clueless of his surroundings or where his sword lay on the ground. I looked at him and back to the sword that was only a few feet away and made a run for it, grabbing it before he realized it was missing.

"Calandra!" I shouted, tossing it over to her. She staggered to her feet, attempting to catch it, but Kelvin intercepted it.

Yanking Calandra up by her hair, he held her hostage with the sword to her throat.

His eyes glazed over, bloodshot—his pupils dilated so wide the whites were practically nonexistent. Surrounding them, tiny claw marks and chunks of skin were torn and bleeding. "Come any closer and I'll slit her throat, then gut you next."

Calandra cackled—her eyes glazing over until they, too, were void of any life. "Let me go. I want to kill her myself," she snapped. "She's not shit, anyway."

I stepped back. Part of me wanted to run from whatever the hell was happening, but I hadn't come this far to flee.

"Ooh. What do you think, Aeron? Should I let her go? What a beautiful irony that would be. Friend killing friend. You'd know about that, right, Elowyn?"

"I think you're a pussy who wouldn't have made it this far if it weren't for me," Aeron spat. "So why don't you shut your damn mouth so I can fucking think for once!"

I slowly backed away from them, swallowing hard. There was venom in those sprites' bites. Venom that turned them vile.

Angry.

Wrathful.

Running a hand down my face, I contemplated my options. There was no escaping. I needed to face this head-on.

Luck wasn't coming to help this time, and I was going to kill or be killed.

"Where do you think you're going?" Aeron demanded, stalking over to where I stood.

"Ugh, cut the shit, and kill her already. It's pathetic," Calandra said, Kelvin's blade still at her throat. She didn't seem to mind—in fact, she looked amused as she watched with delight—and eagerness in her eyes I'd only seen in the king's. The glee radiating from her made her lean into the blade, the edge cutting into her skin.

I swallowed and tried to wet my dry mouth. "Yeah, Aeron, kill me. Unless, of course, you're all talk."

He cursed under his breath and lunged for me. Rage filled dead eyes.

There was no time for fear as I blocked his attack, and his next, my arms straining to keep up with his hasty movements. There was no room for mistakes. One wrong move and he'd overpower and disarm me.

I cursed as I whirled to the right, thrusting my blade toward his knee, but he leaped out of the way, coming back with even greater force.

"She almost took out your kneecap." Kelvin laughed and sounded deranged. "And you call me a pussy!"

Aeron whipped around. "What did you call me?" he yelled, charging at Kelvin like a bull.

Everything happened in a blur—Kelvin shoved Calandra to the ground, using her as a decoy to trip him as his sword came slashing down.

Aeron leaped out of the way, avoiding Kelvin's blade. But he crashed into the ground, scrambling to get to his feet as soon as he made impact.

"Calandra, behind you!"

"Go to hell, Elowyn," she seethed, ignorant of Kelvin as he swung his blade back.

I lunged toward them—toward Calandra—plunging my sword into Kelvin's side. Then I ripped it out, exposing his meaty insides.

His eyes widened as he stumbled back, and back. His arm falling to his side as blood sprayed from his ribs.

I stabbed him again.

And again.

"What did you do?" Aeron screamed as he raced over to Kelvin to save him, but he wasn't quick enough.

Kelvin stepped off the edge—his body weightless for a moment—and tumbled toward the ravine below.

I knew I should feel bad. Guilty, even. But I was numb, and he deserved it. He was going to kill my friend. Even though she continued to look at me as if she wanted to kill me, I knew it was the trial. It wasn't the real Calandra I'd grown to call a friend.

The bridge appeared to our right, and I grabbed her hand, forcing her along despite her protest as Aeron picked up the sword and made a beeline toward us. The planks ached and whined under each step—Aeron hot on our heels.

There wasn't time to feel the tremble in my knees as the bridge shook. Or the fear that'd gripped me in the beginning.

"What's going on?" Calandra panicked. "Is the trial over? Who died? No! Is it me? Am I dead?" Her grip tightened around my hand, and I peeked over my shoulder at her, relieved to find hazel eyes that'd returned to their normal size.

"No, you're not dead. But if we don't get off this bridge in two seconds, we will be."

Calandra huffed her understanding.

I pulled her along, neither of us slowing until we made it back to the landing.

TWENTY-SEVEN

The chatter in the mess hall drowned out around me as I stared blankly ahead at Calandra. Numb was my new normal. I took comfort in the absence.

Her lips moved, but I couldn't hear what she was saying over the whooshing sound in my ears. It'd been two days since the last trial—since I'd killed Kelvin—and I still didn't feel any remorse. Talon said it was shock. Denial. But I knew it was deeper than that.

I was aware of what I'd done, and if I had to go back and redo it, I'd do it again in a heartbeat. Kelvin might not have been as much of a monster as Aeron, but I refused to sit back while the people I cared about got hurt. Not anymore.

"Elowyn. Hello, Elowyn..."

I shook my head—refocusing—and the chatter returned to full volume, assaulting my ears. "I'm sorry, I didn't hear you. What'd you say?"

"I was saying how we haven't had a chance to talk after the trial, and I feel bad I've not been able to thank you properly. I was such an asshole." Her brows formed crests of wrinkles between them.

Poking the brown mush around on my plate, I shrugged. "It's all good, you had no control over it. It was him or you, ya know? The decision was simple."

"Yeah, I guess. There are only two more trials left. What are we going to do if we both make it to the end? I don't think I'll be capable of killing you, Elowyn. Even Aeron."

"You'd be surprised what you're capable of when it comes down to it. But there's no point worrying about it until we must, okay? Just eat." I chewed on my words. Telling her not to worry was rich, especially coming from me. Who was I to give advice when I couldn't turn off my thoughts?

Calandra grimaced. "You haven't touched your plate."

I didn't need her to feel bad for me or worse, worry about me. But the truth was, I didn't have an appetite. It wasn't because of what I'd done or because I was sad. I was tired. The kind of tiredness you felt in your bones that only a weeklong sleep could fix—if only that was a luxury I could afford.

So, instead, I mustered a smile. "I ate some earlier," I lied. "To be honest, I only came down hoping I'd catch you to make sure you were okay. I need to meet Talon to train in a few, so I'm going to get some fresh air first. Do you want the rest?" I pushed the tray in her direction.

She scrunched her nose and giggled. "No thanks. If I have to look at any more brown mush, I'll throw up all over the table."

"Yeah, I get that." I picked my tray off the table and stood. "Hey, if I don't see you around before the next trial, try to keep your chin up, okay?"

Calandra nodded, and I smiled.

"Remember, we'll cross that bridge when we get there," I reaffirmed.

I dumped my food into the trash and slipped out of the mess hall, into a quiet part of the castle.

Thoughts of Talon and whatever was transpiring between us plagued me. One—two moments of stupid, reckless, impulsive decisions, and I couldn't get him off my mind. In the quiet moments, he'd invade the space left behind. In the moments not filled with danger, despair, or grief, it was only him.

But I didn't need that.

I needed to be focused on the trials and getting out of this star-forsaken place because both of our loved ones depended on me. I certainly shouldn't be thinking about what it'd mean for us when this was all over.

It was reckless. Foolish. Yet, it didn't stop me from yearning for his touch.

Insufferable fae prick.

Rounding another corner, the large glass doors to the outdoor gardens came into view when a hand latched onto my throat, slamming my body into the stone wall.

I struggled to breathe as Aeron squeezed my windpipe, his lips furling into a cold-blooded snarl. "You stupid bitch!" he spat, droplets of saliva misting my face.

The corner of my vision darkened.

I clawed at his hands, trying to pry his fingers off me. "I—I'm sorry," I choked. "I didn't—"

"Oh, don't you worry, sweetheart. I'll make sure you're sorry. I'll make sure you suffer, you worthless bastard." He squeezed my neck tighter.

I tried flailing my legs—kicking and scratching at his chest and hands—but he didn't let up. My head felt light, my body limp.

If I could only get him off.

The rest of my vision faded fast, my heart slowing to an unnatural rhythm when Talon appeared behind Aeron, whose blue eyes were lit with feral rage. I reached for him, but his focus locked on Aeron, seizing him by the back of his collar.

My eyes fluttered closed, and when they opened, he'd been thrown off me and to the ground.

"You so much as lay another finger on her outside the arena walls and I'll end you, do you understand?" Talon stepped on his throat to keep him obedient.

I slid down the wall and sucked in a breath. Aeron struggled to catch his, flailing under Talon's weight.

"I know I didn't fucking stutter the last time."

Aeron smiled wickedly as Talon pressed down, his neck crunching under his foot, and I stilled, nervous about what was coming next. Seconds passed before he finally nodded in agreement. His face had become a pale blue as he curled into a ball on his side.

I dropped my head back, my pulse beating out of my ears.

Talon extended his arm, and I reached for his hand. "Are you okay?" He helped me up to examine my throat.

I nodded, stretching my neck. "Yeah. Yeah, I'm fine. Let's just..." I pointed to the doors.

Talon released me and stepped over Aeron, opening the doors for me to pass through.

"What were you doing over here?" The concern in his voice was subtle, but it was hard to miss.

And it made my chest warm.

"I needed to clear my head and thought maybe taking a stroll through the gardens would help." My voice sounded raspy as I rubbed my throat.

He arched a brow at me.

"I wasn't trying to run away again." I held up my hands. "It's ... I don't know. Everything feels heavy."

"You need to talk about it, Elowyn. Killing someone— regardless of how well deserved it may have been—is traumatic. You can't keep pretending it didn't happen." His hand rested on the hilt of the dagger at his hip.

"It's not about that. I'm talking about us—or whatever this is." I fingered the end of my braid, keeping my eyes on the ground. "It needs to stop."

A beat of silence passed.

We continued along the cobblestone path, passing the tall golden shrubs toward the conservatory. The sun glowed in the sky above, the golden landscape around us basking in its rays. For such a cruel and barbaric realm, it sure was beautiful. From the moment I stepped foot into Faerway and laid eyes on that picturesque field of flowers, it had me transfixed. Something inside me had clicked into place.

Talon stopped walking. "I agree." The distance between us was painful, and my stomach sank. I knew it was for the best, but it didn't make it hurt any less. "It never should've gone as far as it did." Every word pushed us further apart.

The air turned thick, and I forced back my feelings, hands becoming erratic at my braid. "There are only two more trials left—I'm sure we can put it behind us. It's not like it meant anything."

My heart sank into my chest as he continued walking while I remained where I stood, watching as he strolled away. Surely, he felt the same. He was doing all of this to get his family back. This was all going to end, eventually. Either by my death or going home. Both of us needed a distraction. That was it.

My back stiffened at the sound of the prince's nasal tone. "Ms. Rosewood, fancy meeting you for a stroll."

I cringed, turning around to face him.

"What brings you out here this beautiful afternoon?" he inquired. "I'd thought you'd be busy training."

"Just taking a break before we head back in," Talon replied from my side.

My shoulders sagged.

Prince Bowen looked from me to Talon and back. "Hm. I

see. Well, thank you, guard, but I'm sure the human can reply, no?" He snaked his hand across my lower back, guiding me away from Talon, toward a more secluded part of the courtyard, and it took everything in me not to recoil at his touch. "So, what brings you to the gardens this afternoon?"

"Getting some fresh air. My days here are numbered, so I figured I'd try to make the best of it." I peered up at Talon for reassurance, but he kept his sight focused ahead. His jaw clenched.

"I see, I see. Did you enjoy yourself at the ball the other night? You disappeared far too soon. A shame, if you ask me." His hand came up to my shoulder and squeezed.

I balled my hand into a fist. Who did he think he was? I wanted to smack his hand off me and punch him in the nose for being presumptuous, but I knew better. Males like him didn't take rejection well. Being denied wasn't part of their experience.

"I had too much faerie juice—it was best I went to lie down. I'd gotten pretty sick." The stolen moment Talon and I had shared in the kitchen that night swarmed my thoughts, my skin tingling in response to his soft, caressing touches that harassed my dreams.

Talon tensed beside me as if he was recalling it as well.

The prince laughed. "You can never have too much fae juice, Ms. Rosewood. The only actual solution is to have more. I wish you would've stayed. And to have seen you in my gown, well, that would have been a delight."

An elegant gazebo loomed ahead. Golden vines weaved through the cedar slats, mixing with bronze leaves and flowers. It faced a clear pond filled with an assortment of fish, covered by the shade of a magnificent willow tree. Shade that I suddenly wished would shelter me from the burning palms of the prince.

I took a deep breath and flashed him my most sincere smile as he took my hand in his, helping me step up into the gazebo.

"Speaking of," he continued, taking a seat on the wooden bench that faced the pond, motioning for me to do the same.

I hesitated, looking to Talon for confirmation before my attention was stolen once more.

"I've been thinking. Seeing as how you didn't need help with a dress, I wanted to offer you something *more* desirable. I have some pull on what goes on around here, you know." He leaned back. "Perhaps your freedom?"

My spine went rigid as I sat beside Prince Bowen, keeping as much distance between us as possible. I looked at him. His blond hair glistened in the sunlight and matched the golden landscape around us. A prince among prosperity, he fit in as easily as the bronze leaves among gold.

"My freedom?" I pressed, swallowing the lump in my throat. "As in, going back home to Wendover?"

Prince Bowen waved his hand. "Yes, of course."

"Why?"

Talon rested his shoulder against the archway and cleaned his fingernails with a small knife.

"Why not?" the prince pondered, giving Talon a side glance. "I'm feeling generous. After all, I'm not my father." He paused. "Of course"—he pinned me with expectant eyes—"I would like something in return. A favor, if you will."

Disappointment twinged in my chest. There was a catch— and there always was with the fae. I noticed Talon clench his jaw and briefly roll his eyes in annoyance before he leveled his expression back into neutrality.

"Like what?"

"Your time. A night of pleasantries, to be exact." He adjusted himself on the bench, rubbing his hands along the top of his pants. He appeared sincere. Nervous, even.

And for a quick moment, he didn't appear to be the evil,

maniacal heir to his father's corrupt court. Rather a sad, lost soul yearning for connection.

"The power you hold, Elowyn. It almost brings me to my knees. I'd give you your freedom just for a night with you. It's a shame we couldn't spend more time together at the ball." His eyes cut to Talon.

Only a night? That didn't sound too bad.

I mulled over his words, trying to find the loophole, but couldn't find anything that stood out. Nevertheless, there was no doubt in my mind it was too good to be true. Too simple. And I knew when it came to the fae, nothing was ever simple.

Yet, part of me dared to take him up on it.

Talon cleared his throat. "While as tempting as your offer sounds, Elowyn and I must get back to training"—he fingered the air, signaling it was time to leave—"these next two weeks are imperative with it being the last two trials and all. I'm sure you understand."

The prince and Talon stared each other down.

I sat there awkwardly, tugging at the hem of my shirt, attempting not to appear as awkward as I felt. The look on both of their faces hinted at violence, and I sucked in a breath. Getting as far away from either of them before that threat came true became imperative.

Only, the promise of freedom was within reach, and the thought of turning it away made my insides crawl.

"You keep speaking for the human as if she has no voice of her own." The prince pulled his attention away from Talon and looked at me. His expression was once again welcoming. "Elowyn, you're entitled to relax. You mustn't train every moment of the day—you wouldn't want to burn yourself out, would you? Please, allow me the honor of your company."

"I don't think I made myself clear," Talon snarled, flicking his small knife up his sleeve as he strolled over to me. "There will be no time for socializing."

The prince chewed on a smile, evidently amused by Talon's warning.

"Now, Elowyn," my *keeper* commanded me.

I stood, conflicted, giving the prince a weary smile of my own as I rounded Talon's side. Further and further away until I was back in the main courtyard.

"Keep walking," Talon said. He came up beside me, grabbing my arm.

The warmth of his touch made me trip, and I tried pulling my arm from his grasp for balance. "Let go of me," I demanded, keeping my voice hushed.

"Stop fighting, the prince is watching us." A warning.

I angled my head over my shoulder, attempting to get a glimpse of Prince Bowen.

But Talon yanked me forward once again and growled. "Stars, for once in your damn life, pretend to be a compliant human prisoner. He's suspicious enough as it is."

"That's your own fault." I thrashed again. "Maybe if you would've let me handle it and not let your jealousy take over, he wouldn't be suspicious."

Talon huffed a laugh, slammed his shoulder into the glass door, and shoved me inside the castle. He wasted no time dragging me through the corridor toward the training room.

"Let's get one thing straight," he said, cornering me between the wall and the training room door. "All I care about is winning the trials." He pulled open the door and forced me inside. The familiar musty air smacked me in the face. "And I'd be damned if he tricked you into a never-ending night of stars only knows what, making you forfeit them." He stalked over to the wall of swords and grabbed a dagger, tossing it at me without warning.

This was going to be a challenging session.

Twenty-Eight

My stomach burned as I splayed out on the ground, sweat dripping down my neck, pooling in between my breasts. It was scorching hot in this stupid room. And I didn't have much more left in me before I passed out from heat exhaustion.

"Get up and go again," Talon said from his spot against the wall. He crossed his legs at the ankles, appearing perfectly content as he snacked on an apple, not a lick of moisture on his skin.

I cursed him under my breath.

"I've already done five rounds of sit-ups." I used my wrist to wipe away the sweat beading on my forehead and upper lip. "How many more do I have to do?"

"Until I say you're done," Talon replied without looking up at me.

I rolled my eyes—not jealous my ass. He had some nerve taking his frustration out on me. Especially when he'd agreed that what happened between us meant nothing. I didn't know why that bothered me. Maybe a part of me wished he would've challenged me, tried to prove I was full of it, but he'd surrendered without a fight.

"No, not until you admit it." Huffing a breath, I got to my feet and crossed my arms against my chest.

Talon cocked his head to the side. The corner of his eyes wrinkled as his soft lips pulled into an amused smirk. "And, tell me, what exactly am I admitting to?"

"That it did, in fact, mean something to you." A zap of energy pulsed between us.

"You're going to need to be more specific. Much more specific." His smile grew larger until his sharp teeth were on full display.

"Seriously, Talon? You know what I'm talking about. Stop playing games."

"I'm afraid I'm dreadfully lost, firefly." Talon shrugged. "Please, enlighten me."

I shook my head, biting the inside of my cheek to keep my irritation in check as he toyed with the apple in his hand. "Us kissing, asshole. It wasn't just nothing to you."

Talon sunk his teeth into the apple, his tongue lapping at the pale flesh to gather all the juice. He watched me intently, then chewed. "Ah, that," he said and wiped his bottom lip clean with the pad of his thumb. "You said yourself it meant nothing. Why do you care what I think?" His brow raised expectantly as he continued to chew.

"I don't. I only want you to admit you're full of shit."

"And you're not?" The knowing look he gave me had me shifting on my feet, a warm blush creeping up my neck.

"No."

Talon laughed. It was deep and gruff and made my insides swirl. "I see." He rose to his feet, stretching. My heart skipped as he approached. "Well, in that case, training will be over when you hit a perfect bullseye."

"What? Why? You had me conditioning for over an hour. My arms feel like noodles."

He stopped short of me, his hair tickling my forehead as he leaned down, his lips meeting my ear. "You should have thought of that before you lied to me." His warm breath on my skin sent defiant shivers up my spine. "Now move."

I remained where I stood, frantically getting my thoughts in order.

He strolled past me to the other side of the training room.

It meant nothing—we were both under a ton of stress. Each of us carrying the weight of impossible expectations. We needed an outlet. A mind-blowing, deeply satisfying distraction. It was normal. It meant nothing, yet the more I tried to rationalize it, the harder it became to convince myself it was true.

Where did the truth rest, anyway? It certainly wasn't always black and white. Could we exist outside of this? After...

Inhaling a sharp breath, I grabbed a bow off the rack, balancing it in my hand as I seized a quiver of bows next. I could do this.

Readying at the mark, I pulled the cord taught.

"Keep your sight above the bullseye." Talon sat to my right in a wooden chair, analyzing my form. "The arrow naturally arches down, so you'll better your odds at hitting your mark." He tore into the apple.

"Noted," I deadpanned, aiming my bow straight ahead. Steadying my hands.

I did what he suggested, keeping my focus above the bullseye. Letting out a slow breath, I released the arrow, watching it fly and land a foot away from the mark.

It was hopeless. I dropped my arms, defeated.

"Not bad. You need to relax a little more. Try dropping your shoulders."

I grabbed another arrow from the quiver and tried again.

Dropping my shoulders and letting out a breath—watching in resignation as the arrow bounced off the stone wall onto the ground below. Talon didn't bother to conceal his amusement this time as I let out a string of curses—tempted to *accidentally* release an arrow at where he sat.

My lips pursed. If only I didn't fear the consequences. He'd keep me there all night if I pulled something like that.

Dropping the bow to my side, I faced him, fist clenched. "Please, I wouldn't want you to hold back at my expense." I threaded another arrow through the string.

"Sorry, it's just—" He contained his laughter and said, "I knew we were going to be here a long time—I didn't realize the extent of how bad you were on the bow."

I rolled my eyes. "I'm pretty sure we were all witness to my botched attempt during assessments. You knew what you were getting yourself into." Talon stood up and stalked over to me, his lips pressed together with bewildered amusement. "I assumed it was fear. I couldn't have expected half of what I'd be signing up for." He motioned for me to turn around and grabbed the bow from my hands. "Here, hold it like this." Talon stood behind me and repositioned my hands, keeping his grip on mine as he brought the bow up to my shoulder.

I tried to concentrate on the target, but every fiber in my body was on fire, unable to focus on anything but his touch as his calloused fingertips tickled my skin.

My back pressed into his chest as he pulled me closer to his body, and it took every ounce of strength in me not to arch into him.

Talon's grip on my waist tightened as if he sensed my thoughts, his lips grazing the shell of my ear as he spoke. "Now adjust your stance ... like this." I could smell the crisp apple on his breath and wanted to taste it on his lips. His voice was low and deep as he positioned me—my ass grazing against the bulge in his pants—and he held me in place. His hand traveled further up my waist.

I was too consumed with his nearness to form coherent sentences. I attempted to blink away the lust that fogged my brain. My treacherous body betraying every logical thought I'd tried to convince myself to believe. I wholeheartedly wanted him.

He ripped something open in my chest that yearned only for him. Wanted him. Refused to be satisfied by anything but him.

Talon let his fingers trace up my arm, to my neck, where he tucked a strand of hair behind my ear. I leaned into his touch, and he held my face in his palm.

"Stars, I love the way your body reacts to my touch. It's so damn sexy."

Goosebumps erupted along my skin as his warm breath caressed my cheek, and I angled my head to meet his gaze, our lips inches apart. All I could focus on was his soft, plush lips. I'd forgotten all about the bow in my hands.

But the weight of it straining my arms brought me back to reality. "I have to admit, seeing how jealous you got was kind of sexy."

Talon brushed his sweet lips against mine—a phantom touch that filled me with magic. "Being jealous would imply I wanted something I couldn't have, firefly."

I rolled my eyes.

And he kissed me once more before pulling away. "Now, quit trying to distract me. Focus on the target."

"Me?" I laughed. "You're the one—"

"Shh." Talon placed a finger on my lips to silence me. "No need to point fingers."

I scowled at him as he turned my chin back to center, winking at my expense. Sucking in a breath, I cleared my mind and counted back from five. Then I released it, dropping my shoulder as I pulled the string back.

"There, perfect form." Talon removed his hands from my arms. "Now." He paused. "Let it fly."

I allowed the arrow to soar from my fingers, holding my breath as it neared the target and directly hit the bullseye.

"That's my girl," Talon purred.

~

My chest tightened—blood. There was blood. And it was everywhere.

It coated my hands and arms as I blindly felt my way down the dark hallway, only the dim light from the candelabra guiding my way.

I'd never been on this side of the castle. It was cold and bleak and smelled like mildew. There was no kaleidoscope of colors cascading through the iridescent windows, no ornate decorations, or gold-plated plants. It was lifeless.

Draining my energy with each step I took.

The hairs on the back of my neck stood at attention as a warm pocket of air brushed past me, engulfing me like a tidal wave, stealing my breath away. I leaned against the wall and struggled for air, wheezing, and coughing with such force I became lightheaded.

"Help me, Elowyn!" a muffled voice cried out.

I held the candelabra in front of me, frantically searching the darkness for who the voice belonged to, but the hallway was empty. I didn't have it in me to keep looking.

My lungs burned. My coughing fit grew more intense, and I dropped to the ground, feeling like I'd inhaled poison.

"Elowyn, I'm in here! Please!"

A door materialized across the way.

I rubbed my eyes, unsure if they were playing tricks on me, but as my vision came too, it was still there. My lungs were screaming at me to turn back.

"Help! I'm in here!"

Setting the candelabra on the ground, I crawled toward the door, but it kept moving further and further away. Reaching it was impossible. Breathing was impossible.

The cries became more frantic with each passing second. I fell to my side, needing a moment to gather my breath when a fire erupted—black smoke filling up the space.

I gripped the hair at my scalp, panic searing my chest.

"Elowyn! Why did you do this to us?" a voice screamed.

I used the collar of my dress to cover my nose and turned back, only to be met by a wall of fire preventing me from going any further.

"You did this! It's all your fault!"

The wall of fire encircled me, blocking the door where the voice sounded. Every door in the hall rattled as they tried to escape, and I curled into a ball, covering my ears to block out their screams—trapped in a deadly maze like they were.

"Get up, Elowyn. Reach within," the familiar voice penetrated my thoughts.

I jolted up, whipping my head around the room to find who spoke, only to spot my mother and Breana on the other side of the flames—the hem of their dresses both catching on fire. The words allowed me to breathe, if only momentarily.

I used what was left to warn them. "Run!" I shouted. "Go, get out of here!"

But they didn't. Their haunted eyes locked onto mine as they came closer, the fire spreading up their garments.

"Now, Elowyn!" the voice boomed again.

They kept approaching.

Fear locked in place, forcing me to watch in horror.

I needed to do something. Anything.

Shaking my head of the destructive thoughts, I closed my eyes and did as he instructed, channeling every bit of strength and emotion until it welled to the surface.

I grasped the raw energy in my palms, its frigid intensity numbing my fingers.

Then I opened my eyes—black shadows unleashing from my hands—evaporating the flames and everything in my sight.

～

"Elowyn!" a voice roared from somewhere beside me.

My eyes ripped open, and I sat up, inhaling a deep, full breath. The smell of smoke still lingered in my nostrils. On my hair.

Talon sat at the foot of my bed. His hair appeared disheveled as he ran a hand through his onyx strands.

"Fucking stars." He huffed, resting his forearms on his knees. "It sounded like you were being murdered."

I rubbed the back of my neck, soothing the ache that throbbed deep in my muscles. He remained quiet, allowing me the space as I woke up, blinking my eyes into focus as I got my bearings.

Golden sunlight cascaded through my window, reflecting off the mirror, blinding me.

"How long have I been asleep?" I pulled my legs to my chest.

"Maybe an hour—or two? I was finishing up my shift and heading back to check on you when I heard your screams at the end of the corridor."

My face warmed. "Did anyone else hear me?"

"Aeron's still in the dining hall, if that's what you're wondering." He stood from the bed, concern furrowing his beautiful features. "I know you don't want to, but you need to talk about Kelvin's death."

"This has nothing to do with Kelvin."

"So, what's it about then?"

I didn't know what to say. How could I explain the reasoning behind these nightmares when I didn't know myself? They were because of Lilian. My mother. My fears. All my insecurities and feelings I try to ignore.

I twisted the ring around my finger, ashamed to look at Talon. I didn't want his pity.

Talon stood and paced the room for a moment before he sat in the chair beside me, resting his forearms on his knees. "How long have you been having these nightmares?"

"It's really not that serious—"

"How long, Elowyn?" He pinched the bridge of his nose.

"A month, maybe. Please don't make it a big deal, it's fine. They don't happen all the time."

"You should've told me instead of suffering through it alone. I could've helped." He furrowed his brows as if he were trying to make sense of it. "Some of the things you said..."

My pulse quickened. "Like what?"

"Ah, you know. Like how sexy and charming you think I am—"

An incredulous laugh escaped me as I relaxed back into my own skin, and I tossed a small pillow at him. "You're such an ass. I'm being serious."

He dropped his head, shaking the smile off his face as he flipped the pillow in his hands. I got the impression he wasn't telling me everything, and it made me uneasy.

"Do you remember any of these nightmares?"

I shrugged. "No, not really. Most of the time, I'm trying to save my mother. Or I'm the reason she dies or some combination of the above." I wiped my hands along my sheets. "Honestly, it's more of a lingering feeling, like, I'm..." I shook my head, huffing a laugh. "It's stupid."

Talon rose from the seat and sat next to me, running his thumb along my jaw, his eyes searching mine. What I would've given to have met him at a different time—one where it'd be possible for whatever this feeling was to flourish instead of being snuffed out. We wouldn't be accepted on either side of the river, not together. It was an unfortunate reminder that I couldn't and shouldn't feel this way. How he got past my defenses and found that soft part inside my chest was beyond me.

I hated it.

I loved it.

"Don't put your feelings down like that, firefly." He gently gripped my chin. "Tell me."

I sighed as he released me. "I don't know, I feel rotten. Like I'm this bottomless pit of darkness. Like I suck the light of everyone around me."

Talon appeared lost in thought as he absently traced his fingertips along my collarbone, a slight frown on his lips. "You're not rotten. I know for a fact since you've come into my life, you've brought nothing but light. A lot of irritation, but light."

I rolled my eyes, biting back a smile—hating yet loving how easily he made me laugh. "You're such an ass, you know that?"

"So, I've been told." He cupped my face, his smile slowly fading as his expression turned serious. Eyes searching mine before he spoke. "They're only dreams, firefly. Don't read into them, okay?"

I nodded. It was what I'd told myself enough times.

His focus flicked to my lips before he let his hand fall from my cheek. "Why don't you try to take your mind off it and finish that drawing?"

"Or you can stay," I blurted, surprising myself. Butterflies swarmed my stomach at the thought. Usually, I could keep those intrusive thoughts under control. Yet, it seemed, as my fondness for him grew, that was getting harder and harder to rein in. "Do you have a deck of playing cards? Or we could do a puzzle if you have one of those? I could just ... use some company right now." The words felt immature as they spilled from my mouth, but all I knew was that I didn't want him to leave. It was as if his presence alone kept the bad things lurking inside me at bay. "If you don't have somewhere else to be, that is."

He frowned and stood from the bed—for a second. I thought he would say no, and my chest constricted with embarrassment. I opened my mouth, ready to backpedal, when he turned around, revealing a smile that threatened to rip me in half.

"I suppose since you asked nicely." Talon winked. "But don't think that adorable pouty face will do you any favors. I play to win, firefly. Always."

Twenty-Nine

"What! That's not fair! You're totally making these rules up as you go." I laughed, splaying my cards out in front of me for Talon to see. "I've played this game a hundred times. I know for a fact, an ace of spades is worth more than the queen of hearts."

An impish grin tugged at the corner of his mouth. "Not in Faerway, firefly. I hate to break it to you, but humans have butchered this game over the centuries. You're the one playing it backward."

"Or maybe you're just a sore loser. Have you considered that?" I leaned back in the chair, stretching my arms above my head.

The sun had begun its descent, dripping a pink and orange watercolor mosaic onto the world below that painted the chamber walls a golden hue. A few hours and five games later, I learned how to spot his tells. The way he smiled when he lied. How the corner of his right eye twitched when he was deep in thought. My favorite, however, was the way his jaw feathered when I outwitted him.

Stars, how badly I wanted to lick those corded muscles

while I threaded my fingers through his soft hair. I shifted in my seat, licking my lips with the thoughts.

"Except, that's impossible. I never lose, firefly." He winked. "You should know better than that by now."

"You just hate being told no."

"Same thing." He waved a hand. "One more game before we call it a night?" His tone was hopeful, and it matched my heart.

I nodded, our gazes lingering on each other a beat longer than normal before he looked away with a smile.

His fingers riffled the cards into a bridge, shuffling and cutting the deck with ease before he dealt them out with one hand.

I swallowed hard as he swiftly flicked the cards from the deck, imagining all the different things his nimble fingers were capable of doing.

Talon noticed me watching—more like drooling—and winked again, turning the skin on my neck into a blazing inferno.

Despite the eye roll that followed, the truth of the matter was I loved this. Being with him. It was the most relaxed I'd felt in weeks. The most I'd laughed.

I didn't know what the future held or if it was the last time I'd ever enjoy someone else's company, so I wanted to soak up every second. Clearing my throat, the room became charged with anticipation as I picked up the cards. A palpable energy buzzed through my body when our fingers brushed and created an electrifying tension. There was no way I'd be able to forget him should I make it out of this hellhole. And I wasn't sure I wanted to.

He pushed me to my limits. He believed in me. Refused to let me give up. Called out my bullshit.

Loathe as I was to confess it—and I doubt I would to him —I wouldn't have survived so long without him.

I fanned my cards to face my chest and concealed a smirk. It was nearly a perfect hand, with almost a full run of tens and a set of spades. As much as I didn't want this night to end so quickly, the satisfaction of beating Talon would be well worth it.

He flipped over the top card, revealing an eight of clubs that I could either pick up in exchange for one in my hand or pass.

"Pass."

Talon arched a brow and picked it up for himself, placing a two of hearts in its place. "I hate to break it to you, firefly, but I already have this game in the bag." He leaned back in his chair, letting his foot graze the side of my calf as he crossed his ankles.

My eyes flickered to the table, but I wouldn't let him distract me. Talon played dirty. This time, it wouldn't work.

"Always so confident. It's kind of cute." I pulled from the stockpile and stuck my tongue out at him—a king of spades. He had no idea what was about to hit him. "Too bad it's near-sighted."

Talon laughed, deep and full of that rare boyish charm that filled me with warmth in the places that usually felt cold. "I'm sorry, can you repeat that? I stopped listening after you said I was cute."

I kicked him under the table. "Stars. That would be the only thing you heard." He shrugged as if to say I should've known, and I kicked him again. "Go asshole, it's your turn."

We went back and forth, collecting and discarding cards in tense silence until we were halfway through the deck. I knew there was no way he had a better hand—I was sure of it.

I'd formed three separate melds that included a run of spades and diamonds, as well as a set of tens. It was as perfect as it could get. I beamed with delight while I waited for Talon to take his last turn and knocked on the table, signaling the end of the game.

And that I won.

Talon sucked his teeth, trying but failing to not look upset —the big baby—and splayed his cards on the table. He had a few good sets and a run of hearts, but it wouldn't be enough.

I smiled as I laid mine down and leaned back in my seat, enjoying the pitiful expression that wrinkled his forehead.

He really did hate losing.

It was glorious.

"If I'm not mistaken, this beats your high score, no?" I teased, stacking the cards back into a pile before handing them to Talon.

He dropped his head and chuckled. "Mhm. I'll let you have this moment, firefly. But the gloves come off next time."

He wished.

Rising from the table, I straightened my back and eased the strain in my neck with a slow roll. Eventually, I found myself drawn to the large bay windows and wandered over.

The once bustling courtyard of fae below had grown silent and empty from my viewpoint. Gone was the array of colorful folk parading about, some who dressed in eccentric fashions, while others wore nothing but rags. Curiosity itched to the surface as I wondered where they went after nightfall. If they lived in the castle or on the outskirts of the surrounding city. A small part of me yearned to find out. To dive headfirst into the culture. To explore.

In a realm as beautiful as theirs, with equally fascinating individuals, there had to be more than met the eye.

I strolled over to the bed and flopped onto the mattress with a thud. A million emotions swirled inside my chest. "I can't believe there's only two more trials left," I said after a moment, keeping my gaze locked on the ceiling. "I'm trying not to think about it too much. It sends me into a panic if I do, and I get shaky and nauseous." I wanted to look at him but didn't. "And I'm not ready to die, Talon. There're so many things that I want to do. Places to see. Foods to eat." I wrung my hands. "I'm terrified," I whispered.

There it was—the truth I'd been trying to run from. The truth that seeped into my dreams

The bed dipped as Talon laid down next to me, propping himself up on an elbow. "You're not going to die, firefly." He laced his fingers with mine and pulled me closer.

"You don't know that. Aeron's out for blood. The king is absolutely mad. When we step into that arena in a few days, anything can happen. None of us stand a chance."

"You're right. I should just start preparing your obituary now. What a tragedy, I was just starting to like you too."

My jaw dropped, and I shoved him in the shoulder.

"I'm kidding, I'm kidding." He laughed and brought my hand to his mouth, lightly kissing each of my knuckles.

The delicate touch of his lips on my skin turned me to liquid, and I had to make an effort not to squirm closer to him. "Mhm, you better be."

"Or what?" Talon pushed, his eyes growing dark. He ran his knuckles along my rib cage before his hand settled on my waist.

I sucked in a breath. That familiar, relentless pull between us sparked to life as we watched each other, my pulse raging in my veins. "Or I'd challenge you to a duel."

His head tipped back with laughter. "Okay, settle down, firefly. I wouldn't want you to hurt yourself."

Forever insufferable.

"One of these days, I'm going to put you in your place." I playfully shoved Talon in the shoulder, and he tickled my ribcage, pulling me with him as he rolled onto his back.

"Give me your worst," he challenged.

Through my fit of giggles and several minutes of attempting to find his vulnerable, sensitive spots, I found myself on top of him, straddling his waist. My thighs ached to clamp around him tighter.

His smile was feral. He adjusted himself underneath me.

Our faces inches apart.

I took in his sharp features, remembering to breathe as my laughter subsided—wondering if Talon could feel my erratic heartbeat. Stars, what I'd give to look at him forever. No painting or illustration could ever truly capture his other-worldly essence. My chest ached as I traced his jawline with the pad of my fingertips, our noses brushing as he leaned up to kiss me. The memories of him wouldn't be enough.

I pulled away at the last second, biting back a smile. "You don't think I was going to let you kiss me that easily, do you?"

Talon shrugged. "I was hopeful."

The night of the faerie ball replayed in my head. How passionately he claimed me in that dark, secluded hallway. How every nerve ending had caught fire and turned my insides into molten lava. The way my body reacted to his touch was unnervingly hypnotizing, yet the thing that stood out the most was how badly I craved more—and how often I fantasized about it. About Talon.

Maybe it was the fact my mortality was inching closer by the day, or maybe I yearned for physical connection, whatever the reason, I couldn't stop myself from trailing kisses down his neck, relishing in the way his chest rose and fell with deep breaths.

Stars, how badly I wanted him. To feel him.

Talon flipped me onto my back, taking advantage of my momentary distraction, and ran his fingers along the underside of my breast.

I arched into his touch, my skin purring with bliss. I needed more. So much more.

His lips grazed my jaw, tracing the curvature of my ear with his tongue. "You should know I always get what I want, firefly."

His rough timbre sent shivers up my spine, and my legs tightened around him involuntarily.

"And what is that, exactly?" I breathed, gripping the hair at the nape of his neck.

Talon's lips tickled my skin as his tongue licked the tip of my nose. "You. Always you."

His hands found their way to the hem of my shirt, his calloused fingers grazing my stomach, and I arched into his touch again.

My fingernails sank into the tension of his shoulders while his hands firmly gripped my thighs, drawing me nearer. A low hum reverberated through my body, and I concealed a satisfied smile, tracing my hands down the length of his arms. I was growing more and more impatient with each touch. Each kiss.

I clung to him, holding him to me. Feeling the sharp nips and fervent suction on my throat, I stifled my moans with limited success.

His lips crashed onto mine, devouring any escaping sounds in a passionate collision, swallowing them.

I opened for him. Welcomed his tongue with my own as it dipped into my mouth. Drunk off cinnamon and magic. He teased me in return, rolling and sliding it in and out, taunting me with his slow and diligent strokes while his fingers roamed the back of my thigh.

My body ached for him—it needed more.
More.

My spine tingled as he lifted my top, letting his knuckles trail up my rib cage and leaving goosebumps in their wake. My hips bucked in response, but he was taking his time, relishing my curves. Caressing his hands down my body.

"Run away with me," he said. "When this is all over and you get the cure for your mother, run away with me."

I paused, my skin flushing from his sudden confession. "What? Are you mad? Where would we even go?"

He kissed my collarbone, and I attempted to lock my legs around him—eager to be closer—but he forced them apart, hindering my movement. He kept his eyes locked on mine as he licked and kissed and nibbled his way down my stomach, stopping inches away from where I wanted him most.

"Elkway. There's a clan of witches there that owe me a favor." He paused, his smile growing larger. "What do you say?"

Although the idea was outlandish at best, I'd be lying if I said it didn't intrigue me. Life would never be the same after this—I'd never be the same. If I could restore my mother back to health, why shouldn't I do something that'd make me happy? I'd always wanted to explore the continent and escape the shackles of Wendover. What better opportunity than to do it with someone who set my soul on fire?

If I'd learned anything these past couple of years, it was to appreciate every moment before it was gone because tomorrow isn't promised to anyone. I'd spent far too long putting aside my own wants and needs for the sake of others.

It was time to take back my life. Be true to myself. And, quite frankly, if I survived these trials, I deserved it.

"I'd say you're mad." I laughed.

Talon's lips settled against mine before I could say anything else. "Yeah, you're probably right," he said between kisses.

He pulled me beside him, wrapping me in his arms as he deepened the kiss.

I curled into his warm, safe body, transferring every unspoken thought and feeling into our embrace—each breath

—every glance. My lips were swollen by the time he pulled away, gazing into my eyes as he tucked a strand of hair behind my ear. I turned over in his arms, pressing my back against his chest, fantasizing about the possibility.

His fingers danced along my arm, igniting a delicious thrill that cascaded down my spine.

The answer was simple. I knew as sleep settled into my bones that there was nothing else I wanted to do more.

THIRTY

Two trials remained. Three competitors. And only one heart would beat in the end.

My anxiety worked overtime, imagining scenario after scenario with every step I took. My nerves frayed as we were ushered to the arena, lined up single file like mere cattle.

If I was right, we'd already completed greed, envy, pride, gluttony, and wrath. Only sloth and lust remained. I couldn't figure out what the king would have in store for either of those, not that it mattered. Whatever he planned would be nothing short of impossible, with deadly consequences.

Sirens.

Poison.

Cannibalistic sprites.

Talon's thumb brushed against my hand so quickly I almost didn't notice.

I peered up at him, careful not to move my head in fear of anyone watching, and found a smug grin on his lips.

He had slipped out the other night, after holding me in his arms until I fell asleep. It was the first night in weeks I'd slept well, but the aching sensation I felt when I woke up to find him gone was almost debilitating. I couldn't wait to see him later that day to train—it was another session filled with insinuation and need.

Dagger throwing had never been so easy.

Talon pulled me into a dark enclave as the front of the line disappeared around the corner. Covering my mouth with his to swallow my surprise, he kissed me deep and hungry.

I wrapped my arms around his neck, holding him to me—losing myself to him. In that moment, I didn't care who saw or who knew, or what trouble we could get into. I only thought of his lips and the growing warmth in my belly.

"You *are* mad," I whispered against his lips, and he kissed the tip of my nose.

"You have no idea, firefly."

"Someone could find us."

"You never answered my question." His eyes searched mine, and I shrugged, pretending I didn't know what he was talking about so we could delay reality a bit longer. He growled, nipping my ear. "Don't toy with me, Elowyn. When this is all over, tell me you'll run away with me."

Releasing a breathy laugh, I arched into him. "It doesn't seem like you're giving me much choice."

"I enjoy getting what I want."

"We should get back to the group."

His grip on my waist tightened, pushing me harder into the wall. "Elowyn," he warned.

Kissing him softly, I opened my lips an inch for my tongue to tease his. I knew as soon as I answered, reality would crash down on us, but I didn't want to feel his absence—too afraid it'd be the last time I'd have the chance to touch him. Taste him.

Caressing my fingertips along his jaw, I kissed his cheek and replied. "Talon, when I said you're not giving me a choice, it's because there's nothing else I'd love to do more."

He nuzzled into my hand, resting his forehead on mine. "Then you better make it through this trial. Any means necessary, firefly. Or I swear I'll make you repay your debt in the afterlife."

I smiled, knowing he meant every word, and kissed him once more, savoring every second until he pulled away and guided me out of the enclave and back to the group.

If the stakes weren't already high enough, the future of my heart was now involved.

We approached the cobblestone path that led to the floating set of double doors. I'd grown familiar with the odd markings covering the granite slabs—and the opaque scales that wrapped around the columns on either side. However, its monstrosity never failed to take my breath away. The grandiose crest that floated above shone in the warm sun, the snakes on either side appearing to snap and hiss at the guests who entered the doors below it.

It was a threat.

A promise.

That all who entered would be privy to a savage show.

Talon stopped short of the doors and faced me. "I'll meet you here when you're done."

I straightened my vest, feeling suffocated under its weight. "Okay."

"Okay."

We remained in place, our eyes locked on each other— confirmation that we both knew it was merely wishful thinking. That the stars had already written our fate, and all we could do was pray it was in our favor. I loosened my breath and turned to face the door, tears stinging my eyes as they opened on a wind-less breeze, cold air smacking me in the face.

"Remember, any means necessary."

I wiped my palms against my leathers as I stepped through the portal—gasping in awe of the mountains before me. I stretched my neck all the way to the side to glimpse the top of the peak. Adrenaline raced through my veins, feeling more mortal than I'd ever had in my entire life.

Swallowing my fear, I lifted my chin as I crossed the rocky terrain to where the king sat perched on his throne ahead.

The fae court encased the front of the mountain behind him, their theater seating extending into the sky.

We were going to be expected to climb to the top.

The large white board that donned each competitor's name —once clean and unmarked—was now sullied and with tally marks and crossed-off names. My name was at the top, followed by Aeron, but it meant nothing. It was a ridiculous, sadistic game to satiate the fae's bloodthirsty appetite.

Although, I'd be lying if I said it didn't get inside my head.

The king crossed his legs as we took our spots. All too casual and pleased to be there.

Calandra's face appeared grim and ashen, so I gave her a forlorn smile and took her hand, squeezing it once before looking ahead. Although it was every person for themselves, I knew firsthand what a difference it made to have someone on your side. No one wanted to feel alone—especially during a perilous competition such as this one. I wouldn't resent her in the slightest if she won.

It was just a shame I'd be the one getting out.

I squeezed her hand again. Though it doesn't alleviate any of my guilt.

"Competitors, greetings," the king bellowed. His auburn hair rustled in the wind.

Prince Bowen sat beside him, bored and uninterested as he polished the buttons on his sleeve. However, he looked up when he felt me staring and winked—a sleazy grin taking over his face.

Fidgeting under the weight of his gaze, I averted my eyes to the king, who stared back unblinkingly.

"This trial is all about perseverance and commitment, a simple virtue most of you filthy humans cannot grasp. Today, you will discover what that truly means or die from indolence. The Ashgate Mountains behind you are of the steepest in the realm, and at the top lies a vial of unicorn elixir that will rejuvenate your body and mind, providing you an advantage for the last trial..." he trailed off, almost appearing lost in his mind. "I'd warn you of the obstacles ahead, but that would ruin the crux of the endeavor." He grinned. "Good luck, humans. And remember, those who submit to diligence will reap the benefits of self-sacrifice."

Aeron walked backward toward the mountain with his hands behind his head. "Don't try to keep up, ladies. I wouldn't want you to hurt yourself." He let out a venomous cackle before focusing on me. "Although I have a special surprise planned for you, sweetheart. Retribution, if you will."

Bile sloshed in my stomach as he swiveled on his foot, turning his back to us as he continued toward the mountain.

A wet, thunderous sound pulsated through the air, vibrating my eardrums—growing louder and meatier with each beat. I craned my neck in every direction, looking for the source, when a copper wyvern flew into view, flanking the side of the mountains. Its scales glistened in the sunlight, making it appear like liquid gold as its leathery, membranous wings carried it through the sky. Its shadow below was the size of a small building as it barreled toward us, stealing the breath from my lungs.

Calandra and I ducked for cover as it flew over Aeron's head and shook up dust and rocks all around us.

Aeron's eyes were wide with panic as the wyvern turned around, its sights set on him as it darted back, swooping closer than it did the first time.

My heart hammered in my chest.

I scurried to my feet and raced for the mountains, my shoes slipping on the gravel.

I skidded to a stop at the base of a boulder, wedging myself between two rocks as the wyvern darted behind me—the gust of air that followed burning my eyes and spraying my body with loose dirt.

My vision remained blurry no matter how hard I tried to blink it into focus, and I lost track of where Calandra and Aeron went.

There was no time to worry about that, though, unless I intended to be a wyvern snack. I needed to get to that vial of unicorn elixir before Aeron did.

Rubbing my palms into my eyes, I attempted to dislodge some of the grit that remained before starting up the mountain.

My nails dug into the limestone.

One foot after the other, I climbed further and further, breathless and aching, until my calluses bled and my knees ached.

I stopped to rest for a few minutes on a narrow ledge, my heart beating erratically against my ribcage as I laid on my back, queasy and lightheaded from the height. Keeping my focus on the clear blue sky, I ran my hands along my face, wiping away the beads of sweat. There wasn't much further to go—the tip was within view and was likely a couple of yards away.

I questioned every single moment that'd led me there. Floating on a questionable slab that balanced hundreds of feet in the air, my legs threatened to give out.

My arms burned.

I was next to empty.

The ominous beating of wings drummed from somewhere below, and the blood drained from my face.

I kept as still as possible, moving closer to the mountain until my back was flush against the cool rock.

Aeron emerged to my right, balancing on a crag a few feet above me, oblivious to my position. However, there was still no sign of Calandra. I hoped she was somewhere below, but I didn't dare look down to check.

The ear-piercing shrill of the wyvern's roar sent small rocks tumbling down the mountainside, and I held on for dear life as the ledge rattled beneath me. As soon as the dust settled, I found a small notch in the mountain to stick my foot in and held onto the edge of the landing above.

My hands—slick with moisture—couldn't get a good grip on the stone.

And my foot slipped.

Not able to find another spot to place it, I clung onto the edge by my fingertips. There was no way I was going to make it, and with the wyvern circling back, I'd tumble down with the rest of the debris.

Shit. I was stuck. I couldn't hop down—the ledge was too small.

"Hey, grab my hand!" a voice sounded above, and I peered up, squinting from the sun.

Pulling her black hair out of her face as she crouched down, Calandra extended her hands in my direction.

A flood of relief washed over me. I placed my hand in hers and then my other, getting a tight grip. "I'm going to jump, okay? I'll count down!"

She nodded, glancing to her left to keep a lookout on the wyvern.

"One," I began. "Two ... three..."

I hopped off the small notch, putting my full weight and trust in Calandra as I dangled in her grip. My feet tried to find traction on the wall of rock, but I only met loose dirt and gravel.

The wyvern sounded again, closer. My skin prickled with fear.

"Come on, Elowyn. Pull!"

I pulled against her, the vein in Calandra's forehead threatening to pop as I finally found my footing and shimmied my torso up and over the ledge and onto solid land.

Calandra slammed into the wall behind her, spent and out of breath.

I rolled onto my back, beyond thankful to be on solid mass.

"Girl, what were you thinking?" She yelled, her eyes bulging with anger, "You looked right at me and ran off when I called for you! Were you deliberately trying to kill yourself?"

I sat up, facing her. "I didn't hear you. Then dust got in my eyes, and I wasn't thinking."

"No shit!" She laughed, tossing a handful of dirt at me. "Honestly, it'd be inspiring if you weren't so incredibly thick-headed. Come on." She got to her feet. "Let's go get that elixir before Aeron. Stars, that's all we need is him having even more of an upper hand."

"I saw him hanging at the edge of the bluff right before you saved my ass. He looked scared as shit." I kept close behind Calandra as she trekked up the trail. "Maybe he's cracking."

"Nope, I'm only getting started," an invisible voice said.

She and I paused, looking for where it came from when Aeron hopped down from the tree, landing right in front of Calandra.

She shuffled back, but she wasn't fast enough.

Aeron grabbed her vest and pulled her to him, snapping her neck with his hands.

"No!" I screamed.

Her body fell to the ground. Limp.

"What is wrong with you? Why would you do that?"

I wanted to run to her.

Help her.

Tears stained my cheeks as I sobbed—and my cries lodged in my swollen throat. I didn't know what to do, frozen in fear as I stared down at her too-still body while flashbacks of Lilian and Breana ripped through me.

"It's part of the game, Elowyn. Drop the innocent act. It's pathetic," he spat, stepping over Calandra's dead body and toward me.

I backed up as far as I could until my foot slipped off the edge. My stomach sank. I peered over my shoulder. It was the end of the line. We were too high up, and I felt lightheaded.

Aeron cackled at my expense. Relentless in his approach. "Don't worry, sweetheart. I'll make this quick."

I focused, taking a deep breath as I tried to figure a way out of this. If I could get over to the tree, I could climb away from him.

Keeping my eyes glued on Aeron, I balanced on the ledge.

Closer and closer.

I was almost there when he lunged for me with a feral gleam in his eyes.

Still, I ran and jumped—my arms inches from latching onto the branch. His rough fingers wrapped around my foot and dragged me toward him before I could escape, but I dug my nails into the ground, thrashing in his grip.

"You're only making this harder for yourself." He threw me into a rock.

My temple hit with a crunch, ripping into flesh. Blood dripped onto the gravel beneath me and coated my cheek.

My body went limp.

This wasn't happening. It couldn't.

I wanted to get back home. To see my mother. Sugarfoot. Run away with Talon. I wanted to *live*. Maybe even travel. I didn't have the time to die.

Whatever means necessary. Talon's words rang through my head as Aeron inched closer to the edge.

It was now or never.

There were no other options left.

I kicked and thrashed, trying to shake his hand loose, but he had me in a vise grip. He stopped at the edge, grabbing my ankle, then my calf, and just as he went to reach for my knee, I pulled my leg back, slamming my foot into his stomach as hard as I could.

Aeron stumbled, his feet slipping on the edge.

"You bitch!" He lunged for me, seething.

One last chance.

I slammed my other foot into his knee before he could reach me, but Aeron caught it, pulling me with him as he tumbled off the side of the mountain.

Thirty-One

My cheeks pulled away from my face as I spun out of control, spiraling toward the ground—unable to tell which way was up. I did everything I could. Fought my hardest. Yet despite it all, I plunged to my fate, resigning to my fortune as the tips of the evergreens approached faster and faster.

It was all for nothing.

The shrill of the wyvern pierced the air as it flew toward me, its wings tight at its sides while it dove, swooping beneath my body, and caught me on its back.

I scrambled to hold on to its scales for dear life as we soared back up, watching as Aeron continued his descent, further and further, until the ground broke his fall with a splat of red.

The wyvern squalled, piercing my eardrums as it soared higher, faster—my heart fell into my stomach. I was the last competitor remaining, and yet there was no relief. No satisfaction. Only a festering sensation that something was horribly wrong as I looked back to the clear blue sky, my eyes burning from the force of the wind barreling in my face.

I crouched down, digging my knees into the wyvern's back as the significance of the moment slammed into me.

Holy shit, I was the last competitor remaining! I was on the back of a wyvern, flying through the sky, and I was the last competitor remaining!

I'd save my mother! Run away with Talon. Play with Sugarfoot again.

A wild smile spread across my lips while tears welled over and dripped down my cheeks. *Holy shit! I fucking won!* I never thought I'd live long enough to see the day.

The wyvern came to an abrupt stop at the top of the mountain, bringing me within feet of the elixir before it flung me off its back.

I toppled over, unable to find my footing, and fell to my knees. Not a graceful landing, but I was alive and would take it.

It looked at me curiously, appearing as cautious about me as I was of it.

My limbs wobbled beneath me as I scurried back. From fear. From being back on solid ground. The wyvern approached. Its enormous feet shook the bedrock with each step, and my bladder threatened to release.

"Why—Why'd you save me?" I croaked out. Stars, tell me this creature didn't save me just to taunt me.

"The realm depends on you, Elowyn. I would've flown you far away from here if the king hadn't confined me to these mountains." The wyvern snorted as it spoke telepathically—a burst of hot air brushing my face. It should terrify me, or at the very least, confuse me, but talking to these creatures came as natural as breathing and, after defying gravity, there wasn't much left to be afraid of.

"I don't understand. How do you know my name? Why am I able to hear you? How am I able to hear any of you creatures?"

"You creatures?" the wyvern hissed. "You possess an ability

most would kill for, and you have the audacity to be so flippantly disrespectful? To the same creatures that granted your lineage the ability to communicate with us in the first place? Watch. Your. Tongue." The wyvern took another step, encasing me with its scythe-like wings, and I retreated again, colliding with a boulder.

Stars formed in my vision as I looked up at it—taking in its golden scales and magnificent stature. I was a mere mortal human in comparison. One swipe of its claws and my guts would spill onto the ground. I didn't dare question the wyvern —but what did it mean by my lineage? Why did the realm depend on me?

The wyvern's eyes widened.

"The answer's been under your nose this entire time, and you mean to tell me you don't know whose blood runs through your veins? You're the daughter of my king. The *true* heir." The wyvern nudged me with its head, lifting me to my feet. "You must get out of here safely and reclaim what's yours before it's too late."

I shook my head. "No. No, there's no way that man—that monster—is my father."

"That monster is not my king. To insinuate as much is insulting!"

"Then what are you saying?" I rubbed my temples. The wyvern was confused—mistaken—that was impossible. Stars, I was tired of the riddles. Tired of not understanding and feeling incompetent. "Maybe if anyone just said what they mean around here, I'd know what you all were talking about!" I shouted. My mother was venomously against the fae, I couldn't be one. No. I refused to believe it.

I couldn't be—how?

"That's enough." The scales lining the wyvern's spine raised like hackles. "You mustn't keep wasting time, Elowyn. I've already said too much. Now grab the vial of elixir and let us be on our way."

I wiped my nose and lifted my chin to meet its hard stare—such a magnificent beast. The illustrations didn't do them justice. I wanted to keep probing and get to the bottom of its wild accusation, but the wyvern was right. As much as I hated to leave questions unanswered, the sooner I got the elixir, the quicker I could get home and forget this horrible nightmare.

With a sharp inhale, I turned on my heel and hiked up the narrow path, one foot in front of the other, not daring another breath. It was everything I could do to keep my focus straight ahead until I reached the tiny bottle and pretended like I wasn't one wrong step from falling to my death.

My hand hesitated, and I twisted the ring around my finger before I picked up the elixir and stuffed it deep into my vest, inching my way down the trail to the solid plateau.

The wyvern dropped its head, and straightened its wings, allowing me access to its back. Its webbed wing was like a thick leather blanket under my fingers as I climbed, trying but failing to wrap my arms around its neck.

"Hold on," the wyvern said.

"To what?"

The wind swallowed my words as the wyvern surged forward, my knuckles whitening as I clung desperately to its rugged scales. With closed eyes, I felt my stomach drop as it leaped off the edge. A strangled scream escaped my throat as we swooped to the ground, my lungs growing horse from the force.

The fae court rapidly came into view as we descended, the crowd once shapeless and unrecognizable, now fully defined.

Their cruel faces were laced with disappointment. Others with rage as we neared the ground.

The wyvern skirted to a stop and flung me off its back,

landing within feet of Aeron's splattered body. I glanced away and got to my feet, brushing the dust off my pants.

King Harkin's amber eyes bore into mine as I revealed the pink bottle of elixir from my vest, and Prince Bowen sneered, gripping the armrest of his throne with such force it appeared to bend under the pressure.

I tried not to appear intimidated, tried to hold my chin high, but their weighted stares made me want to claw out of my skin.

The king leaned over and whispered into his guard's ear, and he nodded, summoning his fellow men as he briskly made his way down the stairs.

Time slowed. Blood surged to my ears—muting the commotion. I didn't understand what was going on. Why was everyone rushing toward me? What did I do? I was the last competitor remaining. I should be released from this star-awful prison, yet they were surrounding me as if I'd obliterate their entire court.

I searched for Talon, spotting him just as he hopped over the railing, his expression tight while he rushed to me—the king's guards on his heels.

"Halfling filth!"

"To the gallows!"

The faerie court chanted.

Each voice was louder than the last, slamming into me one after the other at a mind-numbing cadence.

Halfling? What did that even mean?

The wyvern flapped its wings, sending dirt and gravel in every direction. "Fight, Elowyn. Save us."

It flew off in a blink, and I shielded my eyes, looking up when Talon's body slammed into mine. He twisted around to shield me and unsheathed his sword—blasting gold magic from his other palm, sending half a dozen guards to the other side of the arena, rendering them unconscious.

"Run!" Talon demanded as he fought against the six remaining guards.

I didn't wait.

I did exactly as he said and took off in the opposite direction, ducking and weaving as steel blades sliced through the air, missing my neck by mere inches. It was impossible to know who was who in the frenzy of bodies—I could only hope none of the blood splattered on the ground was Talon's as I ran.

And ran.

I was almost to the exit when a guard grabbed me by my hair and pulled me back. His hot breath on my cheek burned like acid.

No, I was too close.

There were only a few more feet to go, and I'd be damned if I didn't make it out alive.

Ignoring the searing pain that ripped through my scalp, I twisted in his grip and kicked him as hard as I could between the legs.

He doubled over with a growl, and I kneed him in the nose, cartilage crunching under the force. I quickly flipped over and crawled away, trying to catch my breath—refocus—when a dozen more guards began their descent from the observation deck above.

Digging my nails into my palm, I breathlessly watched Talon take on the last two guards. With one swift, final motion, he drove his elbows into their skulls and rushed to my side, getting to me just in time before the other guards closed in.

He hooked an arm around my waist and dragged me toward the exit.

We were running too fast. I couldn't match his strides. The

arena blurred past at a dizzying rate, as did the golden courtyard and the labyrinth of trees and shrubs once we entered the forest.

I didn't know where Talon was taking me. Nor did I care. I just wanted to go home. Wanted my freedom. Yet I found myself consumed with an unsettling paranoia, that I wouldn't live long enough to see it happen.

We reached a small bubbling creek deep within the forest and Talon finally slowed, dropping his hands to his knees.

"Fuck!" he yelled at the ground. Every emotion flashed across his face when he finally stood, dragging a palm down his pale face. I'd never seen him so unnerved. He was usually a pillar of strength, yet his foundation was cracking. My stomach tightened at the sight.

"What the hell is going on, Talon?" I took a sharp inhale through my nose, trying but failing to catch my breath. "Why are they chasing us like we're a threat?"

"Because you are." Talon paced the forest ground, muttering to himself—the words barely audible. "How are we going to get through the wards?"

My body went ice cold, and I leaned against a tree to keep the crushing dread that slammed into my chest from knocking me over. "I'm sorry, *what*? What do you mean, we can't get past the wards?"

Talon took a controlled breath to regain his composure and took my hands in his. I wanted his gesture to comfort me—to provide a semblance of reassurance—but the warmth his touch usually provided only left me cold.

"I promise I'll explain everything later, but we need to keep going. You're not safe here." His eyes pleaded for me to understand, but I didn't. *I couldn't.* The only thing I understood was the bubbling frustration that turned my vision black and had me on the verge of exploding.

I ripped my hands away from his and stepped back, shoving

my palms into my eyes to quell the darkness that threatened to spill over. "Dammit Talon, just tell me! Why can't I leave? Stars, I'm so sick of no one saying what they truly mean! I just want to go home! The king said the last one living would be set free, yeah?" I held out my hands and looked around the forest. "I don't see anyone else here, do you? I swear on everything I love I'm not leaving until—"

"You're the fabled princess," Talon blurted. He rubbed his hand along his slacked jaw as if he regretted speaking the words aloud. "Fuck, I'm so sorry. I tried to protect you, but King Harkin figured it out, and if I don't get you out of here, he'll kill you."

My mouth fell open, but I forgot how to speak. Forgot how to breathe, even. I don't think I was. "No. No, that's impossible." I blanched, recalling my mother's words all those weeks ago:

"We had a secret love affair child—the stars weren't in our favor. It's been for your own good to know as little as possible."

The world spun under my feet, attempting to throw me off its axis. The heir to an entire kingdom? I barely scraped by during the trials, yet there were people counting on me to liberate them from their tyrannical dictator? I couldn't. How? I didn't have magic. I had nothing except fool's luck.

"I know it's hard to believe." Talon's eyes pleaded with mine, but I looked away, unable to stomach the pity that coated them. "I wish there was another way for you to find out, but you need to understand how much danger you're in. You're part faerie, Elowyn. A halfling. To the court, you're an abomination, but to King Harkin—a threat to his throne."

A halfling. It didn't make sense, and yet it explained everything. Like every missing part of myself snapped into place, as if I'd found the missing answers to all my questions.

My ability to talk to animals.

Why I always felt different.

The inexplicable way I felt deeply connected to this realm and never my own. It should've brought me comfort, a sense of peace, but I only quivered with fear. I wanted to tear out of my skin. I felt dirty. Revolting. I couldn't be like these evil creatures. I couldn't be one of them.

"Wait. You knew this entire time?" I asked, although my question came off as more of a demand.

He approached with caution, but I took a step back, not wanting to be anywhere near him. "Elowyn, you need to let me explain."

"I don't need you to explain anything," I spat. "You said all that stuff about running away with you. Made me believe you cared about me, and all the while it was because I'm some fabled princess you hope will save your stupid realm?"

The muscle in his cheek fluttered. "It's not like that."

"No? Then what's it like, Talon? Because not being transparent and omitting the truth—is lying!" I pushed my fingers into my temples, subduing my headache. "Was it fun for you? Hm?" I went on, "Getting a stupid human girl—a halfling— whatever you all think I am, to fall for you?"

"I never lied to you. Everything I said was true!"

It felt like my chest was being split in half as tears stung my eyes. "Yeah, well, we all know the fae are masters at bullshitting. I'm sure there was some half-truth loophole verbiage in there somewhere."

"That's not true, and you know it. What did you expect me to say?" His hands shot out from his sides in exasperation. "By the way, Elowyn, you're a halfling and heir to the entire Faerway kingdom? Hope that doesn't fuck with your head. Good luck with the trials?"

I scoffed, shaking my head. "So, this was all a big, elaborate charade to pacify me, then?"

"For fuck's sake, Elowyn, that's not at all what I'm saying." He growled. "You're choosing to hear what you want to hear—"

"No, for the first time, I'm hearing you loud and clear, Talon. You're no better than any of the other fae in this stars-forsaken place. I knew it was a mistake to fall for you!"

"Damnit, Elowyn, why are you doing this? We can talk about this later."

I didn't know if I was being irrational or if I meant anything I said. I didn't know anything except I had an overwhelming urge to claw out of my skin and scream. Or cry. Or both.

Talon didn't hesitate this time and continued to stalk toward me despite my objections until my back was flush against a tree.

He cupped my face, pulled me toward him, and rested his forehead on mine. "I knew you were stubborn, firefly, but you're not thinking straight. I've never lied to you. I'll explain everything, I swear it, but please let us leave. I don't want to restrain you."

Stars, he was beautiful. It was all I could do to keep from touching him—to run a finger along his tanned skin and trace his sharp features. To kiss him. But his words held me prisoner. I'd grown too comfortable with Talon, cared too much about him to trust my judgment. Regardless of his intentions, or if he blatantly lied to me, you couldn't have one without the other.

What was hope if not a lie we told ourselves about the future? I tried to control the shake in my voice as tears seeped from my eyes. "I can't even look at you right now."

"Firefly," he started, but just when he opened his mouth to finish that sentence, the king's guard ripped through the shrubs, silencing him.

He thrashed against an invisible bond as he was flung back-ward, being dragged through the dirt and mud toward the shrubs they'd come from. It didn't take long, however, before Talon ripped through the bond with a flash of magic and was on his feet—sword drawn.

He went toe to toe with a familiar-looking guard, letting him get a few hits in before Talon whipped around and slammed his blade down, cutting the guard's hand clean off.

A few more desperately ambitious males flanked his right, attempting to take him down, but one by one Talon sliced open their insides and tossed them aside with as much effort as a sigh.

I slipped behind the large oak—my eyes locked on the carnage in front of me—hoping if I remained out of sight long enough, they'd forget I was there when a cold blade pressed into my throat.

I remained as still as possible as metal encased me, preventing me from escaping.

They pinned my arms behind my back.

"Talon!" I screamed, bucking and thrashing under their firm grip as they forced me out of the forest.

I caught his wide-eyed expression just as they pulled me beyond the bushes. His concentration faltered just enough for a blast of magic to hit him in the chest.

An ear-piercing scream escaped my throat as I watched Talon fall to his knees, watching helplessly as they hauled me away until he was no longer in sight.

"Talon!" I sobbed, repeating his name over and over again when an invisible gag slapped over my mouth, silencing my wails.

THIRTY-TWO

My brain throbbed against my skull.

I couldn't move.

Couldn't think.

Slumped in the corner of the cell, I stared straight ahead, unblinking. The irony wasn't lost on me—how I've come full circle to the place it all began. It was funny.

And I was the so-called fabled princess?

I'd laugh if I had the energy. I'd never stood a chance. At least I wouldn't have to play along with the king's stupid games —or be paraded about to amuse bloodthirsty fae. It was time to meet my fate. It was finally over. Everything. All of it.

My chest tightened.

I'd never get to see Talon again or feel his soft touch. I fought back tears and hugged my legs to my chest, our last conversation replaying in my head.

"You're no better than any of the other fae in this stars-forsaken place. I knew it was a mistake to fall for you."

That couldn't be our last conversation. Sure, I was upset he withheld information, but that didn't mean I hated him. I just needed time to process it.

Stars, if I had only shut up and listened, we wouldn't be in this situation. I banged my head into the brick wall. I was going to die, and he was going to think I believed nothing we experienced was real. When, in reality, I was the damn coward.

All my efforts would be in vain.

Sugarfoot would forever wonder where I went.

My mother would die never knowing what happened to me.

I ran my hands through my dirty, matted hair as tears leaked from my eyes, dripping onto the hay below.

The sound of metal clinked together rhythmically from somewhere deep within the dungeon. I cocked my head toward the corridor to hear it better. It almost sounded like keys attached to someone's hip.

My heart raced. The sound grew closer and closer with each step, and I shuffled to my feet, clinging to the metal bars for support, hoping it was Talon coming to get me.

An older, stocky fae guard appeared before me instead.

I tried to hide my disappointment, but an audible whimper formed in my throat despite myself. "Where's Talon?" I demanded, matching him stride for stride until we reached the cell door, where he inserted a long metal key.

He said nothing as he slid it open and entered my cell, his blank expression an ominous sign of what was to come.

"I'm not going anywhere until I know where he is." I staggered backward, cursing the walls that kept me contained. My fingernails dug into the grout behind me, cutting into skin as I pressed my body as far into the wall as possible.

The fae man's lips curled into a cruel smile as he grabbed my arm, forcing me forward and twisting it around until it was behind my back.

I thrashed in response, but his grasp on my hands only grew stronger, shoving me out of the cell. Burrowing my feet into the ground, I tried to resist his authority, but it was no use. He pushed me in front of him like I was nothing more than a slight inconvenience.

"Oh, don't yous worries yous human filth." His thick accent was hard to decipher. "I'lls take yous to that treacherous, nos good, halfling bastard."

A pit formed in my stomach as he let out a gruff laugh and jolted me forward.

I tripped, but he kicked me along, disregarding the yelp that escaped me from his rough touch. Even when Talon first escorted me through this same hallway, he wasn't that aggressive. But that didn't matter. The pain came in second to the fear gnawing at my chest.

Talon was in trouble, and I needed to get to him— help him.

The stocky fae guard laughed again, casting a spell that rendered my body limp, and I fell.

The periphery of my vision dimmed as he seized my ankles, pulling me forcefully to his side. My eyes blinked once, twice, before they rolled into the back of my head.

The cloudless sky above was painted a beautiful shade of cerulean—the same color it had been when I crossed the Dolorem River all those weeks ago.

I enjoyed that moment—the sliver of time in between dreams and reality when you couldn't remember anything. Not your hair color or your name. Not even where you were. It was peaceful. Blissful. You could be anywhere and anyone you wanted to be.

If that was purgatory, I didn't want to leave.

However, my bones soon ached, and my skull throbbed, as

did the crushing weight of reality that came collapsing down with it.

Gone was the illusion of who and where I was, replaced with the familiar sinking feeling in my chest that refused to be ignored.

Talon is in trouble.

I sat up and lightly stretched, feeling my spine pop into place as I took in the surroundings.

But there was nothing.

Only an empty field that stretched for miles until it reached the edge of the skyline, meeting a tall, lean silhouette.

I squinted.

"Talon!" I yelled, rushing to him before he disappeared. Before I realized that this, too, might be a dream. I wrapped my arms around his middle as I inhaled his familiar scent, my heart warming from our embrace. "I thought I'd never see you again," I sobbed, relief washing over me. "I'm so sorry about what I said. I didn't mean any of it. I was so worried! Stars, I couldn't—"

"Let go of me," Talon warned.

Looking up at him, my brief moment of relief was ripped away, leaving me cold and disoriented. His focus remained straight ahead, his jaw set, and his body rigid. It was like he was standing at attention before the king.

I released him, confusion rippling through me while I stepped back, the fae court revealing itself above.

"Welcome, Elowyn, to your final trial," King Harkin announced from his place on the throne above. Prince Bowen sat at his right, his legs crossed as he puckered his lips, blowing me a kiss.

My hand flew to my mouth to conceal my shock—and the bile that climbed up my throat—as my eyes darted back and forth between the king and Talon.

The faerie court above remained quiet, the disgust on their face hard to ignore. Thumbing the ring on my finger, I stood beside Talon, keeping a painful distance between us.

I wanted to tell him how I truly felt and take back all the harsh words I'd said. But the nagging dread in my bones told me I wouldn't get that chance.

King Harkin leaned back against his stolen throne. "I can see the confusion on your face from here." He cackled, tracing a finger along the embellished armrest. "I admit, despite how much I'm relishing in it, you must've seen this coming."

I unfurled my brows, refusing to give him the satisfaction of being able to read me anymore.

"The truth is a dangerous thing, wouldn't you say, Elowyn? It has the power to upend the very foundation of our realm." His neck turned a deeper shade of red with each word he spoke. "As is any interference in our sacred trials!"

Talon blinked—his expression bored as the king spoke. The defiance that radiated off him was contagious and fueled King Harkin's anger, his harsh glare impaling us like an arrow.

"Your fervor isn't virtuous. It's revolting and makes a blatant mockery of our principles! Let's see if you can overcome your lust for the unattainable or if it will be the very thing that thwarts you from obtaining what you desire most."

My heart thumped hard against my ribcage as he looked between us—a wicked smirk pulled at his mouth as two swords materialized at the toes of each of mine and Talon's feet. My head whipped over to Talon, who still faced ahead, refusing to acknowledge my presence at all.

I wanted to scream. I wanted him to look at me—give me a glimpse of what was going through his mind instead of that stoic, unreadable disposition.

Stars, I couldn't breathe!

"Talon Warwick, prove your loyalty to this court by

succeeding in this trial, and I'll release your family—and restore your honor. Kill for your desires or be killed for your transgressions. The trial begins at the sound of the bell."

The fae court didn't disappear like they normally did.

No, they remained in the sky, their haunting presence a painful distraction.

Talon bent over and grabbed his sword, finally facing me as he got into position. My heart sank as I followed suit, picking mine up with trembling hands.

His eyes were hollow like he hadn't slept, and a shadow of stubble ran down his jaw. He looked horrible. Still unearthly beautiful, but gut-wrenchingly anguished.

My heartstrings pulled taut as I longed for him. To be his distraction. To show him how much I truly cared for him.

His lips pulled into a weak smile. "Don't hesitate, firefly," he whispered. "When that bell rings, kill me. Get out of here, don't look back."

I shook my head, tears welling in my eyes as every fiber in my body rejected the idea. "No," I choked. "No. There has to be another way."

The bell sounded, and I flinched, the sword almost slipping from my damp fingers. Talon didn't move, nor did I—my feet stuck in place.

"You need to make a move. Come on, just like we've practiced." He raised his brows expectantly as he slashed his blade through the air, our swords connecting as I blocked.

"You're going to have to do more than that, firefly," he pressed, coming at me again.

I took a step back and swung my blade down, blocking his attack once more.

"I won't kill you," I said as we continued our usual sparring method. "I refuse to."

Talon upped his pace, taking me by surprise, and I struggled to correct my footing. "I'm dead either way, Elowyn. If you think the king will spare me, you've learned nothing."

He pierced his sword toward my stomach, and I leaped back. "What was that for?" I demanded, thrusting mine toward his side as he spun out of the way.

"For that"—he lifted his chin toward me—"to get under your skin." He came at me again, and again, each time more forceful than the last. My blood pumped hard through my veins with each new attempt he made at forcing my hand.

"That's not fair." I ducked his blade. "I don't want to do this! You can't force me to do this!"

He laughed, twisting around to kick my feet out from under me. I rolled out of the way as his blade came pummeling down, lodging into the grass below.

"I don't care what you want right now. You're leaving here, and that's final."

"I think I should have a say in this," I demanded, scrambling to my feet, blocking his sword as it swung toward my thigh. "What about your sister?"

"As if your mother doesn't matter?" The tip of Talon's blade nicked my ankle, sending me crashing to the ground.

I yelled out in pain, clutching my leg as crimson liquid stained my skin. "What the fuck!" I seethed. "That fucking hurt!"

"Get up!"

Baring my teeth, I silently challenged him before I stood, slashing my blade down toward him.

He leaped to the side easily.

"You're a prick, you know that?"

Talon smiled. "That's it, firefly, keep going. Tell me what else you can't stand," he said, nicking my ankle once again.

I yelled through gritted teeth, hopping backward as I held my leg. "Insufferable! A lowly fae brute!"

Talon laughed, but he didn't let up, forcing me to keep blocking his every move—one slip-up. That's all it would take. And his blade would cut into more flesh.

"You're holding back on me. I didn't take you for a coward," he taunted. "Guess I was wrong."

I shoved my blade toward him, tears leaking from my eyes as I clamped down on my anger. "Please stop." I swatted at my wet face. "Please don't make me do this, Talon. I won't be able to live with myself!"

A familiar cruel smirk tugged at his mouth, one I hadn't seen in weeks, and I shuddered. "Pathetic, worthless, human. What was any of this for then, hm?" he demanded, quickening his pace—quickly closing in on me. "Your wretched performance is shameful. You're embarrassing me. My training."

He nicked my hip, and I cried out, slumping over in agony. He kept moving faster. His swift, nimble movements were too difficult to match.

"Screw you," I cried, holding my side as blood dripped through my fingers onto the ground.

Tears streamed down my face—and not from the pain. Talon wouldn't let up until he got what he wanted. Until he was lying on the ground, taking his last breath. He knew every single one of my triggers. Knew exactly what buttons to push and how to get under my skin, and he was only going to use it to his advantage—become more and more spiteful until I cracked.

I'd hate him if I hadn't already fallen for him.

"You and I were a mistake." He sucked his teeth, and I shook my head, refusing to believe it. "If I could go back and undo all of it, I would. You were right. It meant nothing. You meant nothing."

My throat tightened as I searched his eyes, but the once bright emerald orbs were now jaded. I might as well have been looking at a stranger. My heart ached for the Talon I'd grown to love, but he was nowhere to be found.

He flipped his sword in his hand, grabbed it on its side, and drove the hilt toward my ribs.

I hopped back, barely avoiding the solid metal handle before it could slam into my rib cage, when Talon grabbed me by my collar, trapping me in place. I thrashed under his grip as he cocked his arm back, flicking the sword out from his body and catching the hilt in his hand.

"You promised me any means necessary, Elowyn. I'm calling in my debt."

"Please stop." I sobbed. "Please, we can think of something else."

"You gave me your word."

Everything felt like it was moving in slow motion as I quietly begged him to stop.

My vision blurred with tears. I brushed quivering fingers along his cheek, hoping his gaze would find mine. Praying to the stars this would end and he'd realize there was another way, but it was fruitless.

He swung the blade toward my center. His hard-set eyes challenged me to do it—his lips mouthing his final words as I drove my blade into his stomach.

I love you.

Thirty-Three

My sword slipped from my grasp, the clang of it hitting the ground not registering with me, as I watched Talon crumple, the once triumphant smile fading from his face. I fell down beside him, cradling his head in my lap, gently brushing his damp onyx hair away from his eyes.

"No, no, no, no," I cried. "Please wake up. I'm so sorry. I'm so sorry, please. Wake up."

My fingers trembled against his smooth skin. I pressed my forehead to his, tears dripping onto his cheeks. What the hell did I do?

The guards flanked my right, and I wrapped myself around Talon's lifeless body, refusing to let them take him out of my sight. Refusing to be without him. There were so many things left unsaid. So many truths left unspoken.

Guilt ripped into my chest.

The guards attempted to pry him out of my grasp.

"Let go of me!" I screamed, resting my head on his chest, desperate to keep him close. To feel his warmth until his body went cold.

But they were too strong. Too powerful. They showed no mercy as they blasted me with magic, catapulting me into the air.

I landed hard on my back—knocking the wind from my lungs—and I struggled to breathe. Not that I was worthy of it after what I'd done.

Slowly turning on my side, I attempted to crawl toward him. "Please!" I gasped. "Please, don't take him away!" Dropping my head onto the grass, I coughed, taking quick, sharp breaths as I fought for air, collapsing onto my stomach when I finally did.

I didn't know if I was thankful or not—what made me deserve air when I took Talon's away?

Lewis.

Breana.

Calandra.

All of them dead. Each one of their deaths was preventable.

And for what? To appease the king's sick fetish?

I couldn't let it be in vain. I needed to get up, stop feeling sorry for myself, and face the king.

So, I stood on weak feet, my knees threatening to bow from beneath me, and I pushed through it, straightening my back and lifting my chin as I faced the king.

A malicious smile spread across his face while he clapped—slow and calculated as a methodical cackle escaped his too-thin lips.

"Well done, Elowyn. Well done. I admit your tenacity and perseverance far exceeded my expectations. To think I underestimated you. The lengths you were willing to go for your freedom, while admirable, were delusional and futile."

My heart thumped hard against my ribcage, my entire body going numb.

Futile.

I bit my bottom lip to keep it from quivering, the contents of my stomach threatening to spew onto the ground by my feet. This wasn't happening. It couldn't be. I prayed to the stars—wishing there was more to his statement. That I was hearing him wrong. But the harrowing connotation that loomed in the air almost brought me to my knees.

"You see, Elowyn, I own you. You are my prisoner. Indebted to me for as long as I find comparable to the kindness I've shown you. *The mercy*," the king hissed the final words.

Tears streamed from my eyes, drenching my cheeks.

Don't let them see you falter, Talons' voice played in my head, and I sniffled, clenching my jaw in defiance. Despite the tears, despite my tremors, I was fuming. Anger oozed out of every pore, and I clenched my fists, taking his insults to the chin.

"I can't have a disgraced halfling bastard child running around, tainting our bloodline, and consorting with our kind. I refuse to let my court believe I would allow such an abomination to occur."

"You're a liar!" I yelled.

The king tipped his head back with laughter. "Ah. Typical small-minded human, your crossbreeding must have stunted your intelligence."

Prince Bowen turned red as he shook with amusement, not wanting to interrupt his father.

"I never explicitly stated when you could go free, Elowyn. Many conclusions can be drawn from implications. It's your own ignorance and shortsightedness that caused you to end up here."

With a flick of his wrist, King Harkin commanded the same guards that carried Talon's lifeless body away to come summon me—to take me to where I'd surely rot.

I watched them from the corner of my eye, noting their

every movement as they approached. My sword was too far to even think about putting up a fight, not to mention with whatever magic they possessed, I wouldn't stand a chance. But I couldn't surrender without a struggle.

Two guards flanked either side of me, capturing my arms in theirs as they hauled me away. I thrashed, kicking at both of their legs and groins, to no avail.

"You think your court admires you?" I screamed, making sure everyone in the court heard me. "They're terrified of you! You're a power-hungry dictator who feeds off those weaker than you. That's not a king, it's a coward!"

Even as the distance between the king and me grew, the menacing smirk on his face was hard to miss. He looked around at his adoring court—who all cheered and egged him on—before he willed himself to look back at me. Nothing but distaste in his eyes.

"Coward!" I screamed. "I earned my freedom! I did everything you asked and survived every trial! I proved my worth! You're a disgrace to this realm!"

He sucked his yellowed teeth. "Ah, that's the beauty of it all, Elowyn," King Harkin bellowed. "Just as sin promises judgment, virtue comes with its own punishment."

The familiar stale air of the dungeon singed my nostrils long before the darkness had consumed me.

I coughed, spitting the dirt from my mouth as I sat up and dusted myself clean. There was too much of it. Between that and bloodstains, I couldn't tell which was what. My leathers were in tatters, my palms covered in cuts from the previous trial. My bones throbbed. My thoughts raced. One of my boots was missing. I couldn't even fathom when or where I lost it. When Aeron tried to pull me off the mountain? On the way to the cell?

Letting out a sigh, I settled into the same corner I'd grown fond of. The one that gave me the perfect vantage point of whoever came and went. Not that anyone ever did. The dungeons were and always had been deathly quiet, providing no signs of another living soul. To think Talon's sister was down there. It didn't seem possible. I didn't know what to believe.

I couldn't even trust myself.

I pushed the heels of my palms into the side of my head to soothe the pounding sensation that ravished my skull when a glimmer caught my attention from the corner of my eye. At first, I thought I imagined it, hallucinating from hunger or apoplexy, but it shimmered again—its shape fully apparent.

A dagger.

Its sharp tip was a harrowing reminder of how easily my sword had pierced Talon's flesh. I cringed, desperate to rid my mind of the image. How would I live with myself?

Wrapping my arms around my knees, I rocked back and forth—my eyes locked on the dagger as if it were going to jump up and stab me. In a way, I wished it would. Wherever we went after this, it sounded much more appealing.

I crawled over to it, gripping its steel handle in my fingers, admiring its weight. The size. A deep belly laugh erupted from somewhere inside me, echoing off the brick walls. It wasn't funny. No, the king wanted me to end it all. Like the trials, he hoped I'd do his dirty work for him. I was over the mind games. Tired of fighting.

Flipping the dagger in my hand, I entertained dark musings.

"You did it," a small voice squeezed. "Congratulations."

Pipion.

Clearing my throat, I placed the dagger in my lap and turned to her, my tone bored when I asked, "And what's that exactly?"

"Fulfilling your destiny." She blinked, licking her paw to clean the back of her ears.

I looked down and huffed a laugh, balancing the dagger on the tips of my fingers. "Don't tell me you believe I'm the fabled princess, too. I'm an abomination, Pipion. Death follows me everywhere. How am I to fulfill a destiny I don't know the first thing about? I'm a failure. Worthless." The silence felt too loud as I admitted it to her—to myself—my heart aching as I watched her bright eyes turn sad. I didn't want to believe it. But with everything that's happened, it was hard not to. I had so many questions—ones only my mother could answer.

I motioned around the cell. "I mean, look where we are. Back in the same place we first met. I'd hardly call that a win, Pipion. It's a tragedy." To think I'd believed for even a second I'd make it out alive. Make it home. That was the real joke: that for a moment, I thought I was capable. I rolled my shoulders, popping my neck.

"Elowyn," Pipion squeaked as she hopped onto my legs. "You have only just discovered who you are. The gifts you bestow. *This,*" she enunciated. "This is only the beginning." Distant shouting rang, and she raced to the bars, her tail alert while she peered out of the cell. "Get into the corner!" Pipion ordered, shooing me aside. "It's happening."

"What's happening?" I scurried back into my spot in the shadows, thumbing the ring on my finger until my skin was raw.

She didn't respond.

Swords clashed together as a struggle ensued, reverberating off the stone walls.

I held my breath while the seconds ticked past, counting the number of grunts and groans and obscene phrases, before everything abruptly went quiet.

Slow, deliberate steps followed, approaching my cell when a dark figure attached to the sound came to a stop before the metal bars. They waved their hands, opening the door as if pushing aside a curtain.

I swallowed hard when they entered, their presence sucking up all the air. Dominance and power rolled off them, and I knew they could kill me with a snap of their fingers.

Cringing, I pressed myself as far into the brick as I could, dagger at the ready, when they removed their hood.

Wavy, raven-colored hair spilled out against their forehead, sweeping in front of familiar emerald eyes. My heart sank.

It wasn't possible.

Snapping my jaw shut, I dropped the dagger and scrambled to my feet—hurrying to him as fast as I could before he disappeared, and collapsed into his strong, secure arms.

Sweat and iron overpowered his usual teakwood scent as he picked me up, gripping the back of my neck as I wrapped my legs around his torso.

Talon.

My Talon.

Alive—not dead.

Not rotting in a forest somewhere, but here in my cell. Holding me.

I couldn't stop the tears that flowed as I grabbed his face, pulling his lips to mine—savoring his taste and the warm sensation that grew deep in my belly. Talon didn't hold back. He claimed my mouth, taking what he wanted without reservation.

It was feral. Wild. And for a moment, my surroundings disappeared, and I forgot where we were.

Shoving out of his arms, I hopped to the ground, pounding my fists as hard as I could into his solid chest. "What the fuck!" I yelled, tears continuing to roll down my cheeks as I laid into him. "How! You were dead, I killed you!"

Talon captured my hands, pulling me back to him. He held my head to his body as I fought him, trying to wrangle free from his grasp, but I surrendered to it.

The cathartic rhythm of his heartbeat simmered my rage, and I loosened my breath, sinking into him. I didn't care how it was possible. I only cared that he was here.

My Talon

He brushed a strand of hair away from my wet face as he kissed the top of my head, my voice a whisper, "But your heart stopped."

"No, firefly, it just slowed to an undetectable rate," he said into my hair, kissing me once more before he pulled away, cupping my face. "I'd taken a preventative tonic moments before stepping into that arena that'd heal any injuries I'd receive. It was a risk you wouldn't plunge that sword into my heart, but one I was willing to take. I wanted to tell you. Stars, I hated hearing your cries, but I needed your reaction to be authentic so the king wouldn't suspect anything."

"I don't understand. Why—"

"I'll explain everything later, firefly. But right now, I'm here to make good on a certain promise that not even death can keep me from breaking." A knowing smirk curled his lips. "If we plan on getting out of here before the king realizes you're gone, we need to go now."

Talon raised his brows expectantly as he held out his palm, his eyes searching mine as he awaited my decision.

As if I needed to consider anything.

Without wasting another second, I laced my fingers in his

and followed close behind, twisting down different corridors, deep underneath the castle, to avoid being spotted.

Even as darkness consumed us and anxiety eclipsed my thoughts while we ran into the unknown, I'd never felt more alive.

Free.

I was finally going home.

THIRTY-FOUR

Numbness spread to my elbows as we inched through the narrow section of the underground tunnel, our bodies compressed to the limit to avoid getting stuck. Exhaustion weighed on me, every muscle aching, while Talon took the lead, skillfully navigating us through the intricate passageway.

"Are we almost there?" I fanned away a large cobweb—my skin crawling as it wrapped around my hand.

"Just around this corner." Talon contorted his body to fit through the stone, and I followed until we reached a dimly lit tunnel somewhere deep under the castle. I shimmied out of the shaft and hopped to my feet, flexing my arms to work blood back into them. Beams of light emitted through the metal gate at the end, and I felt thankful to be out of that wretched, dirty space.

Talon ducked into the shadows, and pulled me with him, our bodies slamming together. "Listen, when we get to the opening, run until you reach the stable. Don't stop, no matter what. Understood?"

My eyebrows furrowed as I processed what he was saying. "What? I—"

"Promise me, Elowyn. There's a witch that lives in the woods. Her name is Minerva. Find her if anything happens."

"I'm not going to leave you." I squared my shoulders to meet his tight stare. He was mad if he thought I wouldn't fight alongside him. There was too much at stake—and I was done running. And I was certainly done being afraid. "So, save me the lecture and give me a weapon because we both know I won't take no for an answer. This is my fight, too, Talon."

He clenched his jaw as he chewed on my words, likely devising a way to convince me otherwise. But it was a moot point. I motioned for him to get on with it, and with begrudging reluctance, Talon unsheathed the dagger at his hip and placed it in my palm.

I would've chuckled under different circumstances, but it didn't stop a pleased smirk from tugging at the corner of my mouth.

"Watch my right, got it?" His hand didn't leave mine as he spoke. "And don't you dare, for one second, try to save my ass before your own."

He pulled away before he could change his mind and pushed the metal gate open with quiet stealth, the muscles in his arm taut as he used the other to reach for me.

Guards materialized from what appeared to be thin air as soon as we stepped out, drawing their swords.

Talon held them back, casting balls of light from his hand, sending several of them flying back.

"Elowyn, go!" He demanded, keeping his focus ahead.

Magic continued to spew from his free hand as he fought the others off with his sword, blood spilling onto the ground. A rogue guard on Talon's right watched me, calculating my every breath with predatory stillness when he lunged at me, running at me faster than my legs would allow.

There was a flash of light, followed by a snarl, and a wolf appeared in his place—his blade-like fangs ready to tear into my skin.

He rapidly closed the distance between us and gained traction, roaring as it pounced at my back.

I fell, flipping onto my side just in time to capture its front legs, fighting against the fae to avoid razor-sharp claws.

We struggled—fighting for the upper hand—yet neither of us got anywhere. Rolling and struggling on the ground, I punched and kicked at its open belly, but its fur was like a shield.

Its thick saliva splattered on my face, disrupting my vision, and my hand slipped, giving the wolf an opportunity to swing its heavy paw at my head.

I curled into a ball to shield my head when it slumped—its weight crushing my ribcage when an invisible force flung it to the side, sending it into a ditch.

Sitting up on my forearms, I watched Talon stroll toward me, leaving a pile of bodies in his wake. He rolled his neck—as if slaughtering a dozen guards was a mere inconvenience—appearing unfazed without a fleck of dirt on his olive skin.

He sheathed his sword as he offered his hand, helping me up.

I used my sleeve to wipe my cheek. "How did he do that?"

Talon placed a hand on my back and led us to the pasture, looking over his shoulder to make sure no one was following us. "Well, most fae have some sort of elemental magic. They can manipulate water, control fire. Some, like myself, have solar magic and can harness light. Others, like that one, can shift at will."

"Into anything they want?"

"No, it's usually fated. There's very few who can control what they shift into."

The grass crunched beneath our feet as we picked up our pace, trying to reach the forest ahead before anyone else came after us.

I peered at Talon. His shoulders were back, his chin tipped up, not appearing the least bit concerned with whatever we may encounter.

The confidence he exuded, the arrogance—once repulsive —now comforted me.

I swallowed a smile. "So, you guys can wield this magic whenever you want, without consequence?"

"Ah, there's always a consequence, firefly. He likely won't be able to shift for days now. It's a delicate balancing act—the well only runs so deep until you burn out. I've seen far too many fae push their limits and exhaust their power entirely." He shrugged, resting a hand on the hilt of his sword. "I knew someone who shifted into a falcon one too many times and could never shift back out of it."

My eyes widened as I imagined the horror. "What about you? What are your limits?"

Talon grabbed my arm, forcing me to a stop.

I opened my mouth to question why, when he placed a finger over his mouth, silencing me. His body went rigid as he listened to our surroundings.

"We need to go. There's more coming." He had picked up on a sound in the distance, too far away for me to hear.

Talon pushed me into a run, and we sprinted for the forest, keeping our momentum until the shelter of trees hid us from view. We kept running until we reached the edge of the field where a wooden stable sat beside a creek, hidden deep within the thicket. Its tin roof was rusted over and worn from the sun due to years—if not decades—of neglect.

The soothing sound of trickling water washed over me.

We stepped inside. Small beams of light seeped through the cracks between the wooden slats, illuminating the settled dust and dirt that covered the beams. Hay littered the ground, stacking high into the corners while horse bays lined the back wall. It was quiet.

"What is this place?"

"It was an old stable we used years ago to deliver goods to fae on the outskirts. However, when King Harkin rose to power, he felt it was no longer necessary. He said it took up 'too many resources.' As if providing food to those unable to make the trek to the city was too much of a burden." He strolled to the middle bay, pushing the upper leaf open.

A dark bay mare neighed.

I approached the stall, and she reared at me as I peered through the barn door.

"Woah! Down girl," Talon soothed. Unlatching the brass lock, the bottom door opened with a whine, and he stepped in, rubbing his palm along the bridge of her nose.

She snorted.

"Shh. It's okay, Zephyr," he continued, stroking her black mane. "It's Elowyn. You remember me telling you about her, don't you?"

I waved—unsure what else to do—in a pathetic attempt to show her I wasn't a threat. "Is this your horse?"

"She was your fathers." A distant smile pulled at his mouth as he spoke.

Butterflies swarmed my belly. Just when I'd grown comfortable and accepted the feelings I had for him, Talon pulled the rug from under my feet, and I was back to where I began: conflicted and confused. He'd held such a heavy secret without so much as revealing an inkling of suspicion.

How would I know if—when—he was keeping something

else from me? I wanted to trust him, but how could I when I couldn't even trust my intuition to know the difference?

"She sprained her leg a few years back," he continued. "King Harkin insisted we put her down. So, I took her to the healer. Watched as they sharpened the axe, but I couldn't do it. I brought her here instead."

My stomach dropped as I looked at the beautiful, healthy horse before me, unable to imagine how anyone could think she deserved to die. "Why would he do that?"

Watching him care for the horse pulled my heartstrings taut.

His compassion.

The gentle ease with which he mollified her.

It was an entirely different side to him, and it warmed my chest despite my unwillingness.

"Because she was King Gareth's personal horse. Harkin did a number on her because of that."

The horse snorted, finally settling.

"She's skittish of strangers now, unfortunately." Talon tipped his head toward Zephyr as he plucked a sugar cube from the pale. "Try talking to her," he said and dropped a few cubes into my palm.

I looked from the horse to him as I chewed the inside of my lip, unsure of what to say to calm her.

"My apologies, I didn't mean to alarm you, I'm only trying to get back home," I tried. "My horse, Sugarfoot, is waiting for me. So is my mother, hopefully."

The likelihood I'd find my mother in a condition less than poor was now an all too real probability—one I'd forced myself not to think about this entire time. I couldn't escape it now. Whether I was ready to admit it, I was going to see for myself. And when I did, I'd have to learn to live with it.

Zephyr nickered, scuffing a hoof against the dirt. "It's good to finally meet you, Elowyn." Her voice was as smooth as silk. "Although I could do without that *rodent* in your pocket."

Startled, I jumped back—moments away from ripping off my vest—when Pipion poked her head out. Her enormous eyes were apologetic as I fell against the bay wall, placing a hand over my heart to calm my nerves.

"I didn't want to stay behind when everything went down." Pipion rubbed a paw over her eye. "But you were so preoccupied, there wasn't a good time to tell you."

"Yeah, no shit." Pushing off the wall, I rubbed my brow. "Is it okay if she comes along?" I held a sugar cube between my fingers, and her tongue jutted out, sweeping the treat from my hand in one swift, wet motion.

"I suppose if that'll make you happy, Elowyn." Zephyr snatched another cube while I wasn't paying attention. "Keep it stowed away. Stars help me if that rodent so much as touches me. I will stomp it without hesitation."

I huffed a laugh, opening my palm to give her the rest of the cubes. "Deal. You can handle that, right, Pipion?"

She squeaked her understanding—burrowing back into my vest—as I watched Talon bridle the horse.

He latched a saddle onto her back as if he'd done it a hundred times over and swiftly mounted her, adjusting himself before extending a hand to me. "You ready, firefly?" His eyes were bright.

I swallowed, looking over my shoulder at the castle in the distance where my friends' lives had ended too soon. A pang of sorrow twisted in my chest, and I turned around, placed my foot into the stirrup, and flung my other leg over.

For them, I told myself.

I held onto the back of the saddle, but Talon grabbed my wrists, wrapping my arms tightly around his stomach.

"You need to hold on," he said, letting his fingers linger on mine to make sure I stayed put.

I bit my lip, ignoring how his warm scent enveloped me as I did what he ordered. Ignoring how my breath hitched as I strad-dled his back—bringing with it images of the last night we shared. How perfectly we fit together. How undone he made me.

I squirmed, trying to find relief from the building pressure, and he squeezed my thigh. His touch remained and never wavered. Even long after he commanded Zephyr out of the stables.

We rode for hours.

Day turned into dusk as we traveled—further and further from the castle. There was no sign of life. No forest creatures. Only towering evergreens, endless forest vegetation, and the rhythmic sound of Zephyr's hooves clapping against the undergrowth.

Everything blurred together, flashing by at a dizzying rate, and I closed my eyes—my legs aching from sitting so long.

"Can we stop for a minute?" I stretched my back. "I think I'm going to be sick."

"We're almost there." Talon covered my hand with his and squeezed. "You see that cottage up ahead? That's where we're going."

A small stone house came into view, wrapped in flowering vines. It looked like a drawing out of a storybook with its black, tin roof arching to a point and the plumes of smoke billowing out of the chimney. Even as we advanced, it remained but a quaint structure—making me wonder how we'd both fit.

"Where are we?" I asked.

Talon helped me dismount. He held me close as I stumbled into him, kissing the top of my head. "The witch's house I told you about. You didn't think we'd leave without the cure for your mother, did you?"

I whipped around to look at him, a mixture of wonder and gratitude filling my chest. "She has the nightingale?"

Talon caressed a thumb along my cheekbone and cupped my chin—a strong, sure gesture—and he nodded. "I should warn you though, Minerva's an ancient, powerful being. She never does anything without wanting something in return. Let me do the talking, okay? Follow my lead."

I shuddered, my stomach twisting into knots while I watched Talon tie Zephyr off on a nearby tree, shielding my arms as a deft wave of wind brushed past, rustling the leaves.

The atmosphere thickened, a heavy blanket smothering the air, and we approached the wicker door. It opened wide—ready to devour us—revealing a gaping black hole on the other side.

"After you." I motioned Talon ahead.

He rolled his shoulders, an impish smirk lifting at the corner of his mouth as he slipped his hands into his pockets. "Chicken," he said, disappearing into the cottage.

Flipping my finger to his back, I stayed behind. Listening. Waiting to hear if any commotion broke out. For any shrieks or cackles indicating a struggle. But I was met with deafening silence. Even the wind stilled—the forest around me growing dark.

The hair on my neck stood as I stepped forward, on high alert for anything that could be lurking in the near distance.

"I think I'm going to wait out here," Pipion said, startling me. She hopped out of my pocket and scurried onto a bed of grass several yards away. "I'll be here when you get back. Don't look her in the eyes too long—she'll turn your heart to stone."

Perfect.

I turned back to the cottage, second-guessing my decision. The last time I ignored the stories, it didn't work out for me very well. However, I didn't come this far to stop now.

I took a deep breath, muttered to myself, "Well, here goes nothing," and slipped into the darkness.

THIRTY-FIVE

"Talon!" I yelled, feeling my way around the darkness. Trying to find something, anything, that could help me gather my bearings. But there was nothing—only blind faith as I continued forward. "Where are you?" I called out again.

Wiping my palms against my pants, a twinkle of light appeared ahead, growing larger with each step I took.

It flickered and darted to the left and then the right, shooting back and forth haphazardly until it came to an abrupt stop at the tip of my nose.

My eyes crossed at its nearness, and I took a step back, the soft light warming my face. It called to me—a welcoming invitation—and I reached for it, hesitating for a moment before I touched it with my index finger.

As soon as I did, everything around me exploded. A kaleidoscope of colors twisting and expanding.

I folded like paper between pockets of air, spinning and tumbling, until I crashed face-first into a black and gold ornate rug. Air shot from my lungs, and I rolled onto my back, choking as I learned how to breathe again.

Talon appeared above me, his hair shielding only part of his expression. He looked down at me, bemused. I wanted to smack him as he helped me to my feet. "That's one way to make an entrance."

I rolled my eyes, brushing my clothes back into place, ignoring the sting in my palms and how he watched me. "Yeah, well, you could've warned me."

Talon smiled. "Where would be the fun in that?"

Placing a hand on the small of my back, he guided me out of the foyer and into a sitting room. The cottage was much larger than it appeared from the outside. The huge, frameless windows on the north end of the home opened to the bright, immense moon—illuminating the space. Golden frames of all shapes and sizes covered the walls, as did an assortment of potted green plants. Wicker baskets and jars filled with herbs, bookshelves stacked with grimoires, and random trinkets filled every room. There wasn't an empty space to be found.

It was cozy.

Welcoming, even.

"She's placed a glamor on the house," Talon offered, noticing the wonder on my face. "It's to detract any wanderers that may come across it. The portals to ward off anyone who's bold enough to enter that has ill intentions."

I roamed over to the crackling fireplace, holding my hands near the open flame, warming my wind-blown skin. "What happens to them? The ones that do."

"Some say they're torn into a thousand pieces and used for Minerva's spells."

The side door in the kitchen creaked open to reveal a petite, blonde-haired woman. "Oh, don't lie to the poor girl, Talon," she said as she entered, placing an empty jar on the wooden table. Her navy-blue dress flowed with each movement and swept across the stone floor as she glided over to us. Her pale skin looked almost see-through; it glowed under the moonlight —she was entrancing.

I shifted my weight between my feet.

"A witch cooks two lost children in her oven one time and suddenly we're all bad." She chuckled, holding out her hand. "I'm Minerva."

Her touch was light and soft, like the rest of her appearance. "Elowyn."

Minerva looked me up and down. "So, you're the one they whisper about," she stated. "You defied the king."

I gulped, looking behind her at Talon for support. He'd made himself comfortable on a deep purple chaise lounge, his legs crossed at the ankles, seemingly asleep when his eyelid popped open, and he winked. So happy one of us took this seriously.

Forever an arrogant prick.

"I didn't defy him. I won fairly."

She smiled, flashing her sharpened teeth. "Yet you're on the run."

I nodded, trying to pull my hand away.

But her grip tightened. "Curious. That's not what I hear." She turned my palm over in hers, her eyes growing wide. "Oh, what a beautiful ring. It's so unique. Please, child, where did you get this?"

Her grip loosened, and I could finally rip my hand back and tuck it under my arm. "From my mother. It was my father's ring."

Minerva's smile stretched across her face. "Very curious." She stared at me for a moment—her icy gray eyes bore into mine until she snapped out of it. "I say, how about some tea, hm? And you can explain what brings you two to my home."

She whisked away on a breeze back to the kitchen where a

kettle sounded—convenient timing for someone who didn't know we'd be arriving.

"Talon, are you sure this is a good idea?" I whispered as he stood from the chaise. "She won't poison us or anything, will she?"

"No." He smirked. "Well, lest you offend her, that is."

My stomach dropped, and I whipped my head toward Minerva—carefully watching her as she prepared the tea and noted everything she used. If she thought I'd defied the king, would she stupefy me and try to drag me back to him?

No, Talon wouldn't let that happen. Unless, of course, she drugged him too.

Talon's low, husky laugh brushed against my ear, breaking me free from my thoughts. "There's nothing to worry about, firefly." He squeezed my hand. "We'll be on our way soon enough, okay?"

I nodded, allowed him to lead me into the kitchen, and sat down in a metal chair at the wooden table. Bushels of thyme, sage, and rosemary hung from the ceiling, filling the room with a savory aroma that blended nicely with the brewing tea.

Talon took a seat next to me, pulled a knife out of his sleeve, and began cleaning his fingernails. A bored habit of his I'd picked up on.

"So, Elowyn. What brings you all the way to my neck of the woods?" Minerva placed two small porcelain cups down and filled them with tea. "Sugar?"

I shook my head.

"We were hoping you could help us," Talon said. "We need the nightingale elixir."

"I see." Minerva poured herself a cup and joined us at the table, dumping a spoonful of sugar into her tea. "That's a specialty blend for respiratory ailments, you know. What do you need an elixir such as that for?" She took a sip and placed her cup back down.

"My mother," I offered. "She's sick, and her medicine's run out. I crossed into Faerway because I remembered a story about the nightingale and thought if I could find it, it'd cure her." I shrugged. "But obviously, that didn't go as planned."

Bringing the cup to my nose, I inhaled—containing an audible sigh of delight as my mouth watered. If the witch thought it safe enough to drink, it should be okay, right? I looked to Talon, who did the same, taking a sip as well to reassure me.

Without giving it another thought, I emptied the liquid into my mouth. My chest and belly warmed as it slid down my throat. It was even tastier than I could've imagined. A blend of lemon and chamomile that instantly relaxed my nerves.

Minerva set her cup down. "How is it, my dear?"

"It's delicious. I've never known tea to have such flavor. Normally, it tastes like dirty pond water, but this?" I took another sip. "I could drink it all day."

She reached across the table, placed her hand on mine, and smiled. "It's an ancient recipe. I can try to find it for you if you'd like."

I opened my mouth to tell her how much I'd like that when she interrupted me and asked, "Have you ever had your palm read?"

Talon and I shared a look, taken back by the sudden change of subject.

"I'm sorry, it's one of my many specialties," Minerva continued. "And I'd be delighted if you allowed me the honor of reading yours while you're here."

It never interested me—tarot, crystals, palm readings—it all seemed nonsensical. However, that was before arriving in Faerway and experiencing all the magic. Before learning all the stories were true. It was hard not to be slightly curious now, if only to not offend her.

"Yes—I mean, no. No, I've never had a palm reading. I'd love that."

Butterflies swarmed my stomach as she pulled my hand toward her and unraveled my fingers, running hers along my palm.

"Ah yes. A nice, strong headline, just as I suspected. You're wise—bullheaded even." She chuckled, pointing to the line that ran directly under my index finger. "This line here, your heart line, indicates you can be quite ruthless and impulsive. This will be your downfall—you'll need to be careful."

I sucked in a breath. My downfall? I didn't like the sound of that. However, she continued, running her fingers along mine, observing, and pressing the skin on my palms to get a better look. Her face gave nothing away as she twisted and turned my palm up and down and over, checking every angle.

"Yes, you have much to offer, my dear," she went on. "With much luck and love on your side. You'll be powerful because of this—almost unstoppable, but not without its challenges and sorrow. Your future is bright but also filled with darkness, my dear. Hold on to the light so it doesn't consume you."

Minerva released my hand, and I pulled it into my lap, wringing my fingers together. I wasn't sure how I was supposed to feel about any of that. My downfall. The darkness that could consume me. My head ached as I mulled over her words, trying to find a semblance of comfort but fell short of nothing.

Talon cleared his throat. "Well, as touching as this moment is, can you help us or not, Minerva? We must get back on our journey." He leaned back in the metal chair and stretched his legs. Despite the size of the kitchen, his tall frame took up most of the space—the room shrinking around him. His eyes never left hers as he continued to clean his fingernails, the sharp, polished blade a promise that he'd be leaving with the nightingale one way or another.

Minerva glowered at him and clicked her tongue. A wicked gleam shone in her eye as she turned her attention back to me. "Always in such a rush, this one. Fae have endless time and yet no patience. Riddle me that one."

Talon rolled his eyes.

She stood from the table, holding up the body of her dress as she twirled and swayed through the kitchen—stopping when she reached a shelf of labeled bottles, varying in different sizes. She ran her fingers along each one before plucking out a small purple vial, no bigger than her thumb.

"Here we are, the nightingale elixir," she sang. "An elusive remedy that can kill as quickly as it can cure. Three and a half drops every hour for one day and not a second sooner."

My skin went cold as she placed it in my palm, turning it.

"I think this should cover it." Talon reached into his pocket and pulled out a cloth bag and tossed it in the center of the table.

"Oh, no, no. Your coin isn't necessary. This visit has been far more valuable." Minerva took my hand. "Thank you. It was a pleasure meeting you." She turned to Talon. "The next time you show up here unexpectedly, I'll give you a tail."

A smile curled up his lips, and he touched my elbow, signaling it was time to leave. "It was nice seeing you too, Minerva."

"Remember what I said, Elowyn," Minerva said, her touch cold. "Don't let the darkness consume you."

THIRTY-SIX

Zephyr carried us through the inky shadows and deep into the untamed forest as Talon skillfully navigated us around trees and branches. I felt exposed to whatever lurked beyond my sight, the skin crawling on my back. We needed to stop and make shelter somewhere—especially when things like drowlers existed. I shuddered at the memory.

We rode for another hour until we eventually slowed to a trot, coming to a full halt in a circle of trees. "What is this place?"

Talon grabbed my waist as he helped me dismount the horse next, rubbing the side of my arms to warm me. He lifted his chin. "Look up," he said.

I did what he asked—my mouth gaping open at the sight of the treehouse above. It appeared multi-leveled, with sections of it hidden behind thick hemlocks and a wraparound deck. It was secluded—like our own private oasis—and I basked in the privacy it'd provide from the creatures that wandered the night.

I hummed, turning to Talon briefly before approaching the hanging ladder. "Please tell me we're going to sleep up there."

A low chuckle formed in Talon's throat as he tied Zephyr

off to a tree. "Mhm. Now let's go before the wispings come out."

"Wispings? What is that?" I peered over at Zephyr, and then Pipion, who was curled into a ball inside Talon's satchel. "Will they be okay if we leave them here?"

"They'll be fine, now go."

I stepped onto the first rung and continued up and up until I reached the wooden deck overlooking the forest canopy. "Where are we?"

He pulled me to him as he joined me on the terrace, and I inhaled his warm scent, smiling into his chest. Being in his arms was like taking a deep, long overdue breath. Gone were the worries of tomorrow and what the king was planning. He planted me firmly in this moment.

"Rahway—about ten miles from where I grew up," Talon said. "My father built this treehouse for us when we were kids." He took my hands and led us inside, the floorboards creaking under our weight. It was a simple setup fit for growing children, with a small table and a few chairs. Books and children's toys—soaked in dust—rested on untouched bookshelves, hidden by the large tree trunk that jutted through the space. Ghosts of memories played under the large skylight. I imagined a young Talon running around causing havoc, then took in the murals painted along the walls.

"I thought someone would've torn it down by now," he continued. "Imagine my surprise when I came across it a few years back on patrol. Since then, whenever I find myself in the area, I come here to rest."

"Have you thought about restoring it?"

Talon wiped his hands down the side of his pants, while he walked to the far back corner of the treehouse. "Maybe one day when I have a family of my own," he said over his shoulder. "Only time will tell."

"You should. This place is beautiful, it shouldn't go to waste."

Talon pulled out two bedrolls and a few blankets from a storage chest and piled them onto the floor, making a pallet on the ground for us to sleep on. He motioned for me to sit, and I flopped down—my bones sighing with relief as I stretched out.

After an entire day on horseback, it felt amazing to rest my aching back and breathe in the stars that splattered the inky sky. Hundreds—thousands—of them glittered through the skylight, casting soft shadows into the treehouse.

The backdrop to countless love stories.

The gatekeeper of even more secrets.

This moment was a mere blip in time compared to all they'd seen, and yet for me, it was everything. The thought was terrifyingly beautiful.

How every breath, thought, laugh, and tear would one day become stardust and fade into oblivion—lost amongst the sea of constellations. And I would be nothing but a memory.

I shook off the chill that ran down my spine, this moment suddenly feeling much, *much* bigger. More important. Maybe all this pain and struggle wouldn't be for nothing? Maybe I was, in fact, destined for something greater. To be the fabled princess.

My head lolled to the side to find Talon looking out the window, appearing far away in distant memories. I could drink him in all night—savor his beauty. The way his hair brushed the tips of his eyelashes. How his long, nimble fingers curled around the hilt of his weapons as he unstrapped them from his body. The veins in his forearms and his satin-like skin.

I wanted to trust him again, but the nagging voice in my head screamed danger. What else was he keeping from me? What other secrets was the night hiding?

Talon turned and met my gaze as if he sensed me staring,

and my heart fluttered. There wouldn't be any other way to find out. I sat up and rubbed my hands against my pants, bracing myself for answers I wasn't sure I was ready for.

"We should probably talk about it, Talon."

He raised his brows in question, and I cleared my throat.

"About how you know more about me than I do."

Talon's chest rose as he took a deep breath and strolled over to the pallet of blankets. "Something wicked has festered in this realm long before your father died. He tried to get ahead of it, but..." His knee brushed mine as he laid down, propping himself up on his elbow. "You should know that this entire realm—who *you* are—your father wanted to keep you from all of it. Made me swear, should anything happen to him, that I'd continue to do just that." Talon's lip pulled into a frown. "I checked on you and Deirdre as often as I could, but when the trials began, my visits became less and less frequent."

"Seeing you in that forest was the last thing I expected. It'd been years since I'd seen you, yet there you were: a lamb amongst wolves. And there was nothing I could do about it." His lips pressed into a hard line, and his brows furrowed, as if recalling the memory was physically painful for him. "You don't know how badly I wanted to let you go. But I couldn't. Not with the other guards present. Had I known your mother was sick, Elowyn... If I could've done something sooner." He shook his head. "I hated myself for it. I needed you to hate me for it, too. So, I pushed you. Tried not to get attached, but it was impossible. The way you pushed back. Your strength. Your fire. You were my speck of light in complete darkness. *My firefly.*" The air in the room grew thick with each confession that left his lips, and my chest felt heavy. "I couldn't let anything happen to you—not because of the promise I made to your father—because I was selfish. Because I wanted—needed—more time with you. But by the time King Harkin figured it out, your fate was sealed. As was mine for protecting you. So, when I learned he'd gone back on his word, there was no logic—only pure rage—as I fought to get to you."

There'd always been something so familiar about Talon. Maybe that ancient voice inside me knew just how intrinsically woven together our lives were. It would explain why, despite my initial contempt, I'd always felt safe with him. Even when I believed he wanted me dead. Talon had always been my protector. *My guard*. He had kept to the shadows and risked his life to do whatever was necessary to keep me safe. His loyalty may have been to my father, but he would lay down his life for me. I couldn't believe I'd think he'd ever lie to me, especially when he'd never given me any reason not to trust him. He'd been nothing but supportive. Encouraging.

I didn't need to hear anymore.

My lips crashed onto his, and I pulled him to me—needing to eliminate all the distance that remained. Magic danced on my tongue, igniting every nerve. Every bone. Filling me—completing me. A part of me felt undeserving of his devotion after everything I'd put him through, but all I wanted—*needed*—was to show him how much it meant to me.

Talon rose to his knees, pressing his body into mine as he laid me on the pallet of blankets, his rough hands in my hair.

"I'm so sorry, firefly." His voice was barely a whisper, breaking our kiss as his lips found my neck, licking and sucking above my collarbone. "Please forgive—"

I arched into him and pulled him closer, meeting his tongue stroke for stroke to silence him. "You have nothing to apologize for," I said between breaths. "I should be the one asking for forgiveness. I didn't mean any of the cruel things I said. I was just angry. Confused."

He sunk his teeth into my neck, and I moaned, biting my lip.

A wicked smile curled up the side of Talon's lips as his mouth found mine and his hips rocked against me, wanting and ready. His kisses soft and diligent—nothing like the rushed, desperate frenzy of stolen touches back at the castle. No, Talon was taking his time, savoring me as if he had all the time in the world. His hand slid down my body, appreciating every curve along the way until he reached my waist. Deft fingers caressing my skin.

Talon leaned down, brushed his nose along mine, and kissed me.

I reached for his waistband, feeling for the clasp, but he pulled my hand away and pinned it above my head. "No, firefly. No. Tonight, you're mine. I'm going to show you exactly what you do to me."

The weight of his body on top of mine drove me wild, and my hips bucked, desperate to meet his. Desperate for more. His firm grip had me crying out, and I hooked my legs around his waist, guiding him to me, but he resisted. Teasing me.

More. I needed more.

Insufferable prick.

"Every fucking dream I have revolves around you, every thought," he said against my lips, and I drank in every syllable, writhing with pleasure as his tongue trailed down my neck. "Let me show you what you do to me, Elowyn." My name never sounded so beautiful. Like a sacred oath, as it rolled off his tongue—with such tenderness and promise, my chest threatened to rip open. "Let me show you how consumed I am by you." Talon scooped me into his arms then and unclasped my vest, pushing it off my shoulders as he removed my shirt.

My fingers trailed down his stomach until they reached the hem of his shirt, and I tugged it over his head, pulling him back to me, unable to stand the separation.

Talon smiled against my mouth and grabbed a handful of

my breast, working the button on my pants with the other. He helped me pull them past my hips, cradling my head in a kiss while I shimmied them off, and tossed them to the side.

My bare legs chilled as the crisp air brushed my skin, and Talon's eyes darkened. His gaze swept over me as I lay before him in only my undergarments. Slowly and deliberately.

Talon removed his pants and let them fall to the ground, appreciating my body a little while longer before he removed my thin gossamer barriers, leaving me completely exposed.

A hum of his appreciation settled over me. "Stars, firefly, you're so fucking perfect," he said, kissing my forehead while he buried himself inside me.

His eyes fluttered closed as he savored the feeling. Talon's mouth fell open with a breathless sigh, and I gasped.

He brushed his thumb along my lower lip as he pulled out, lightly moving in and out until I adjusted to his size. He covered my mouth with his, swallowing my moans as he continued to rock against me with diligent, easy strokes. His hand never left my breast, his other tangled in my hair as he entered me, worshiping every inch of my body, slowly picking up speed.

Demanding.

Unadulterated moans fell from my lips.

He filled me, my hips meeting his stroke for stroke.

Talon's low, deep groans sent me over the edge as I came undone around him, his rhythm never slowing as I grew wings and flew, pleasure rippling through me so intense stars exploded in my vision. The corner of his mouth lifted into a grin at my completion, and I fell limp. His eyes rolled into the back of his head as he came with me, the growl that escaped him splitting me in half.

Talon pulled me to his chest as if I'd actually fly away and kissed my shoulder, gathering my hair to the side, licking the salt-slicked skin at the nape of my neck.

I shuddered in his arms, interlocking our fingers, and my breaths labored, exhaustion pulling me into its grips.

I turned around and nuzzled my head into the crook of his arm. "Please, never leave me again."

"Not even in my dreams." He kissed the tip of my nose, tucking a stray piece of hair behind my ear—his gaze serious. In his arms, I was safe.

And in that moment, I knew that no matter what happened, as long as I had him, everything would be okay.

Thirty-Seven

We made it to the Dolorem River the next morning before the sun rose in the sky, neither of us knowing how long we had until the king's guard caught up to us. All we knew was, that despite how perfectly our bodies molded together to shield each other from the brisk morning air, there was no time to waste if we wanted to keep whatever advantage we might've had. If any.

I could've stayed tucked away in his treehouse, curled up with Talon, for eternity. Or at least held onto that moment a little longer before reality came crashing down like an unforgiving wave—relentless and unabated. Before everything changed forever.

My heart leaped into my throat as we approached the shore, an odd stillness settling over the forest with each step Zephyr took as if it held its breath, waiting to see what'd happen next. That made two of us. A few short weeks ago, I'd looked across this same river with hope and eagerness.

Today, I returned to where my nightmare began.

The water glistened under the sun's rays, mocking me—the only proof it was alive.

The trials. Escaping death.

None of it would matter if we couldn't escape—if Talon's plan failed. If *I* failed.

"What if the wards are still in place?" My fingers flexed on Talon's side as I tried to calm my nerves, but despite my best efforts, my heart still raced in my chest. It was the question I was dreading to ask—the one that hung around my neck like a noose.

Everything weighed on one simple answer.

He covered my hands with his and wrapped them around his middle.

His touch calmed me immediately. I relaxed into him, taking in his scent and gentle touch, wondering what our future looked like. If one even existed past the shoreline. I shook the thought away.

"Then we keep running." Talon shrugged. "And we'll keep running until I get you somewhere safe and find a way through the wards to help Deirdre. My promise won't die in vain here, firefly. I swear to you." Talon clicked his tongue and cued Zephyr into a trot, leading us into the river before I could protest or read into his response. I held onto him as tight as I could as the water inched up our waists, the cold water stealing my breath—a warning of just how lethal it could be.

A reminder of the dangers that lurked beneath its surface.

I fought through the shock and took a deep breath, resigning to the river's demands, and clamped my teeth down on my quivering lip.

Pipion scurried out of Talon's bag and crawled up my torso, reaching my shoulder just as Zephyr's hooves dropped off the stream bed and the water reached our collarbones.

I looked up, searching for images within the clouds, trying to distract myself, only to find flashbacks in their place. I winced. My leg burned as I recalled the searing, hot pain of the water wraith's claw cutting into my flesh—and the infection that brewed after. The fever. The fear that threatened to strangle me. My throat swelled just like it did when the river swallowed my screams, and I coughed, my eyes brimming with tears.

My stomach lurched—it wasn't real, I reminded myself. I was safe. Talon promised they wouldn't harm me while in his company, and I knew with every fiber of my being that was true.

Yet I couldn't allow myself to relax. Being in the same wraith-infested waters had the hairs on the back of my neck standing up with each fluttering movement.

"How are you doing back there?" Talon squeezed my forearm. "You haven't taken a breath in over a minute."

I rested my forehead against his back and closed my eyes, taking a long drawl of air back to the present moment.

Pipion giggled. "I think she's struggling,"

I would've flicked her off my shoulder if she wasn't the perfect wraith bate. "Nope, I'm good," I forced out, my lungs straining. "I'm good. Just want to get back on dry land. *Now.*"

"We're almost there, I promise. Only a few more yards."

I hummed my reply, peeking open an eye to see for myself. The hint of pine and moss wafted into my nostrils, replacing the lavender scent that was uniquely Faerway's.

I spotted the tattered remains of my rope on the ground, still loosely tied around the trunk of the tree. My satchel, however, was nowhere to be found. I wondered if that was nature's doing, picked off by animals to make nests, or if a search party had come across it when I never came home. The thought of my mother receiving my belongings without me in tow was almost enough for my tears to well over. The distress. The anguish.

I swallowed hard.

I would make it right—there was no other option.

We were so close.

But just then, a sharp, spindly fin broke the surface of the water and circled the rear of the horse, disappearing under the murky water. A ripple brushed against my back, and I broke out in a cold sweat.

No, not again.

The memories came back with a vengeance, and I squeezed my eyes shut—my spine tingling with fear, and I silently pleaded for Zephyr to move faster. Quicker.

"Please, please, *please*, hurry," I pushed, my arms aching as I clutched Talon tighter, trying but failing to disappear into him.

He tapped his heels into Zephyr again, and she picked up speed, gliding us through the water as swiftly as a fish. The wraith followed beside us—a menacing smirk on her thin lips while her spindly black hair trailed behind her like ink.

Taunting me.

Relishing in my fear.

Hunting me now that it'd latched onto my scent.

It felt like an eternity before Zephyr's hooves finally reconnected with the stream bed and pushed us up onto the shore, my full body weight returning to normal as she shook her mane dry. I looked back at the river as we trotted ahead, meeting the same beady gaze of the water wraith who'd attacked me weeks ago, snapping her sharpened teeth at me before she swam away.

Shuttering, I averted my eyes and rested my chin on Talon's back.

Talon vibrated with laughter and gave my thigh a reassuring squeeze. "You can loosen that death grip now, firefly. We won't make it far if you cut off my air supply."

I let my hands fall to his waist and rolled my eyes. I couldn't believe it; it was truly happening. With nothing left standing in our way, the stars were finally in my favor.

There should've been a rush of excitement that swelled in

my belly the deeper we traveled into the dense forest. However, I couldn't shake the fact that something didn't sit right.

Maybe it was the overgrown canopy.

Or maybe I'd grown used to the enchanting faerie landscape.

Whatever the reason, the leaves in Wendover felt washed out and dull. *Bland*. Something was off, yet I couldn't put my finger on what—even the air smelled different.

My bones didn't hum with the same vivacity they did in Faerway, and a deep, ancient yearning inside me itched to be unleashed.

When I'd traveled through this forest all those weeks ago, life felt fragile and hopeless. Like each step threatened to snap me in half. I couldn't have imagined what the stars had in store for me or who—what—I'd become. The man I'd meet.

I held that scared, meek girl I used to be close to my heart, slightly envious of her blind optimism. Surely, life was bound to look different after experiencing such emotional turmoil, right?

A pit formed in my stomach, wondering how my mother would react when I told her about everything that had happened. Once she drank the nightingale elixir and the initial shock wore off, there was no doubt she'd give me a piece of her mind.

As much as I dreaded the inevitable lecture, I longed to hear her voice again, even if her words were coated with disdain. My chest swelled, and I pictured the dormant fire returning to her eyes—the rose hue to her cheeks.

I bit my lip to keep my smile at bay, not wanting to get ahead of myself, but as we broke through the tree line, it became impossible to suppress. There were a hundred questions I couldn't wait to ask that'd keep us talking until dawn. I could already hear the crackle of the fireplace while I nestled under a blanket and talked in circles. My mother's face terse as she gave me her undivided attention.

I wondered if she'd be able to see past her bias of the fae and accept Talon, let alone allow him into our home, especially after she learned about what I'd endured.

If I was able to, she could also, right? After all, she had fallen in love with my father.

The nagging voice in my head told me it wouldn't be that simple.

A few minutes later, the small cottage that'd raised me formed at the bottom of the hill—its stone walls and cherry wood door welcoming us. My heart caught in my throat, stealing my breath.

Home.

I'd almost forgotten what it looked like.

Tears burned my eyes, blurring my vision before I quickly wiped them away, afraid if I blinked, it'd disappear. After weeks of doubt and torment—there it was.

I could almost smell the cinnamon burning inside. Although I'd begged the stars to bring me back home, I hadn't actually believed it would happen.

Being there was so surreal—overwhelming.

Talon looked over his shoulder, flicking his chin toward the house. "Go on," he said. "We'll be right behind you."

My jaw fell open, but I remained frozen, sputtering incoherent sentences. I wasn't sure what I was attempting to protest—perhaps it was shock. Perhaps I was overflowing with so much happiness my body didn't know how to handle it all.

"Go, firefly." Talon nudged me.

I closed my mouth and nodded, wiping my palms along my pants before I flung my leg off Zephyr and hopped onto the ground.

It felt like a dream.

Everything that had happened these last two months was meant to keep me away—prevent me from getting my happily ever after—but there it was. *I won*.

"Elowyn!" an unusual, disembodied voice rang inside my head.

I looked around, my eyebrows knitting tightly together looking for the source, when I spotted Sugarfoot across the field in her usual spot under the oak tree. She reared on her hind legs, kicking her hooves through the air as she neighed loud enough for the entire countryside to hear. "Elowyn, you're home!"

I slapped a hand over my mouth, allowing the tears to well over and flow down my cheeks, fighting the verge of completely losing it right there. My Sugarfoot. Her white coat shone in the sun, looking as healthy as ever.

"I'm here, girl!" I yelled back.

My legs carried me faster than they ever had before—the wind drying my damp face—until I finally reached her. I threw my arms around her neck and clung to her, letting out a squeal of happiness. Sugarfoot nudged me with her nose in a fit of excitement, nickering and snorting as I ran my hands through her coarse mane, laughing through the tears.

Stars, I had missed her so much.

Zephyr was wonderful, but nothing could ever compare to my girl. I never wanted to leave her again.

She neighed loudly. "I missed you so much. I thought you weren't ever coming back! We've been worried sick!"

"I know, I know. I'm sorry." I kissed the tip of her snout and reached into my vest, pulling out the vial of nightingale—the deep purple liquid like a melted jewel. "But it wasn't for nothing. I got this."

Sugarfoot's eyes widened. "Oh yay, you got it! I knew you could do it!" She twirled in a circle, her tail bouncing with each movement, and I laughed. Stars, it was good to be home.

"You'll never believe what I endured to get it, either." I wiped the lingering tears from my eyes, my cheeks hurting from smiling so hard. "I have so much to tell you."

"I never doubted you for a second, Elowyn. You are your father's daughter, after all."

Your father's daughter.

One simple comment had me tumbling back down from the clouds, disorientated and in a haze. Not that I was surprised Sugarfoot knew my father. However, it was unsettling that everyone knew but me.

My hand dropped to my side, wiping my palms down my tattered pants, and looked down—my clothes matching the disarray of emotions coursing through me.

"Zephyr?" Sugarfoot asked, but her question wasn't directed at me.

Confused, I turned to find Talon on the back of a rearing Zephyr, trying to calm her as she proceeded to gallop straight at us. He leaped off her back just as she and Sugarfoot collided, frolicking and playing like they hadn't seen each other in years.

Talon approached and folded his arms across his chest while he relished in their moment. "Sugarfoot was part of your father's fleet," he said after a moment. "When he learned Deirdre was pregnant, he gave her Sugarfoot to help make her travels to their meeting spot easier."

My brows shot up. "She was my father's too?"

He nodded.

I looked back at the two long-lost friends enjoying their reunion, and warmth filled my chest. It was perfect—everything was—yet a sadness tugged at my heart despite it. I felt guilty for surviving. For having hope. A deep festering shame threatened to pour from my eyes as I thought about Calandra and Breana and the life they'd never get to experience.

I sniffled, wiping my running nose with my sleeve. I'd imagined returning home a million times, yet nothing could've prepared me for how emotional I'd be. Conflicted.

The cottage door creaked open behind me, stealing my attention to find my mother on the stoop. My legs trembled underneath me, threatening to give out, but Talon held onto my waist, keeping me steady.

Her brown eyes were bright as they locked onto mine—she'd wasted away to nothing. Even worse than I'd left her. The sleep gown that covered her was more like a sack, and it hung on her shoulders. A mixture of guilt and relief, sadness and joy surged through me as I started toward her.

Praying she'd understand. *Forgive* me.

The tears I blinked away moments ago leaked down my face freely, along with a shrill of delight that scratched the back of my throat.

Mother.

She was beaming with happiness as she started down the stairs, her bony knees knocking together with each weak step. I couldn't get to her fast enough. Weeks' worth of doubt weighed me down like lead as life moved slowly around me.

The scent of her floral perfume hung thick in the air—the tips of our fingers brushing—when an arrow penetrated her stomach, and her knees cracked against the ground.

THIRTY-EIGHT

I stumbled back, slapping a hand over my mouth to contain the scream that exploded in my chest as she looked from me to the arrow, confused. Blood dripped from her mouth, staining the stone pavers below.

She instinctively ripped it out, collapsing to her side. My bones turned to liquid, trembling as her nightgown turned bright red and blood pooled around her body, draining the little color left in her cheeks.

Time stopped, yet somehow, I kept moving.

Existing.

Breathing.

It shouldn't have been possible. Surely, I'd fallen through the fabric of time and disappeared into nothing.

However, the scream that escaped me reverberated inside my skull, reminding me I was, in fact, still very much alive. I didn't know what to do—*what was I supposed to do?*

I gripped the hair at my scalp, hoping to pull a thought from my worthless head. This couldn't be happening. I prayed it was a dream, just another nightmare that I'd soon wake from, but the blood only spread further from her body, dripping off the steps. Pooling around us in inconceivable spurts.

I fell to her side. "Mother, Mother, please stay with me," I begged, cupping her pale face in my hands. "Please, Mother, I'm here. I'm sorry." Blood coated my shaking hands as they moved along her face. There was so much—too much blood.

Commotion to my right pulled my attention over my shoulder, spotting Talon rushing toward a dozen guards that emerged from the tree line, his sword drawn and ready.

They hunted us. Tracked us there.

Waited for the perfect moment to strike.

The king didn't care if I escaped. No, what better punishment than to take the one thing I was fighting for?

The one person who kept me going.

My vision blurred with tears as I looked back down at Mother and grabbed her rigid fingers. "I'm here, Mother. I'm here. You're going to be okay, alright? You're going to be fine. Just stay with me. *Please.*"

Her lip twitched as if she were attempting to smile, and I swallowed the lump in my throat. Even when facing death, she still tried to comfort me.

"Your ring, darling," she rasped. "Where is your ring?"

I looked at my hands—stained red—and found them bare, but I couldn't bring myself to worry about that as her breathing labored and her eyes glazed over. Fear or wonder lit her expression as she looked to the sky.

"Oh, my love ... so beautiful."

"Please don't go. Not yet. I—I can fix this." I sobbed, shuffling around my vest for the nightingale vial, my damp fingers slipping on the smooth glass. "I can fix this. Just hold on. Please, Mother."

But my plea went unheard. She took a final breath—her eyes locked on the blue, cloudless sky.

"No, no, no! Mother!" I cried.

No.

No.

An unnatural sound escaped me as I convulsed with shock —as if the grief was too violent for my mind and was trying to escape through my bones.

I wanted to hug her tighter one more time.

Tell her how much she meant to me.

Roll my eyes at one of her silly jokes.

But the person who'd tethered me to this world was gone, and I'd never get her back. I'd never hear her words of guidance or affirmations ever again. Never feel her unwavering love. Her warmth.

My mother was dead. *Dead!*

I cried into her hair, my lungs straining to be quiet as I pleaded for the stars to give her back—to go back in time and get to her sooner. Never leave.

What was I supposed to do?

I curled into myself, hugging my mother to my chest as I rocked her. Us.

It was all my fault. All my fault!

I covered my mouth to contain my wretched sobs, my head feeling like it was going to explode from all the pressure.

Reach within, Elowyn.

The words still made no sense—they never made any sense —yet every fiber of my body surrendered, digging deep until I reached an endless void.

Frustration and anger welled from the darkest cavities of my soul, replacing the harrowing sadness that threatened to rip me apart, and I pulled.

Summoning it until the simmering rage came to a boil, overflowing out of me and into the world.

I stood as inky shadows spilled from my hands, slithering

and hissing along the ground toward the guards like a viper ready to attack.

They tried to run—they even bothered to scream—but their efforts were in vain. I clenched my fists instinctively, commanding the shadows to constrict, and watched with delight as they coiled around them, silencing their cries and dissolving them into nothing.

Talon staggered back—not in horror—but in amazement as I plucked them off one by one, no longer in control of my body or thoughts.

More and more shadowed tendrils spilled from my palms and amassed a force to be unrivaled by humans or fae.

An icy chill spread through my limbs, tunneling my vision, but I kept pulling, accessing a depth I never knew existed and allowing it to consume me. Submitting to the shadows' demands until I had nothing left to give.

Until darkness bled into the whites of my eyes and suffocated everything living and bright.

Orbs of golden light forced their way to the surface. The blast of Talon's golden magic was the last thing I saw before I collapsed to the ground.

I awoke in my living room, wrapped in a blanket on the sofa beside the crackling fireplace. It took a moment for me to gather my bearings and realize where I was—how I got there—when everything came flooding in at once.

My mother.

The guards.

The inky shadows with a mind of their own.

Kicking the blankets off my body, I shot up, wincing from the splitting headache that followed, and I doubled over, too weak to move. It felt as if my very essence had been devoured, the meat sucked clean from my bones, leaving me hollow and empty.

That was grief, I told myself. Grief and nothing more.

However, I couldn't sit here and do nothing. Not when my mother's body was growing colder by the minute. I gathered enough strength to stand—going where and to do what I didn't know—when Talon rounded the corner.

"Woah, easy now," Talon said, placing a hand on my shoulder as he sat beside me, the cushions dipping from his weight. "You did a number on yourself—you need to rest."

I didn't bother fighting him. Instead, I sank back into the sofa, pulling my knees to my chest as he wrapped the blanket around my trembling body.

"She's dead." My voice was flat and detached, but it was all I could muster. "There was nothing I could do, Talon. I couldn't grab the nightingale fast enough. I did all this for her, and for what? She'd still be alive if I never did!" My throat constricted. "What am I supposed to do, Talon? I don't know what to do. I —I didn't even get to hug her!"

Talon pulled me to him and held me to his chest, stroking my hair away from my blood-stained face. My cries came out in hopeless sobs, but his hold on me never wavered. He said nothing as I grieved, nor did he try to offer any words of sympathy. But I didn't need him to. There were no words that would make any of this feel better—nothing that would take this pain away.

Instead, he offered me something finer—something I'd been too proud to admit I needed until now: love.

I cried until my eyes went dry and my sobs turned into haphazard sniffles.

Talon placed a gentle kiss against my temple and held me tighter, as if afraid I'd disappear back into the shadows.

In my darkest moment, I'd never felt so seen—so understood.

He kissed away the lingering tears from my bloodshot eyes. "Your mother raised a strong, capable woman, firefly. She knows how much you loved her, and she'd be so incredibly proud of what you accomplished and how hard you fought." He gripped my chin and lifted my gaze to meet his. "Don't you dare, for one second, blame yourself for what happened. You had nothing but pure intentions."

"Is that what you'd call killing those guards? Because I enjoyed every single second of it, Talon. My bones bathed in their screams. I wouldn't have stopped if—" I swallowed the words before I could utter them, ashamed of how much I liked it. "I'm a *murderer*. How can you sit here and say my mother would be proud of that?" She wouldn't have been.

"Because you're a fighter, Elowyn." The deep timbre of his voice cut through me like glass, and I straightened. "She knew that better than anyone. Now, I'll be damned if I'm going to sit here and listen to you throw yourself a pity party when you only did what you had to do to survive."

"Killing those guards wasn't for survival. I didn't know I was capable of that until they were dead. Where'd that even come from, anyway? How is it possible to access magic I never knew I had?" The question burned my tongue like acid. I waited for him to reply, my chest swirling with uncertainty. No, it hadn't been for survival. It was revenge and rage.

"It's not completely unusual for a halfling to wield magic, although it's typically diluted to a much more basic form."

I tucked my hands between the nook of my knees, afraid of the darkness that lurked beneath their surface. "So, what I did ... that's not normal, is it?"

"Nothing about you is normal, Elowyn." Talon went quiet for a moment, deep in consideration when he finally cleared his throat, cupping my face in his hands. "No, your father had an insurmountable well of magic. There was a strong possibility you'd inherit his abilities." Talon's thumb brushed along my bare finger, his face pale as he looked at my hand. "Where's the ring, Elowyn?"

I shrugged. "The last time I remember having it was in Minerva's cottage. Why, what's wrong?"

Talon cursed, running his hands through his hair as he stood and paced the length of the room. "She must've taken it off when she gave you the palm reading. The duplicitous wretch! I should've known."

"I don't understand. What does my father's ring have to do with anything?"

Talon came to a stop between my legs, kneeling to meet me at eye level. "Elowyn, that ring's sole purpose is to keep powerful, unpredictable magic in check."

I raised my eyebrows expectantly, waiting for him to continue. Another secret.

"It'd allow someone the ability to access an exonerated amount of magic with no consequence." His face turned solemn.

"What do you think Minerva plans to do with it?" My heart ached. All I wanted was to grieve, but fate had other plans for me, it seemed.

"It's not her I'm worried about. And if I'm right, we need to get it back before it falls into the wrong hands. Or worse yet, your ability consumes you."

"Your future is bright but filled with much darkness, my dear. Hold on to the light so it doesn't consume you."

My blood turned cold. Whoever wanted the ring didn't need it for themselves. They needed *me* to be without it. There was only one person I could think of who'd want that—who'd benefit from my demise.

King Harkin had killed my mother, robbed me of the chance of knowing my father, and destroyed my sanity—leaving me in scraps for the vultures to feast upon. He wouldn't get away with that again. I was the rightful heir to Faerway, and I planned to claim my throne. Planned to take back everything that was mine. Even if I died trying.

Talon and I shared a look as we both came to the realization. A silent promise loaded with fury and retribution.

I was no longer sad.

No, I was far worse than that. But that was the thing about pain: no one usually cares until it turns into rage.

"Whatever means necessary, right?" I asked.

"Whatever means necessary."

ACKNOWLEDGMENTS

When I set out to tell the story of Elowyn in *A Fate so Wicked*, I was in the midst of grieving my mom. I knew it'd be a story unlike anything I've written before, and I was determined to finish it. For me. For my mom. For anyone who has experienced tremendous loss. For those who'd cross oceans for the ones they love. I see you and appreciate the strength you have to keep going. The world needs more people like you.

Despite blind determination, writing a book was mentally harder than I could've expected, and it wouldn't have been possible without an amazing support system.

To my Discord writing friends, I'm so happy I found you weirdos. Thank you for all our inside jokes, late-night conversations, and the countless kicks in the ass when I wanted to throw in the towel. I love you all so much.

To my boys, James, and Tyler, for your patience. There were many late-night diners and microwaved meals while writing *A Fate so Wicked*. Thank you for being understanding, inquisitive and holding me accountable. You're the biggest blessings in my life.

To my love, Nick, for being so supportive and encouraging me to go after my dreams. Your unwavering belief in me means the world. You're everything I've ever searched for.

To my best friend of 26 years, Rebecca Susan, for listening to my indecisive ass talk in circles until I finally made a decision (and for putting up with my tantrums when I feel overwhelmed).

To my editor, Ellie Race, for understanding my vision and helping me polish this story into something beautiful.

To Mikyn, one of my wonderful ARC readers, for your eye to detail. I appreciate your help so much!

Last and most importantly, thank *you*. The reader. The dreamers. The oddballs. Thank you for giving my story life and being the reason stories like mine can exist. I hope you enjoyed reading it as much as I did writing it.

About the Author

K.E. Austin was born and raised in the tropical paradise of South Florida before relocating to the North Georgia mountains with her family. Growing up, she escaped into faraway lands, reading anything that made her believe that one day, she, too, would discover she had magical powers (although, the jury is still out on that one). When she's not spending time with her family and chasing waterfalls, she enjoys writing emotionally charged characters with compelling plots that feature high stakes and mysterious love interests.

Follow K.E. Austin on social media @itskeaustin

Made in United States
Orlando, FL
22 October 2024

53002254R00245